Also available from

GENA SHOWALTER

and HQN Books

**And look for the next two books in the
Original Heartbreakers series**

The Hotter You Burn

The Harder You Fall

Coming soon!

GENA SHOWALTER

THE
Closer
YOU
COME

HQN™

HQN™

ISBN-13: 978-0-373-77962-8

Recycling programs
for this product may
not exist in your area.

The Closer You Come

www.HQNBooks.com

Printed in U.S.A.

To Emily Ohanjanians for your invaluable feedback and sheer awesomeness, and to Jill Monroe, Roxanne St. Claire, Lily Everett/Louisa Edwards and Deidre Knight for listening to me, encouraging me and praying for me!

CHAPTER ONE

Strawberry Valley, Oklahoma
Population ~~7,413~~ 7,416
Drive Slow and See Our City,
Drive Fast and See Our Jail

BROOK LYNN DILLON was not a fan of mornings. Or afternoons. Or evenings. When a girl reached a certain level of exhaustion, every time of day sucked.

She'd bypassed that certain level, oh, about seven years ago when, at the tender age of eighteen, she'd begun working at Rhinestone Cowgirl. Despite what every tourist passing through town assumed, the RC wasn't a strip club, thank you very much, but an up-and-coming jewelry store.

Her five-hour shift always kicked off at the butt crack of dawn, or as her mom used to say, before the rooster crows. Afterward she had sixty short minutes for a little R and R—the Reading and Reviewing of any new past-due notices—before working a ten-hour shift at Two Farms, the only "fine dining experience" within a fifty-mile radius. The description came directly from the owner, never mind that his idea of fine dining was using shiitake mushrooms in the beef Stroganoff instead of regular ones.

Today wouldn't have been so bad if her sister had completed her own shift at Two Farms, but halfway to the finish line, Jessie Kay had taken off without saying goodbye, and Brook Lynn was forced to take over her tables to save both their jobs. At least her sister left a note in her locker.

Don't stay in tonight. Go out and get drunk. Or, you know, at least pretend to be drunk. Your prudish ways are ruining our good name! XO JK

Brook Lynn had never hustled so hard for less reward. Her back and feet ached, and she wanted to go home and fall into some sort of coma even more than she wanted to win this week's lottery. Fifteen million and counting!

But here she was. Her best friend, Kenna, had called to tell her Jessie Kay had taken her own advice and gotten trashed, partying hard at the Glass house, acting as if the male attendees were going to die if she didn't give them a little mouth to mouth.

When Jessie Kay had a few too many "party favors," she became very...popular. A good-time girl. Brook Lynn, Miss Responsible, had never been a good-time anything. Too many worries balanced on her shoulders.

Tonight's worry? Tomorrow's possible front-page headline of the *Strawberry Daily*: Former Beauty Queen Turned Slacker Fails to Control Her Whoremones—Again.

Not on my watch!

Brook Lynn stepped out of her car, a one-wheel-in-the-grave beater she'd named Rusty. Like a vacuum, her pores opened up and sucked the stiflingly hot air straight into her body, and not even the sweet, addictive scent of wild strawberries and magnolias made it better. She wiped a sudden sheen of sweat from her brow and marched up the dilapidated porch steps, her gaze sweeping over one of the largest homes in the parish.

A hundred-year-old farmhouse in need of brand-new everything. White paint had chipped away, revealing rotten siding. Multiple wood slats had come loose, and the seal on several of the windows had broken, allowing moisture to pool between the panels.

Not altogether beautiful, but the fifty-two-acre spread had come with a greenhouse, a small dairy, two barns, a work shed, vegetable gardens and wild strawberry patches, all surrounded by hand-set stone walls.

Harlow Glass recently lost her family's sprawling estate, and Lincoln West, a newcomer in town, had snapped it up. He was obviously more tech savvy than manual laborish, considering he'd done no actual work that Brook Lynn could see. Which made sense, she supposed. He'd just moved from Oklahoma City to enjoy good ole country living in Strawberry Valley, and it was common knowledge that big, bad city boys spent the bulk of their time sleeping around, coiffing their hair and posting pictures of food on the internet.

Brook Lynn had interacted with the guy on more than one occasion, and shockingly enough, she'd come to admire his dry wit and puffed-up ego. He loved to brag about his own magnificence, but the hint of humor in his tone always saved him from falling over the edge into obnoxious.

Have you ever seen a body this perfect? No. And you never will, Brook Lynn. The good Lord has an A game, and I'm proof.

For a guy who spent all day behind a computer, he certainly was buff. And because she *hadn't* seen a body as perfect as his, she hadn't been able to rebuke him. But then, she had yet to meet his two roommates. Maybe they were hotter.

Problem was, West's friends kept to themselves. Not

once had she seen them in town. Of course, that hadn't stopped Jessie Kay, who had a habit of looking for love in all the wrong places. She had not only met the two other newcomers to Strawberry Valley—she'd also already slept with one. Beck...something. Gossip claimed he was a player of players and had totally worked his way through the over-twenty-and-under-forty female population in the city before moving here, looking for fresh lady meat.

The other guy... Jase was his name, she thought. Less was known about him. To her knowledge, he hadn't hooked up with a Strawberry Valley resident, though there had been a sighting or two and plenty of interest. Older women whispered he was "hunkalicious" while younger girls giggled nervously behind trembling hands.

A cacophony of voices seeped through the cracks around the front door. Brook Lynn wiped the dust from the upper panel of glass and peeked inside...and oh... crap. She hadn't expected so many guests. At least thirty people congregated in the living room, drinking beer, talking and laughing, and there were indications of others in the hallway and kitchen. Most were in their mid-to-late twenties, so Jessie Kay had gone to school with them—and the rumor mill about her actions this evening had likely already started spinning. These people wouldn't turn a blind eye to the fight to come, either.

And there *would* be a sister-versus-sister fight. Jessie Kay always resisted her own rescue.

Brook Lynn reached up and switched her inner ear implants to silent. The devices were a couple of years old but still deemed experimental, used to treat cases of hyperacusis as severe as hers—hearing everyday noises at such a blaring volume, it sometimes felt as if acid had been poured inside her ears. They allowed her to experience a sublime state of deafness whenever she desired. Which she did. Often.

Without bothering to knock, she stepped inside the house. Through a thick haze of cigar smoke, she saw the home's interior hadn't had any work done, either, and was in even more desperate need of refurbishment. Wallpaper had yellowed with age and peeled at the corners. The white shag carpet was stained and threadbare in places. In complete contrast, the furniture scattered throughout looked brand-new, flawless.

Finding no sign of Jessie Kay, she moved deeper into the house, reading lips along the way. A skill she'd honed over the years.

"—would never have guessed he was such a citidiot," the recently divorced Charlene Burns was saying. "But after tonight's antics?"

Citidiot. She had to be talking about West or one of his friends. They were the only city boys to move here in forever.

"I know!" Tawny Ferguson replied with a nod. "It's so, so sad."

"Can we really blame him, though? Smog probably putrefied already damaged brain cells. But Jessie Kay? That girl has no excuse. Trying to steal *my* Beck before throwing herself at Jase was *such* a slutty— Oh, hey, Brook Lynn." Charlene flashed a faux-bright smile and even managed an enthusiastic wave.

Brook Lynn held up her index finger and said, "One."

Both girls darted away as fast as their feet would carry them.

Over the years, Brook Lynn's count of three had served her very well. The only warning anyone received before her "viper's tongue" was unleashed. It was known for drawing blood and leaving internal injuries few could survive, all because she'd flayed Jessie Kay's ex-boyfriend with a verbal tongue-lashing. Once! But that's all it had taken. A legend had been born, and that legend had only grown—without any real help from her. Nowadays most folks would rather have their nose and mouth stapled shut—after being waterboarded—than clash with her.

A tap on her shoulder sent her wheeling around. "Kenna," she exclaimed, happy to see her friend.

The lovely redhead greeted her with a much-needed hug. "I lost track of Jessie Kay, but I guarantee West knows where she is. That boy has his head on a swivel. Come on."

Brook Lynn followed close behind and wished, not for the first time, that they could just pack up and run away together, leaving the rest of the world behind. But Kenna had a six-year-old daughter to think about. Not to mention a smoking-hot fiancé. And Brook Lynn, well, she had Jessie Kay, who would self-destruct without her.

Well, self-destruct *faster*.

Kenna led her through an overcrowded game room, where people hovered around a massive, elaborately carved pool table set in the frame of an old car, but no one actually played the game. Probably because a plastic sign hung from an aged chandelier, right over the center of the felt. Touch And Regret.

Another door led to a spacious kitchen. Though the walls were atrocious with an even uglier, darker yellow paper, the appliances were stainless steel and clearly fresh from the factory, the counters a lovely cream-and-rose marble. Someone had done some work in here, and her heart pinged with envy. *My dream kitchen in progress*.

Kenna stopped and waved her arm toward the sink...
where Brook Lynn spotted West. He was in the middle
of a conversation with a man she'd never met.

"I've got this," she told her friend.

Kenna cupped her cheeks in an effort to gain her full
attention. "You sure?"

"Very. Go back to Dane before he starts hunting
for you." Dane Michaelson, once the most sought-after
bachelor in town, was now the reason Kenna breathed.

"I happen to like when he hunts me," Kenna said,
wiggling her brows. "Think Animal Planet goes wild."

"You make me sick. You know that, right?"

"Don't be jelly. Your time is coming." Kenna kissed
her forehead before taking off.

Brook Lynn's time wasn't even close to coming. She
had zero prospects. And with that depressing thought,
she focused on her quarry. As usual, the sight of West
arrested her, even in profile. Not because she was attracted to him—she wasn't—but because, on top of that
ultrafine body he liked to boast about, he had a face
worthy of decorating the most beloved romance-novel
cover. With his shaggy dark hair and piercing, soul-
ful eyes, every unattached female in town was ready
to throw herself at him—and many already had. But
though he was nice, even charming and supersmart, he
could have been standing in a full swatch of sunlight,
and darkness still would have clung to him.

She did *not* need another fixer-upper in her life, and
there was no question the guy would require work.

According to Kenna, whose fiancé had the inside
tract, West allowed himself to date one woman per year,
for two months. No more, no less. When the clock zeroed out, he dumped the poor, dear thing for some rea-

son or other that sounded purely made up and never spoke to her again.

How crazy was that?

The guy with West was just as spectacular in appearance, maybe more so. Masculine and muscular, yet almost pretty. His eyes were a perfect honey gold, though his hair couldn't decide between blond and brown. Not that it mattered. The different colors blended together in beautiful harmony. Even his eyelashes started out black before curling into golden tips.

Brook Lynn read their lips to the best of her ability, considering they weren't looking directly at her and she didn't know their speech patterns, picking up snippets of their conversation and filling in the rest.

"It's only been six months," Honey-gold said.

"Yes, and I want him to survive the next six," West said. "This is going to cause problems."

"Not with me."

West glared at his friend.

"What? What'd I say that's so bad?"

"The fact that you don't know makes it worse."

West and Dane were working on some kind of project together, which meant Kenna, who was never far from Dane's side, and Brook Lynn, who spent what little free time she had with her best friend, had interacted with him more than anyone else in town. A few days ago, she'd asked him flat out why a guy who so obviously enjoyed the fast-paced city lifestyle had moved here—other than it being the greatest place on earth, of course. He'd merely turned on the charm, saying, "Why, to make all your dreams come true. You're welcome."

And now she had to try to get straight answers out of him. Peachy.

Determined, she walked over and tapped West on the shoulder.

He focused on her, a rebuke clearly poised at the edge of his tongue. When her identity clicked, he switched gears and grinned in welcome. "Well, well. If it isn't the girl I want by my side if ever zombies attack."

"*When* they attack," she corrected. It was only a matter of time. And yes, she was one of *those* people. A believer. "Where's Jessie Kay?"

The two men shared a look before Honey-gold took her hand and kissed her knuckles. "Hello, beautiful. I'm Beck, and if you'll give me thirty minutes of your time, I'll make you forget your friend and most assuredly your name."

Ah. The infamous Beck. Number two of the bachelors three. "Jessie Kay is my older sister, so I won't be forgetting her, I promise you. But if you seriously possess the skill to make me forget my name, I swear I'll find a way to marry you. Still interested in a hookup?"

Something akin to panic flashed over his features, though he managed to mask it quickly. "Forever with a beauty like you?" he said in the same easy tone. "You're only whetting my appetite, darling."

Women fall for that? Really? She focused on West—before she gave in to the temptation to teach Beck a lesson he'd never forget. "Where is she?"

West pushed out a breath. "You sure you want to know?"

She dropped her chin to her chest, her gaze staying on him and narrowing. "This conversation is fixing to start annoying me."

Beck chuckled. "*Fixing* to start?"

"Something they love to say here. Just go with it."

West frowned and said to Brook Lynn, "You do realize I'll be breaking all kinds of bro-code rules if I tell you."

"Better you break the rules than I break your face."

"Fair enough." Looking suddenly and inexplicably irate, he said, "She's in Jase's bedroom."

Jase, their other friend? Jessie Kay had turned her sights from Beck to him? Meaning Charlene Burns hadn't been blowing smoke. Great! "Where is Jase's bedroom?"

"Third door on the right," West said, even pointed.

Beck slugged him in the arm. "Dude. What if they're still busy?"

Busy? As in exactly what she suspected?

A tightness came over West's features but he shrugged. "Her corneas will burn, but they'll heal."

"Dude," Beck said again. "There *is* such a thing as privacy."

Leaving the pair to their argument, she stalked out of the kitchen and down a hallway. The couples who'd migrated this way were pressed against the walls, making out, so no one noticed her. She came to the correct door and prepared to knock, announcing her presence… only to hesitate. If Jessie Kay was totally tee-rashed, the guy was taking advantage of her, and if Brook Lynn gave him any warning, he would stop whatever crime he was committing and hide the evidence. He needed to be caught red-handed.

Then again, if she walked in and interrupted two consenting adults while they were getting "busy," her corneas would indeed be burned.

What was more important? Her sister or her eyes?

Okay, then. Decision made.

Brook Lynn turned the knob. Or would have, if it hadn't held steady. Dang it! Locked out.

Well, too bad for Mr. Hand-in-the-Cookie-Jar. A lock wasn't actually a problem for her. Brook Lynn's con man of an uncle had taught her how to pick anything with a tumbler. And hustle at pool. And cheat at poker. He'd actually taken her allowance every time she'd lost during a "practice" session.

She backtracked, avoiding the kitchen, and soon came to an office with a Keep Out sign posted on the door. Please. After confiscating two paper clips from the top drawer of the desk, she returned to the bedroom door. A quick insertion and twist…yes!…and she was able to push her way inside.

The lights were on. A man stood at the far edge of the bed, pulling a black T-shirt over his head and oh… wow…*wow*. She caught a delectable glimpse of olive skin and a delicious eight pack that could only be made from adamantium. A maze of intriguing tattoos she would have liked to study in-depth decorated much of his chest, but unfortunately the material covered him a second later, hiding the visual feast of sexy.

One thing became very clear very fast. West and his supposed most perfect perfection could suck it. There was a new and even juicier slice of beefcake in town.

Beefcake paused when he noticed her, snaring her with the most intense green eyes she'd ever seen, making her shiver. Why? Those were not bedroom eyes; they were far too cold for that. They were frosty, practically arctic…but they were also an invitation to do whatever proved necessary to warm the guy up.

She watched as those beautiful, sensual eyes narrowed.

Mortified to be caught staring, she cleared her throat. "Are you Jase?"

He gave a clipped nod. "I am."

Only two words, and yet she had trouble tracking the motion of his lips. They'd thinned with displeasure, his tone probably stilted and stinging.

"Who are you?" His gaze swept over her as he ran a hand through his dark hair. The strands stuck out in spikes. "How'd you get in here?"

Never admit to your crimes. Uncle Kurt's voice reverberated through her head.

Never follow your uncle's advice, baby girl. And there was her beloved father, just before he'd died.

Never forget lies are poison. Her cherished mother.

All three, now gone. A pang in her chest.

"Maybe you forgot to lock the door?" she suggested. It wasn't a lie, but it wasn't an admission, either.

"Maybe I didn't." His lips were thinning again.

She shrugged. "Faulty lock? Who's to know?"

He arched a brow. "Did you come here hoping to be spanked?"

Her heart rate kicked into overdrive, the organ pounding against her ribs, as if she'd just been shot up with enough adrenaline to revive a dead horse. "No, I didn't, but you're certainly welcome to try—if you want to have your balls surgically removed from your throat." Had threats of bodily harm replaced proper meet-and-greets, and she just hadn't gotten the memo?

"What do you want?" he asked, crossing his arms over his chest.

Was he trying to intimidate her? She studied him more intensely—and got caught up in his appeal. He wasn't classically handsome, but then, he didn't need to be. His features were rugged, total male, with a nose slightly out of alignment and a square jaw dusted with inky stubble, leading to a tattooed neck. Two necklaces hung just over his sternum, one an oval, one a cross. He had wide shoulders, leather cuffs anchored around his wrists and silver rings on several fingers.

He wore jeans that weren't fastened and combat boots that weren't tied. Clearly he'd dressed in a hurry. And he could be talking to her right now, but deaf as she currently was, she wouldn't know it. She returned her attention to his mouth. Once again it was a hard slash.

"I'm sorry," she blurted out. "I need you to repeat that."

He frowned. "Who are you?"

"Brook Lynn Dillon. I'm looking for my sister, and I was told—" Movement atop the bed drew her gaze. "She's in here with you," she finished. If Jase said anything else, she didn't know and didn't care anymore. She approached the bed.

The person beneath the covers stretched before sitting up, pale, shoulder-length hair falling into place around a sleep-soft face Brook Lynn recognized all too well. Relief blended with an irritation she didn't understand as her sister blinked over at her.

Jessie Kay's lips were moist and red as she clutched a sheet to her naked chest. "Brook Lynn? What are you doing in here?"

She wasn't wasted, as Brook Lynn had feared, but she was clearly exhausted—from too much pleasure. The irritation spread and spiked.

"What do you *think* I'm doing?" she demanded.

"Well, the first thing that pops into my head is— annoying the crap out of me."

A typical Jessie Kay response. "Just…get dressed," Brook Lynn said. "Let's go home."

"No way. You go." Her sister settled more comfortably against the pillows. "I'm good right where I am."

"Too bad. It's late, and we have to work tomorrow."

"Actually, *you* have work. I'm calling in sick."

"No, you are *not* sticking me with a double two days in a row," Brook Lynn said. "I'll tell Mr. Calbert the truth. You know I will."

Jessie Kay shrugged, unconcerned.

How are we related? "I'm very close to losing my temper with you." Brook Lynn had only three goals in life: save money, buy Rhinestone Cowgirl and turn her sister into a viable human being.

Love the girl, but I don't know how much more I can take.

Jessie Kay loved her, too, and hadn't purposely set out to make her life hell. That was just collateral damage.

"Calm down, Warden," her sister said. "No need to blow a gasket."

Warden. A nickname Jessie Kay had given her at the age of fifteen. Brook Lynn gritted her teeth, saying, "Get dressed. I mean it."

Her sister's eyes, a darker shade of blue than her own, flashed with impatience. "I told you. I'm not going anywhere." Jessie Kay said something else, but she'd turned away, and Brook Lynn couldn't follow the movement of her lips.

"I'm on silent," she interrupted. "I need to see you."

Jessie Kay immediately turned toward her, but her gaze got caught on Jase, and she flinched. Before Brook Lynn was able to comment, her sister rushed out, "Okay. All right. I'll get dressed. Jeez."

Brook Lynn dared a glance at Jase. He hadn't relocated from his spot at the end of the bed, his muscled arms still crossed over his chest. His frosty gaze was locked on *her* rather than the woman he'd just slept with, and she gulped.

"We'd appreciate a little privacy," she said, praying she wasn't breathless.

He gave a single, clipped shake of his head. "Sorry, honey, but this is *my* room."

Honey? Had she misread his lips? "Well, we want to borrow it for a few minutes."

"I doubt you could afford my rental fee."

Depended on the currency. Shivers? Tingles? She currently had those in spades. He exuded the most potent levels of testosterone she'd ever encountered, her deepest instincts recognizing him as the kind of guy every girl should have by her side when the zombie apocalypse occurred.

After a marathon viewing of *The Walking Dead*, she and Kenna had even mapped out survival plans A, B and C. Glomming on to the first strong (and handsome) man they came across just happened to be the heart of B. Plan A, her personal favorite, revolved around kicking zombie butt while stealing supplies from other survivors—girls had to do what girls had to do—while C boiled down to burning the entire world to the ground.

"Can you at least *pretend* to be a gentleman and turn around?" she asked.

"I would—if I knew how."

A quiver ran through her, nearly turning her muscles to jelly. She should not find his unrepentant bad-boy admission sexy. No, she definitely shouldn't. Somehow she managed to look away from him. He'd just slept with her sister, so he was now and forever off-limits.

Jessie Kay scanned the spacious room. "Anyone seen my shorts?"

A pair of cutoffs and a tank were wadded up next to Brook Lynn's feet. She picked up both and tossed them at her sister. "Well? Aren't you going to apologize for missing five hours of work?"

"Uh, why would I apologize?" Jessie Kay tugged on the shirt. "I'm not sorry. Besides, I barely had any customers."

"All of your tables were full with changeovers every hour. Meaning I had to hustle—without a break—to meet the demands of your customers as well as mine. Which was impossible! I made mistakes and lost tips." A single penny counted when you had so few.

"I'll make it up to you, swear," Jessie Kay said, shimmying into the shorts while still under the covers. "Don't worry."

Another spark of anger burned through Brook Lynn. "Have you come into a secret inheritance, or will I be forced to dig into my savings yet again to pay your share of rent and utilities?"

"Hey! I'm totally keeping track of every cent I owe you. I'm going to pay you back."

It may be too late then, she wanted to scream. Her future happiness had a time limit. Edna, the owner of Rhinestone Cowgirl, had given her until the end of the year to come up with the money to buy the place.

Brook Lynn might not be passionate about her creations, but owning that little jewelry shop was her only viable road to success. And *that* she wanted with every fiber of her being. She had already begun to make plans. She would pay to have a webpage created and sell her jewelry to people all over the state of Oklahoma, not just to the residents of Strawberry Valley and the seasonal flood of tourists. She would finally stop living day by day and actually live for tomorrow.

Her sister stood and patted her on top of the head.

"Hate to break it to you, little sis, but your jewelry store is just about as useless as a cow squirting water."

Useless?

Useless!

"I just don't want you unhappy," Jessie Kay added, throwing fuel on the fire.

The burn of simmering anger became a bomb of rage, exploding inside her. Unhappy? Unhappy! What did her sister think she was now?

"Well, maybe *I* don't want *you* to end up like Uncle Kurt," Brook Lynn gritted out.

Jessie Kay gasped. "Dude. That's *so* harsh."

Most definitely.

Years ago, one of the massive machines at a nearby dairy farm exploded, killing half the workforce. Many Strawberry Valley residents were employed there, including their dad. He had been pronounced dead at the scene.

Their mother had done her rock-solid best to raise them, but occasionally she'd been so desperate for help she'd called her con-artist brother. And when she later drowned—God rest her precious soul—Uncle Kurt, their only remaining family, had moved to Strawberry Valley "for good" to care for them. Brook Lynn had been fifteen at the time and Jessie Kay seventeen, and though they'd been old enough to see to their own needs, they'd still required a legal guardian. But Kurt had stayed only long enough to collect the life insurance.

Jessie Kay gave her a little push, snapping her back into focus. "I'm nothing like that dirtbag. You take that back."

"Never!" Brook Lynn returned the push. She only ever resorted to physical violence with Jessie Kay.

Her sister slapped her shoulder.

Brook Lynn delivered a slap of her own. "I'm fixing to start counting, Jessica Kay."

"One," her sister mocked, knowing her ways better than anyone.

"Two, three." Forget battling with words. With a screech, Brook Lynn launched forward, crashing into Jessie Kay. They fell into the mattress and bounced to the floor, where they rolled around in a struggle for dominance. When they bumped into the nightstand, the lamp teetered…tumbled down and shattered. The damage barely registered as they continued to wrestle. Brook Lynn managed to come out on top and pin her sister's shoulders with her knees. She forced the girl to slap her own face.

"Why are you hitting yourself, Jessie Kay? Huh? Huh? Why?"

Her sister twisted left and right, trying to dodge the blows.

Warm breath fanned the crown of Brook Lynn's head as strong arms banded around her, and a masculine scent saturated her awareness. Jase.

"Let me go," she demanded. "Let me go right now."

His hold only tightened. He hefted her over his shoulder fireman-style and strode out of the room.

CHAPTER TWO

JASON—JASE—HOLLISTER carted the petite bundle of fury into the backyard. She fought him every step of the way, the little wildcat, but he held on as if she were a well-deserved war prize. The party guests watched with wide grins, enjoying the show. A few even followed him, no doubt curious to see how the scene would play out.

He resented their presence, actually hated that they were here. Truth be told, he liked to keep his two friends close and everyone else at a distance. His head wasn't screwed on right on the best of days, and today wasn't the best of days. He hadn't had a best day in a long time.

Behind him, the firecracker he'd just slept with shouted, "Put my sister down this instant, you overgrown Neanderthal!"

If he hadn't already regretted sleeping with Jessie Kay before Wildcat had stormed into his bedroom—she was also known as Brook Lynn, apparently—he would have regretted it now. Before moving to Strawberry Valley a few weeks ago, he'd decided to end his sexual bender. A five-month carnal odyssey, Beck had called it, not quite realizing how right he was. It *was* an odyssey. Straight into hell. Jase had expected pleasure, maybe a little fun, but he'd had trouble relaxing around the women, and it had made for bad sex, great guilt and even worse memories.

Tonight had been more of the same, another regret to add to his ever-growing list. He'd had trouble focusing, constantly on alert for a sneak attack.

The nine-year habit would be hard to shake.

Besides, the move here was supposed to be his fresh start in a place that represented everything he'd never had but had always craved. Roots, permanence. Peace. Wide-open spaces and community support. A clean canvas he'd hoped to keep clean, not mar by creating a perfect storm of drama, pitting two sisters against each other.

Too late.

Though he'd had no desire to shit where he ate, so to speak, and mess everything up with a scorned lover, he'd had a few beers too many tonight, and Jessie Kay had crawled into his lap, asked if she could welcome him to town properly, and that had been that.

At least he'd had the presence of mind to make it clear there would be no repeat performances, no blooming relationship. He'd earned his freedom the hard way—and he would do anything to keep it.

Women never stuck around for the long haul anyway. His mother sure hadn't. Countless foster moms hadn't. Hell, even the love of his life hadn't. Daphne had taken off without ever looking back.

Light from the porch lamps cast a golden glow over the swimming pool, illuminating the couple who'd decided to skinny-dip. They, like everyone else within a ten-mile radius, heard the commotion; they scrambled into a shadowed corner.

"Pay attention, honey," Jase said to Brook Lynn.

"This isn't a lesson you'll want to learn twice. You throw a tantrum in my room, you get wet." Jase tossed the little wildcat into the deep end, hoping to calm her down.

Jessie Kay beat at his arm, screeching, "Idiot! Her implants aren't supposed to be waterlogged. She's supposed to cover them with a special adhesive."

Please. "Implants are always better wet." He should know. He'd handled his fair share.

"They aren't in her boobs, you moron. They're in her ears!"

Well, hell. *I'm on silent,* she'd said, the words suddenly making sense. "Way to bury the lead," he muttered.

Brook Lynn came up sputtering. She swam to the edge of the pool and climbed out with her sister's help, then arranged her hair over her ears before glaring up at him, reminding him of an avenging angel.

He'd hoped the impromptu dunk would lessen her appeal.

He'd hoped in vain.

Water droplets trickled down flawless skin the color of melted honey. The plain white button-up and black slacks she wore clung to her body, revealing a breathtakingly erotic frame, legs that were somehow a mile long, breasts that were a perfect handful...and nipples that were hard.

Those traits, in themselves, would have been dangerous for any man's peace of mind. But when you paired that miracle body with that angel face—huge baby blues and heart-shaped lips no emissary from heaven should ever be allowed to have—it was almost overkill.

Damn, I picked the wrong sister.

Well, what was done was done. Another piece of broken glass in his conscience. Another memory to leave a sticky film on his soul, like a spider determined to catch flies.

"I'm sorry about your hearing aids, or whatever they are," he said, "but catfights aren't allowed in my room. You should save all disputes for the next JELL-O Fight Night."

She watched his lips. Her eyes narrowed, an indication she'd understood him.

Without looking away from him, she said, "Jessie Kay, get in the car. If I have to start counting again, you'll regret it."

For the first time that evening, her sister heeded her command and took off as though her feet were on fire.

West and Beck arrived a second later and scoped out the scene: a gorgeous woman who was soaking wet, probably chilled, stood as still as a statue, her hands fisted at her sides, while Jase couldn't seem to look away from her.

"What the hell happened?" Beck demanded, running a hand through his hair.

"This is between him and me." Brook Lynn pointed to Jase. "You guys go inside."

"Your hand is bleeding." West frowned and reached for her.

"I'm not your concern." She stepped away, avoiding contact, and would have toppled back into the pool if Jase hadn't caught her arm.

With her sex-kitten curves, he was surprised by the slenderness of her bones. Even more shocked by the soft silk of her skin, the warmer-than-melted-honey temperature. She wasn't chilled, after all, and the longer he held on, the more electric the contact proved to be, somehow cracking through the armor he'd spent years erecting around his emotions, until he practically vibrated with the desire to touch *all* of her…to hold her…

To devour.

What the hell?

He released her with a jolt and widened the distance between them. His inner armor wasn't something he maintained just for grins and giggles. It was for survival. As a boy abandoned by his parents and sometimes mistreated by fosters, he'd learned emotions were a weakness that could be used against him. To feel something for a person or object meant he'd placed value on it—whether for good or ill.

Feel nothing. Want nothing. Need nothing. For the most part, the motto had served him well. There had been times the armor vanished, the darkest of emotions consuming him…pushing him to do things he shouldn't. Trouble had always followed.

Brook Lynn peered down at her wrist, as if she'd felt something she couldn't explain, before focusing on him, her eyes narrowing once again.

To Beck and West, who'd remained after her command to leave, Jase said, "Get everyone inside. I'll handle her."

The two glanced between him and the girl, and he knew they wanted to protest. Tension thrummed from them both. But then, tension always thrummed from them both. They loved him, but when they looked at him, they only saw him through the dark-tinted glasses of a shared past, a trip they'd taken together through hell. Their guilt and shame always radiated below the surface.

They blamed themselves for the worst years of Jase's life, a time he would have been far better off dead. It was the reason West had once battled a drug addiction, and Beck still refused to connect with anyone for more than an hour, maybe two if the girl was good. Whether they admitted it or not, they wanted to make themselves suffer the way Jase had suffered. The way he sometimes suffered still.

"Get everyone inside," he repeated. The gossip vine in this town worked faster than a cable modem, and he had no desire to be the topic du jour. He guarded his privacy the way other people guarded their most valued treasures. Maybe because he had a lot more to hide.

Really, in today's digital world, there was no such thing as a secret, and the citizens of Strawberry Valley would learn about him soon enough. He just hoped they didn't attempt to run him off with pitchforks and torches.

"Now," he added.

This time his friends obeyed. Once the backyard had been cleared, however, they returned to his side.

West offered Brook Lynn a towel. She failed to notice, her attention somewhere in the distance, where tall oaks and blooming magnolias stretched across the acreage. The wild strawberries growing along the forest floor were his favorite part of the property, vivid red fruit that sprang from flowers of the whitest white, with sunshine-yellow centers. A landscape more beautiful than anything he'd ever thought possible.

"Brook Lynn," he said, but still she paid him no heed. Were her hearing aids ruined?

Guilt pricked at him.

West tapped her on the shoulder, and she yelped.

When she noticed the towel, she accepted with a quiet "Thanks."

"You guys head inside, too, like she said." Jase hiked his thumb toward the house.

West put his back to Brook Lynn and said softly to Jase, "Tell me you're not thinking what I think you're thinking."

What? That the girl looked good—and would look even better in his arms? Too late. Just as quietly, just in case, he replied, "I'm not going to try anything with her."

Beck gave Brook Lynn his back, as well. "Jase, you just threw her in the pool. I'd say your chances of anything but a catfight are slim. The only thing left to do is finesse the situation, and that just happens to be my forte."

Allow Beck to *finesse* the delicate beauty? A bead of anger rolled through Jase, surprising him. He'd never directed his temper at his friends. The night's activities must have screwed with his head more than usual.

"Besides," West added, "you can't afford trouble."

No, he couldn't. He'd endured his fair share already.

"What if she decides to file a complaint with the sheriff?" Beck's gaze was grim.

Panic prickled the back of Jase's neck.

"Whatever you guys are saying about me, stop. If you'll figure out the cost for repairs," Brook Lynn said, nudging West and Beck aside to peer up at Jase, "I'll reimburse you for the lamp and nightstand."

After what he'd done, she thought *she* owed *him*? And get serious. As if there was any way in hell he would ever take her money. He'd heard her argument with her sister, knew the two were barely scraping by.

"Go." He gave his friends a push toward the door. They reluctantly returned to the party, not because they thought it was the right thing to do, but because they felt they owed him. "I ruined your hearing aids, honey. How about we call it even?"

Her hands immediately went to her ears. To ensure her hair was still in place, hiding them?

The self-conscious action did something to his chest. Made it hurt.

"How about we don't," she said.

He ignored her, saying, "Your hand might need to be stitched." Fat drops of crimson trickled from the cuts the lamp shards had caused.

Her chin lifted another notch. "I'll be fine."

"At least let me get you a bandage."

She watched his lips, took a moment to decipher his words and shook her head. "No, thanks."

So polite. So distant.

So not worth the hassle.

He'd apologized. He'd offered to pay and had even suggested he play doctor. Now there was nothing left to do but make an exit. "Whether you believe it or not, we *are* even. It was nice meeting you, Brook Lynn. Let's do this again in never." He turned away, fully intending to put her and her sister in the "better off avoided" category of his life.

"Wait," she called, and for some reason, he stopped. "What are your intentions toward Jessie Kay?"

He closed his eyes. *Don't need this drama.* Slowly he turned and said, "You pinned her down and made her slap herself. You seriously care?"

"I do," she replied, fire crackling in the blue depths of her eyes.

Lying had never been his thing. "I have no intentions. Tonight was a one-and-done experience."

The fire intensified. "So that's it? You just screwed her, and now you're dismissing her?"

"That about sums it up, yes." In fact, he was pretty sure he was done with all women for a while. When things settled and a need for companionship grew, he might think about contacting Daphne. She already knew some of the horrors he'd endured as a kid, the sins he'd committed as a young man. Though she didn't know everything he'd been through as an adult—he shuddered, recognizing soul-deep he would never discuss certain things, even with West and Beck. He could have something good with Daph, something permanent. She'd had her reasons for leaving him, and they'd been good ones.

But what could *he* offer *her*? It would be impossible to build a future on the crumbling foundation of his past.

And…looking at Brook Lynn now, his body said *to hell with Daphne, take this one*. The girl smoldered with life and vitality, and he experienced another unbearable urge to grab on to her and hold tight. Warmth spilled through his veins, causing his skin to prickle.

This reaction wasn't as much of a mystery as the others. Until six months ago, he'd gone nine years without a woman. Of course his body wanted the one that was nearby.

"Jessie Kay is a person," she said. "She has feelings."

"So am I. So do I."

Brook Lynn's skin flushed to the deepest rose, the change startling, mesmerizing. Irritating.

"She also knew what she was getting into," he added.

"I made sure of it before I ever escorted her into my bedroom."

Brook Lynn removed one of her sensible flats, but rather than throwing it at him as he expected, she dumped out the water. "Do you do this often, then?"

"Do what?" he asked.

"Seduce and abandon women."

He laughed; he just couldn't help himself. "Honey, you must not know your sister as well as you think. *She* came on to *me*." Just a few weeks ago, she'd done the same to Beck. Not that either of them had put up much of a fight or ever complained. "At first, I even told her no."

"Are you saying she *forced* you?"

He lost his grin in a hurry, dark waves of rage breaking through his armor, rushing over his mind. His hands balled into fists.

He took a deep breath. *Feel nothing. Want nothing. Need nothing.*

Tone flat, he said, "No. I was willing. And now, this conversation is over." He turned before he did something he would regret—too many of those already— and once again began to walk away.

Once again she called, "Wait."

Something must have been seriously wrong with him, because he faced her, snapping, "What?"

She stepped back, as if frightened.

"What?" he asked more gently.

"I really am sorry for the damage I caused in your room." Her features softened, making her appear vulnerable in the most tantalizing way, rousing protective instincts he hadn't known he possessed. "I *will* pay for what I broke."

He recognized integrity when he saw it and respected the hell out of it. To so many people, words were just a means to an end. To him, words were a bond. Jase wouldn't prevent this girl from doing what she felt was right.

"I'll mail you a bill," he said, deciding he wouldn't charge her more than twenty dollars for items he'd spent well over two grand on.

"Thank you."

"And I'll pay for the damage to your hearing aids." He wondered why she had them in the first place. Had she suffered with deafness all her life?

"No." She shook her head with confidence. "I was out of line, barging in on you and Jessie Kay and then starting a fight in your room. I don't blame you for tossing me in the pool," she admitted, surprising him. "I can't in good conscience allow you to pay for anything."

He made sure she had a perfect view of his face. He wanted no misunderstandings between them. "Refusing payment isn't going to do you a bit of good, honey."

She peered at him for a long while, silent, before recognizing his own determination and sighing wearily. "Fine," she said. "Whoever owes more can deduct what the other owes and pay the rest."

"Agreed. And now…" He motioned to the back door of the house.

"Dismissed?" With a *humph*, she stalked around him—but didn't head toward the house. She exited the yard through the side gate. He followed at a discreet distance to make sure she reached her vehicle safely.

She climbed into a rust bucket that couldn't have been close to street legal.

"Are you okay?" her sister asked. "What did Jase say to—"

Jessie Kay's voice was cut off by the slam of Brook Lynn's door. As the engine sputtered to life and the headlights blinked on, Jase returned to the house.

West and Beck were waiting for him inside his bedroom, where they knew he couldn't avoid them.

Beck reclined on the bed, flipping channels on the TV. West sat beside him, tossing pieces of popcorn in the air and catching them with his mouth.

"Hiding from your own party?" Jase asked.

Both glanced over at him.

"I'm the crotchety old man who doesn't like having people in his space—after I'm done with them." West threw several pieces of popcorn at him and missed. "I'm currently done with them."

"Old?" Jase arched a brow. "We're twenty-eight."

"*Physically* twenty-eight. But our souls? Those are older than dirt."

Beck grabbed the last handful of kernels and stuffed them in his mouth. "I don't mind people in my space, but we're currently out of fresh lady meat, and you know I never go back for seconds."

Exasperated, Jase said, "Then why did you invite everyone over?"

They peered at him, expectant. Guiltier than usual.

"Maybe we thought you could use it," West said, his tone thick with emotion.

"Whatever you want, you get," Beck said. "No questions asked."

They were trying to make up for everything he'd lost. He wished he could comfort them, reassure them, but he'd never even been able to comfort or reassure himself. "For future reference," he said, "a party isn't the way to make me happy. I'd rather be alone than surrounded by strangers."

More guilt from West, sorrow from Beck. Regret from Jase.

"I wanted to move here," he said. "We're here. That's enough." Six months ago, he'd asked the two to find him a new place to live. Somewhere outside city limits, where the crowds were thinner and the pace slower. West had connections out here, and what he'd described had enthralled Jase. Trees, hills, the closest neighbors miles away. And when the isolated famansion—farm-mansion, as he'd heard it called—suffered a foreclosure a short time later, the two had uprooted their entire lives, unwilling to let him make the move on his own. True, the estate needed a little TLC, but that was something Jase excelled at and was actually enjoying doing.

Beck had lived next to a golf course and West inside a room adjacent to their plush office suite in downtown Oklahoma City. Each place had been purchased soon after they'd created and sold some kind of computer program, hitting it big, and even when they'd made far more money, investing a huge chunk for Jase, they hadn't bought bigger and better. Change had never been easy for either man. Jase knew that well, hated change himself, but the two had been willing to move here for him.

Besides, it wasn't as if he would have survived the past nine shudder-inducing years without them or as if he'd have any kind of life now.

"Remember when we first met?" he asked, switching topics. Anything to distract the pair.

West cracked a smile. "The fosters had no idea their

request for troubled adolescent boys to guide and nurture would lead to the three of us joining forces."

Beck snorted. "I believe the mother—what was her name?—told my social worker we were fully capable of building an actual Death Star to destroy the world."

They'd been eight, and the ten months Jase had spent living with the boys had been the best of his life, an unbreakable bond forming. Even after the system split them up, they'd never lost touch. They'd occasionally attended the same school or lived in the same neighborhood, but at sixteen, when they were able to pool the money they'd earned doing odd jobs, they'd bought a car, and that had been that. It had been the three of them against the world. Still was.

These men were the only people in the world Jase trusted. The only people he would *ever* trust. They were his family.

"Hey. What's with the reminiscing?" West asked. "You wouldn't be trying to avoid the mention of a certain girl…Brook Lynn Dillon?"

Jase rolled his eyes, even as his body quickened with…yearning?

"I'll take that as a hell, yes," Beck said, his grin wide and irreverent. "He hoped to avoid."

"Are you wanting a gossip fest? Why don't we paint our nails and give each other back massages?" Jase asked.

"Yes," the two deadpanned in unison.

"I call dibs on the pink polish," Beck added.

"No fair." West pretended to pout. "I wanted the pink."

"You guys aren't ridiculous and immature *at all*."

"But you love us anyway," Beck said.

He did, and they loved him. "West, go kick everyone out of the house. And if you leave any popcorn crumbs on my sheets, your blood will soon join them. Beck, haul ass to the kitchen and cook your famous morning-after special. I'm starved."

"On it." West flew out of the room.

"Can do." Beck grinned as he passed, even paused to pat Jase on the shoulder. "It's not morning, but you sure did get screwed, didn't you."

CHAPTER THREE

Two weeks after "The Dunking," the state of Brook Lynn's life should have improved by leaps and bounds. What was the saying? When you were at the bottom of a pit, you had nowhere to go but up.

Somehow she'd managed to burrow deeper.

After she'd gotten Jessie Kay home from the party, the implants had basically short-circuited, causing massive headaches, uncontrollable dizziness and extreme nausea. She'd had to have them replaced the very next day with a surgery that accumulated thousands of dollars in medical bills. Insurance had refused to pay, citing the devices were still experimental. A ridiculous excuse. But Jase hadn't yet contacted her to settle their debt—thank God he'd insisted on paying his part—and she desperately needed the money.

The new implants required three days of complete bed rest to heal and attach to her canals properly. Three days without pay. As soon as she'd recovered, Jessie Kay had taken off for who-knew-where, looking for a man to console her after Jase's rejection. For two days after that, Brook Lynn had been forced to work double shifts.

Jessie Kay had come back, only to take off again and return last night. Now Brook Lynn called her sister's cell to tell her to keep her butt home and rested for tomorrow, but she went straight to voice mail. Dang it! The girl was off carousing again, wasn't she?

Argh! Her sister sometimes reminded her of a mouse in a wheel, spinning, spinning, but never going anywhere. Of course, the same could be said of herself, she realized with a sigh, simply in a different way. Jessie Kay chased guys. Brook Lynn chased Jessie Kay.

Perhaps it was time for a change.

Perhaps? Why was that even a question?

As she began cleaning Two Farms for closing, she thought back to the "fun list" she and Kenna had created a few weeks ago. Fun—something neither of them had ever really experienced. The list of activities was supposed to spice up their lives. The plan? Try every flavor of Ben & Jerry's ice cream, text I hid the body to a random number. Be Cinderella for a day, and eat a real Krabby Patty. Get a tattoo, TP someone's house, solve a case with Sherlock and Watson. Ask out a boy. Throw a drink in someone's face, gulp blue Gatorade out of a Windex bottle. Jump into a body of water with all of their clothes on. Spy on someone. Oh, and speak with a fake accent for an entire day.

The last was the only thing Brook Lynn had done. Meanwhile, Kenna the overachiever had done *everything*. Dane had made it his mission to ensure she checked off every item on the list.

Brook Lynn simply hadn't had time for the others. Or, to be honest, the inclination. But…maybe she needed to start despite her lack of enthusiasm. Just pick something and go, go, go. Like…asking out a boy… even seducing one.

An image of Jase flashed through her mind. What he might have looked like minutes before she'd entered his bedroom. Naked, flat on his back and hard as a rock.

No! Oh, no. Jase? She recoiled...even as she shivered. The man had used and discarded her sister, leaving no doubt he would use and discard Brook Lynn. If he even wanted her. So, ask him out? No. Nope. Never. The guy she picked would give her what she hadn't had since the death of her mother: security.

A long-term commitment with a nice man with a nice income and the unending patience required to deal with Jessie Kay without sleeping with her, flirting with her or hurting her feelings seemed like just the ticket.

Attainable. Surely.

He had to live in Strawberry Valley, be over twenty but under forty, and he had to have had steady employment for at least a year. He had to be stable, reliable and in no way a fixer-upper. So, of all the eligible men in town, that left...

A few too many, surprisingly enough. To narrow the playing field, she decided he could have zero history with Jessie Kay. Well, well. That left only one name. Brad Lintz, the supersweet owner of Lintz Automotive. He came into Rhinestone Cowgirl every so often to buy a present for his mother, sisters, an aunt, a handful of nieces, whoever happened to have a birthday, and he always said something to make Brook Lynn laugh. Once or twice she'd even suspected he wanted to ask her out.

Brook Lynn...would you do me the honor of...would you, uh...show me that necklace again?

Could she put on her big-girl panties and actually make the first move? She never had before. Part of her had always feared the slightest hint of aggression would lead the man to assume she would settle for as little as Jessie Kay did: a single night of sexual pleasure. And she wasn't casting stones. She understood her sister. Despite what everyone thought, sex wasn't a frivolous, sterile transaction for Jessie Kay. It was a means of finding the acceptance and affection she craved, if only for a short while. A craving that only grew every time she woke up in bed with a guy, expecting more from him, and he made her feel as if she'd committed the cardinal sin of moving too fast. Too fast, after he'd slept with her.

None of the guys heard her crying in her bedroom the next day.

Brook Lynn, too, had often wondered if a moment of comfort would be better than no comfort at all. But then she would remember doing what felt good today often led to regrets tomorrow.

Of course, on the other end of the spectrum, doing what scared her today often led to happiness tomorrow. So... Yes. For a chance at improving her life and finally having fun, she could put on her big-girl panties.

She would go see her doctor tomorrow after her shift at the RC, get on birth control—just in case—and then go to Brad's shop. Her stomach began to twist into a thousand tiny knots of nervousness already.

"My office, Brook Lynn." Her boss's voice echoed through the empty restaurant, startling her from her thoughts. "Now."

Mr. Calbert sounded gruffer than usual. Was he going to yell at her for Jessie Kay's absence or the plates Brook Lynn had broken or the orders she had screwed up—or all three? Yeah, probably that last one. The knots in her stomach tightened. But at least the new implants were doing their job, leveling out the noises around her while allowing her to distinguish certain nuances.

"On my way," she called. She trudged into the break room to grab her purse from her locker.

Heart hammering, she entered Mr. Calbert's office. He was in his midfifties with thinning hair, glasses as thick as her wrist and a build that suggested he enjoyed tasting the foods he served.

His office was small, crammed with file cabinets and a desk too big for the space. He was already seated, drumming his nails impatiently. When she eased into the chair across from him, he got straight to the point.

"Your sister was a no-show. Again."

"I know. And I'm sorry." When Brook Lynn had seen Jessie Kay this morning, she'd been hunched over a toilet, vomiting her guts out from too much to drink, her mascara running down her bright red cheeks.

You going to be okay for work? Brook Lynn had asked.

I'll be there. Jeez! I'm not a total slag.

Mr. Calbert shuffled papers around, saying, "Why do you put up with that girl?"

Because Jessie Kay had done whatever was necessary to keep Brook Lynn fed after Uncle Kurt had taken off. Because she'd comforted Brook Lynn when they'd lost everything. Because her sister was all she had left.

"That has no bearing on our conversation," she said, raising her chin.

"Actually, it has everything to do with our conversation." He propped his elbows on the desk and rested his forehead in his palms. That did not bode well. "Look. I like you. I do. I think you're a good girl with bad problems, and that's what makes this so difficult, but this is a business, and it has to be done."

Dread slithered through her, a boa with every intention of choking her out. She could guess where this was leading and vehemently shook her head. "Don't do this, Mr. Calbert. Please. I need the money."

He lifted his head, his hazel eyes bleak. "I'm sorry, Brook Lynn. I loved your parents. They were nice people, and I respected them, but I can't rely on you anymore. You're too tired to work as much as you do, but I can't cut your hours because you always beg me for more. You break things—"

"I'll pay for them."

"—and you get a ton of orders wrong."

"I apologized to everyone."

"You put peanuts instead of croutons on Mr. Crawford's salad, and he had an allergic reaction. I have to pay his medical bill and for his mental anguish!"

"Anyone could have made that mistake." But okay, all right. Yes, her mind had been zapped by all the extra hours and tasks she'd taken on. "At least now Mr. Crawford knows his EpiPen is working properly," she tried.

Mr. Calbert shook his head. "I need to be able to rely on my staff."

"But—"

"I can't rely on you or your sister. You and Jessie Kay are fired, Brook Lynn. Effective immediately."

JASE HAD JUST finished off his third beer of the evening, knowing it wouldn't be his last. He had seriously dark emotions to drown, and by hell, he was going to drown them. If he failed, he'd get in his car and head into town to see *her*.

The new bane of his existence, Miss Brook Lynn Dillon. He hadn't been this obsessed with a woman since Daphne.

Daphne. Yeah. He'd think about her. Unlike Brook Lynn, the thought of her actually mellowed him.

He let his mind drift to the night he and Daphne had met. They'd both been sixteen, and while he'd earned money repairing and washing cars, she'd worked at a fast-food joint. He'd gone in for a burrito and had come out with her phone number. They'd spent the next two years together, inseparable, and had been saving to rent an apartment together.

She'd represented the future. Stability. And unlike most of the foster families he'd lived with, he'd wanted her to stick.

"Want a beer?" Beck asked West.

They were congregated in the game room, their sanctuary. Beck and Jase were playing pool, while West watched. Or, more accurately, thought about something; the guy had been lost in his head for the past half hour.

"No," West finally replied, and Beck breathed a sigh of relief.

Jase observed the entire exchange with a frown. Beck had been testing West's resolve to remain sober more and more lately, and he couldn't figure out why. But then, the two had a history he knew nothing about. So many years' worth of memories made without him.

He never had a problem convincing himself he was fine with it—until moments like this.

"You aren't an alcoholic, West," Jase pointed out.

"But I *am* a recovering drug addict," West said. "Alcohol is my gateway."

West had gotten high for the first time nine years ago, and he'd stayed high for the next three.

Dark eyes grim…haunted, his friend admitted, "I wasn't even feeling the temptation…until recently."

"What changed?" Jase asked.

"What else? The time of year."

Lightbulb. The oncoming anniversary of Tessa's death.

Tessa had been West's first and only girlfriend. The two had met mere days after Jase first encountered West and Beck. She'd lived down the street, and while Jase

and Beck had grown to love her like a sister, West…
he had grown to love her intimately, desperately. The
pair had been halves that depended on each other, rather
than wholes that complemented each other, and West
had never recovered from her loss.

I'm never going to end up like that.

Brook Lynn's image drifted through his head, taunting him. He gripped the edge of the table, nearly snapping the wood.

Tessa had dropped out of high school her senior year
to waitress full-time and help her mom pay bills. Later,
though, she'd passed her GED exam. Her deadbeat mom
hadn't cared enough to celebrate, so West had promised
to throw her a party. He'd toked up instead. She'd left
the apartment they'd all shared with a sad smile, saying it didn't matter. But afterward Beck confessed he'd
seen her crying as she'd driven away.

That night, she'd crashed her car into a lamppost.

Sweet, beautiful Tessa had died at the age of nineteen.

"I get it. The anniversary of Tessa's death is three
months away," Jase said. According to some of the tales
Beck had told him, West spiraled more and more, drinking, flaking on clients, even picking fights. Soon after,
he picked a woman, showered her with affection and
gifts and ended things in exactly two months, as if he
was willing to give happiness a shot because it was
what Tessa would have wanted, but he didn't feel he
deserved more than a taste.

"Yes," West responded, head bowed, "and I'll be fine
this time. I will. I'm not going to limit what you can do
because of a weakness *I* have."

"For a smart man, you can be really stupid." Jase
clasped him by the nape and stared him down. "We

help each other. Every day. Every hour. Every minute. What makes you think I'd want anything to do with something that bothers you?"

"You've lost so much already."

Yes. More than either man knew. Jase had shared only a few of the atrocities he'd suffered—and committed— during the years of their separation. He could barely stand to think of them. "So have you," he said. "A scholarship to MIT, and soon after that, Tessa."

Pain flashed in dark eyes that had already witnessed the worst the world had to offer.

"You've been clean six years," Jase said. "During that time, you've created and sold different computer programs and games I won't pretend to understand, and you've made us richer than we ever dreamed by investing the profits for us. Cut yourself some slack."

"Put that way, I *am* pretty awesome," West said, the barest hint of a smile revealed.

"Though only a close second to me," Beck said, thumping his chest like a gorilla.

The doorbell rang before Jase could pop them both in the back of the head.

Everyone displayed different variations of dread.

"Bet it's one of Beck's women, coming to request seconds," West said.

Beck lined up his shot. "Too bad. The candy store is currently closed."

West snorted. "If only it stayed closed for maintenance. These women are upsetting my schedule."

Jase had noticed West's time-management and schedule-building skills had only gotten sharper over the years, though he'd done his best to relax and pretend he could roll with spontaneity. In reality, he'd always lived by a regime, preferring to have every minute planned.

Another round of ringing echoed from the walls.

"Don't everyone rush to the door at once," Jase said.

Beck peered at West. "Do me a solid and get rid of her."

"Happy to, but you'll owe me." West strode from the room.

"Like that's anything new," Beck called. The amused vibe vanished in a blink. He tossed Jase a look rife with concern. "He'll come through this, but it's going to be hard. I'm glad you're here. It's been rough going it alone with him these past few years."

"Whatever I can do to help, I'll do."

"Just keep reminding him that you're here." As Jase got in position to drill the eight ball into the far right pocket, Beck switched gears, starting a joke. "So, an angel walked into a den of iniquity."

The word *angel* made him think of Brook Lynn again, and certain parts of his body began to ache for contact. Every day since he'd met her, he'd gone into town to give her that bill she was so determined to pay and to reimburse her for the implants he'd ruined.

If he were honest, settling their debt had little to do with his frequent trips.

He'd wanted to talk to her, to find out what it would take to break through all of her stubbornness and prickly anger and make her smile. To prove she wasn't as beautiful as he remembered…or as soft and warm. But every time he'd seen her, he'd realized she was *more* beautiful—and probably softer and warmer.

She worked at a jewelry shop Monday through Saturday, and while there, she wore her pale hair in some kind of intricate knot on top of her head, thick locks at her temples tumbling down to frame her exquisite face and, he was sure, to cover her ears. She usually had a pair of magnifying glasses over her eyes and a small pair of needle-nose pliers in hand. Once, as she had helped a guy with grease stains on his hands and overalls, she had talked with her hands, laughing happily at whatever he'd said to her.

Jase had experienced a wave of anger he hadn't understood then—and didn't understand now—and had left before Brook Lynn could spot him.

But he'd gone back again and again.

Most evenings, she worked at Two Farms, and because she was usually the last to leave, she often had to walk to her car alone. Anyone could hide in the shadows, jump out and perform a grab-and-stab. Or worse. And okay, yes, she got points for carrying what looked to be pepper spray, but she lost even more for not paying attention to her surroundings. She was like a Disney princess, practically dancing and singing, "I'm so ready to be disarmed and mugged!"

Did she not realize even small towns had crime?

Case in point: he could be cited for stalking. Hence the multiple beers and his desperation to stay inside the house tonight. He would not risk a legal battle for anyone.

He sank the ball and smirked at Beck. "You going to tell me the rest of the joke?"

"Not a joke. A fact." His friend motioned to the entrance with a tilt of his chin then wiggled his brows.

Jase looked, and yep, he had to agree. An angel *had* walked into a den of iniquity. Beside West stood Brook Lynn Dillon.

Hauntingly beautiful. And completely off-limits.

The urge to touch her, to hold her, bombarded him all over again, and he had to grit his teeth against it.

Feel nothing. Want nothing. Need nothing.

"Hey, Brook Lynn," Beck called. "You're looking mighty fine today—which can mean only one thing. You came to ask me out. Well, it's your lucky day, pretty. I accept."

Jase hit his friend in the arm and muttered, "Don't flirt with her," before he could think better of it.

Beck frowned at him. "Who was flirting? I was baring my soul."

The conversation ceased to matter when he noticed Brook Lynn's eyes were swollen and red, as if she'd been crying. There was a cut on her bottom lip, as if, in her despair, she'd chewed a little too hard.

He threw down his cue. If someone had hurt her—

His hands fisted at his sides as he closed the distance.

Her gaze landed on him and widened. Gulping, she stepped away from him. "Do you, uh, know where Jessie Kay is?"

Had he scared her?

"No," he said, careful to moderate his tone. "I haven't seen or spoken to her."

Her shoulders slumped with defeat and, if he wasn't mistaken, a big dose of fatigue. She worked far too much, couldn't get much more than a few hours of sleep each night. While he admired her fortitude, rarely having seen anyone push themselves so fervently, he knew she couldn't go on like that forever. Soon she would break down. If she hadn't already.

"Are you okay?" he asked. "How are your ears?"

Chin trembling, she said, "They're better. I can hear." A second later, the trembling stopped, and determination darkened her eyes. Stubborn side engaged. "By the way, I never heard from you, so I didn't know which of us needed to deduct the money. I just took a guess at how much I owed you." She stretched out her hand. In her palm rested three crisp one hundred dollar bills.

He jolted back as if she'd just offered nuclear waste, wondering how long she'd had to save for so little. "Hell, no. That's way too much." A single penny was too much, he decided. "The lamp was ugly, so you did me a favor. I should probably pay *you* for getting rid of it. And the nightstand has a crack, nothing more. It's no big deal."

Brook Lynn breathed a sigh of relief as she stuffed the money in her purse. "If you're sure…"

"I am. Now, how much do I owe you for the implants?" he asked.

She shifted from one foot to the other. "They… weren't cheap."

"That's fine."

"Like, over two thousand dollars not cheap." She whispered the amount, as if scandalized. "If your furniture cost something similar—"

"No." He didn't blink. "I'll bring the money to Rhinestone Cowgirl tomorrow. The full amount."

She looked taken aback. "You know where I work? Never mind. Everyone knows. I don't…I can't accept so much…I—"

"Just say thank you and save us the trouble of arguing. You won't win."

She rubbed at her temples in a clear effort to ward off an oncoming ache. "Thank you."

Better.

"And now," she said, squaring her shoulders. "I guess there's nothing more for us to say."

He hated himself and his weakness for her, but he

wasn't ready to be parted from her, even though he knew better than to try to hang on to anything. The longer you had it, the more it hurt when it was taken away—and it was *always* taken away. "I'll walk you out."

"No need," she said, turning on her heels. "I'll be okay on my own."

"Okay or not, I'm still walking you out." He would not be like the double-douches at the restaurant and leave her on her own.

She'd definitely gotten the implants fixed. Without reading his lips, she had a ready reply. "If your goal is to make sure I make it to my car, feel free to watch me through the window. You do like it when women walk away from you, do you not?" She disappeared through the doorway.

"Poor Jase. Denied and burned at the same time," Beck said, shaking his head with mock sympathy.

West grinned. "Would you like some aloe vera for your soul, Jason?"

He flipped both of them off, choosing levity over man-pouting, and raced after Brook Lynn.

The moon seemed to have withered into a small hook, its golden glow hidden by clouds. The air was fragrant with the sweet scent of the magnolias, roses and strawberries growing along the edges of the house, turning what should have been a creepy night into a time for lovers. His hands curled into fists.

Brook Lynn stiffened as he came up alongside her, but said nothing to rebuke him.

"Pepper spray," he said, noticing she carried her weapon, at least. "That's good."

"Oh, this isn't pepper spray." She held up a tube of hand sanitizer. "I don't want to hurt people, just germs."

This is a joke. Has to be. "So if a mugger leaves you bleeding on the street, at least you won't contract a case of the sniffles. Is that it?"

"A mugger?" She scoffed at him. "Where do you think we are? The city? There hasn't been a mugging in Strawberry Valley since Wanda Potts decided to role-play with her husband and steal his virtue."

"I don't care what's happened in the past. I want you armed for the future."

"Hello. I *am* armed." She waved the sanitizer in his face. "The world is going to spiral into a zombie apocalypse one day...unless we get proactive and do something. It's called germ warfare. Look it up. I'm doing my part."

"That's not what germ— Never mind. You fear *zombies*?"

"Fear? No. That's Kenna. I'm actually looking forward to battling the undead. I plan to collect their heads like trophies."

Why was that so damn sexy?

Hint: *everything* about her was sexy. Even the fact that she was clearly a hot mess. He'd never actually met someone who believed zombies were a real possibility.

His legs were longer than hers, his stride faster, so he reached her car first and opened the door for her. She didn't get in right away, pausing to blink up at him. Confused by the gesture? Did she not expect the men in her life to be nice to her—or did she not expect *Jase* to be nice?

Either answer would have annoyed him, he was sure, so he didn't bother asking.

"You're headed home, right?" Knowing her—and as much time as he'd spent watching her, he was beginning to learn—there was a chance she had a third and fourth job.

"No. I have to find my sister. She and I are due to have a chat."

Wait. He shifted, blocking Brook Lynn from sliding into the car. "You have no idea where she is. How do you know where to start looking?"

"I feel like you should already know the answer to that," she said, a little sass to her tone. "Did you or did you not sleep with her?"

He glared, not appreciating the reminder.

"Fine." She held up her hands, all innocence. "I'll be starting with the bars."

"And you're going to…what? Go inside every one you come across between here and the city?"

He expected her to deny it. *Wanted* her to deny it. Instead, she softly announced, "Yes. But don't worry. This won't be the first time. Everyone pretty much knows me now and leaves me alone."

Oh, hell, no. This delicate female had no idea how to protect herself from predators. Zombie or otherwise. He would stake his life on it. And yet she planned to trek through seas of drunken men who were only looking to score? Who may not take kindly to being rejected?

"I'm going with you." The moment the statement registered, he cursed. He couldn't help her the way she needed without finding himself in a whole lot of trouble she wouldn't understand. He added, "West and Beck are going with us." Problem, meet Solution.

Her surprise was immediate. Not used to anyone doing anything to help her with her sister? The idea alone made his chest throb, and he couldn't blame coincidence this time. For some reason, this woman affected him in a way no one else ever had.

Would Daphne affect him even more deeply, now that they were adults?

"I couldn't ask—" she began.

"You didn't ask. I'm telling."

Her eyes narrowed, her golden lashes nearly fusing together. She opened her mouth to snap a sharp reply, he was sure, before her shoulders sagged with defeat. "All right. Thank you."

Determination could only carry a person so far, and she'd reached the end of hers.

He called for his friends, explained the situation; they didn't hesitate.

"We'll find her, no problem," Beck said.

"Grab your keys," Jase said to West. "We can re-schedule pool time."

"You don't have to reschedule—" Brook Lynn began, but Jase gave her a withering glare, and she changed her tune. "I'll drive."

West glanced at Brook Lynn's junkyard clunker and grimaced. "I insist we take my car."

"I don't want to use up your gas," she called as he stalked back into the house.

Much better to use West's gas than what little there had to be of hers. "Come on." Jase helped her settle into the backseat of West's Mercedes.

"Why are you doing this?" she asked, even more confused. "You don't like Jessie Kay, and you don't like me, but you're still willing to help us?"

"I never said I didn't like you," he informed her, moving in beside her.

As his friends claimed their spots up front, she looked at him, her lovely face illuminated by the ve-hicle's interior light, her expression almost...sad. "I've learned that actions speak so loudly, words often don't need to be uttered."

"Well, I think my actions tonight are proving I like you just fine." Liked her far too much.

As they motored down the country roads, he turned and gazed out the window—anywhere but at her—hoping to stop the now-constant ache, end the conversation and shatter his awareness of her in one fell swoop.

He accomplished only one out of three and cursed.

Brook Lynn sat so close to him, the heat of her enveloping him, the scent of her filling his nose, and both fogged his mind.

They passed through his favorite part of town, where different-colored buildings formed connecting lines on each side of the road. Some of the buildings had tin roofs, some shingles. Some were flat; some were pointed. Some of the walls were made of red brick and some of wood. But every single one had character, as if they had come straight out of a painting.

Brook Lynn shifted, rubbing her thigh against his, breaking his concentration. His hands itched for contact... How easy it would be to reach out and twine their fingers.

Hand-holding? What, I'm in junior high now?

"Jase," Brook Lynn whispered and sighed warily. "I like you just fine, too. You're actually a pretty nice guy."

Kind words. For him. The least-deserving person on earth. If she knew half the things he'd done...hell, even a tenth of the things he'd done...she would have kept her lips zipped. But she didn't know, and he reached for her without thought, the need to connect with her stronger than the need to remain self-contained, distant.

Who am I?

The moment his hand covered hers, she visibly relaxed. He tightened his grip, actually clinging to her. *I've helped soothe her. Me. And maybe...maybe she's soothing me, too.* At least a little. Because even though desire for her was building, turning his body into a pressure cooker, he experienced wave after wave of peace. As if the world could catch fire and burn around him, and it wouldn't matter. He was finally where he needed to be, doing what he needed to be doing.

Might not know who I am, but I know I need more of this. Which was the very reason he forced himself to release her.

CHAPTER FOUR

JASE REVERENTLY LAID Brook Lynn on one side of his bed while Beck just sort of plopped Jessie Kay on the other. Both girls were passed out, though for different reasons. Brook Lynn was exhausted. Jessie Kay was trashed.

The lamp on the nightstand cast soft beams of light over Brook Lynn, and Jase found himself standing there, unable to move, staring like a creeper. He'd never expected to meet the real Sleeping Beauty. Silky blond hair spilled around a face as delicate as an antique cameo. Her lashes were so long they curled at the ends. Her heart-shaped lips were red, plumped...begging for a kiss.

A muscle flexed deep in his gut.

"Jessie Kay?" she muttered, the girl clearly never far from her mind.

"She's fine. She's right next to you," he said quietly, not wanting to yank her from that sweet place between sleep and wakefulness. "Beck is tucking her into bed right now."

Her eyes remained closed as she burrowed deeper into the covers. "Home?"

"My home. You slept through most of the search."

"Have to tell her...we...fired."

She and her sister had been fired...from Two Farms? Surely. It was the only job they worked together.

Her earlier tears suddenly made sense. That muscle in his gut flexed all over again.

He'd learned a lot about Brook Lynn tonight, and he'd liked every detail. She was dedicated. Loyal. Kind. Caring. Determined. Sweet.

Too sweet for me.

Only a fool would fire her. And knowing her situation? The fool had to be a major asshole. Somehow she had become a mother to her older sister, and she was a damn good one.

"Jase?" Beck's voice whispered through the room.

He glanced up. His friend now stood in the doorway, waving him out. Though he hated to leave, he dragged his feet into the hall, shutting the girls inside.

In the kitchen, West gripped a beer in each hand. His eyes were darker than usual, reflecting the shadows underneath.

Beck cursed under his breath. "Seriously?"

"No need for a hissy, Becklina. These aren't for me." West handed a beer to each of them. "You've both earned a drink. And don't even think about refusing."

In unison, they claimed a spot at the table.

Jase clinked his bottle against Beck's. "Congratulations. You got twelve numbers during tonight's mission. It's a new record."

"Yeah. An all-time low. I must have been off my game somehow," the guy said with a slight pout.

West rolled up his shirtsleeves. "Beck's lack of success is not tonight's top story. This just in—Jase has feelings for Brook Lynn." He waved his hand around the center of the table. "Discuss."

Feelings? Him? He slammed the bottle on the table with more force than he'd intended. "You're wrong. I barely know her, but even if I did feel something—

which I don't and never will—I won't go after her. That delicate Southern flower would cut and run the moment she learned the truth about me."

West frowned at him. Beck patted his shoulder. Both radiated the ever-present guilt and sorrow he hated so much, as if they were to blame for even this.

He loved them, but sometimes he couldn't stand to be in the same room with them. It hurt too much.

"Besides, if I wanted Brook Lynn, why would I be thinking about finding Daphne?" he asked. "Tell me that."

"Daphne?" Beck shook his head, hanks of hair falling over his forehead. "Why the hell are you thinking about her? She left you when you needed her most."

"Maybe *I* left *her*," he said. He might have blamed her for their split at first, but then he'd gotten over himself and reviewed the situation through her eyes. His actions had presented her with a clear-cut choice: a life of misery with him or a chance at happiness without him. It wasn't brain surgery.

West scowled at him. "You were forced to leave her."

"No. No, I wasn't. I chose to do what I did, and the decision cost me."

Silence descended, tense, oppressive. Jase looked away from his friends, his gaze skipping over the room. *Have got to finish repairing this place.* It was time. They were settled in, and they weren't going to move. Not again.

The yellowed wallpaper had what looked to be strawberries scattered in every direction. He'd already replaced the chipped and stained laminate counters with marble and the parquet floor with stone, only to stop. Some part of him recognized the house had become a metaphor for his life. Bits and pieces fixed up, the rest a crumbling wreck.

While a little manual labor would change the house, nothing would ever change him.

"Jase," West said. "Forget about Daphne. We need to talk about the reason you won't admit you're developing feelings for Brook Lynn."

Seriously. When had these two become such pusses? "I have no feelings," he insisted. "I'm too screwed up."

"We're *all* screwed up," Beck said. "But that doesn't stop me from trying."

"Boy-o, you haven't been trying," West said. "You've been plowing, sowing the proverbial wild oats."

If people were clay, then the past was the pair of hands on the spinning wheel, shaping…shaping…*mis*shaping. They'd each been dried and hardened damaged. The only way to change them now was to break them. But Jase had been broken before and had tried to glue the pieces of himself back together. Had suffered in ways he wouldn't wish on his worst enemy. He was different now—worse.

He would *not* break again.

"Forget about me. You're avoiding the heart of the issue, Jase," Beck said softly, leaning back in his chair. "We all are, and it's not doing us any good. So I'm just going to say it. Because despite the fact that we all did what we did together, we've never spoken the words aloud."

A stilted pause as Jase shook his head. They hadn't spoken the words aloud because he couldn't bear to hear them.

"Nine years ago," Beck continued, "we committed a terrible crime. The three of us. Together."

Not ready to do this. Jase drained his beer then drained Beck's. "Enough."

The color faded from West's face, but still he said, "We killed someone."

Jase went still. Why were they doing this to him? As if he would ever forget.

West, looking haunted, said, "They deemed it voluntary manslaughter."

"You refused to name names and testify against us to reduce your sentence," Beck added, "so you were given the maximum penalty."

"I know. I know all of this," Jase snarled, his rough voice echoing off the walls. "Enough!"

Damn it, the girls.

He twisted in his chair to watch the door in the hallway. A minute passed…two…three… To his immense relief, it never opened.

He released a breath he hadn't known he'd been holding. He never wanted Brook Lynn to discover he was an ex-con. A murderer. That he'd committed the crime not in self-defense but in white-hot rage.

"I expected the purging of the poison to make me feel better," Beck said, slumping in his chair. "Instead I only feel worse."

"Yeah," West said, just as despondent. "That kind of sucked."

Jase's mind drifted to the hours before his entire world had come tumbling down…when he and the boys had been so hungover they'd slept the day away. Tessa had come barreling into the apartment, tears streaming down her cheeks, waking them. It had taken a while, but West had finally gotten the story out of her. She'd gone to a party with her girlfriends and one of the guys there—Pax Gillis—had followed her when she left and raped her in her car.

Even now, bile burned his stomach at the thought.

They'd gone after the guy and beaten him bloody, and it should have stopped there. But even after Pax passed out, their rage hadn't cooled. They'd continued to whale...and whale...until finally stopping no longer mattered. The damage was done.

Even though Jase had paid for the crime—again and again—guilt had plagued him ever since, almost as bad as prison. Almost. Books and movies often tried to depict the horrors of life behind bars, but they weren't even close to the reality. There was no privacy. Few privileges. Food he wouldn't serve to dogs. Hour after hour spent with nothing but memories—and other inmates. Constant threats of violence...rape. Carving weapons in secret simply in an effort to protect yourself, all while living with the knowledge that years would be added to your sentence if you were ever caught. But what else could you do? Let someone shank you?

Been there, done that. And he had the scars to prove it.

Jase would rather die than go back.

"I know you." Beck returned to subject one. "You prefer commitment. Need it. But ever since your release—"

Speaking over him, Jase said, "The boy locked behind bars was not the man who emerged. I've changed."

"The core of you hasn't." Beck pegged him with a hard stare. "You've been settling for randoms, and I don't know why. I mean, I know why *I* do it. Panties melt off whenever I enter a room, and it'd be criminal not to do something about it. But that's not the reason you do it."

"I know why," West said softly. "You don't think you're good enough. You don't think you deserve better."

He pushed to his feet. "This is the last time I'm going to say it. Enough." A familiar rage brewed, dark and hungry.

Calm. Control.

His friends only wanted the best for him. He knew that. Just as he knew they thought they owed him for letting him take the fall for them, not realizing they'd long ago paid their debt in full. And not just for the money and the house. They were the only visitors he'd had his entire time behind bars, showing up at least twice a week. They'd offered ears to listen and, as puss as this sounded, hearts to care. Not that he'd ever shared the worst of his experiences.

They didn't know he would never trust anyone else and would always assume the worst of everyone around him. That he would never stop looking over his shoulder, expecting to be attacked. No woman would ever be able to put up with that for long. If one even wanted to be with an ex-con.

Brook Lynn was the one who deserved better.

So was Daphne. Hell, so was Jessie Kay.

Damn it! He'd come to Strawberry Valley desperate for a clean canvas, but all he'd done was paint it black.

"I'm going for a walk," he said. *Have to get out of here.* There was a pond deep in the heart of their land where the fish practically jumped into his hands. The little slice of tranquillity might be just what he needed.

Beck glanced at the clock on the wall. "It's 2:00 a.m."

"I think I can handle the dark," he said, trying for a

dry tone. Deep down, he knew his words weren't exactly true. There was darkness in his mind, in his soul, and he'd *never* handled them. Would he ever?

CHAPTER FIVE

BROOK LYNN LIFTED her arms overhead, arched her back and extended her legs while pointing her toes. As she stretched, the heavy ache of slumber gradually receded from each of her limbs. Sunlight spilled over her, warming her. The seductive scent of masculine musk mixed with the pleasant fragrance of honey and oats enveloped her, fusing with the very fabric of her being. The softness of the sheet beneath her paired with the comforter above her made her feel as though she'd been swathed by clouds. It was, quite simply, heaven on earth. Something she hadn't experienced in a very long time. If ever.

The only thing that would have made the moment better was a bowl of her French toast casserole, baked with layers of fresh bread, heavy cream, brown sugar and the pecans that fell from the tree shrouding her front porch.

Her stomach rumbled, all *get up and prepare this* now.

She blinked open her eyes. An unfamiliar—no, slightly familiar—setting greeted her. A single window was draped by navy blue curtains. Minimal furnishings: a bed, two nightstands and a dresser. The wood floor was scuffed. Realization struck, and she frowned. She'd been here once before—and it had not been an enjoyable experience.

Realization struck a second time. This was Jase's bedroom.

She jolted upright, her heart a wild cascade against her ribs as she zeroed in on the damage she had caused here. The nightstand with *a crack, nothing more* looked ready to crumble. The "ugly" lamp was a porcelain beauty marred by a crater.

The dark brown comforter on the bed—moved.

Gasping, she scrambled back…falling off the edge of the bed and hitting the floor with a loud thump. She jumped to shaky legs, ready to defend herself from—

"Jessie Kay?"

A soft, sleepy moan registered, followed by a breathy sigh. Relief poured through Brook Lynn as her sister rolled to her side, soon returning to a sleep coma anyone suffering with exhaustion would envy.

A quick scan proved the girl was unharmed and fully dressed, missing only her shoes. Brook Lynn was fully dressed and without shoes, as well, wearing the same T-shirt and shorts she'd worn last night. But though she searched, she found no sign of their footwear.

Bits and pieces of memory teased the fringe of her mind. Searching bar after bar with West and Beck while Jase opted to guard the car. At some point she must have fallen asleep. She had a vague recollection of Jase carrying her to his bedroom. For a moment, she'd thought she was floating. Then she'd felt a strong heartbeat against her temple…steel-hard arms undergirding her…the most delicious heat wrapping around her.

Why hadn't Jase taken her and Jessie Kay home? To *their* home? And dang it, where was her cell phone? If she didn't call Edna soon, there would be hell to pay. Who was she kidding? There was already hell to pay. The clock beside the bed proclaimed 10:03 in bold red

numbers. Brook Lynn was seriously late. And if she lost *that* job…

She stalked into the bathroom, took care of business and washed up quickly, brushing her teeth with paste on her index finger. It wasn't ideal, but the only other option was using Jase's toothbrush, and she would rather die than allow his mouth to come that close to hers, even by proxy.

Her reflection revealed a bedraggled mess with rosy cheeks and eyes sparking wildly. With anticipation? Excitement? No, no. Of course not. More like frustration and annoyance.

In the hallway, the scent of bacon and eggs saturated the air, causing her mouth to water and her stomach to rumble all over again. She hadn't had a decent meal in… Crap, when was the last time she'd had a decent meal? There was rarely enough time to shop or cook, even though she loved to do both, so she usually snacked on bread and cheese at Two Farms.

Won't be able to do that *anymore.*

Before she could work up another cry over the loss of a major source of income, the sound of banging registered. She followed the noise to the kitchen, where two plates piled high with food rested on the table. Somehow she found the strength to keep walking *without* snatching a piece of bacon—or twelve.

Hinges creaked as she pushed her way outside. The temperature instantly rose…oh, if she had to take a guess, she'd say seven hundred degrees. Bright rays of sunlight burned her eyes.

Squinting, she padded onto the cement. "Ow, ow, ow." It burned, too! She jumped onto the soft grass, two black birds taking flight in front of her. She scanned the yard—and finally found the source of the bang-

ing. Jase, with a hammer. *Shirtless* Jase. Muscles honed from intense manual labor bulged as sweat glistened and trickled down tanned skin and more tattoos than she'd realized. One of his arms was fully sleeved, the colorful ink wrapping over his shoulder and covering his pectoral. On his other side, his rib cage and torso were etched with intricate designs. A handful of what looked to be letters rose above the waist of his shorts.

Am I drooling? I'm probably drooling. Wow. Just wow. He was major man-candy. Gourmet. The house specialty. He radiated the most sublime sex appeal, the kind that shattered the most ingrained resistance and battered the staunchest inhibitions, and he would definitely satisfy even the most intense sweet tooth. He worked the hammer with masterful expertise, as though he could fix anything, anywhere, anytime, and she had to admit it was total girl porn.

How she longed to close the distance and study every inch of him more closely. Study, yes…

Perhaps touch…

He paused to wipe his face with a rag, and she almost moaned at the increased deliciousness of him. If *almost* was the new word for *loudly.*

He looked up and stilled.

"Brook Lynn." His sunglasses were light enough that she was able to watch his gaze travel over her slowly, leisurely.

Her body reacted as though physically caressed, tingling and aching in her most intimate places. Heat flash? Maybe. Probably.

"Good morning," he said, his voice a husky rasp just as sexy as the rest of him.

"Morning." She gulped and wiped her hands on the side of her wrinkled shorts. *Don't gawk at his chest.*

Certainly don't glance lower. "My phone. My keys. Shoes." *Making words should not be this difficult.* "Do you know where they are?" Better.

"Phone and keys are in the kitchen. Shoes are in your car."

She must have been too focused on the noise—and then the food—to notice the phone and keys. "Well, then. Thank you. For everything," she added, only to hesitate. "But, uh…I'm a little confused about why you didn't just take Jessie Kay and me to *our* home."

"Two reasons." He set the hammer aside. "I didn't have permission to enter your residence, and Jessie Kay had had too much to drink. She needed to be monitored, so…" He shrugged.

So he'd acted like the gentleman he'd once claimed he wasn't. "Well, thank you. Again," she said and turned to retreat inside. Only then, with her gaze off him and a little distance between them, was she able to breathe.

How did he affect her so strongly? And how could she make it stop?

"You didn't eat," he said, coming in behind her.

Her eyes widened as she rounded on him, her breath hitching when she discovered he was close enough to touch. Close enough to press against, male hardness to female softness, if only she leaned forward the slightest… little…bit. *No! Bad Brook Lynn! Bad!*

Then his words hit her. "That feast is for me?"

His nod was slow, and his gaze hot on her, as if he'd sensed the direction of her thoughts. "Your sister, too."

Needing no further encouragement, she sat at the table and dug in, soon caught up in a whirlwind of different tastes and textures, moaning with rapturous delight. Yes, she would have added a few other spices to take the flavor to a whole new level, but all in all the meal rocked her socks.

When she finished, she dabbed at her mouth with a napkin. *Oh,* now *I'm ladylike?* She looked up to find Jase had removed his sunglasses, but hadn't pulled on a shirt...and he was staring at her as intently as she'd stared at him. It was disconcerting. Especially since his features were blank, and she couldn't read him.

A blush burned her cheeks, and she cleared her throat. "Don't judge me." *Or my new food baby.*

He arched a brow. "Is that what I was doing?"

Surely. "Well." She cleared her throat again. "Anyway. My compliments to the chef."

"That would be Beck."

Never would she have guessed the pretty boy had a skill that didn't involve a mattress and a panting partner. "Did he train at the Institute of Divine Cuisine and Hellish Addiction?" Jessie Kay had often accused Brook Lynn of sneaking into classes.

"More like the Institute of That Was Fun, But Now It's Time for You to Go."

Nice. "You guys and your one-night stands," she said and rolled her eyes.

"Is that *judgment* I hear, angel?"

Angel? The endearment proved a thousand times more personal and tantalizing than "honey," shocking her to the core. Of course, he'd meant nothing by it. She figured he probably used the words interchangeably with every female he encountered—even with her sister. But...

I'm still reeling.

"No judgment," she said and stood. "And now it's time for me to jet." *Before I do or say something more stupid.* "I'm late for work, so...this is goodbye."

His gaze still locked on her, he stepped closer to her, too close for comfort. She should have backed up, if only out of a sense of propriety, but she remained in place. He crossed his arms over his massive chest, those green eyes heating, burning. A sign of...arousal?

The provocative scent of him filled the air between them; it was masculine, sultry and heady, and it fogged her thoughts. It must have. Why else would she have continued to gaze up at him instead of running away?

"Jase?"

"Brook Lynn."

Her heart must have heard music her ears couldn't pick up, because the treacherous organ whipped into a frenzied beat, perhaps even doing cartwheels. Her breaths began to come faster, and shallow. *I'm panting. I'm freaking panting.* She shifted from one side to the other. He took another step toward her, as if compelled, then another, the last whisper between them vanishing.

He's the predator, and I'm the prey.

Need more space. Now!

Finally, the synapses in her brain connected, and she hopped backward. As one minute ticked into another, relief remained just out of reach. In fact, she'd just made everything worse, her body aching...desperate to be close to him again...determined to hold on to a strength unlike any she'd ever encountered...to be held on to, as if she were precious, as if she were worth anything, worth everything.

The distance had the opposite effect on him. He snapped out of...*whatever they'd been doing* and gave a clipped shake of his head. He massaged the back of his neck and even took a step backward on his own, asking, "How much money do you make at the jewelry store?"

No way. No way he'd gone there. "What size is your penis?" she snapped.

He didn't miss a beat. "Ex-large."

His balls were that size, too. "Well, my paycheck isn't your business." It was so pathetic, she almost wished it wasn't *her* business.

She carried her empty plate to the sink, at last spying her phone and keys…right next to a check for two thousand dollars, made out to her. She nearly hyperventilated as she clutched the small piece of paper to her chest. It was more than she'd ever had in her possession.

"I don't…I can't…"

"Don't even think about refusing," he said.

"I…I won't." She couldn't. And she couldn't face him, this man who'd just saved her from certain financial ruin. She'd finally do what her body wanted and throw herself at him. "Thank you."

"You're welcome."

Her phone vibrated, signaling a text had just come in. She checked the screen to find three missed calls and four texts, all from Edna.

You're late, Brook Lynn. I'm going to assume you meant to call and alert me?

Edna had never learned to abbreviate.
Where are you??????? the second text read.
Third: Are you coming in today or not?
Fourth: THIS IS VERY UNPROFESSIONAL MISS DILLON. PERHAPS YOU AREN'T SERIOUS ABOUT WORKING HERE OR BUYING THE SHOP.

Just peachy. "I've got to go," she said on a sigh. "If you could give Jessie Kay a ride home, I'd appreciate it."

Brook Lynn continued to do her best to avoid looking at him, although her reason for doing so had changed. Reminded of her sister...reminded of what this man had done to Jessie Kay, *with* Jessie Kay, a flood of guilt swept through her.

I shouldn't want to hold him or be held by him. I should want to slap him.

Jase opened his mouth, closed it. He ran a hand through his hair, the thick muscles in his arms knotting, his body radiating a frustration his facial features failed to project.

"I'd...like to offer you a job," he finally gritted out.

That was what bothered him? The thought of offering her a job?

Wait. Back up. He actually wanted her to work for him? Shock forced her to meet his gaze once again. His eyes were darker, deeper...infinite. She shivered, her tone breathless as she asked, "A job?"

He inclined his head, saying more easily, "As my assistant."

"Your assistant?" When had she become an echo?

Another incline of his head.

"I don't understand," she said. "Why do you need an assistant? What do you even do?"

"I live."

"You live." Echoing again. "What does that mean?"

He scrubbed a hand over his face. "Look, I have to fix this place up, make sure it's safe. Habitable. I can't do that if I'm always leaving to buy supplies."

"So you'd want me to buy supplies?"

"Among other things," he muttered.

"What other things?" Love-shack cleanup? Finding all the panties stuffed in his mattress?

"This and that."

"Wow. You're *so* informative." But she needed another job. Desperately. Her Rhinestone Cowgirl wages weren't enough to survive *and* thrive. "How much would you pay me? What hours would I work? Monday through Saturday, I wouldn't be able to start until sometime after noon. And why do you want *me*?"

The words reverberated in her head, the burn returning to her cheeks. "I mean," she added, "what skills do you think I bring to the table?" She'd graduated high school, sure—barely. After her mother died, she'd stopped caring about her grades. And after Uncle Kurt left, she'd been too busy working any odd job she could find, trying to make money and remove some of the burden from Jessie Kay's shoulders. Delivering newspapers and running errands for her neighbors hadn't exactly allowed her to build a sought-after skill set.

Jase thought for a moment, sighed. "You're loyal and dedicated, two of my favorite things. In an employee," he was quick to add.

Her brow furrowed as she considered his words. "How do *you* know I'm loyal and dedicated? This is only our third conversation."

His expression said *do we really need to get into that?*

No, she supposed they didn't. The answer was simple. The way she chased after Jessie Kay.

"I'll pay you five hundred dollars a week," he said.

What! Did he expect her to hand over a kidney, too? Did she care? The greatest opportunity of her life had just presented itself on a maple-syrup-soaked breakfast platter. And, really, the job would be easy. A basic fetch and carry, with a little of *this* and *that* on the side. Baking? Getting rid of one-night stands?

Done, done and done. With a smile.

But she couldn't rush into anything, had to chat with her sister, weigh the pros and cons. "I need a day to think about it," she said.

He nodded, as if he'd expected such a response. "Call me tomorrow."

"I'll need your—"

"My number is already programmed into your phone."

Uh… "How is it programmed into my phone? I didn't add it."

"No, you didn't. But I did."

How— Oh! There was no pass code to safeguard her list of contacts—because she couldn't afford a new phone and had to make due with an old flip.

Her hands curled into fists. "You had no right to do that."

"Delete it, then," he replied, shrugging. "Whatever."

"Delete what?" Jessie Kay strolled into the kitchen, looking as fresh as a daisy. No sign of a hangover, which hardly seemed fair. She patted Jase's behind as she passed him, saying, "Hey, handsome. You sure are looking good this morning."

His lips almost—almost—deepened into a scowl as he backed away from her. Did he ever feel anything? Really feel?

"What?" Jessie Kay asked with an unrepentant grin. "Just appreciating the machinery. Nothing wrong with that."

Brook Lynn battled an intense surge of jealousy at the thought—

Jealousy? No, no. Indigestion. Almost definitely for sure there was a chance indigestion was all it was. "There's food for you on the table," she said, and her sister immediately changed directions. "After you eat,

Jase will drive you home." The *indigestion* grew worse. "Stay there. Please. After my shift at Edna's, we need to talk."

You were supposed to go see your doctor and ask out Brad today.

Well, crap. *Forget the doctor and Brad. Forget the fun list.* Opening lines of communication with Jessie Kay was far more important. How would her sister react to Jase's job offer? Happy for her? Envious?

"Dude," Jessie Kay said. "Don't we have a shift at the restaurant tonight?"

As if she cared. Heck, as if she really would have shown up.

"News flash. We got fired."

"What?"

"Mr. Calbert fired us. He said he couldn't rely on us anymore."

"Us? Or me?"

"Both of us. I got looped in because I couldn't hack double shifts all the time."

"Well, he did us a favor. *I* did us a favor." Her sister shrugged. Actually shrugged. "That job sucked donkey balls."

"Maybe, but we needed it." Brook Lynn sighed. "Just…make sure you're home when I get back from Edna's. We need to talk about things. I mean it."

"Sure, sure." One slice of bacon vanished, then another, and her sister moaned with delight.

"I don't think you heard me. You go home, you stay."

Jessie Kay rolled her eyes. "I'm not a total slag. I said I'll be there, so I'll be there."

"Like yesterday at work?"

"Extenuating circumstances."

"Such as?"

"I'd lost most of my stomach lining and probably a lung."

That was fair. "All right." Brook Lynn allowed herself a final glance at Jase—those dark eyes were still locked on her. She shivered, cursed herself and her apparent weakness for the forbidden and left the house.

BROOK LYNN PARKED her car in a lot a few blocks from Rhinestone Cowgirl. Edna claimed the spaces in front of the shop needed to remain free for customers, but the truth was she considered Rusty an abomination.

She wasn't wrong.

As the sun glared, Brook Lynn raced down the sidewalk. People she'd known her entire life waved and hollered out greetings.

"Running late?" Virgil Porter asked from his rocker. Though he owned Swat Team 8—*we assassinate fleas, ticks, silverfish, cockroaches, bees, ants, mice and rats*—he often sat with the owner of Style Me Tender Salon across the street from the jewelry store, playing checkers.

"Unfortunately," she replied. In a town this small, everyone knew everyone else's schedule.

"Explains why Edna was pacing the sidewalk, telling everyone who passed you'd broken her heart," Mr. Rodriguez said. He gave the best buzz cut in a twenty-mile radius. His only competition, Rhett Walker, gave what Mr. Rodriguez referred to as "bootleg butchers" in his mother's garage.

"Edna's going with a broken heart?" Peachy. Usually, whenever Brook Lynn messed up, she went with betrayed trust.

Brook Lynn flew through the shop doors so late she'd

missed more time than she would actually work, a horror of horrors for a perpetual early bird.

"I'm so sorry, Edna."

The owner of the RC leaned against the counter and crossed her arms.

Brook Lynn expected to be scolded, wanted to be—*deserved it*—but in the ensuing minutes Edna somehow made her feel as if she'd dropped an H-bomb on the town.

Oh, the guilt trip.

"Do you know how many frantic calls I had to deal with this morning, people wondering if I was going out of business?" Edna asked.

"No, ma'am."

"Two!"

Wow. That many?

"It ruined my entire morning, Brook Lynn—*you* ruined it. And after everything I've done for you."

"I'm sorry, Edna," she said again. "I promise to bring you a Swiss enchilada casserole tomorrow. Your favorite."

Edna dabbed at eyes that weren't even close to watery. "You were once my favorite, too. I loved you like the daughter I never had." Edna had always been one of those people who craved the sympathy hardship bought her and milked every situation to her advantage. "It's like my heart is breaking right inside my chest."

"You actually *have* a daughter," Brook Lynn pointed out.

"Yes, but she's such a disappointment. You never were...until today."

Ouch.

Edna puttered around the shop, dusting display cases

that didn't need to be dusted. She was a short, round woman with miraculously unlined skin and a pretty crop of silver hair. Her cheeks were always rosy, and to be honest, she could have passed for Mrs. Santa Claus... until she opened her mouth.

"Caroline moved to the city to attend massage school, you know," Edna continued, stuck on the topic of her daughter. "Never mind the fact that *I* have back pain and could use a healing touch every now and then."

Brook Lynn faded in and out of the ensuing lecture about giving being better than taking, offering the occasional "Mmm-hmm" and "You're so right." *Heard this a thousand times before.* But at least they were back on familiar territory.

Then the words "If you're serious about buying this shop one day..." caught her attention.

"I am," she rushed to reply.

"Yes, but if you're truly serious—"

"I truly am."

"I mean truly, *truly* serious, then you'll show up on time," Edna said with a sharp stare. "Every. Single. Day."

"Absolutely." Brook Lynn would offer no excuses for today's tardiness. She'd heard too many over the years and had learned to hate them.

They had it coming, baby girl. Always courtesy of Uncle Kurt.

Dude. I had to. That beer was calling my name. Always courtesy of Jessie Kay.

So, even though this was one of Brook Lynn's first official offenses at the RC, she made no effort to defend herself. "I promise you it won't happen again."

Edna released a long-suffering sigh. "We'll see."

"I'd be happy to stay super late to make up for it."

"That might be a start." Edna gathered her purse and strolled to the front door, saying, "I'm headed to my new book club. We're deciding whether to call ourselves The Strawberry Bookcakes or Strawberry Fields of Books." She gave another heavy sigh before saying, "I'm not sure I'll recover if I missed the vote."

More guilt. "Which one are you voting for?"

"Not sure yet," she replied and disappeared outside.

"If you don't know," Brook Lynn muttered, knowing Edna would never hear, "why do you even care which name is picked?"

The next few hours passed without incident...or a single customer. As Brook Lynn gathered her tools to create a spectacular necklace for the window display case, sure to draw the eye of those passing by, she phoned Kenna to tell her about Jase's job offer, keeping her phone on speaker to save herself from having to press the device against her implants.

"Are you going to take it?" her friend asked.

"Yes. No. Oh, I don't know."

"He's offering a lot of money."

"Yes." She could be debt free in a little over two years. The impossible finally made possible.

"So what's the problem?" Kenna asked. "Do you think there's more to the job than he told you?"

"Like washing and ironing the clothes his myriad lovers leave scattered on the floor? Yes."

Crackling silence over the line before Kenna chuckled softly. "What is that I hear in your tone? Is that *jealousy*?"

"What? No!" More calmly she repeated, "No. I've been battling indigestion today."

"Indigestion. I see."

"You see? What do you think you see, Miss Starr?"

Sweet, tinkling laughter echoed. "I see fun times ahead—for me. By the way, I've booked an appointment at some place in the city for you and Jessie Kay to try on bridesmaid dresses. And I will, of course, reimburse you for any time off work—" A gasp. A low, needy moan. A giggle. "Dane. Stop."

Well, well. Her fiancé had arrived. *Never far from her side.*

A pang of envy as the man whispered, "I'll stop when you've given me everything I want," and oh, wow, his voice was so low, so hot, even Brook Lynn shivered.

I want a happily-ever-after like theirs. Surely I've earned one.

"Brook Lynn," Kenna said, breathless.

"You've got to go. I know. Love you."

"Love you, too. But oh, oh. Wait a sec. I meant to tell you I would be eternally grateful if you would make me a smoked chicken salad sandwich with fresh-baked bread…like, tonight for dinner, maybe? Because you love me and want me happy. I've got a craving."

"You've always got a craving." When they'd lived together, Kenna had left little sticky notes all over the house, begging for this or that sandwich.

"She meant to ask for two sandwiches." Dane's voice shot over the line.

"I meant two sandwiches," Kenna said. "I can have the ingredients waiting at your house and pick the sandwiches up later…"

"You know I can't resist your pleas," she said.

"You're the best!"

"I know." *Click.*

Brook Lynn sighed, wondering if she should rethink her plan to stop by Brad's auto shop after work and just do it, live a little. Her shoulders drooped. No, he still didn't rate higher than her conversation with her sister. Or, for that matter, Jase's job offer. Or her sister's lack of employment. Or past-due notices. Fingers crossed she and Jessie Kay discussed everything without a single argument.

She still wasn't sure how her sister would react to finding out her lover—her onetime lover—had asked *Brook Lynn* for help. As if she'd been rejected by him—again?

Can't do that to her.

Well, then, decision made. As easy as that.

Tomorrow, she would find another second job. Virgil at Swat Team 8 had just lost Kenna and might be willing to take a chance on Brook Lynn. He wouldn't pay nearly as much as Jase, but killing bugs might be better for her state of mind than killing the hopes and dreams of his scorned lovers. Plus, the job wouldn't hurt her sister's feelings. It also wouldn't test Brook Lynn's resolve to avoid the most delicious of temptations.

And he *was* delicious, wasn't he? Still wrong for her, and nothing her life needed, but 100 percent melt-in-your-mouth delicious. And kind of emotionless. What was up with that?

Doesn't matter. Not my problem.

At the end of her shift, she drove straight home, more convinced by the minute that she'd made the right decision. But Jessie Kay's car wasn't in the driveway, and she wasn't inside the house.

Brook Lynn baked the sandwiches for Kenna and Dane, and chatted with the pair for half an hour when they came to collect the food.

She had made sandwiches for Jessie Kay and herself, as well, and wanted to eat them together, but as she waited for her sister to return, one hour bleeding into two, hunger got the better of her and she caved, devouring her own.

She watched two old episodes of *The Walking Dead.* She paced the living room, watched another episode of *The Walking Dead* and practiced severely cool headchopping moves. And…still there was no sign of her sister.

Finally she could stand it no more and texted:

Where R U?

Duuuuude, her sister replied. Lost my phone. Will call U when I find it!

UR srsly telling me U can't find UR phone? she texted back, wanting to scream *You're using it right now!* How drunk R U?

Only had a few, swear! But sis! Sis! My liver was a bad girl 2day & NEEDED 2 B punished.

Attached was a photo of Jessie Kay and her favorite partner in crime, Sunny Day.

Sunny's parents had probably thought "so cute" when they'd come up with the name. Brook Lynn's verdict? So not.

The two were in quintessential selfie mode—Jessie Kay was bent over, lips parted in a perfect O, while Sunny held a paddle at her bottom. Sweat dotted both of their brows. From dancing? Probably. Men stood all around them, practically drooling.

Another text came in, the misspellings out of control.

Knw eve prom 2 all bt came we postpo? Plese?? Pleas???????

Translation: know we promised to talk, but can we postpone? Please? Please?

Beads of anger rolled through Brook Lynn. From the moment their father died, she'd done her best to protect her sister from any sort of emotional pain. She'd even upped her already stellar efforts after their mother died. And *this* was the result?

Brook Lynn had known she needed to change her ways, but this just cinched it. If she wanted different results, she had to do something different. And she would start by refusing to coddle Jessie Kay.

Yay! a part of her cheered. *Finally.*

She wouldn't feel guilty about this. She wouldn't! She'd had enough.

She scrolled to Jase's number in her address book. After only two rings, he answered, the roughness of his voice greeting her, bypassing the usual hello, how are you and getting right to business. "Nice to hear from you, Brook Lynn."

Shivers danced through her. *This is stupid, dangerous for my peace of mind.* But she said, "I'll take the job," before she could talk herself out of it. "Most days I can be there shortly after noon, but tomorrow I can't make it till two. After my shift at Rhinestone Cowgirl I have a personal errand." Her doctor was good about getting her in whenever she had a spare hour. Because yes, she was sticking with the birth-control part of her plan no matter what.

"Two is good." His breath crackled over the line. "I'm looking forward to seeing you." Something about his tone…

It was deep as always, but it sounded like…a promise? Or a warning?

"Me, too," she whispered.

CHAPTER SIX

JASE MIGHT HAVE made the biggest mistake of his life. Then again, he'd done nothing illegal and wouldn't end up in prison, so...

Nope. Somehow this was still a top contender for Worst Mistake Ever.

As another knock sounded at his front door, this one faster and louder, he trudged into the entryway. He knew Brook Lynn waited on his porch, eager to begin her first day as his "assistant." Eager...dreading—little difference.

What the hell am I going to do with an assistant?

It was the last thing he needed or wanted. Until she'd mentioned the loss of her second job. He'd hated the thought of her struggling to find another, one that might not pay as well, then working herself to the bone and slogging her way into an early grave.

He'd tried to prepare himself for his first boss-employee encounter with her, but a man couldn't ever really prepare for torture. And that was exactly what the situation would be. Somehow, she made him feel as if he'd been stripped and strapped to a rack, his chest carved open and his every nerve ending exposed.

And I signed myself up for a daily dose.

Tense, girding himself for impact, he opened the door—the sight of her utterly stole his breath. Silky hair hung around her shoulders in gleaming, platinum waves. Wide, baby-doll eyes that should only ever sparkle with passion were now hardened with determination, but no less arresting. She wore no makeup, and he found he liked the natural rose flush on her cheeks, the golden tips at the ends of her lashes. Liked the sheen of moisture left on her lips as she traced her tongue over the plump bottom one.

That deep, throbbing ache kicked off in his chest, and he gnashed his molars in annoyance.

Feel nothing. Want—

Screw that. He wanted something. He wanted her.

He simply wasn't going to do anything about it.

Her T-shirt read Math Problems? Call 1-800-$\{(10x)(\ln\{13el)]-[\sin(xy)/2.362xl$. A pair of faded jean shorts displayed the spectacular length of her legs to perfection. So did the scuffed, dirt-caked cowgirl boots.

Was his tongue hanging out? The girl could probably rock a garbage bag.

"Reporting for duty, sir," she said, the words flippant…but the little tremor in her voice betrayed her agitation.

He remained in place, blocking her from entry. "First things first. What made you change your mind about working for me?" He'd wondered all night.

Her eyes narrowed, her lashes practically fusing together. "Maybe I used the eenie meenie miney moe method."

"Do you also settle arguments by sticking out your tongue?" *I shouldn't be thinking about her tongue.* "Never mind. Don't answer." He waved her inside.

She stopped in the living room and stuffed her hands in her pockets. "Are West and Beck here?" How hopeful she sounded.

Did she not want to be alone with him? *Not irritated*

by that—thrilled. "West is in the city for business. Beck is out trying to find a place in town for him and West to set up shop."

"And probably sleeping with his real-estate agent," she mumbled. "What do West and Beck do, anyway?"

"Create different kinds of computer programs and games." Jase was as far from tech savvy as possible. Being cut off from society for so long meant everything digital that was so commonplace for everyone else was alien to him. He wasn't even sure how to use some of the apps West had put on his phone.

"Why don't they just work from home?" she asked, her tone now reverent, as if working from home was a dream everyone entertained. "I mean, it's not like they're going to drum up a whole lot of business in Strawberry Valley."

"They drum business all over the world, wherever they are, but they aren't their most productive while I'm making repairs on the house. Or so I've been told." He motioned to the peeling wallpaper. "The boys are part of the reason so little has been done."

Beck, far more than Jase and West, hated change—which was surprising, considering he changed lovers almost every night. Jase had to ease him into each and every home improvement. And West, well, he liked to plan every detail down to the studs—which usually took months.

"Ah." Caught up in their conversation, Brook Lynn forgot to be leery and smiled up at him. The amusement brightened her entire face. "Gave you a verbal spanking for your noisemaking, did they?"

So bright...blinding me to everything else. Making the ache a thousand times worse.

"Nah, they know better than that," he managed, rubbing the spot just over his heart. "I finally kicked them out so I could get started on the larger tasks." *Not* because he'd wanted to be alone with Brook Lynn.

"Why don't you work with them?" she asked. "Considering how close you guys are, I mean."

"Cubicles and computers aren't my bag."

"Are you a silent partner, then? Is that how you guys met? Business?" She blinked and shook her head, as if she'd just realized something important. "You know what? Forget it." She lifted her chin, squared her shoulders. "We might as well get started. What's my first assignment?"

Good question.

He looked around, considering his choices. Something easy. Maybe something that required very little bending over—or a *lot* of bending over.

He must have taken too long to reply, because she added, "How about I give you a detailed history of your house? It's been in the Glass family for a million generations, but there is now only one Glass left. Harlow. She refused to get a job when her mom died, which is how you guys were able to snatch it up, I guess. She was the town bully once upon a time, before becoming a recluse. She's a year older than me and still hangs around town, though no one knows where she's living right now."

Detailed history...or cautionary tale?

"I promise not to bully you. Now, start with the living room," he said, "and end with the kitchen." That way, she'd feel as though she'd contributed something to his day without actually straining herself. And he could make himself scarce so that he wouldn't have to see any bending or not bending.

"You mean...clean them?"

"Spotlessly."

She pursed her lips. "So I'm a maid, as suspected."

"You're an assistant."

"An assistant who cleans your house."

"Good for you. You catch on so quick." He patted the top of her head and tried not to marvel at the silky softness of her hair—or to think about twining a lock in his fist and angling her head for better access to her lips.

What the hell was wrong with him? Since his release, he hadn't kissed a woman. Not even the handful he'd bedded. Not because he thought kissing was anything special. It wasn't. The less distraction, the better, especially while already vulnerable.

Brook Lynn neither stepped away from him nor batted his hand away. "It's funny to me. You truly aren't afraid to lose that hand," she said, utterly calm. "But okay. Fine. Where are the supplies?"

"You'll find everything you need under the kitchen sink. And now, I need to return to my own work." He left her then, forcing himself to walk away.

What else could he say to her, really? Besides, getting chatty with her would be a huge mistake. Already she'd asked a question he hadn't been prepared to answer. *Is that how you guys met?*

His past was his business and not a topic for conversation.

He shut himself outside, hoping the distance between them would help him relax. He only tensed further. It was almost as if he…missed her? Already? She was just so bright, a total contrast with his mind, which was always so dark. He felt drawn to her, and it both ramped him up and soothed him. It was difficult not to crave her presence.

Had to be the summer heat. Yeah. Definitely the

heat. The air was thick with humidity, already stifling. He removed his shirt and picked up his hammer. He'd finished repairs on the shed just before Brook Lynn arrived, knowing it was always best to ensure his tools had a proper place for storage before he took on any other projects. Without tools, a man couldn't work. Without work, Jase would have to listen to his own thoughts.

He labored on the house for an hour...two...replacing slats on the shutters. His gaze constantly strayed to the kitchen window, his desperation to catch a glimpse of Brook Lynn maddening but undeniable. The first time she appeared, he struck his thumb with the hammer and had to choke down a curse. He was grateful she never glanced in his direction.

When he finished with the shutters, he moved on to siding, removing and replacing damaged panels. Sweat continually poured from him and had he been alone, he would have stripped bare and jumped in the pool he'd repaired the first week he'd moved here.

What would Brook Lynn think about *skinny-dipping*?

She'd let him know, that was for sure. Girl was opinionated. He didn't have to wonder where he stood with her, a trait he liked. In prison, inmates smiled to his face and stabbed at his back. In a few of his foster homes, parents laughed with him at lunch and had hushed, closed-door conversations about him after dinner.

Not that every moment of his life had been terrible. There'd been good times. A lot of good times. With Beck and West. Tessa. Daphne. A few foster families. But the bad times had been so damn bad, they often completely eclipsed the good. Could he even remember the last time he'd laughed?

What had Brook Lynn's childhood been like? She

seemed well-adjusted, if a little overly concerned with her sister. Straitlaced. Normal. The kind of girl who would fear a guy like him, once she discovered the truth. He wouldn't be able to blame her.

Keeping her at a distance was now his only defense.

Tomorrow he had a meeting with his new parole officer and— Jase stiffened as problems crystallized. Brook Lynn wouldn't understand a day off so soon. And what if his parole officer ever came for a surprise home visit while she was here?

Damn it, he should have thought this through. Now it was too late.

He'd give her the list of supplies he'd planned to pick up. She could— No, she couldn't. Her beater of a car wouldn't be able to hold pipes and wood planks and boxes of marble. He didn't even want her trying to carry those things.

He'd tell Beck to let her borrow the truck. And for Beck to go with her, do all the heavy lifting.

Jase stiffened all over again. He didn't like the thought of Brook Lynn and Beck spending time together. Alone. In a cramped space.

"Thirsty?"

Her voice startled him, and he almost reintroduced his thumb to the hammer. Damn it! He never lost awareness of his surroundings. He'd trained himself to listen for every incoming footstep, every whisper of movement. That kind of OCD diligence had saved his life on more than one occasion.

In an act of self-preservation, he threw the hammer in the toolbox. As he climbed down the ladder and faced her, this new bane of his existence, she held a glass of ice water out for him.

The thoughtful gesture unnerved him. "Thank you,"

he muttered and drained the contents. The chill of the liquid soothed the dry heat in his throat.

"You're welcome." She took the empty glass from him and stepped away. "So…three women have already come to the door looking for Beck."

"So few?" *And what do you think of Beck, Miss Dillon?* He looked her over, noticing the streak of dirt on her cheek, the smudges of grease on her shirt. *So adorable.* "How old are you?" he asked then flinched at the accusation in his tone.

Most women would have glared at him. She didn't miss a beat. "Twenty-five. What about you?"

"Twenty-eight." Considering he had the life experience of a gutter rat, he felt decades older.

"Have you ever been married?" she asked.

There was only one reason the answer would matter to her, and it caused him to shoot harder than those steel pipes he was going to ask her to buy.

"No," he rasped. "No wife." He'd had a few girlfriends before Daphne, but nobody nearly as serious.

Daphne had seemed to accept him just as he was… until his sentence was handed down, and she realized she'd have to live without him for almost a decade— more than that, he wouldn't be the same when he got out. He'd be different. An ex-con. Harder. Probably mean as hell. Teenagers never fared well behind bars.

He'd begged her to stick around, to trust him, promising to be whatever she needed the day they were reunited. Part of him had still been a little boy, desperate to hold on to some kind of family.

She'd sobbed while she'd walked away, but she'd still walked. He'd cursed her, apologized, begged some more. She hadn't turned around, hadn't even slowed. It had hurt then, and yeah, it still hurt now, but he saw it for what it was. Self-preservation. He couldn't blame her for that.

Had life treated her well? Hell, maybe she was married with a dozen kids. Maybe not.

What would he say to her, if he saw her again? *You were the best thing to happen to me. I miss you.*

Was that still true? And would the man he had become even appeal to her? If she found out some of the things he'd endured throughout the years...would she react as fearfully as he suspected Brook Lynn would?

"Jase?"

Brook Lynn's voice, gentle now, summoned him out of the dark mire of his head. He blinked and found her standing directly in front of him, her cool, dainty palm resting on his knotted shoulder. His hands were fisted, he realized, his nails cutting into his skin. Razors seemed to have grown in his nose and lungs, turning every breath into an act of torture.

Steady. When his gaze met hers, she dropped her arm and backed away.

"So...uh...yeah. I've finished the living room and kitchen." She ran her bottom lip between her teeth, suddenly nervous. "What would you like me to do next?"

Put your hand on me again. Never let go. "Nothing." He cleared his throat. "Go home." *Before I do something stupid.*

"But I've only worked three hours."

Only, she'd said. "Your check isn't contingent on the number of hours you're here, honey. Simply on doing what I say."

She shook her head, saying, "Why don't I clean the bathrooms?"

He did *not* like the thought of this girl scrubbing toilets. "No bathrooms."

"Bathrooms," she insisted. "Then I'll wash up and cook dinner. Unless you have plans?"

He bristled. "No bathrooms. No dinner."

"I'll take that to mean 'no plans.'"

"If you want to do something, clean the garage."

"Great. I will. After I take care of the bathrooms." With a saccharine-sweet smile, she skipped into the house.

"Stay away from the bathrooms. That's an order, Brook Lynn," he called. "My word is law."

She waved at him through the glass door...and might have also flipped him off.

Did she think she could do whatever she wanted without consequences?

Well, she would have to be taught differently.

Anticipation zinged through him, so strong it was almost a shock to his system.

Boom!

The noise sent Jase to the ground, already reaching for the hammer, the closest weapon. Sweat beaded at his temples, trickled down, and he had trouble catching his breath—until the purr of a car engine registered, and he realized a vehicle had simply backfired.

He lumbered to unsteady legs. His heartbeat refused to calm, bucking in his chest like a horse trapped in a stall.

It's okay. I'm okay.

At the end of the day, feelings didn't matter. They were unreliable. He chose to believe he was okay, so that would be that.

Once he regained his composure, he toiled over the shingles. A few more hours passed, and he somehow managed to maintain his focus until Brook Lynn stuck her head out the door.

"I spilled cleaner on myself. I need a shower and a shirt," she said. "Would it be okay for me to use your bathroom and dig through your closet?"

Just like that, she fried what was left of his brain. A thousand cars could have backfired, and he wouldn't have noticed.

Shower—she would be naked. Water—it would drip down her body, catching in all the places he longed to lick. A towel—the cloth would rub all over her curves, caressing her skin. His shirt—something that had touched his bare skin would soon cling to hers, his scent fusing with hers.

Hard. As. A. Rock.

"That's fine," he gritted out.

"Thanks." She vanished.

A few more hours passed, and he spent almost every minute imagining the things she was doing to herself. At last the sun began to set on the horizon, dusting the sky with a wealth of gold, pink and purple, drawing his full attention. He stopped what he was doing, utterly transfixed.

While locked away, he'd missed the simple things most. The everyday things he'd once taken for granted. Sunrises and sunsets. Holidays with his friends. The smell of fresh-baked bread and—

Fresh-baked bread?

He sniffed, and sure enough, he caught the telltale scent of yeast. His mouth watered. Almost in a trance, he made his way into the kitchen. Brook Lynn stood at the stove, stirring something in a pot, and oh…damn. Her hair was still damp from her shower, curling at the ends. The shirt she'd chosen read I'm In for the Win, and even though it was too big for her, she made it look like something out of a high-fashion magazine.

My every fantasy made flesh. She was gorgeous. Sexy. And completely within reach...

He rubbed at the newest ache in his chest.

And a meal made from scratch? That was something he'd never really had, even in foster care, where most of the dishes he'd eaten had come from boxes or cans.

Brook Lynn noticed him and waved the steam away from her face. "I hope this shirt isn't one of your favorites."

It is now. "No," he managed.

"Good. I'm afraid I dribbled sauce on it. Oh, and I'm assuming you like cheesy chicken spaghetti and rolls because that's all you had the groceries for."

He had no idea if he liked them or not. He hadn't even bought those groceries. They'd arrived yesterday, a gift from one of the women hoping to sleep with Beck a second time. "We'll have to learn the answer together."

"Well, you're in for a treat," she said, the heat flushing her cheeks to a deep rose. "Everything will be ready in forty-five minutes."

A lump grew in his throat, and he wasn't sure why. "I'm going to shower." Desperate to escape her, he stalked to his bedroom, locked himself inside.

His bathroom smelled of disinfectant and gleamed like a diamond, and all he could do was curse. Damn that girl. She'd cleaned it, even though he'd forbidden it. *Did I honestly expect anything less?*

He showered quickly, toweled off and dressed. He moved toward the door, only to realize he wasn't quite ready to face Brook Lynn. The urge to touch her still plagued him—and it was stronger than before. He wanted to shake her...then make everything better with his mouth.

Sick to his stomach, he sat down and wrote out a

very long, very detailed list. Then, and only then, his mind centered on her upcoming chores, did he return to the kitchen; he placed the list, a wad of cash and a key on the counter.

Brook Lynn looked at everything, looked at him and arched a brow in question.

"Your chores for tomorrow," he said, gazing past her. The ache in his chest bloomed with renewed force. "Also money to pay for the supplies, and a way into the house. I'll be gone. Personal business."

"Well, I *am* your personal assistant. Right?"

He rubbed the back of his neck. "I have to go."

"Go?" she echoed. "Now?"

This minute. This second. "I...I'm sorry." He strode out of the kitchen...out of the house, not turning back.

SHOCK HELD BROOK LYNN immobile. He'd left. He'd really left. *Without* telling her about his plans for the evening. *Without* tasting the food she'd slaved over. *Without* commenting on all her hard work.

Uncle Kurt had taught her a lot of things she would be better off not knowing, but there was one fact he'd unwittingly driven home. When actions contradicted words, actions won. Every time.

I love you, girls, Uncle Kurt had said. But leaving them destitute wasn't an act of love.

Just now, Jase's actions had said plenty. She wasn't important to him. Her efforts weren't important. But okay. All right. She wasn't here for back pats and flattery. *Show me the money.* She had worked for grumpy, gruff Mr. Calbert, and she could work for—gorgeous—gruff Jase. Probably. Maybe.

At first, she'd hardly gotten anything done. She'd been too busy peeking out the windows, savoring the sight of him and his mighty hammer, trying to avoid his notice whenever he'd glanced her way. But then she'd somehow found the strength to force him out of her mind and buckle down. She'd cleaned as if the Lord Himself planned to come for a visit, no speck of dust left behind. And, surprise surprise, she'd enjoyed every moment of it, knowing she was making Jase's life just a little bit better, the way he was making hers better. So of course, she'd started thinking about him again... about his strength, his tattoos and his hands...all the naughty things he could do with them.

Then she'd walked past his bedroom and remembered finding her sister in bed with him.

Anger and indignation had hit Brook Lynn, and part of her had even yearned to quit. If only giving up were in her nature. The other part of her had demanded she take a stand and let Jase know she was no pushover. He'd tried to baby her, which was why she'd disobeyed his orders. She'd expected a thank-you afterward, maybe even an admission that he'd been wrong. Hello, backfire.

She put the casserole in the fridge without baking it and left a note on the counter with heating instructions. She bagged the rolls, leaving an air pocket to prevent condensation, and finally read over his list— nearly fainting.

Clean the entire house. Even the rooms you cleaned today. All except for the game room, which you are to avoid. Did you get that, Miss Lynn? AVOID.

Grocery shop. At least two carts' worth.

Bake three cakes—one for every owner of the home. There WILL be a taste test.

Wash the windows. Even the hard-to-reach ones.

Wash and fold the laundry.

She shuddered, wondering if he sorted his laundry like

most other men—"filthy" and "filthy but wearable"—
and wondering why she wasn't horrified by the thought
of handling his underwear.

Iron everything in my closet.

*Rearrange the furniture in the living room. Lady's
choice. Take a picture, then put everything back the
way it was.*

*Stack the wood outside. Never know when a cold
front will come in.*

The slam of a door startled her, and she glanced up,
her heart beating in time to the newcomer's pounding
footsteps. Had Jase returned?

Beck rounded the corner, flooding her with disappointment. No, no. Not disappointment. Relief. Of
course.

He drew up short when he noticed her—and grinned.
"Well, well. My Christmas present came early this year.
West scheduled a late night out, and Jase is obviously
gone, considering his car is missing, so it's just you and
me, all alone. Whatever should we do?"

Flirting? Really? He probably couldn't even help
himself, it was so ingrained. While Jase had showered,
two other women had come knocking, wanting to speak
with "my Beck." They'd also demanded to know who
the hell Brook Lynn was and what the hell she was
doing in My Beck's house. The blatant hostility had
merely amused her.

"I don't know if Jase told you," she said, "but he hired
me to be his assistant." Maid. "And then he had to go…
somewhere."

"An assistant, huh?" Beck pointed at her, waving his
finger to indicate her entire head. "You should probably
wear glasses and put your hair in a bun."

"Why?"

"For the role-play. Fully committing to your character makes all the difference."

She nearly choked on her tongue. "We are *not* role-playing. I really am his assistant." Maid.

"If you say so."

"I do. And now I'm leaving. Office hours are officially over."

Beck held out an arm, stopping her from passing. "Hold on a sec, pretty. Your car isn't parked out front."

"That's good, because I walked." There was no reason to use up precious gas when this house was only a mile—or three—from Rhinestone Cowgirl.

He gaped at her. "So…Jase left without giving you a ride?"

"Clearly." Or were they talking about role-playing again? In which case the answer would still be the same. "I'll be fine," she said.

"You sure will, because I'll be driving you to your car." Beck scanned the kitchen and sniffed. "After I eat. Something smells amazing, and I'm not just talking about you."

Good to know. "Hungry?" she asked.

"Starved, actually."

She placed the casserole in the oven. "It'll be ready for consumption in twenty to thirty minutes."

"Just enough time for a shower." He undid the top button of his shirt. "Looks like you could use one, too. Why don't we conserve water and do it together?"

"I would rather be stabbed in the kneecaps before walking on hot coals."

"So…maybe next time?"

"Maybe never."

"Your loss." He winked at her before disappearing around the corner. A door shut.

Another knock sounded from the living room. Another of Beck's women?

With a sigh, she strode to the foyer—and found Jessie Kay on the porch.

"What are you doing here?" Brook Lynn asked with a frown. Her sister had been too hungover this morning to chat about the new job.

"What are *you* doing here?" Jessie Kay removed her sunglasses and stepped inside without an invitation.

"I work here. Something I would have liked to discuss with you."

The statement of fact was met with a glower. "Was that last night?"

"You know it was."

"Well, did you account for Jessie Kay Standard Time?"

Meaning, what Jessie Kay agreed on shouldn't ever be counted on, and it was Brook Lynn's bad for assuming otherwise. "No. I actually thought you'd keep your word for once."

"Then this is on you."

Brook Lynn shook a fist in front of her sister's face. "You are *such* a pain."

"As if that's news." Jessie Kay flipped her hair and shifted from one foot to the other. "So, where's Jase? I brought him a seven-course meal. Me…and this." She held up a six-pack of beer.

She was still interested in him? *Stomach twisting.* "He's out, but that shouldn't matter because you two aren't dating. I told you what he said. He isn't looking for a relationship."

"Oh, my darling sis. What do you call a man with only half a brain? Gifted. Jase doesn't actually know *what* he wants. I've decided I have to show him."

Stomach twisting harder. "You're wrong. Jase knows what he wants." It wasn't her sister…and it wasn't her.

Jessie Kay stared her down and glowered. "What's with you today? Why are you so snappy?"

"Just because." Because she was tired and hungry and sore, and Jase had been rude, and she didn't know where he was or what he was doing—didn't know *who* he was doing. And it wasn't her business. She was his employee and would never be anything more. She shouldn't *want* to be anything more.

"What'd Jase hire you for, anyway?" Jessie Kay asked, running a fingertip along the top edge of a chair. "What is it he needs?"

"Help around the house." From someone just desperate enough to agree to slave labor.

"So you're his maid?"

"Executive assistant. Now, go home. Please. And actually wait there this time. I'll be right behind you, and we'll talk about everything that's happened."

Jessie Kay protested.

"One," Brook Lynn said.

Her sister hurried onto the porch. "Dude. You are such a pain."

"I know. We can discuss that, too, if you so desire." She shut the door. In the kitchen, she waited for the casserole to finish baking, and when it did, she placed the sizzling dish on top of the stove before writing a note to Beck. Short and sweet.

Had to leave, BL

Outside, darkness had fallen, the only light spilling from the porch. She switched her implants to a lower setting, allowing more sound than usual to filter into her ears. Despite the discomfort, she needed to be able to pick up on certain noises, like the snap of twigs or the grunt of the undead. She clutched her industrial-size hand sanitizer close to her chest the entire trek, making it to the RC parking lot without incident—

Only to find Jase standing beside her car, his own parked behind it. He looked as if he'd just stepped out of a violent windstorm. His hair was disheveled, his clothes wrinkled and askew.

Had he tangled with a tornado?

When he spotted her, he crossed his arms over his chest.

"What are you doing here?" she asked, her heart pounding wildly.

"Beck called me. Said you'd taken off…that you were walking. Alone."

And that was a crime? "He didn't lie."

Motions clipped, he opened her door for her. "If I don't like you walking out of Two Farms at night, what makes you think I'd like you walking three miles through a forest and down a darkened street?"

Had Jase feared for her safety? "Well…"

"Do not *ever* leave my house on foot again, Brook Lynn. Do you understand?"

All she could do was blink over at him. "Or what?" Seriously. She wanted to know.

"Or…" He cursed under his breath. "You'll get a very stern lecture. Now go home and drive safely." He climbed inside his own car and backed away from hers, but he didn't speed away. No, he waited until she was sealed inside her own vehicle.

"He's a closet gentleman," she muttered, awed by that fact. Yes, he'd done other nice things for her. Helping her search for Jessie Kay. The job. The pay. But for the most part, he was emotionally closed off or running hot and cold, and he seemed to care about nothing.

Who was the real Jase?

She waved as she passed him, even smiled. He didn't wave back, and he definitely didn't smile. But he did follow her home and take off the moment she made it inside.

She had no idea what to think about this new revelation of his character...*actions mean more than words*... but she would be lying if she claimed she wasn't looking forward to their next interaction.

CHAPTER SEVEN

JASE'S MEETING WITH his parole officer had gone better than expected. He'd been placed on unsupervised parole, which meant there would be no more monthly meetings and fewer random drug tests. He could mail in his dues and wouldn't be subjected to monthly inquisitions about his activities, finances and future plans.

Almost over. Less than six months to go.

Finally. An end in sight.

Jase longed for the days he would no longer have scheduled reminders of a youth spent behind bars and the reason he'd been sent there. Or of all the times he'd been placed in the shoe, forced to spend twenty-three hours of every day by himself, locked inside a too-small room, his "good days" taken away from him.

In prison, every thirty days of excellent behavior earned an inmate forty-four days off his sentence, while every infraction meant those days were tacked back on. Needless to say, he'd had a lot of infractions.

He now sat on the sidelines of a field, watching West and Beck coach the Strikers, a youth soccer team the two had sponsored long before earning enough money to actually do so, made up of boys and girls trapped in the system, whether through foster care or simple financial aid.

"Edward, my man," West called from one of the goals. "That's the way. You're doing great."

A little girl approached him and asked a question. West listened intently before demonstrating the proper way to kick a ball. Beck—who loved playing soccer but had always hated being teased about his name—was currently helping a redheaded boy improve his goalie skills.

Jase envied his friends. He would have loved to share his own knowledge of the game, to actually make a difference in someone's life, but these kids had dealt with enough crap. They didn't need the hassle an ex-con would bring to the table. And as soon as their guardians learned about his past, there would be a hassle and he would be asked to leave.

"Which one is yours?" A thirtysomething brunette placed her lawn chair next to his.

He spared her a brief glance, noticed the yellow sundress hugging generous curves—but he wasn't even close to tempted. "I'm friends with the coaches. Just waiting for them to finish up."

"Ah. The coaches the mothers can't stop talking about. I swear, more moms watch the Strikers practice than any other team on the planet."

He nodded, saying nothing else. Encouraging a conversation of any sort wouldn't be wise. Mistakes were the stepping-stones to ruin, and Jessie Kay had taken him too far down that path already.

Brook Lynn, on the other hand—

Would only take him further, he decided. He'd tossed and turned most of the night, images of her in his shower, naked, wet, using his soap and his shampoo, playing on a continuing loop in his mind. This morning he'd woken up on the verge of climax and gasping her name. Knowing how soft her skin was and just how sweet she tasted would likely turn him into a frothing-at-the-mouth he-beast with only one goal: sinking inside her no matter the cost.

Maybe that wouldn't be such a bad thing, though. Maybe he would forget her afterward, just like he'd forgotten so many others.

Stop rationalizing, seeking permission.

"Go, Johnny, go!" the woman beside him called. "Yes! Yes! That's the way. Oh, baby, I'm so proud of you."

It was clear she loved her son, and a pang of envy hit Jase. He'd been six years old when his mother had packed up and abandoned him in a crumbling, run-down apartment, knowing she would soon be evicted. Days had passed before the super found him.

Being a parent wasn't a responsibility he would ever want or welcome, but he was damn sure he'd never abandon his own child like that.

"Good going, Ryan," Beck called.

If anyone would understand his issues about childhood abandonment, it was Beck. The guy's mom had taken off soon after his birth, and the father he'd rarely ever seen had left him with one aunt after another before signing away his parental rights and moving out of state without even saying goodbye.

How could parents be so uncaring? How could people be so cruel?

Like I have the right to judge anyone.

A sudden prickling at the back of his neck had his gaze darting here and there. Some part of him must have sensed danger his eyes hadn't yet found. A handful of parents loitered nearby... A man a little younger than him leaned against a car parked at the curb, shading his eyes with his hands as he watched the field...

A snow-cone stand had a line of kids from other teams. No one watched him. No one looked to be packing heat.

Jase forced himself to relax. He wasn't in danger at a freaking Little League practice.

A whistle blew, and Strikers scattered across the field, returning to their parents. West and Beck began picking up cones and balls. Jase rolled his shoulders in an effort to loosen the knots forming there before standing and jogging to the field to help.

He reached Beck, and they bumped fists.

"How'd the meeting go?" Beck asked, stuffing the cones in a bag.

"Better than expected. I've been upgraded to unsupervised."

"Dude," his friend said, sounding like anything but a millionaire businessman.

"I know."

They shared a quick grin.

West dumped a basket of soccer balls into the bag. "I need a picture of the two of you in this moment. I'll create a GIF and tag it with the phrase I Just Found Out I'm Awesome. You Might Want to Get Yourself Tested."

"It's funny because it's true," Beck said with a nod.

"My results would be negative." Just like all the others, thank God. Jase had paid a visit to his doctor immediately after his release. He'd had a full workup done and received a clean bill of health. But months had since passed, and he'd been with multiple women. He'd used a condom with each of them, but maybe he should do another round of testing. Not because he had any interest in unprotected sex with anyone particular. Of course not. Never. Just for his own peace of mind.

"You guys ready?" West hefted the oversize bag behind his shoulder. "I've allotted myself two hours for lunch."

"More than ready." Beck kicked into gear. "I'm starved."

West snorted. "You're always starved."

Deadpan, Beck said, "I also think I want to take two hours *and eight minutes* for lunch."

West punched him in the shoulder. "Forget it."

Jase drank in their easy camaraderie.

On the way to their cars, three moms blocked Beck's retreat in an effort to "question" him about upcoming practices and games. Those need-answers-now questions sure were punctuated with a lot of giggling, but Beck responded as if the upcoming championship depended on the words that left his mouth. Somehow, despite his seriousness, he managed to flirt with each of them. But then, flirt was his default setting.

West glanced impatiently at the time on his phone. "Beck. Man. My two hours are already running down."

"Pencil me in for another minute," Beck said before returning to his convo with the women.

Jase didn't stick around to hear the rest of the mating dance, but met the boys at their favorite dive. A hole-in-the-wall located in one of the rougher areas of Oklahoma City. Surrounded by government housing, with gang signs spray-painted on every wall and streets littered with potholes. His home turf.

They ate greasy burgers and heart-attack fries, and for a while, it was just like old times, when they had teased each other and laughed, nothing between them but a bond thicker than blood.

But the reprise didn't last long. A clatter of breaking dishes sent Jase hopping to his feet, a butter knife clutched in his white-knuckled grip.

Horrific memories flashed through his mind. Memories that had been seared in his brain, a disease without a cure. Darkness he couldn't shake. Inmates surrounding him, forming a wall so the guards couldn't see what was happening. A cold shiv pressing into the back of his neck. His clothes…ripping…

He was already panting, gaze darting around the restaurant, searching for the threat.

"Everything's fine." West unfolded an inch at a time in an effort not to spook him and gently rubbed his nape. "You're safe, man. You're safe."

Safe? Was he? The prickling at the back of his neck had returned.

When he realized people were staring at him with strange looks on their faces, he squared his shoulders and reclaimed his seat, setting down the knife. He pushed his food away, no longer in the mood to eat, and though his friends tried to return to their previous conversation, the laid-back solidarity of before was gone, the tension and guilt back.

West finally released a bitter laugh. "There's no good time to bring this up, so I'm just going to do it now. As you probably know, the anniversary of Tessa getting her GED is coming up."

And her death.

Beck tensed. "We've still got a few months to go."

"Yes, but what I want to do takes time and planning." West caught a bead of condensation trickling down his water glass. "I plan to throw her a party. The one she always wanted. The one I promised her but never gave her. I would have done it already, but…"

But Jase hadn't been around, and Tessa would have insisted on having him at any celebration in her honor. Another rock of guilt his friends still carried.

The lines of tension bracketing Beck's eyes softened. He gently asked, "Are you sure this is a good idea?"

"Tessa's death wasn't your fault," Jase said. "You don't have to sentence yourself to life without the possibility of happiness, clinging to her memory."

"Her death *is* my fault," West said. "A life sentence is far less than I deserve."

"Her death has *never* been your fault." Tessa had always been an up-and-down kind of girl, but her ordeal with Pax Gillis had shredded her. Months passed, but she'd never recovered emotionally. She'd cried every night, but she'd cried especially hard the night she'd died, and Jase often wondered if she'd lost control of the car, as the police report had claimed, or if she'd intentionally crashed.

The Gillis family had been hounding her, blaming her for Jase's actions. If she hadn't lied about the assault, they'd said, Jase wouldn't have come after their son.

"You weren't there," West snapped. "You don't know."

"No," he replied quietly. "I wasn't there." *I was rotting behind bars.*

The Gillis family had protested every time he'd come up for parole, which was another reason he'd remained behind bars as long as he had. But then, last year, Pax's dad had died of a heart attack, leaving only the mother and the little brother. Jase remembered them from the trial. A small, slender woman who'd never stopped sobbing and a punk kid with a Mohawk, who'd had more piercings and tattoos than Jase.

West closed his eyes, pinched the bridge of his nose. "I'm sorry. I shouldn't have spoken to you that way."

"Forget about it." But Jase knew he wouldn't. He never did. "I have."

"I feel like I'm living Moore's Law," West muttered.

"Uh, you're smarter than the rest of the class, bro," Beck said. "You'll have to explain that one."

West shrugged. "Over the history of computing hardware, the number of transistors in a dense integrated circuit doubles approximately every two years. In other words, my brain is the hardware and my memories grow stronger as time passes."

That made two of them. "Why don't I ask Brook Lynn to help us with the planning?" Jase said, getting them back on track.

"Good idea," Beck said. "Since she's working for us and all."

Jase swallowed a protest. *She's mine, not ours.*

West rubbed two fingers over his jaw. "I've been meaning to ask... Are you sure it's smart to have the little blonde firecracker hanging around the house all the time?"

No. "Why?"

"Why?" Beck arched a brow. "Did you really just ask me *why*? Dude. You nailed her sister."

"So?" *Don't like the reminder.* "You did, too."

"So you both admit to being idiots. May we move on?" West grumbled, a surprising amount of frustration in his voice.

"Exactly," Beck said, speaking over him. "The situation is complicated. And yes, I can roll with it. But can you? I've seen you, man. And I can't believe I'm having to point this out yet again, but you watch Brook Lynn like you're drowning, and she's the only life raft."

"You must be going blind," Jase ground out. "I have never looked at *anyone* that way."

"My eyes, like every other part of me, are working just fine, thanks. But if it's the analogy that bothers you, I can give you a more palatable one. You look at that girl the way I look at her casseroles. As if there's about to be a party in your mouth."

West pushed his plate of leftover fries away. "I told you guys what would happen if you messed around with a Strawberry Valley girl. I *told* you, but you did it anyway. You've got no one to blame but yourselves."

Beck flipped him off, and Jase threw a wadded-up napkin at him.

West held up his hands, all innocence. "Hey, we've all agreed I'm the smart one in our little band of brothers. Why the attitude now?"

"Your IQ might be higher," Jase said, "but your street cred definitely sucks."

"True that," Beck said.

West laughed, the sound of it rusty. "Tell me you didn't just *true that* me. Because if you did, I will have to deduct serious points from *your* street cred."

"What do I care?" Beck spread his arms wide. "I've got points to spare."

The two continued to argue good-naturedly, the tension draining once again, and Jase soaked it up, knowing there'd soon be another drought. This was something else he'd missed. This most of all. Smack-talking, enjoying the company of his friends. Smiling till it hurt. Just...*being*, no worries intruding.

The insults continued as they cleared their table and headed outside.

I'm kind of jealous of people who haven't met you.

If ignorance ever goes up to $5 a barrel, I want drilling rights to your head.

A handful of bikers arrived, removing their helmets, locking up their gear. One glance, and Jase had them pegged as trouble-seekers. He'd encountered plenty of guys just like them in prison. They had a chip on their shoulder the size of a two-by-four and always had something to prove.

His assessment was soon confirmed. Just to be contrary, one of the younger guys stepped in West's path, causing West to bump into him.

The biker snapped, "Why don't you watch where you're going, man?" and shoved him.

West plowed into Beck, who plowed into Jase. Of course, all the bikers laughed as they gathered around their comrade in a perfect show of unity.

West rolled his shoulders, saying, "Instead of watching where I'm going—" his tone even, perhaps even anticipatory "—why don't I teach you how to move out of my way?"

"I vote...yes," Beck said with a cold smile.

West and Beck were not afraid to fight anyone. Even a group of anyones. And they were damn good at it. But Jase was better. He turned "dirty" into "downright filthy." The only problem? His opponents tended to end up in the ER—or dead.

Fear of returning to the life he'd despised screamed: can't risk it. He was so close to finishing parole. Proving a point by knocking the bikers down a peg or two would help nothing but his pride.

Jase grabbed his friends by the arm and dragged them away, going around the bikers, who snickered. One even called, "That's what I thought. Cowards."

Rage joined the rest of Jase's emotions. Despite his armor, he'd never been able to rid himself of the switch inside his mind; it was either flipped to "fight" or to "calm," but rarely anything in between. And it was difficult to blaze from "fight" to "calm" in an instant—the two were such different states, and really, he could only flip that switch so many times before a wire shorted out and he just…went…*insane*.

Beck drew in a deep breath. "Sorry, man. I'm sorry."

West paled, scrubbed a hand down his face. "I didn't think… Jase, I'm sorry."

He waved the apologies away. He understood the instinctive need to annihilate all challengers, to protect what was yours.

Brook Lynn's angelic face flashed inside his mind, and he quickly blinked to clear it. She wasn't his, and she would never be his, but even still, desire for her sank claws in his chest, cutting deep and holding on. He wanted her, and it was time to stop denying it, even though admitting it was more dangerous to his peace of mind.

"Let's head home," West said, and Beck nodded.

Jase's car was parked beside theirs. He paused to say, "Do me a solid and take the long way," before climbing inside.

He wanted a few minutes alone with Brook Lynn. What he would say to her, do with her—to her—he wasn't sure, but he was looking forward to finding out.

CHAPTER EIGHT

OUTDID MYSELF, IF I do say so, well, myself.

Brook Lynn stacked a packet of papers she'd found haphazardly stuffed inside Jase's underwear drawer, a blush heating her cheeks. He'd told her to clean everything, so everything she was cleaning. His room was her final chore—one she'd been putting off all day. This task was her last.

Her gaze latched on the words *Department of Corrections*, and her heart skipped a beat. Was he a cop? A parole officer?

The idea…intrigued her.

Would he have hunted down her uncle Kurt and forced the man to return her mom's life-insurance money?

Super Jase to the rescue!

And oh, the sexiness of *that* image.

Red alert! If she wasn't careful, she would fall deeper into like with him.

Frowning, Brook Lynn finished tidying the dresser. As she strolled through the house for a final inspection, avoiding the game room as instructed, she slapped her hands together in a job well-done. She hadn't moved the furniture around, but she had added feminine touches to the decor, and they were—in a word—ah-mazing. A lace doily over the coffee table. Colorful, decorative pillows on the couch. Bowls of lavender potpourri on the mantel. And for her own amusement: boxes of tampons in the bathroom cabinet for any overnight guest who might be in need.

She'd talked with her sister at last and had actually received a blessing for this new gig, though not for the cash Brook Lynn would make. Oh, no. Jessie Kay planned to use her as an excuse to visit…and a direct line of communication to Jase.

My sister still wants him. And I still…don't like it.

But what could she do about it? What could she say? Her attraction to him was wrong on every level.

There was only one right way to proceed. Let Jessie Kay do her thing, and resign herself to being Jase's personal assistant, nothing more, nothing less. She would work hard—would give this her all. In return, Jase would treat her and her efforts with respect, never again requesting she do more than was humanly possible. And she would inform him of that the second he returned. She had balls, dang it. Yeah. That's right. She had big, fat lady balls.

Hinges on the front door creaked. Footsteps sounded.

"—told you to take the long way," Jase was saying.

"Don't recall agreeing to that," West said. "Do you?"

"Nope," Beck replied, laughter in his tone. "But I do wonder why you wanted to be alone. Would it have anything to do with offering hands-on instruction to the staff?"

"You both suck," Jase muttered.

In the kitchen, she gulped, her lady balls shriveling. Bossman had finally come home.

"Go ahead and admit— What the hell?" Beck demanded.

Silence.

Tense, oppressive silence.

They'd noticed the new decorations.

"I...don't even know what to say right now," West gasped out. "I think I need to add a breakdown to my schedule."

Seconds ticked by. No reaction from Jase. Or maybe he'd spoken so quietly she hadn't heard him. A real possibility. For the past hour, her inner ears had been itching as though bees buzzed inside. Never having experienced anything like it, she wasn't exactly sure what was going on.

"Brook Lynn," Jase called.

Well, she'd certainly heard *that*.

"Back here," she replied, trying not to tremble.

Jase entered the kitchen alone, and oh, wow. His presence somehow caused the air in her lungs to evaporate in an instant, leaving her lightheaded. There would never be a better example of raw masculinity. He wore a black tee that hugged his muscular biceps and displayed a good portion of his tattoos. His jeans were ripped, the hems tucked haphazardly into combat boots. He wore his necklaces, his silver rings and the leather cuffs around each of his wrists.

Total bad-boy hot.

Never knew that was my thing.

He met her gaze, and she would have sworn she detected a hint of...mirth? Maybe even approval? But they were both so well contained, she couldn't be sure.

"The changes are nice," he said.

What! It was one thing to suspect approval, but quite another to have it confirmed. "Thank you?" *She* liked the changes; they were everything she would have wanted in her own home, if she hadn't spent her entire adult life counting every penny.

"But you have to return everything to the way it was," he added.

"What!" The word escaped her this time. "Everything?" she asked, her brows drawing together.

"Everything."

"But…"

"No buts."

Caveman speak for *subject closed*. "But why?" she insisted.

"Because I said so."

The most frustrating words in the history of the world!

"I'm sorry," she gritted out, "but that's not good enough for me."

Jase peered at her for a long while before saying, "You did too much too fast." He looked past her, to the counter. "What are those?"

From cryptic to inquisitive in a blink. Someone needed to explain the effects of whiplash to him. "Those are special deliveries for Beck. An array of desserts from countless women who stopped by throughout the day."

Charlene Burns had come with strawberry muffins and a word of warning: *Do yourself a favor. Don't get involved with these men, darlin'. They're users, each one of them.*

Brook Lynn had wanted to quip, *And you will be the exception to their use-and-lose rule, which is why you've come back for more?* but had somehow found the strength to hold her tongue.

Newly legal Missy Thompson had come with strawberry cake and questions. *Has Beck said anything about me? Do you know if he likes brunettes or blondes better? Because I can rock either look. Will you give him my number?*

Even Harlow Glass stopped by, though Brook Lynn had gotten the feeling she hadn't come to scope out the guys. Instead, the black-haired, blue-eyed beauty had just thrust out a plastic bag of fresh wild strawberries she'd most likely plucked from the field out back—and had probably spit on. The girl had once been famous for her cruelty. But she had shyly—a trick, surely—asked to come inside to chat. Suspicious of her intentions, Brook Lynn had flatly refused.

But...I have to tell you...there's a man... He's come to the house and... the girl had stumbled out.

A man? Brook Lynn had finally relented and moved aside to allow the girl entrance, saying, *If you're doing this to hurt me in some way, there will be hell to pay.*

Harlow scanned the foyer and turned puke green before backing up, apologizing a thousand times and leaving the house in a hurry.

Brook Lynn could hardly believe the seemingly timid, softly spoken mouse was the same bold femme fatale who'd once terrorized kids at school. Including Kenna. Brook Lynn remembered holding her friend time and time again while she sobbed about the awful things Harlow had said.

If her new demeanor was the real deal, something had happened to the girl. More than the loss of her mom and her home. Or maybe that was what Harlow wanted her to think. For once in this small town, rumors were scarce. All Brook Lynn knew? Harlow had left public school in the middle of her junior year in favor of being homeschooled. She'd stayed in town, but few people had seen her out and about. And when they had, she'd kept her head down and her pace swift, discouraging any kind of interaction.

For now, Brook Lynn wasn't going to worry about

what Harlow had said, some strange man who may or may not have come to the house to do…something? Nothing? And how did Harlow even know that?

"No one's gotten the message yet," Jase said. "The way to a man's heart is *not* through his stomach."

"Duh. It's through his ribs."

"Funny." He pointed to the platters. "There's a bite missing from each one. Why?"

"I thought I'd do my due diligence and test everything for poison." Nothing compared to her creations, and that wasn't bragging; that was pure fact.

"If there *was* poison, what would you do? Feed it to me anyway?"

"There's only one way to find out." With her sweetest smile, she offered him a fork.

He took it, saying, "If I die today, you'll be the first one the cops question."

"I'm willing to risk it."

The corners of his mouth twitched as he motioned to the stove, his first undeniable display of amusement. It did funny things to her insides. "That casserole is still intact. Why?"

"I made it, and it's fresh from the oven." Steam wafted all around it, scenting the air. This one contained chicken and waffles, even maple syrup, and it was one of her favorites. "But it's for Beck, not you," she said. "I'm sure you already have dinner plans." *Oops. My bitterness is showing.*

His gaze landed on her and narrowed. "Tell me, honey. Between the two of us, who do you consider the boss, and who do you consider the employee?"

The starch in her spine dissolved. How could she expect him to respect her if she wouldn't respect him?

"You are the boss," she said without any heat. "Would you like me to fix you a plate?"

"No," he grumbled, and after the fuss he'd kicked up, she kind of wanted to slap him. Then he added, "I'll do it," and totally redeemed himself.

He stalked past her, careful not to touch her, and gathered a plate and ladle. The itch intensified in her ears, and she scratched gently, always making sure hanks of hair covered the big, bulky implants. Everyone who'd ever seen them had either flinched or stared in morbid fascination. A few kids had even called her Frankenlynn.

Jase filled his plate with the casserole she had prepared and faced her with a frown. "Are those waffles I'm seeing? Mixed with *chicken*?"

"Does it matter?"

"Yes."

Lord save me. "Just try it."

Standing there, he scooped up a forkful…and then simply peered at the sample with distaste. She rolled her eyes and approached, claiming the fork and shoving the food into his mouth.

His eyes widened as he chewed. "What else did you put in it? Crack?"

"Only a little," she said, deadpan. Then she flinched. Maybe she shouldn't have teased a cop about drugs. Former cop? But he didn't even blink at her comment. "While you eat I'll just go and remove the *necessary improvements* I made in the living room. Even though I don't understand why you asked—commanded—that I do it."

"I'll just stay in here, eating my crack," he replied, his attention never straying from his food. "But come back in here when you're done."

The way to every man's heart might not be through his stomach, but it certainly looked to be the way to Jase's. Not that she wanted his heart.

She entered the living room and found West and Beck doing the work for her, and not happily. For the first time the perpetually upbeat guys were actually scowling. Beck's motions were clipped as he ripped away the doily, dumped out one of the bowls of potpourri and swiped up the pillows.

He noticed her and gritted out, "You can't just change things, Brook Lynn. Especially when everything was perfect the way it was."

So…it wasn't the fact that she had turned a bachelor pad into a chick paradise? It was simply the fact that she'd altered the hobo-hideous design? *Too much too fast,* Jase had said. Got it.

"Why don't we keep the rest of the potpourri?" she suggested. "It smells so nice and—"

He tossed the remaining bowls of potpourri out the window, then did the same with the garbage bag of items he'd gathered.

O-kay. She made a mental note to retrieve everything on her way to the car. Today she'd driven straight to the driveway to avoid the awkward ride home Jase would have insisted on giving her. Maybe she would reintroduce the potpourri tomorrow and pray Beck failed to notice. Bottom line: the house wasn't yet a home; it was simply a place to stay, as generic as a motel. She would be doing him a favor, and one day he would see that. Surely.

It will be for his own good, she thought.

Her sister's voice mocked her. *Warden always knows best, doesn't she?*

Ugh. How many times had Jessie Kay spoken those words? Countless.

Maybe Brook Lynn should leave things alone. Allow Beck and West to deal with their demons—whatever they were—on their own, without any "help" from her.

Nah. Not my style. When she noticed a problem, she wanted to do everything in her power to fix it.

"Brook Lynn. You done yet?"

Jase's voice sent a shiver traipsing along already sensitized nerve endings. "I suppose so." Feet suddenly as heavy as boulders, she trudged into the kitchen. He sat at the table, a plate in front of him and another steaming in front of the chair beside him. He motioned for her to take it.

The moment she settled, he said, "Don't change things, all right. Beck doesn't like it."

"Figured that out on my own, thanks."

"Yeah, but I wanted you to hear it from *your boss*."

Had stressing those last two words really been necessary?

"You're in charge," she said, somehow managing *not* to roll her eyes. "I get it."

"Good."

"Why doesn't Beck like change?"

Jase stiffened, his fork pausing midway to his mouth. A haunted gleam darkened his eyes, turning the emeralds into stormy onyx. "He has his reasons" was all he said. "We all do."

And they weren't pleasant reasons, she realized. Like maybe a change in his past had devastated him so terribly he now preserved what he could of his present.

After the death of her dad, she'd experienced a similar reaction, not wanting his things to be altered in any way. "I'm surprised you and West convinced him to move here."

He shifted in his seat, inching away from her. "How long have you lived in Strawberry Valley?"

Message received. Beck wasn't her business. "All my life," she said.

"Must be nice, having roots."

Meaning he'd never had them? The thought saddened her. "A lot of the people here have their quirks, but when my mom died, they really stepped up to the plate to help Jessie Kay and me."

"How old were you?"

"Fifteen."

"What happened?"

"Long story."

"Then you should probably get started."

"I'm sure you've got better things to do," she began, shifting uncomfortably.

"I don't. Talk. I want to hear."

She rarely shared the gruesome details, but his desire to know eased her reservations. "Well, we'd lost our dad years before in an explosion at Dairyland. Every year since we would spend a weekend camping in his favorite spot. I don't know if you've noticed, but there's a river that runs through the north edge of town. He loved it there. We would plant flowers in his honor, but that year Jessie Kay was doing twirls and tripped on a rock, and she dropped the flowers in the water. She dove in after them, and our mom dove in after her. The current was strong and swept them away. I gave chase on land, screaming for help, but no one was around. Jessie Kay finally managed to drag Mom to shore, but she...she was already dead and neither of us could revive her."

"Jessie Kay blames herself?"

"Yes." Nothing Brook Lynn had said had ever changed the girl's mind. She cleared her throat, once, twice, waiting as the trembling in her chin stopped. "Speaking of my amazing sister, did I tell you she bakes the best strawberry cookies in the history of ever?" Truth. *If* Brook Lynn helped her do the baking.

He blinked at her, as if he wasn't quite sure how the topic had veered so drastically.

"Do you like strawberry cookies?" she asked.

"Who took care of you?" he asked, focusing only on that. "Jessie Kay had to be...what? Seventeen?"

"Yes. An uncle came to stay with us for a while."

"Was he good to you? Were your parents?"

"My parents were *awesome*, the best of the best. Mom used to tell us she loved us with all her heart, adored us with all her mind and would always momma-bear-protect us with her whole body." She smiled with fond remembrance. "My dad called us his favorite princesses and built us castles made out of blankets."

His face expressed a mix of awe and sadness. "And your uncle?"

She lost her smile in a hurry. "He was as far from awesome as humanly possible. He was a thief, a liar and a deadbeat. He only came around when he needed something or to convince Jessie Kay and me to help him hustle. *People trust kids,* he'd say. Then he took off with Mom's insurance money."

"I'm sorry, honey." The tension in his voice confused her.

She continued anyway. "You want to know what's silly about the whole thing? I was sad when he was gone. He was the only family we had left."

Jase wiped away the beads of sweat that had popped up on his forehead. "Where is he now?"

"Dead. About a year after he left us, he conned the wrong person." Desperate to learn more about Jase, she asked, "What about your parents?"

He finished the meal without responding, drained his glass of water.

Clearly, even though she'd shared some of her most painful memories, he'd just shut down yet another subject. But fine. Whatever. She was disappointed, but she could roll. "Did you know that Jessie Kay is an expert dancer? She took ballet classes for years. Really knows how to move."

Which he'd probably learned while he'd had her in bed. Ugh.

A muscle jumped in his jaw. He stalked to the sink, ignoring praise of her sister a second time.

"Did you know Jessie Kay was once crowned Miss Strawberry Valley? She was only eighteen." Some people—cough, Charlene Burns, cough—liked to say she'd won simply because she was an orphan and the judges had felt sorry for her.

Some people were idiots.

Again, nothing from Jase.

Guilt, such an insidious creature, slithered through Brook Lynn. Because part of her *liked* his lack of reaction.

I'm a terrible sister. Jessie Kay had dibs and that was that. Besides, Brook Lynn would never be able to overlook the fact that Jase wanted what she didn't: something temporary.

Also, the guy she ended up with had to be reliable in every way. Like, say, being emotionally accessible, willing to share his past and his secrets. She had to be able to trust him with her heart, mind and body, and had to know he would be there for her every step of the way.

With a sigh, she picked at her food. She really needed to do as planned and ask out Brad Lintz. He fit all of her criteria. And he wouldn't treat his former lovers this way—refusing to acknowledge their very existence.

Stop thinking about having fun and actually have some. For once.

"By the way," Jase said. "It was good."

Her brow wrinkled with confusion. "What was?"

"The casserole."

Well, duh. "Obviously." He'd eaten half the pan. "You should taste my sandwiches."

"If the sandwiches are better than your casseroles, I'm officially putting in an order for tomorrow's dinner."

"Done. Hey," she said. "Would you mind if I take some of the casserole to Jessie Kay?"

"Why would I mind?"

"Because you paid for the food," she said then yawned. The trials of the day had finally caught up to her…and the itching in her ears had worsened with the movement of her jaw. She dropped her fork to gently scratch.

"Take as much as you'd like. Always." Jase leaned over and pinched a lock of her hair, rubbing the ends between his fingers. "You've had a long day. You should go home."

She really should…but for the first time in a very long time she didn't think she'd fall asleep the moment her head hit the pillow. Her blood suddenly ran too hot, and her heartbeat came too strong. She wanted to be here, talking with Jase—being touched by him. For Jessie Kay. Of course.

"Do you have a new list of chores for me?" she asked.

One of his brows winged up. "You finished the other one?"

"Just like Cinderella before the ball." Well, well. Something else to check off the list she'd made with Kenna. Be Cinderella for a day. Although, actually attending the ball and meeting Prince Charming would have been more fun than the chores part of her day.

Another undeniable twitch at the corners of his mouth. "How?"

He sounded shocked. Had he deliberately set out to make her fail? "I may or may not have enlisted the aid of the women who came over looking for Beck."

He crossed his arms over his chest, saying, "Cinderella did not have help."

"I beg to differ. She had mice."

His dark eyes sparkled. Was he fighting a laugh? *Go me!*

Beck stormed into the kitchen, his charming facade utterly gone. He waved a stack of papers and photos in Jase's face. "There were phone numbers and printed selfies taped to my bedroom walls."

The laugh Jase had been holding back finally burst out, and Brook Lynn marveled. He wasn't as rugged-looking when he laughed, but he was just as appealing. Maybe even more so. His entire face lit up, his features softening, making him appear years younger. Almost…boyish.

"Blame Brook Lynn," he said, hiking his thumb in her direction.

She offered Beck a sugar-sweet smile as he focused all of his anger on her.

"There's a line," he growled. "A line you just don't cross."

"Got it," she said with a nod. "But, uh, I'm not actually the one who put the photos there."

"You let someone else in my room?"

She nibbled on her bottom lip. "It's not like you haven't had a parade of women march through it already."

"By choice—while I was there. Who did you allow into my room? I want a name."

"I could give you a name, but I'd have to give you six to be accurate, and to be honest, I—"

"Six," he echoed hollowly.

"Yes." She'd barred those same women from stepping one foot inside Jase's room, choosing to take care of his space on her own. "The girls were clearly interested in *being* with you again," she said with a blush. "I figured you'd enjoy another go. Who wouldn't? They were hot little totties."

Beck opened his mouth to blast her, she was sure, but Jase moved in front of her.

"Enough," he said. "She's sincerely sorry and won't do it again. Isn't that right, Brook Lynn?"

"Right," she said with a jaunty salute as she peeked around Jase. "Consider me the room's new chastity belt."

Beck drew in a deep breath and slowly released it, his animosity draining. "Let's not get carried away. I'm allergic to chastity belts." Just like that, Beck the Sweet and Charming was back. He noticed the array of desserts and shook his head. "As many strawberries as you country girls eat, you'd think someone would taste just like the fruit. So far no luck."

"You're *taste-testing* your way through the residents?"

"And loving every moment of it." Beck helped her close her mouth before he sauntered off.

"What about you?" Brook Lynn asked, unable to stop the words from escaping.

Jase turned and met her gaze. He sobered instantly, the intensity of him suddenly crackling, her awareness of him suddenly *smoldering*. She found herself pushing to a stand, facing off with him. A battle. But what was the prize?

"What about me?" he asked softly.

"Who do you want to taste-test?"

His pupils expanded, the black spilling over the emerald. "Are you offering?"

Yes. "No." She shook her head, determined to mean it. "Never."

He ground his teeth and took a step back, breaking the spell. "Good."

"Yeah. Good," she repeated softly. She scratched at her ears, cleared her throat. "Well," she said and cleared her throat again. "Like you said, I should go."

His nod was clipped. "I'll walk you out."

She offered no protest, knowing it would do no good. "Thanks."

Outside, the air was a perfect blend of warm and cool. The moon hid behind clouds, a few stars glinting from their perch of black velvet. The only swath of light came from the single-bulb lamp on the porch.

Jase opened her car door, and as she moved around him, misjudging the distance, she accidentally brushed her shoulder against his arm. Both of them hissed, as if they'd just been burned.

Tremors rooted her in place. She stood in the open space between door and car, peering up at him. In the darkness, with thin ribbons of golden light seeping from the car's interior and falling over him, the wind caressing strands of his hair over his brow, he could have stepped straight from her fantasies.

The scent of him enveloped her…honey and oats, like the soap he used…and it was both pleasant and comforting; she only wanted to get closer to him. Her blood heated, and her skin tingled. She forgot the discomfort in her ears. Forgot all the reasons she'd told herself to avoid this man.

Like he'd done in the kitchen, he reached out and pinched a lock of her hair between his fingers. A compulsion? She hoped so. A lance of pleasure sped through her, and breath snagged in her throat. What would he do next? What did she *want* him to do?

His head lowered…lowered a little more…coming closer and closer to hers. Anticipation consumed her, the heat and tingles growing worse.

His fingers moved to her jaw and tipped up her face. Preparing her for his kiss. She knew she should close her eyes, but she didn't want to miss a moment of this.

For a long while, his mouth hovered over hers.

She breathed him in. He breathed *her* in. She tensed, eager for contact. Ready for it. Her belly quivered. She'd been kissed before—of course she had—but this would be her first kiss with a man so intense, so closed off, yet seething with such quiet savagery. And it would be wrong for her, wrong *of* her, but almost…necessary.

"Jase." *Do it. Please.*

The sound of her voice caused him to stiffen. He dropped his arm to his side, severing contact.

"See you tomorrow, Brook Lynn."

Just like that, he walked away. Leaving her confused, angry. Determined.

The only problem was, she didn't know what she was so determined to overcome. Her attraction to him...or his resistance to her?

CHAPTER NINE

SLEEPING PROVED IMPOSSIBLE for Brook Lynn. She tossed and turned in bed, thinking of nothing but her almost-kiss with Jase.

Why had he stopped?

Did it really matter?

Sometime between falling onto her mattress and rising to take a shower, she'd made a decision: she would overcome her attraction to him, and that would be that.

There were too many problems stacked against them, anyway. Jessie Kay. Brook Lynn's employment. His attitude. Oh, his attitude! Smoldering one moment, ice-cold the next. Always annoying.

Besides, she still wasn't interested in a fling. *Give me long-term or give me nothing.*

Right?

"Jessie Kay," she called, banging on the girl's bedroom door. "What do you want for breakfast?"

Silence greeted her.

She peeked inside—no one was in the bed draped with sheets covered with silly pandas or anywhere else. Peachy. Had her sister even come home last night? Brook Lynn tromped to the kitchen…where she found a note. And a glass jar with a giant spider trapped inside.

Dude! Do you see what was waiting in the kitchen for me? The devil! I managed to catch it—you're

welcome. Now you get to kill it. All I ask is that
you check for a pulse afterward to make sure he's
really, really, *really* dead. Love, JK

PS: I would have killed it myself, because I'm
tough like that, but I was in a hurry to go out and
make us some dough. You're welcome x 2.

"You are deathly afraid of spiders, and you know it,"
Brook Lynn muttered to her absent sister. And Jessie
Kay, out making money? *I'll believe it when I see it.*

After freeing the spider outside, Brook Lynn decided
to forgo breakfast and made her way to the Rhinestone
Cowgirl. Strawberry Valley was just beginning to rouse.
Shop owners were outside, dusting off sidewalks while
Closed signs flipped over behind them.

She waved to Mr. Rodriguez. Virgil hadn't yet arrived to begin their next checkers game. There was
Wanda Potts, taking pictures of her storefront to post on
Twitter and Facebook. She sold "designer" clothing—
meaning, she'd designed them. Next door, Donut à la
Mode was being unlocked. It was nice, seeing the same
people, the same sights, every morning. Comforting.

When Brook Lynn stepped inside the RC, she was
ten minutes early and more fatigued than usual. Her
eyes burned, and her feet dragged. And her ears! The
itching had only gotten worse. If this kept up, she'd have
to call her doctor and pay for a checkup she couldn't
afford.

Maybe she could get an advance from Jase...

No! No way. She wasn't going to treat him like a
piggy bank. He was her boss, and he was a person. A
distant person, sure. Gruff, but a natural-born protector. Look how quickly he'd stepped in front of his friend
simply to stop the guy from yelling at her.

And she was still insanely curious about his past. How bad would it be to look him up online?

Oh, who cared? She plugged his name in a search engine. Jase Hollister.

Not much popped up. He had no Facebook page that she could find, no Twitter account. But she *was* asked if she'd meant Jessie Hollister, Jake Hollister, Jason Hollister or Jane Hollister.

Jason seemed the most obvious choice, so she clicked on it...and oh, wow, there seemed to be thousands of them. She narrowed the search to Jason Hollister in Oklahoma. The first thing to pull up was Hollister Co. at Penn Square Mall, followed by a few links to people on Facebook and LinkedIn. But none of the pictures matched the Jase she knew. There was an article about some kind of fight to the death between teenagers, but again, the picture next to it looked nothing like her Jase. The boy was far too scrawny.

The bell above the door tinkled, signaling the arrival of the first customer of the day, and she glanced up to see a young man she'd never before met standing in the doorway.

"Can I help you?" she asked. Tourist? Just passing through?

He had sandy-colored hair and wore a wrinkled white button-down and black slacks. He scratched his arms as he glanced behind him nervously before retreating outside, the door closing.

O-kay.

Brook Lynn closed the search window just as the bell tinkled again.

"Got your dating-911 text," Kenna said as she glided to the counter, her red hair bouncing over her shoulders. "What's up?"

Oh, yeah. In her delirium last night, Brook Lynn had contacted her friend. But in the bright light of the morning, discussing Jase seemed like the worst idea ever.

"Dating-911?" she asked, playing coy. "That doesn't sound like me, does it?"

"Gonna play the dumb-blonde card, are you?"

"Why not?" she said with a shrug. She scratched her ears. "I've got a full deck."

Kenna chuckled. "You typed, and I quote, *do you know what's worse than zombies eating your brains? Liking a man who's slept with your sister.*"

"Someone needs to invent an app to stop people from making foolish admissions in texts," she grumbled.

"I bet West could do it. But even if he manages it, it's too late for you. So...are we talking about Jase or Beck?"

Why not admit it, just put it out there? "Jase."

"Oh," Kenna said, and she sounded disappointed.

"What? You don't like him?"

"I like him just fine, but of the two guys he just seems less attainable."

She gaped at her friend. "Less attainable, when Beck is a certified man-whore?"

"Well, yeah," Kenna said. "Jase is like a wall of ice. Dirty, dirty ice," she added with an appreciative, dreamy sigh. "But ice all the same."

"Ice can be melted, you know." And with Jase, it had. At least for a little while. Once he'd even laughed with her.

I want to see him laugh again.

Kenna patted her arm, saying, "It can also refreeze."

"True." Hadn't it already?

Did she *want* him to melt for good?

No, no. *No fixer-uppers, remember?* She'd decided

to go after Brad. The safer choice. The smarter choice. Being with him wouldn't get her canned or hurt her sister. Which was the reason she'd also texted *him* last night, asking him to stop by the shop whenever he was free.

"I won't go after Jase," she said on a sigh.

"Oh, Brook Lynn," Kenna said. "I'm so sorry. I should have kept my mouth shut. I've never seen you look so dejected."

She scratched her ears yet again. "I'm not dejected." *I'm disappointed.*

"I never should have discouraged you. If anyone can melt Jase once and for all, it's you. Besides, the past might have created who he is, but we shouldn't let it define who he can become."

"What do you know of his past?"

"Not much. Dane mentioned something about foster care."

The child of a broken home. Stomach twisting, she changed the subject before she raced out of here to hunt the guy down and throw herself in his arms to offer all the hugs he probably never received growing up. "How are wedding plans coming?"

Immediately snared by the topic, Kenna regaled her with stories of white lace dresses, snobby caterers and shy ice sculptors, all revolving around her crazy soon-to-be in-laws.

One day, I'll *have such awesome problems,* Brook Lynn thought.

The bell chimed, and Norrie, Kenna's six-year-old daughter, came racing inside. Dane Michaelson entered soon after, his gaze heating when it landed on his fiancée, practically steaming the air.

That. I want that.

"Hi, Aunt Brook Lynn," Norrie said, skipping over to embrace her. "Guess what? Dane told Uncle West he's got to get Momma alone soon or he's gonna die of blue baseballs. I didn't know baseballs could be blue, did you?"

Kenna almost swallowed her tongue.

Brook Lynn laughed out loud, but quieted as the itching in her ears grew worse.

Dane closed his eyes for a moment. "That was supposed to be our secret, squirt."

Norrie had a major problem with verbal diarrhea. Every word to enter her ears exited her mouth.

"We better make sure they get some time alone, huh?" Brook Lynn said. "That way his baseballs can return to their original color. So how about you come over this evening and spend the night with me?" When Kenna and Norrie had moved out, Brook Lynn had left their rooms alone, part of her hoping they'd come back.

Maybe I'm more like Beck than I realized.

"Yes!" Norrie squealed with happiness. "Can I, Momma? Please! Please!"

Kenna cast Brook Lynn a grateful smile. "I think that would be wonderful."

"Sweet!" the girl said, jumping up and down.

The bell chimed a third time, and in stepped Charlene Burns.

She set her sunglasses on top of her head, saying, "I could use a moment alone with Brook Lynn, y'all."

Kenna waited for Brook Lynn's nod of approval. Which she gave. Reluctantly.

"Well, okay, then. I guess this is where we say goodbye." Kenna shot Brook Lynn a sympathetic look before departing with her family.

"So," Charlene said, resting her elbows on the counter.

"So. How can I help you?"

"I just wanted to make sure Beck got those muffins I baked him."

I think you mean bought *him.* "He sure did. He even said something about all these strawberries making the girls here taste just as sweet. Doesn't that make you think strawberries are his favorite fruit?" Brook Lynn added, tracing her fingertips over a strawberry pendant. She desperately needed to make a sale today.

Charlene brightened. "I have a collection of Edna's finest at home. I'll wear—"

Brook Lynn tried to look as horrified as possible. "You're thinking about wearing last year's fashion? Are you sure— No, no, I'm, uh, sure that'll be fine. The other girls who came over with treats for Beck will probably wear last year's fashion, too."

"Other girls brought him treats? Who? You tell me right this second."

"I'm not going to name names and start a catfight when I don't even know which of you Beck wants. But if you stick around the store long enough, some of them might just arrive to buy jewelry, hoping to impress him." Not a lie. They *might*.

Feminine calculation gleamed in Charlene's hazel eyes. She bought every item with a strawberry. She would never wear them all, but this way, no other woman would be wearing them, either.

Brook Lynn floated on clouds of happiness the rest of her shift—or would have, if not for her ears—creating new pieces for the display cases. When the bell over the door rang again, she glanced up, expecting Brad—and almost snapped off a finger instead of a wire. *Jase* had just entered the store.

Reeling.

As usual, he looked good. Dangerous and good, as if he'd just stepped from a boxing ring… No, scratch that. As if he'd just come from an illegal street brawl, his dark hair mussed, his emerald eyes bright and gleaming from the high levels of testosterone pumping through his system. A man on the prowl, searching for a willing woman to satisfy.

She set the needle-nose pliers aside. "What are you doing here?"

He waved a piece of paper at her, his biceps flexing. "I have your new list."

Her heart rate picked up speed as she read over what appeared to be a shopping list. Or rather, tried to read over it. Her eyes would not move past number two, her cheeks heating. "Beer. Condoms," she said, peering at him through the thick shield of her lashes.

"Ex-large," he said with a nod. "Maybe ribbed for her pleasure. I'll let you decide."

The bottom dropped out of her stomach. "Is there a specific *her* in mind?"

"Just consider that a collective her."

"I see." She tried to contain her blush as she ticked off another item on the list—and failed. "Hemorrhoid cream? Seriously?"

"I don't know if anyone's ever told you this, honey, but sometimes you can be a major pain in the ass."

Well played, Mr. Hollister. Well played. Clearly he was having fun.

Fun. Again. And at her expense. Well, not anymore.

It's my turn, she thought, mentally adding an item to her own list. She'd turn the tables on him. Starting now.

"Personal lubricant?" she said, eyeing him up and down *without* shivering. *Surely I deserve some type of reward.* "Yes, I can see how you might need that. Or is it for a *friend*?" She used air quotes, letting him know she wouldn't believe him if he tried to take that path.

He set his elbows on the counter and leaned closer to her. "Some women need an extra boost. None of mine ever have, but there's a first time for everything."

The blush redoubled. "Why lice shampoo?"

He shrugged. "There could be an outbreak."

"What about the yeast-infection ointment? The feminine cleansing pads? The vajazzle tattoos?" *Never even heard of that.* "The peekaboo mirror for personal inspection?" She gazed at him and rested a hand over her heart. "Wait. Do you have a hoo-ha fetish?" She batted her lashes at him, hoping he heard the unspoken *bless your heart.*

"Doesn't every man?"

"Well, you can still count on me. I'll take care of everything. You and your hemorrhoids will be feeling better in no time. One day soon you'll even be able to sit in a chair without a cushion."

He rocked back on his heels. "You are not handling this the way I expected."

"Tears? Refusal? Please. I'd buy laxatives, suppositories for constipation, pills to stop diarrhea, an entire box of pregnancy tests and a tube of antifungal cream without a single moment of humiliation."

"Great. Add those to the list. And don't forget you promised to make sandwiches tonight."

The bell tinkled, signaling the arrival of another customer, saving her from having to reply.

Though Brook Lynn stood on her tiptoes, she couldn't see over the wide expanse of Jase's shoulders. When she motioned for him to move, he simply crossed his arms over his massive chest, stubborn to his core.

Fine. She stepped to the side and peeked around

him, her gaze locking on Brad. As he removed his sunglasses, she waited for tingles and heat, *wanted* to experience them, but...nothing.

Peachy. She smoothed her clothes in place and forced a smile. "You came."

"Of course," Brad said, returning her smile with one of his own. "You texted."

Jase tensed, as if the store had just been invaded by zombies.

"Jase," Brook Lynn said, "this is Brad Lintz. He owns Lintz Automotive, and he's a true master of his craft. He's kept Rusty, my car, running for years. Brad, this is Jase. My boss. My other boss, I mean."

Brad held out his hand. "Nice to meet you."

Jase bristled like a porcupine before he pressed his palm against Brad's—and he must have squeezed too hard, because Brad flinched. Jase released him and stuffed his hands in his pockets, as if he didn't trust them, and returned his gaze to her. His pupils had expanded, black completely overshadowing green. A sign of heightened emotion; one she'd seen every time she'd caught a glimpse of herself in a mirror after a fight with Jessie Kay.

He was...angry?

His body language answered the question, shouting *yes!* He grew stiffer by the second and even braced his legs apart, as if he meant to pounce.

"I should go," he said. "Don't forget the list."

As if she would be thinking of anything else.

He stalked out of the shop before she had time to form a reply, acting as if his feet were on fire.

"Interesting guy," Brad said.

"Yes." But he wasn't dating material. Brad, on the other hand...

He was a handsome man, with well-defined features, tidy dark hair and navy eyes. A combination she hadn't seen often. He stood just over six feet—though at six-four, Jase towered over him. He was lean and when not wearing his work overalls, always well dressed.

"What kind of list?" Brad asked.

"Oh, uh, something for work." She tucked Jase's note into her pocket. And now it was time to nut up or shut up and ask Brad out.

What if he says no?

She'd survive. Maybe cry. Big deal.

"Brad," she began. Sweat slicked her palms as sickness churned in her stomach. How should she do this?

Do you know what my shirt is made of? Girlfriend material.

I'd rather die.

I don't have a library card, but do you mind if I check you out?

I'd rather die twice.

"Well," she said, rubbing at her ears. With Jase here, she'd forgotten how badly they'd been bothering her.

"In your text," he said, "you mentioned you had something important to ask me."

"That's true. I do." *Open your mouth. Create words.* "Brad, would you like to go out with me?"

JASE PACED JUST outside the Rhinestone Cowgirl. He should go home. He had a crap-ton of work to do. He felt as if he was being watched, his neck practically burning with an increase of tingles, but he couldn't bring himself to care. Brook Lynn was currently in an enclosed space with another guy. Alone. Jase didn't like that—even though he had no right to dislike it—and things just got worse.

He was boss; she was employee. He'd made sure she understood that.

He still didn't like it.

The girl was chipping away at his armor, and she had no idea she was doing it. No idea that every smile, every joke, every touch between them destroyed a very necessary layer of his protection.

Hell. The armor was already close to disintegrating, wasn't it?

And now this other man wanted her. That much was obvious. The adoration in his eyes had been sickening. And, if Jase had to guess, the feeling was definitely mutual. Brook Lynn had *brightened* when she'd spied him.

His hands fisted, the bones aching. He wanted to stomp back inside that store and kick Brad out on his ass. But of course he didn't. He wouldn't. It would be considered assault. Worse, Brook Lynn might not appreciate his helpfulness.

Nothing but disaster awaited him here.

He picked up the faint sound of footsteps, coming in behind him, approaching fast. Tensing at the possibility of a threat, Jase spun.

An older man dressed in overalls paused to give Jase the stink eye. "What are you doin' loitering outside Ms. Edna's shop, boy?"

Jase breathed, his heart rate slowing. "I'm…thinking."

"Do yourself a favor. Go inside and buy your girl a fine piece of jewelry."

Not what he'd expected the guy to say. "I don't have a girl."

"Guy?"

"No."

"Single, then." The old man looked at the shop door then back at Jase. He shuffled closer and held out his hand. "I'm Virgil Porter of Swat Team 8—we assassinate fleas, ticks, silverfish, cockroaches, bees, ants, mice and rats. You must be one of them city boys who moved here with Lincoln. And I know. Everyone calls him West, but that's his last name, gosh dern it, and I ain't calling no one I've shaken hands with by his last name. It's rude is what it is."

"I'm Jase. And I assure you, that's my first name." Unlike with Brad, he didn't contemplate breaking every bone in Virgil's hand.

"You pinin' for our Brook Lynn, then?"

Yes. No. Damn it. He didn't know what was going on inside him.

Last night he'd wanted to kiss her more than he'd wanted to live free. Something about her called to him. Her delicacy, maybe. All he wanted to do was protect her. Or her stubbornness, perhaps. She did what she thought was right, refusing to back down. Or her wit, even. She'd taken his list and turned it against him.

He smiled despite The Great Hemorrhoid debacle.

"Yes, sir," Virgil said with a nod. He patted Jase on the shoulder. "You ain't the first, son, that's for sure."

How many others were there? Yes, a man would be a fool not to recognize Brook Lynn's appeal, but Jase didn't like the thought of other men desiring what belonged to—

Not me. Never me.

Maybe Brad.

"Sir, I don't mean to be rude, but I'm not comfortable discussing my love life with a stranger," Jase said. He was barely handling a discussion with himself.

Virgil waved his words away as unimportant. "Miss Brook Lynn is a special girl, and she deserves a special man. You special, Jase?"

"No, sir," he said, opting for honesty. "I'm not." The people of Strawberry Valley would be horrified to know just how un-special he really was.

"Well, that's too bad."

A feminine scream suddenly pierced the air—and it had come from inside the jewelry store.

Jase didn't hesitate. He bounded forward, practically shattering glass as he pushed his way inside. He took in the scene in an instant. Brook Lynn was sprawled on the floor. There was some kind of small mechanical device splattered with blood resting beside her. Blood leaked from underneath her hair, down her chin, dripping on the floor.

Brad was crouched in front of her, begging to know what he should do. He was trying to help her, but Jase didn't care. She was sobbing. He shoved the male aside and acted as her shield. She grabbed hold of his wrists, holding on to him for dear life, her eyes wide and overflowing with tears.

"What's wrong, angel?" he asked.

A whimper of pain escaped her. She opened and closed her mouth, but words never formed. Finally, she released him to clutch at her ears.

Her ears. "How can—"

She cringed, even moaned.

"I think she needs—" Brad began, and Brook Lynn whimpered.

Jase rounded on the guy, glaring, and slapped a hand over his mouth. For whatever reason, noise hurt her right now, so there would be no more noise. It was as simple as that.

When he was certain Brad understood another word would get him hurt bad, Jase gathered Brook Lynn in his arms. She burrowed against his chest and cried quietly, her entire body heaving. He pulled the cell phone from her pocket, turned it to silent and thumbed through her address book to find her sister's number.

Texting with such an old phone proved difficult, but he did it. One minute dragged into another, and he had to fight wave after wave of helplessness to keep from drowning. Not knowing what else to do, he carried Brook Lynn to the back of the shop, away from Brad and Virgil, who'd followed him inside the shop. When he opened the office door, the groan of hinges sent her into another fit of sobbing. He laid her on the couch, waited until she'd calmed, and tiptoed out to call the only doctor in her address book. He told the receptionist what was going on and was told he'd get a call back. He barely managed to keep his crap together while he waited.

Five minutes.

Five minutes of utter hell.

Finally, though, a nurse phoned him and he learned that he was to give Brook Lynn the sedative that would be waiting at the local pharmacy and then take her to Baptist Hospital in the city. Jase rang Beck and quietly told him to pick up the medication and bring it to the shop. Then all he could do was wait some more.

CHAPTER TEN

BROOK LYNN BOLTED UPRIGHT, unable to catch her breath or hear a single sound, a residue of panic slowly fading.

Panic? Why? She searched her surroundings for clues. A tube extended from one of her arms, ending in an IV bag. A blood-pressure cuff was anchored to her left biceps. Hospital, she realized.

Ugh. She hated hospitals. As a kid she'd spent countless hours inside sparse, sterile rooms with strangers as roommates, drugged to the max to counteract the constant, uncontrollable pain in her ears.

Her ears!

Frantic, she reached up. The moment she encountered the implants, she relaxed. They were in place and clearly working, deaf as she currently was, and though the motion caused a dull throb to reverberate through her head, like a fresh bruise in the process of healing, it was far better than the itching—and what had come after.

Once again, I'm Frankenlynn. But at least she could function.

The room was small but private, Jessie Kay sleeping in the chair by the window. The blinds were open, allowing her to see outside. Bradford pears, oaks and wildflowers surrounded a busy parking lot.

Memories flooded Brook Lynn. She'd been inside Rhinestone Cowgirl. Brad had just accepted her invitation, and as they'd made plans their hands had brushed together—masculine contact she hadn't experienced in a very long time. But there had been nothing. No spark. No shiver of pleasure or internal tingle. Not like the mere thought of Jase often caused. Brad had leaned toward her and, afraid he was going to try to kiss her, she'd jerked away. She'd stumbled. When she hit the floor, one of her implants had ripped free.

The pain—oh, the pain. Every sound, from the whistle of wind against the shop windows to the patter of footsteps outside, had agonized her. Then Jase had arrived and...she couldn't remember anything after that.

Fingertips brushed over her wrist. Gasping, she faced the culprit. Jessie Kay had woken up and now stood at her bedside. Her lips were moving.

"You'll have to start over," Brook Lynn said, speaking over her sister. "I'm on silent, and I'm not ready to change that. I have to read your lips."

Jessie Kay nodded and, with tears welling in her eyes, said, "I'm so sorry this happened. Sorry I wasn't there to help you."

"It wasn't your fault."

"I know, but..." Features tight with tension, Jessie Kay latched on to her hand and squeezed. "I was with Sunny. She'd just gotten a huge check for the oil leases on her land, and she staked me a few hundred bucks. We went to the casino in the city to try and win more."

Just like Uncle Kurt. Trying to hide her dismay, Brook Lynn said, "And while you were there, you threw a penny in a wishing well and asked that one of my implants fall out?"

"Never! Dude. You know I hate wishing wells."

True story. Jessie Kay feared the *Pet Sematary* effect. "Then I still don't see how this is your fault."

"It just is. For once in your life, don't argue with me."

"Fine. You're to blame. You suck."

A relieved nod. "Much better."

Brook Lynn squeezed her sister's hand in return. "How long have I been here?"

"Two days. You've actually woken up and talked to me a few times before, but the doc told me the drugs might screw with your memory."

Brook Lynn clenched her eyes shut and dragged in a breath. She'd missed two days of work? *After* she'd told Edna she would be more reliable. *After* only two days on the job with Jase. *I'm the worst employee ever.* Both of her bosses had to be tee-icked.

"By the way, Jase is in the waiting room. He hasn't left, not one time," Jessie Kay said, her eyes going wide with awe. But the awe was soon replaced by dismay. "He yelled at me. Told me I was nothing but a drain on you, and I needed to step up and do my part."

Two reactions bubbled up at once…warm flutters dancing in her stomach, anger burning through her veins. Jase had stayed? Had worried about her? He *cared* about her that much? But he'd yelled at her sister, insulted her, when he'd had no right to do so. He didn't know the fires and trials that had molded Jessie Kay into the woman she was. He hadn't been there every time she'd tossed and turned with nightmares, crying out for their parents. He hadn't been there when she'd scrimped and saved to buy their uncle a birthday present—only to find out he'd hocked it the next day.

"I love you," Brook Lynn said. "You know that, right?"

Jessie Kay gave a reluctant incline of her head, wiped away the tears that had sprung up and quickly moved on. "Kenna is here, too. Brad was, but he had to go to work. I'm supposed to call him with a progress report and..." Her gaze shifted. "Hey! No one invited you in here, death-peddler."

A shadow fell over Brook Lynn just before Dr. Murphy claimed her attention.

"Nice to see you, too, Miss Dillon," he replied.

Jessie Kay hated doctors almost as much as spiders, and Brook Lynn could only blame herself. As much as Brook Lynn had cried before and after each of her visits, her sister had learned to associate medical treatment with anguish.

Dr. Murphy was an older black man with a full head of silver hair and eyes the loveliest shade of chocolate. He was one of the most distinguished-looking men she'd ever come across.

"How are we doing, my dear?" he asked with a warm smile.

"Well. I think."

"Good, good. Let's have a look at those vitals."

The exam lasted only ten minutes or so, and as he checked her over, he explained how the tube anchoring the new implant to her ear canal hadn't adhered properly and had come loose, wreaking havoc on her whole system. From her equilibrium to actual brain activity. While knocked out, she'd even had a seizure. But she was on the mend now and could go back to her regular schedule upon her return home tomorrow, as long as she stayed off trampolines and away from jump ropes for the next several weeks.

When Dr. Murphy left, she lumbered into the bathroom to clean up as best she could, which was actually easier than anticipated. Propped on the sink was a plastic bag filled with goodies. A washrag, hairbrush, toothpaste and a toothbrush. A ponytail holder, T-shirt and a nice bar of soap. She returned to the bed feeling ten thousand times better.

Jessie Kay hadn't left from her spot and once again clutched her hand, as if she couldn't bear another moment of separation.

"Thanks for the supplies," Brook Lynn said.

"Do you seriously believe I'm that thoughtful?"

"Good point. Who brought them?"

"Beck, at Jase's order."

Jase again. The man confused and angered her...but he also delighted her. *What am I going to do about him?*

"I was so afraid," her sister admitted. "If I were to lose you..."

"You didn't. You won't. You heard Dr. Murphy. I'm fine."

"Yes, but for how long? You work too hard. You need a break. You deserve one."

"We have bills. More now than ever."

Jessie Kay shook her head, the first hint of a smile revealed, like the sun peeking out from behind dark clouds. "We don't. Jase is taking care of everything."

What! "No. No, no, no."

"Yes, yes, yes," her sister insisted. "You can bury your stubborn side in a cow patty, where it belongs. He's already paid the hospital bill. You think they'll give the money back to him?"

She wouldn't be a drain on him. She would rather die. "They won't, but I will. I'm paying him back even if I have to get a third job." And a fourth one. "Even if I have to sell my organs on the black market!"

"First, I call dibs on your liver. I could use a new one. And I'll expect a sisterly discount. But why can't we let him—"

"I said no!"

"Okay, okay. Calm down." Jessie Kay pursed her lips, as if she'd just sucked on a lemon. "*I'll* get a job."

Please. *Heard that before.*

"I know you're not actually speaking any words, but I don't think you've ever been ruder to me," Jessie Kay said. "Your eyes are saying plenty."

"Well, I hope you're listening. They don't like to repeat themselves."

"I'm listening, all right, and they have a *seriously* dirty mouth." Her sister gave her hand another squeeze. "So…did you talk me up to Jase?"

Sickness churned deep in her stomach. "Of course."

"Did you mention my ability to make any conversation about sex?"

"Somehow that detail got left out," she said drily.

"Well, it's time to put it in." Jessie Kay wiggled her brows. "See what I did there?"

Brook Lynn rolled her eyes.

"I'm going to marry that boy, you know," her sister said with a firm nod. "And I'm going to break him in like a carnival pony then ride him into the sunset for a happily-ever-after. For *both* of us."

The churning and sickness grew worse. *Marry* him? As in, take his last name, sleep in his bed every night and have his babies, marry? "Why Jase? After the way he's treated you, the things he's said to you, why not pick, say, Beck?" *Please.*

"Beck was a mistake. He's like an older brother now. Jase, on the other hand, is the white knight I want guarding my back."

The moisture in her mouth dried. *I can't steal a white knight from my sister. I just can't.*

Not that he was Brook Lynn's to steal.

"We need him," Jessie Kay said. "He can make our lives better."

He could. He was strong. Smart. Funny. Teasing. Passionate. Resourceful. Sexy. "Or he could make our lives worse." *Am I trying to change her mind for her good...or my own?*

Once-bright cheeks turned waxen. "Do you not think I can win him over?" Jessie Kay asked with a tremor. "Do you not think I'm special enough?"

Her sister's vulnerabilities didn't show up often, but when they did...*I would rather have my heart ripped out by a zombie than see that look on her face.* "I think you're the specialest. I know you think he doesn't know what he wants, and that you can show him, but are you sure you should try? Shouldn't a man be willing to fight for *you*? You are a prize, and if he can't see that on his own..."

"Am I, though? Am I really a prize?"

"I think so. Mom and Dad thought so. I mean, are you a total underachiever? Yes. But you're also smart and witty, and you sure aren't ugly."

Her sister snorted. "Your compliments are like poetry." She fluffed her hair. "But you're right. I'm definitely a prize, and he'd be crazy not to want me. I *will* find a way to change his mind. Because I want him. Bad. I've never met a guy so capable and concerned, so willing to step in and make everything better."

A flood of different emotions hit Brook Lynn, one after the other. Anger. Frustration. Worry. Sadness. Regret. Affection. Hope. More anger. Her chest hurt. Her temples, too.

"I texted him a bit ago," Jessie Kay said. "Told him you were up. He'd like to see you."

"No. Absolutely not." *Can't face him right now.*

"But why not? He's your future brother-in-law."

"Because," she gritted out, doing her best not to reveal her frustration with the term. "Just because."

Jessie Kay hesitated, nodded. "Okay. I'll go tell him you're not up for visitors."

"Thank you." Yes, she needed to express her gratitude to him for all he'd done. He'd gone above and beyond what was expected of a boss or even a friend. But with her sister's words clanging around in her head, she didn't think she could bear to be in the same room with him, looking at him, breathing him in. "Tell him, and then head home."

"No, I—"

"Yes. You need to rest, and so do I. Just…find me a notebook and a pen before you go. Please," she tacked on when she realized how rude she must sound. *Warden strikes again.*

Jessie Kay shook her head. "Sorry, sister dear, but I'm here for the long haul. I'm staying, and that's that. I'll be right back." Before she left, she kissed Brook Lynn on the forehead. And, true to her word—for once—Jessie Kay did, in fact, come right back with a notebook and pen.

Expression bemused, Jessie Kay said, "Dude. Jase does *not* like being told no."

"Learned that my first day as his assistant." Her heart drummed erratically. With guilt or longing, she wasn't sure. "Did he leave?"

"No. He's basically moved in to the waiting room, and it'll take a crane to get him out."

He was *that* desperate to see her? Why?

Palms beginning to sweat, she fluffed her pillows and decided to put him out of her mind. He'd leave soon enough. Surely.

"Help me make a fun list," she said. Despite the change

in her circumstances and the looming possibility of having to nail down a third job—*whimper*—she wasn't going to abandon her plan to enjoy life. Not anymore. But the list she'd made with Kenna had failed to inspire her, which was probably why she'd never made a real attempt to work through it. She needed a new one. One tailored specifically to her.

Jessie Kay pulled her chair closer to the bed. "Ohhh. A fun list. You certainly came to the right person."

"An expert."

"Do you want X-rated, PG-13 or PG?"

No need to think about it. "PG-13."

"Boooo, hiss." Jessie Kay made a face and gave her a thumbs-down. "Mild wild girls don't have as much fun."

"This one will."

Jessie Kay tapped her fingers together, saying, "Well, the first thing you'll need to do is flash a room full of men. At a bar!"

Ugh. The crowds. The music. Drunks who might grab what they shouldn't. "No, thanks."

"Write it down," Jessie Kay insisted, pointing to the notebook. "Or I start counting."

"Fine." She wrote "Flash one man, preferably a boyfriend" and said "I'm also writing 'hustle someone at pool and/or poker.'" While she wasn't the biggest fan of the skills her uncle had imparted to her—all those late nights in smoky pool halls and man caves learning with the best—she decided to take something that once pained her and turn it into something that amused her. Kenna was right. The past created who a person was, but shouldn't define who they could become. "Oh, and I'd like to attend a wine-and-cheese tasting."

Jessie Kay's head fell on her shoulder, her eyes closed. She let out a loud, exaggerated snore.

"Am I boring you to sleep?" Brook Lynn asked.

Her sister peeked through her lashes. *To death.*

"Too bad for you. Because I have never been so alive." She wrote down "Drink whiskey straight from the bottle" and "Smoke a cigar." Oh, and "Learn how to properly fight zombies."

The notebook was snatched out of her hand. Jessie Kay read what she'd written and gagged. "When did you become a Victorian maiden living in a paranormal-romance world? Should I write down 'learn to do the scandalous waltz while turning into a vampire,' too?"

Brook Lynn grabbed the notebook and spoke aloud the next words she wrote. "Shave off all my sister's hair. Have a secret identity for a day, and host a mystery dinner."

"Touch my lustrous mane and lose a hand," Jessie Kay said, fluffing the mane in question. "Honestly, you're seriously depressing the crap out of me right now. You need to add 'oil wrestling with a guy dressed like Tarzan.' Oh, oh, and 'holding a long, hard—'"

Looking down at her list, she lost track of her sister's words. She wrote the dreams she'd had since she was a little girl…and a curious teenager. "Rescue a dog from a shelter" and "Dance for a hot guy, preferably the boyfriend I flash."

Jessie Kay might have been the one to take ballet lessons, but Brook Lynn had been the one who'd yearned to spin and pirouette and dress as the swan princess. And, okay, sure, no guy on the planet would find her attempt at ballet sexy. But she could certainly perform some kind of naughty striptease.

What would Brad think of this desire of hers?

What would *Jase* think?

She trembled.

Nope. No. Not going there.

Maybe she needed to forget the men of Strawberry Valley and say yes to the next citidiot who asked her out. He wouldn't be boyfriend material, but he also wouldn't stick around town and gossip about her lack of talent. Of course, he wouldn't settle for a few hip thrusts, either. He'd want all her clothes to come off and her backside grinding into his crotch until he reached a happy ending. Which wasn't actually a half-bad idea, except for that last part...and it would certainly stop Jessie Kay's snoring fit.

A tap on her arm had her glancing up. Her sister's mouth was moving, but her gaze was not on Brook Lynn.

"—be in here," she was saying.

Brook Lynn smelled him before she saw him. Honey-and-oat-scented soap. Tingling and heating, she turned her head and found Jase standing at her bedside. His features were taut, his arms crossed; the muscles beneath his skin flexed. His clothes were wrinkled, proof he'd slept in the waiting room, unwilling to leave her.

And I don't have the lady balls to talk with him? I suck.

"Give us a few minutes," she said to her sister.

"Are you sure?" Jessie Kay asked, looking nervous on her behalf.

No, but she nodded anyway.

After giving her hand a final comforting squeeze, Jessie Kay strolled out of the room and shut the door behind her.

Brook Lynn drew in a deep breath and faced Jase. He wasn't peering at her, but at the wall over her shoulder. He plowed a hand through his hair and stalked to the chair Jessie Kay had vacated. She watched him, silent, unsure. Waiting, hoping. Dreading.

Finally, the wait proved to be too much.

"Thank you for paying the hospital bill," she said. "But I can't accept your money."

That green gaze at last moved...and locked on her. His blank mask was firmly in place. "You refused to see me. Why?"

She racked her brain for the proper response. Her reason had been a good one—Jessie Kay wanted him, and being around him only made Brook Lynn ache for what she couldn't have. She refused to lie, but at the same time she had to protect her emotions.

"I'm choosing not to answer you," she finally said.

"Are you afraid of me?"

"Define *afraid*," she said.

He didn't speak for a long while, and she began to squirm on the bed. Fought the urge to babble. *Yes, I'm afraid of you. Of what you make me feel. Of what would happen if ever I fell for you.*

"You don't have a choice about the money," he said. How like him. He'd ignored her request and changed the subject. "It's already done."

"I know, but I *will* pay you back."

"And I won't accept."

They'd see about that.

"Tell me about your ears," he said.

Suddenly self-conscious, she shifted on the bed. "Without the implants, I hear everyday noises at a higher volume than other people."

"What caused it?"

"I was born that way."

"So you've suffered all your life?"

"I used to wear earmuffs. They helped. And I realize I've missed two days of work," she said, changing tracks, "but you don't have to worry. I'll take care of your list tomorrow."

He was shaking his head before she could finish. "No. You'll be resting."

He was going to treat her like an invalid, wasn't he? "Are you planning to fire me?"

He flinched, as though horrified by the thought. "No."

"Then I'm going to do my job."

"Then I'm firing you," he said simply.

She sat up, grabbed him by the shirt collar and yanked him closer to her. As strong as he was, he could have resisted, and she wouldn't have been able to do anything about it. She leaned toward him until they were almost nose to nose.

"Now you listen to me, Jase Hollister. My ears are messed up and unless there are extreme advances in medicine they will always be that way. Some days, like today, I'm totally deaf. Other days I can hear just fine. I have little machines attached inside and out, and sometimes they have flashing lights. People stare."

His gaze dropped to her lips, and she shivered, almost losing her nerve to continue.

"But that's it," she said. "That's the extent of my problem. I'll heal from this newest surgery, and I *will* work. I will do a good job. You will not baby me. Do you understand?"

His eyes narrowed to tiny slits as he plucked her fingers from his shirt. Something about him...as if the icy husk he surrounded himself with was now melting before her eyes. Cold-blooded? Oh, no. This man suddenly *burned*.

But when next he spoke, his tone gave nothing away.

"You're saying I should treat you like a normal, healthy woman?"

Should I be nervous? "Yes. Because that's exactly what I am."

"Okay, then. That's exactly what I'll do." He let her go and straightened. He smoothed his clothes, gave her one last lingering look and strode from the room—leaving her trembling...and desperate for their next interaction.

Despite his words—and his actions—something had changed in him. Between them. That look...

What would he do when she showed up for work tomorrow?

She could hardly wait to find out.

CHAPTER ELEVEN

JASE RETURNED TO the hospital bright and early the next morning, purpose in his every step. He couldn't stay away a second longer, felt dragged by an invisible chain.

He didn't pause at the nurses' station and didn't care if visiting hours had or hadn't started. He went directly to Brook Lynn's room, the private suite he'd ensured she had. The door was open, and she was perched at the side of the bed, looking fresh and clean with cheeks bright pink and her golden hair gleaming around her shoulders. She wore the T-shirt and shorts he'd had delivered for her.

The shirt had come straight from his closet.

The lingering effects of her illness had fallen away, and the sight of her arrested him. She was a beauty like no other, so it was little wonder he'd been on fire for her all night. Or that she'd awoken needs he'd never known he'd had—needs he would never again be able to ignore. To possess utterly, through any means necessary. To consume wholly. Not just anyone, but her. Only her.

When she'd proudly proclaimed herself healthy, he'd almost pulled her flush against him and kissed her. But she'd looked vulnerable and hauntingly fragile, and he'd found the strength to walk away instead. The need to protect her, even from himself, had proved stronger.

Now here she was, on the bed, looking as healthy as she'd claimed.

He shut the door and moved into her line of sight.

She gasped with surprise—and pleasure? "Jase!"

He paused long enough to ask, "How are you feeling?"

Warmth bloomed in her baby blues. "Totally racer ready. Just waiting for my discharge papers."

"Good." He closed the distance, cupped the back of her nape and pressed his lips to hers.

She opened with another gasp.

No turning back now.

His tongue thrust against hers, and hers reached tentatively for his. A groan escaped her, enthralling him, and just like that, he lost track of his surroundings, his intention to simply taste. His mind centered on only one thing: hearing that sound again.

He urged her to her back, kissing her as if he would die tomorrow. As if she were the last girl he'd ever see. As if her lips held the answer to every question he'd ever asked. Supple and willing, she reclined for him. Her arms wound around his neck, bringing him with her, so that the hardest parts of him were lined up with the softest parts of her. All the while their tongues rolled and thrust in a white-hot tangle.

He tasted cinnamon, a hint of strawberries. A heady combination, addictive when it should not have been. He'd tasted all three flavors before, but they'd never made him feel as though he was floating... melting from the inside out.

He could be locked away for the rest of his life, he decided, but it wouldn't matter because he'd experienced this one perfect moment. Not even Daphne had affected him this strongly—and with so little. But then, her kisses had been those of a teenager in puppy love.

This one came straight from a woman with passions as intense as his own.

Everything he'd felt for Brook Lynn since moment one consumed him, raw and carnal as she arched her back and rubbed her chest against his. Softness without the barrier of a bra, two little beads abrading deliciously...only the thin material of her shirt covering her.

He clutched at her pillow, nearly ripping the material in half, and lifted his head to ensure she could read his lips. "Be still," he told her. If she kept moving like that, the experience would end in mere minutes. "Please."

"Can't," she rasped, her fingers applying pressure at his nape, urging him back down.

Her eyes were glassed with passion-fever, her cheeks even rosier than before. Her lips were red and swollen, moisture glistening over them.

"Damn, you're beautiful."

"And you're wasting precious time." She stopped trying to force him down and sat up, thrusting her tongue in his mouth, as if she'd been starved for him and could not live another second without this.

When she fell back, he went with her, her willing captive. Her nails raked down the ridges of his spine, and he cursed the shirt that prevented skin-to-skin contact. The urge to climb on top of her, to pin her down with the full bulk of his weight, teased him. He would put his hands on every inch of her, strip her, caress her nakedness and drive her to the very edge of release. And the sounds she would make...he would swallow them all.

A low, possessive growl rose from deep in his chest. He'd never heard it before. Not from anything human. It should have scared the hell out of him, but it merely urged him on. He put one of his knees on the bed—on the gurney.

The gurney.

They weren't just in a public place, but in a hospital. Anyone could come in. Anyone could sneak in behind him, attack him.

Jase jolted back, severing contact. His body shouted a protest, his hands closed so tightly he would have sworn he'd cracked the bones. He struggled to catch his breath, to stay in place, away from her. *Have to stay away from her.* How had she made him forget his surroundings, even for a second?

She traced her fingertips over her kiss-swollen lips. "Jase, I…"

She stopped, just stopped. What would she say? *I want more? I shouldn't have done that? You're my boss?*

With a screech, she slammed a fist into the mattress beneath her. "I can't believe this! I'm such a mouth-slut."

The change in her startled him. "You are not a mouth-slut."

Ignoring him, she added, "And do you want to know what sucks worse? You're a superstar stud because you've now mouth-bagged two sisters."

Mouth-bagged? "That would make *me* the mouth-slut, not you." He had a choice: fire her and pursue her, though he could never offer her anything permanent, or apologize, vow to never again kiss her and return to the way things were.

She covered her face with her hands. "We can't do that again. Ever."

He locked his jaw to prevent a curse from escaping. Very well. She'd made the decision for him.

Prying her hands away from her eyes, he said, "You're right. We can't do that again."

She ran her bottom lip between her teeth, a nervous gesture. "You came here to kiss me, not for any other reason. Why?"

Because he couldn't *not* do it. Because he'd never wanted anything more. "Why did you let me?"

"You first."

"A moment of insanity," he said, and she flinched. Okay. Insulting her wasn't a smart move on his part. He added, "Obviously, I'm attracted to you."

Her eyes widened as she squeaked, "You are?"

The magnitude of her surprise caught him off guard. "Has no man ever told you that?"

"Yes. I mean, a few have."

Only a few? Clearly the men of Strawberry Valley were idiots, and yet Jase was struck by a sudden urge to track down the few smart ones and do a little skull bashing. *She's mine!*

He sucked in a breath. No, she wasn't, and as he'd told himself before, she would never be. *Feel nothing. Want nothing. Need nothing.*

"But you…" she said. "You're difficult to read."

He stalked to the chair beside the bed and sat, increasing the distance between them. If he wasn't careful, he would reach for her. Do…more. And if he did more, he would want to try for something serious with her—Beck was right. The desire for commitment was hardwired inside his brain. But if he committed to her, she would own him, but would he ever really own her? And if ever anyone dared hurt her…

I'll do things that will send me right back to prison.

"What's so difficult? I'm attracted to you, as I said, so I kissed you. But I won't do it again. You have long-term written all over you, and I respect that. I just wish I didn't have to be the one to break the news to you. Relationships fail, honey. Always."

BROOK LYNN STUDIED the man she'd just used as an oxygen tank, basically sucking the air from his lungs. There was no lingering sign of Jase's desire for her. His cold, hard mask was firmly in place, his eyes pure green frost, his lips pressed into a hard line.

Miss my tender lover already. But really, he wasn't hers, and that was becoming clearer by the moment. She couldn't allow herself to think otherwise, even for a moment.

"Relationships do not always fail," she said. "I know couples who have been together thirty, forty and fifty years." And she'd think of their names at some point... probably.

"Honey, just because they've stayed together doesn't mean they still make each other happy."

Wow. He wasn't just jaded—he was *jaded.*

Marry him? Jessie Kay didn't stand a chance.

Jessie Kay! Crap!

I'm the worst sister ever born.

Brook Lynn had only one saving grace. In no way, shape or form would Jase and Jessie Kay ever have ended up together. Unlike her sister, Brook Lynn believed a man when he said he wasn't interested in something, or someone, and she wasn't willing to try to change his mind. Why should she? He either wanted to be with her or he didn't. He was either honored to put the work in, to do whatever was necessary to keep her, or he wasn't. There was no middle ground.

Jessie Kay saw a man's reluctance as a challenge.

The harder the battle, the sweeter the victory. What she didn't get? The worse the fall.

Would she view what Jase and Brook Lynn had done as just another hurdle to climb? Or as the betrayal it was?

I have to tell her what happened. Soon. No more putting it off.

Brook Lynn stifled a groan.

"What?" Jase asked.

She waved the question away, not wanting his answer or his opinion. She and her sister had never liked the same man before. And she did, she thought. Brook Lynn wasn't just attracted to Jase. She liked him. A lot. Despite the fact that she'd lined up a date with another man before kissing him. Stupid, stupid, stupid.

"Tell me about your parents," she said, remembering the way he'd shut her down the last time she'd tried to ask about his past.

"I don't even know who my father is," he admitted, surprising her. "While I lived with my mother, different men paraded in and out of our apartment. Could have been any one of them. Or none of them."

Her heart broke for him. Clearly, he *had* seen the worst of relationships. "Did they treat you well? These men?" she asked.

His gaze skidded away from her, sticking to the wall just behind her. "Sometimes. Not always."

The urge to curl up in his lap, wrap her arms around him and offer comfort bombarded her. Only the thought of rejection held her back. That, and Jessie Kay.

"Despite your abysmal experience," she said, "I still believe happily-ever-afters are a possibility. My parents adored each other."

He shook his head, pity filling his eyes. "Given time, who knows what would have happened with them. All relationships, even those that start out great, end up toxic. Why would you want one to last?"

"Not all relationships. What about you, West and Beck? You've been friends for...how long?"

"Since we were eight," he said.

"And do you hurt each other?"

He frowned. "Sometimes."

"Really?" She found that astounding—how had they hurt each other?

"But it's never on purpose, and we always do the kiss-and-make-up thing," he admitted.

"Well, there you go. Your own life has just proved your theory wrong. But tell me more about this kissing."

He snorted. "I don't like to kiss and tell. As for our relationship, we know everything there is to know about each other. We're honest to the point of brutal in a way couples never are. They always keep secrets and blunt the truth, thinking it's a kindness."

She wondered what he'd say if she asked how fat her butt looked in her shorts. "So you don't think a woman can deal with knowing everything about you? Knowing the real you?"

His eyes narrowed. "I'm certain of it. Therefore, I'll amend my argument to state that only *sexual* relationships are toxic."

There was no winning with a man who'd already made up his mind. And *what* had happened to this one to make him so jaded? Had to be more than he'd admitted.

"Have you ever trusted a woman enough to tell her everything there is to know about you?" she asked.

"No."

"Well. Until you do, you can only guess about how

she'll react. And if one woman reacts poorly, it doesn't mean others will react the same way."

He brushed his fingers through his hair, the motion jerky. Was this getting through to him?

"You can't change what's happened in the past," she said, "but you *can* change the path of your future."

He arched a brow, all cocky assurance when he should have caved under her logic. "Want to go there, do you?"

What did that mean? "Are you implying I'm trying to change the past?"

"You're definitely not changing the path of your future. You've allowed your sister to become a chain around your neck."

"I have not! And she certainly isn't a chain."

He shrugged, all *whatever you say.*

Frustrating man! "Enough about her. I want to talk about your attraction to me."

He went still. "And yours to me."

"I never said I was." She'd only thought it, again and again.

"You didn't have to say anything, honey. Sucking on my tongue and sinking your claws in my back told me all I needed to know."

The sudden heat in her cheeks could have warmed the entire building every day of the upcoming winter. "Be that as it may, I'm not interested in a fling."

"Like I told you, I figured you for a long-term girl. But I wouldn't give you a one-nighter even if you begged me."

"But...but...*why*?" He'd kissed her with such passion, and now he couldn't stand the thought of being with her even once?

He massaged the back of his neck, somehow looking

both fatigued and virile. "I seriously think I feel one of those hemorrhoids coming on."

The unexpected comment drained the affront right out of her, and she laughed. He laughed, too, and she wished she could hear it. Whether it was rusty or hearty. The way his face lit, as if he were peering directly into the sun, gave him a boyish innocence she'd seen only once before on him. She…liked it.

He quieted abruptly, acting as though the laughter were his enemy. He scowled and pulled at the collar of his shirt. "Well," he said, and his throat moved with a cough. "I should be going. Like you mentioned, your doctor will arrive soon with your discharge papers." But he made no effort to stand.

Even though she was annoyed with him, and realized he'd avoided her question, she wasn't ready for this stolen moment to end. Here and now, they weren't boss and employee—they were moth and flame. Her lips still hungered for him, tingling, aching. Her hands itched to return to his hair. No kiss had ever affected her so strongly, and he hadn't even put his hands on her!

"Stay," she finally rasped. "Just a little while more."

A wave of relief washed over his features.

"What's this?" he asked, plucking the list from the bed.

Oh, crap. The list! She'd been tweaking some of the finer details while she'd waited for the nurse. When she tried to grab it, Jase leaned back, moving out of reach.

"That is none of your business," she said. "That's what it is."

He smiled, saying, "A *fun* list?" He scanned it and smiled again—only to look up at her with a glower. "These are things you've never done before, I'm assuming."

She squirmed on the gurney. When his stare remained steady, she crossed her arms over her middle and said, "No, I haven't done them."

He relaxed. "Honey, if you flash someone in public, you're likely to start a riot."

Was that a compliment or an insult? "I'll make sure it's private."

"Good." A diabolical gleam entered his eyes. "*We're* private right now."

Oh, no. The ice around him had begun to melt again. A warning sign appeared in her mind, reading *Danger! Danger! You'll end up right back where you started. Craving him, but unable to have him.*

"I'm here for you," he continued, gripping the notebook with so much force, the center bowed. "I will allow you to flash me."

"Oh, you'll allow me?" Her stomach twisted even while desire pooled deep inside her. "Thanks, but I'm going to decline."

"It's not like you have to worry about being groped."

"You think you can resist me?" Jerk!

"You think I'll pounce on you the moment I see your breasts?" he countered.

She glared at him. "Maybe I think you'll be disappointed." Maybe? Ha!

"That isn't even a possibility," he said, confident. "But challenge accepted. Now you *have* to flash me."

"I don't *have* to do anything."

"Oh, I get it." His smile was all about projecting sympathy. "You're scared."

"I am not!"

He held up his hands, palms out. "If you say so, angel. But I believe you're the one who told me actions mean more than words."

Using her own statement against her? She was going to make him *so* sorry he'd gone there. She grabbed the hem of her T-shirt, her hands trembling. "I'm going to do it. You can't stop me."

"Do you see me trying?"

"Once I do it, it can never be undone. You can never go back to wondering." Not that he'd wondered.

Had he wondered?

"I think I can handle it," he said drily and waved his hand impatiently.

Could he? Could *she*?

What if he hated what he saw?

What if he liked it?

What if indecision was the path to insanity?

Either nut up or shut up. I'm not the girl I've always been: reserved, maybe even timid. I'm fun. And now it's time to prove it.

With a deep breath, she flipped up the shirt. Between one blink and the next, Jase had a full-frontal view of her chest. Cold air stroked her skin, making her shiver. Definitely the cold and not his gaze...which was laser-beamed on her...staring so openly, so hungrily, as if he'd been starved for years and she'd just offered him a feast.

He liked.

It unnerved her—thrilled her. Moisture flooded her mouth. Her breasts suddenly felt heavier, the apex of her thighs warming and aching.

"There," she said shakily and returned the shirt to its proper place. "We can now check that off the list."

Jase gripped the arms of the chair. Sweat beaded on his brow. His gaze lingered...lingered...finally lifted and met hers. Slowly he unfolded from the chair. He stood there for several long moments. She waited, tense and eager to find out what he'd do next. What did she want him to do? Kiss her again?

No. Bad!

Touch her—

No! Really, really bad.

But if he tried, would she really be able to resist?

"Leave," she rasped. "You have to leave. Now. *Please.*"

He was already backing out of the room. When the door shut behind him, she realized she could breathe again and sucked in much-needed oxygen.

When Jessie Kay arrived a short while later, a nurse and wheelchair in tow, Brook Lynn had calmed significantly—at least on the outside. She didn't complain when she was helped into the chair and wheeled to the car, even though she could walk just fine.

Once they were on the road, Brook Lynn opened her mouth to confess all, but Jessie Kay handed over her cell phone, a steady red blink signaling a message. Only Edna ever called her.

"Does Edna know why I missed work the past few days?" she asked.

"Yep," Jessie Kay said. "Jase spoke with her."

Jase, yet again.

"Listen to the message for me," she said. "If you don't mind."

"Don't you know it's dangerous to drive while distracted?" Jessie Kay took the phone anyway, saying, "If anyone can do it, it's me. I'm, like, the best multi-tasker ever." She held the phone to her ear, listened… and paled.

"What?" Brook Lynn asked. "What's wrong?"

"Edna…she…she's such a slag, Brook Lynn. A bona fide slag."

"What! Why?"

"I'm so sorry, but she fired you. She said she's going to find another buyer for the store. She said this is the third time this year you've been out for an illness for a prolonged period of time, not to mention when you were late, and she can't count on you anymore. But she's going to give you a severance package, so that's good, right?"

Just like that. In a moment of time, Brook Lynn's entire world came crashing down. Her income shrank. Her dream of owning Rhinestone Cowgirl burned to ash. Now Jase was the only life raft in a great and terrible storm. The guy she was desperate to repay. The guy who thought she was too fragile to work. The guy who'd kissed her once and walked away from her twice.

This was another rejection, she realized. She was always so quick to protect Jessie Kay from them, but honestly, they stung her just as sharply. She stared out the window, silent.

Jessie Kay reached over and squeezed her arm, but all the action did was make her feel worse about the conversation to come.

Maybe Jase was right. Maybe all relationships were toxic, and a girl could never count on anyone. Tears burned the backs of her eyes. Brook Lynn couldn't even count on herself. Every time she picked herself up, she fell back down again. She was tired of falling.

Buck up. Another setback? So what.

But—

No buts! This could be a fresh start. A chance to create a new dream. Something she loved, not just something she happened to be good at. One problem. Unlike the kids who'd always known what they wanted to be when they grew up, she never had. Well, besides the far-flung dream of being a dancer. Considering she lacked skill, and dancing on anything but a pole wouldn't pad her empty bank account, that wasn't an option. So... she had to find something she loved, was good at and that would actually make her money.

Easy, she thought and burst into tears.

CHAPTER TWELVE

JASE DOVE INTO the deep end of the pool. The hot sun beat down, burning his shoulders and heating the water as he swam one lap after another. All around him, cotton drifted through the air, so thick it looked like snow.

After a night of constantly replaying the best damn kiss of his life, craving Brook Lynn, desperate for her, he'd gotten up at dawn to finish shingling the roof. He'd worked like a madman, pouring his sexual frustration into the task.

He'd had a mere taste, and now his body hoped to gorge. He wanted her more now than he ever had before.

He yearned to go to Brook Lynn, to talk to her...to kiss her again—and more, so much more. Hence the laps. If he kept himself busy, he had a better chance of resisting temptation and staying away from her.

The kiss had been a mistake. Clearly. His favorite mistake, yes, but a mistake nonetheless. It had split him open, allowing some of his secrets to spill out. He'd willingly shared bits and pieces of his past with her, leaving him vulnerable, shaky, on edge. And yet, strangely sated.

Can't go further with her. Can't share other secrets.

She thought a woman—herself—would be able to forgive Jase's past, but her uncle had been a no-good con man, predisposing her to dislike anyone who broke the law. She probably wouldn't take the time to distinguish a career criminal from a onetime offender, especially when the single crime was so horrific.

More than that, she clung to hope of a happily-ever-after. He knew better, knew there was no such thing. Did he really want to be the one who destroyed her dreams? Of all his crimes, that would be the worst.

He rounded the end of the pool—and found the object of his torment seated on the other side with her bare feet dipped in the water. He stopped abruptly, nearly sinking to the bottom before he had the presence of mind to tread.

The sight before him... *Killing me.* Flaxen hair glimmered in the sunlight. Tanned skin appeared brushed with hints of copper and gold. A white tank and faded jean shorts hugged the very curves he'd had underneath him almost twenty-four hours ago.

A rush of testosterone...endorphins...whatever revved him up. "I thought I fired you," he said, annoyed by the way his heartbeat sped up.

"Congrats! You've just rehired me." She whipped a small object from her back pocket and grinned at him—a wicked grin that made him as uneasy as it did hot. "To celebrate, I brought you a present."

As he reluctantly swam closer, she lifted her fingers from the object, one by one...and he came face-to-face with a tube of Preparation H.

He barked out a laugh, the burst of humor as new to him now as it had been the last time. "You really are a pain, you know that?"

"Well, I'm not letting you rub the medication all over me, if that's what you're hinting at."

Wrong words. *Provocative* words. He lost his amusement in a nanosecond, his mind trapped by images of his hands moving on her, all over her.

Sinking again... He'd been reaching for his erection, because yes, he now had one, his length as hard as a steel pipe. He'd almost stroked himself in front of her.

"You're not working for me anymore, Brook Lynn." He meant those words, he really did.

"Please, Jase." She clapped her hands together, creating a steeple. "Please. I need this job."

No. Absolutely not. He couldn't be exposed to this kind of temptation every day.

His silence must have propelled her in another direction. "I still owe you sandwiches, remember?"

"Okay, you're rehired," he said, unable to stop the words from leaving his mouth. What the hell was wrong with him? His only excuse was that she gave good lunch. The best he'd ever had.

She rewarded him with a wide, toothy grin. "Thank you, Mr. Hollister. You're a doll."

"Don't thank me yet," he muttered. Though he would have liked nothing more than to climb out of the pool, he continued to tread. He was as far from perfect as she was close to it; his scars might appall her...or lead to questions he wasn't prepared to answer. "You haven't heard your new duties."

"I don't care what they are," she said, completely earnest. "I'll do them."

Oh, angel. You should have kept those words to yourself. The things I want you to do to me...

This time, his silence must have unnerved her, because she began to babble. "I'm going to work for you from sunup till sundown, and every week you're going to deduct a hundred dollars from my paycheck, until I've paid back every penny you spent on me."

"Uh, that would be a big, fat no."

She kicked water at him, saying, "What's yours is mine, but what's mine is mine, is that it?"

"Something like that. Which *is* something you should thank me for, honey." Something he'd never offered to another woman, but knowing her, she would protest. She always—

"Fine," she said and sighed. "Don't take out the money."

He eyed her with suspicion and thought, *Too easy. This has to be a trick.* Would he soon find surprise wads of cash stuffed in his dresser drawers?

Bingo. She was just sneaky enough to try it.

He was sneakier.

"Let's backtrack a bit," he said. "How can you work for me from sunup to sundown? What about your hours at Rhinestone Cowgirl?" When he'd spoken to Edna the day of Brook Lynn's injury, her daughter had just returned to town, and the woman had made it sound as though she would be too busy to man the counter herself, that she would need Brook Lynn more than ever.

Brook Lynn waved a hand through the air, dismissing his question as unimportant, even as her eyes filled with shadows. His skeptical nature shouted a high-pitched alert. She'd been fired, hadn't she?

Part of him was angered on her behalf, demanding he tear the jewelry store apart brick by brick and present the remains to her as a gift. The other part of him just wanted to weep with relief that she would no longer be working herself to the bone.

"If we're going to do this…if we're going to make this—" What? It wasn't a relationship. "This *thing* between us work, there will have to be a few changes. Or rather, rules."

"Agreed," she said with a nod. "And the first is definitely—"

"Uh-uh. I make the rules, honey, not you. The first is definitely no kissing. The second is no thinking about kissing. The third is no flashing me. No matter how badly you want to do it."

"Hey," she snapped. "You practically begged me to do it."

"Be that as it may." Another glance at her magnificent breasts would finally crumble what remained of his resistance. They'd been so plump and round, her nipples as ripe as the strawberries the town was famous for, tightening under his gaze. And damn it, he was sinking again…his hands like heat-seeking missiles. "I'm going to expect you here at eight every morning, and you'll stay until eight every night." It was the only way to ensure his little workhorse wouldn't go out and get yet another job. "And because I'm increasing your hours, I'm increasing your pay."

"But—"

"Nonnegotiable," he said. "You will be on call every weekend. With pay." Again to keep her from getting another job. "I anticipate many casserole and sandwich emergencies in my future."

"But—"

"Agree or not. Those are my terms. The rest is up to you."

"Agree," she gritted out.

"Then it's settled." At last he climbed out of the pool, deciding it was better she see his scars than get the peep show of a lifetime as he unintentionally stroked himself to completion while drowning.

Her gaze followed a trickle of water down his chest, and she gulped. "Anything else?"

His step faltered. Was that *arousal* he heard, turning her voice to smoke?

He swallowed a groan, deciding to drape the towel around his waist rather than his shoulders, hiding his growing erection instead of the damaged tissue left over from multiple fights.

"Yes, there's something else," he said. "Your chores. You're in charge of cleaning the house, grocery shopping, laundry, meals. All meals. Breakfast, lunch and dinner, and every snack in between. And just so you know, we like dessert with each of our meals and even our snacks. You'll also be in charge of writing a positive affirmation every morning."

She blinked up at him. "Maybe you've forgotten, but I was doing most of that stuff already. I've been your non-wife wife for *days*."

He couldn't stop the tide of warmth spilling through him, and it made his tone snappier than he'd intended. "You are not my wife, non or otherwise. Understand?"

She held up her hands, all innocence. "Whatever you say, Mr. Hollister, sir."

When she went prim and proper like that, he just wanted to drag her against him and kiss her breathless.

"I like when you call me sir, Miss Dillon. Let's make that a new requirement." And now he needed distance. "You've got work to do. You're days behind. Just don't do anything too strenuous. I mean it."

"Ten-four, sir."

If he had any hope of abiding by his own rules, he might need even more than distance. He might have to create some kind of emotional rift between them. He knew of only one way to do that.

He led her inside the house, gave her a gentle push toward the couch. "I seriously think you should rest before you begin. You're a delicate flower, and I respect that."

"Flower? Rest?" She glared at him. "For how long?"

"Just a few hours."

"Hours?" she echoed hollowly. "I told you before. I'm not an invalid."

"Maybe I should get you a bell," he persisted. "You can ring it anytime you need me."

She hissed like a cat that had just been poked with a stick. "Do it, I dare you. The bell will only stop ringing after I cram it down your throat."

Wouldn't do to smile at such a threat. He turned away, certain it would be best to end the conversation now.

"Oh, I almost forgot," she said. "Jessie Kay asked me to give you something."

He curbed the urge to take off like a bullet before facing her once again. "What?" he asked, unable to hide his sudden stash of wary. Jessie Kay had been a mess when she'd first arrived at the hospital. She'd clung to him, and he'd comforted her as best he could. She had faults, yes, but so did he. He'd gotten a glimpse at the heart of her, and it was clear she loved her sister. But she'd called and texted him countless times since, asking him out, telling him how much she cared about him, how perfect they would be together.

"This." Brook Lynn held up a strawberry-shaped locket. "You can put a picture of your girlfriend inside it."

He stiffened. Did she *want* him to date her sister? "I don't have a girlfriend."

"I know. But maybe one day you'll find someone willing to put up with you."

"I won't."

"That's what I told Jessie Kay," she announced.

He frowned, not liking her adamancy. He could commit if he wanted. Look at Daphne. If she'd stayed with him, he would still be with her. They'd be married, maybe even have a kid.

A pang of longing hit him, but he quickly quashed it. There'd be no kids. Not for him. Not ever, he reminded himself. He didn't want to be responsible for someone else's emotional or physical well-being. If he screwed someone up the way he'd been screwed up, allowed his own flesh and blood to be hurt, the increase of guilt would finally choke him. He was sure of it.

"Jessie Kay wants to prove a picture of a girl won't burn the skin off your chest," Brook Lynn added. "If you open it up, you'll find her favorite selfie."

Something about her tone stuck with him... Was that jealousy? He wanted to study her features, but wouldn't permit himself the luxury. "Being with her was a mistake," he said softly. "You know that, don't you?"

She hesitated before starting, "But—"

"No. No buts. She's a good girl. Pretty, smart and capable, if only she'd try, but she's not for me. That's never going to change."

"Fine. Sir."

The word he'd meant in jest somehow created the very distance he'd thought he needed between them, but he realized now he couldn't stand it. "I've changed my mind. You'll call me Jase."

"You'll be lucky if that's all I call you," she muttered.

The sun must have shifted outside, because a beam of light suddenly spilled through the curtains, hitting the locket; the beads glimmered, and he couldn't pull his gaze away. Clear stones in varying shades of red were anchored together with tiny black ones. Such exquisite detail, each piece glinting in perfect harmony. He remembered seeing similar trinkets in the shop and being impressed by the craftsmanship.

"Did you make this?" he asked.

Silence.

Finally, he glanced up. Brook Lynn's attention had moved from him to…he wasn't sure where. She would be totally deaf this week, he remembered Jessie Kay telling him.

He tapped her arm, careful not to linger too long on her softness, and when she faced him, he repeated his question.

"I did, yes," she said, her pride obvious.

"I—" *Love it.* "Thank you," he said, carefully placing the necklace in his pocket.

"I'll tell her you were pleased."

"Don't," he said. "That will only encourage her."

Her eyes narrowed to tiny slits. "Sleeping with her also encouraged her."

He thought he heard irritation mixed with another hint of jealousy. As if. *Only hearing what I want to hear.*

He gnashed his teeth. "Rest. I'll be outside if you need me."

"I don't have my bell," she replied with sass.

"All you have to do is shout, and I'll come running."

THIS DAY IS going wonderfully, Brook Lynn thought. *And terribly.*

She didn't rest, and she didn't leave her implants on silent, as ordered; she got started on her chores, listened for Jase and pondered. Her mind was like a playground for naughty toddlers, different thoughts swinging from different parts of the jungle gym.

After her bout of crying last night, she'd picked herself up yet again and decided to put all of her eggs in Jase's basket. And okay, that was a stupid saying, making her think of female eggs and Jase putting his—

Never mind. Now that she was putting all of her *time* and *energy* into her job with Jase—better—she would be able to get a full eight hours of sleep every night. A dream come true! She would get to cook, one of her favorite activities, and still have time for fun. Finally! She and Jessie Kay would be able to eat right because she would ensure Jase and his friends ate right, the four main food groups part of everyone's daily diet: something fried, something with gobs of butter, something with heaps of sugar and sweet tea.

For the first time in a very long time, she had nothing to complain about. She had hope again, all because of the man interested in seeing to her every need.

So...why do I feel so unsatisfied?

Jessie Kay had taken off before Brook Lynn had awoken, so she'd sent her sister a text telling her she'd be at Jase's and afterward, Brad's. It was time to plan the details of their date.

Her sister's response?

Will U B drinking while UR w/Brad?

No.

Playing strip anything?

No.

Having sex?

NO!

Then why the heck R U going 2 see him?

A woman rounded the corner, her short, dark hair mussed, her cheeks flushed from exertion. Her clothes were wrinkled and her button-up top misaligned. She also had on a pencil skirt and mile-high heels, and she was clearly a professional of some sort, not in the hooker sense, but in the someone-who-worked-inside-an-office sense.

She spotted Brook Lynn, skidded to a stop and scowled. "Who are you?"

"Uh, that would be my line." The woman was unfamiliar, not from Strawberry Valley.

Professional tightened her hands around the strap of her briefcase. "Beck told me he was single. If you're his wife—"

"Wife?" she heard from around the corner before the man in question sauntered in and wrapped his arm around Professional's waist. "Nah. She's my permanent side slice, so she doesn't mind sharing me for an hour or two. Isn't that right, pookie?"

"Not right," Brook Lynn said with a shake of her head. "Not ever."

Beck shrugged, unabashed. "She's just mad because I only ever let her role-play the exalted position of wife in bed."

"We have never been in bed together," Brook Lynn gritted out. "Never will."

"You're kidding, Beck. I know you are." His newest conquest relaxed against him. "You have the most amazing sense of humor."

Gag me. Please.

Beck wore a suit and tie, his clothing as straight and

perfect as if they'd just been pressed. Not a strand of his hair was out of place.

He kissed the woman on the temple. "You should take off, pretty. Work is calling your name."

She turned in his arms, and Brook Lynn thought she responded with "I'd rather hear you scream it."

Could he even remember it?

O-kay. My cue to vanish. Brook Lynn moved out of the kitchen. But Beck and his lady lover followed hot on her heels. Or rather, Beck followed, dragging the gal with him.

"Though it pains me to say it, there's no time for a repeat performance." Beck patted Professional on the bottom. "You know I need at least two hours to enjoy you properly, and that's only if I'm in a rush."

The woman ate up the flattery as if he meant it, clinging to the lapels of his suit.

Beck ushered her to the porch and blew her a kiss—just before he shut the door in her face.

Brook Lynn shook her head. "You are the man parents warn their daughters about."

"Thank you."

"Because it was totally a compliment."

He wagged a finger at her. "You're my assistant," he said. "And yet, I strangely do not recall being assisted with this bang and bail."

"Actually, I'm *Jase's* assistant."

"Why limit yourself? You can work for us both. Besides, if Jase had been inside, he would have commanded you to get rid of my date for me."

"You did fine on your own, and you didn't even have to prepare your special breakfast."

"That's because it's lunchtime," he said, as if she were missing a few brain cells. "What are you serving?"

"To Jase? Sandwiches. They'll be ready in thirty. To you? Only advice. If you don't want your conquests to get the wrong idea, don't let them stay the night. Or, I don't know, maybe keep it in your pants once in a while."

"I met Helen…Harriet?…this morning. We came back here for a quickie. Her idea."

"Seriously?"

He walked over and cupped her cheek. "Yes, cupcake. I'm *that* good. And for your information, I would be willing to keep it in my pants, no problem, but I keep getting requests for showings."

She batted him away. "I know where that hand has been."

Unoffended, he adjusted the cuffs at his wrists.

"You need a new hobby," she told him.

For a moment, only a moment, his expression registered seriousness. "Sometimes sex is the only way to keep the darkness at bay."

"Beck," she said, suddenly wanting to hug him.

He grabbed his car keypad from the kitchen counter—apparently he drove some kind of alien vehicle with a keyless start—and flashed her a wicked grin meant to shut down any sympathy on her part. "By the way, I've been tracking down a surprise for Jase. Someone from his past. I don't think he's interested anymore, but he has a right to choose, you know? Anyway, I'm close to success, so for my reward I'd like a ham and cheese casserole for dinner."

"Someone from his past?" If he wanted a meeting with an old school chum, *she* would like to be the one to track the guy down. Because she owed him. Not for any other reason. "And what do you mean, choose?"

"Sorry, pretty, but I only share information that important when I'm naked."

"Then I'll happily go to my grave ignorant of the person's identity and the choice Jase has to make, whatever it is." She motioned to the sandwiches she'd spent the past two hours preparing. Even rapid-rise fresh-baked bread took time. "Take a look at the lunch you're not going to get."

He might have whimpered. "I'll change your mind. Just see if I don't." Beck gave her a jaunty salute before stalking from the room.

Well. While the bread was cooling, she had better check on Jase. He was probably dying of thirst. And she couldn't let that happen, now, could she? She filled a glass with water and carried it outside, the sun hotter and brighter than it had been a few hours ago. She scanned the backyard. The shed Jase had refurbished so expertly looked brand-new. The redbuds and magnolias were in full bloom, the towering oaks throwing umbrellas of shade in every direction. Lovely, but there was no sign of Jase.

"Jase?"

The squawk of black birds was the only response.

She trudged around the side of the house—and that's where she found him. His back was to her, and he was as still as a statue.

"Jase," she repeated and walked around him.

He was staring at his hand. His bloody hand. Crimson pooled in his palm and dripped onto the ground... a discarded hoe.

She gasped, horrified, and dropped the water. "Jase, are you okay?"

He gave no indication that he'd heard her, just continued to stare down at his injury. His expression disturbed her. It was totally and completely blank. As if he wasn't all there, his thoughts far away.

Not wanting to startle him, but knowing he needed help, she gently tapped his shoulder. "Jase."

The contact jolted him out of the trance, and before she could blink, his arm shot out. He shoved her with enough force to send her tripping backward, falling to her bottom. She landed in the cold water she'd spilled, the glass rolling away from her. His face contorted into the darkest, meanest scowl she'd ever seen, scaring the crap out of her. His hands fisted, the blood now pouring from the wound.

He took a menacing step toward her, and she would have sworn she saw her death shining in his eyes. He looked at her as he'd never looked before: as if she were a stranger to him. A faceless threat to be eliminated.

She crab-walked backward, uttering a trembling, "Jase? Please. Listen to me. It's me, Brook Lynn." There was no way she could defend herself against him if he attacked, the strength she'd once lauded enough to kill her.

Fear moved through her like an avalanche, growing stronger, bigger. Consuming her.

He just kept coming. Closer and closer...

"Jase." She lumbered to her feet and held out an arm. A puny move, but what else could she do? "You're scaring me, and I need you to stop. Jase!"

He blinked, skidded to a halt. "Brook Lynn?" Frowning, he shook his head, as if to clear cobwebs. "Are you okay?"

Relief gradually melted the avalanche. "I—I'm fine."

"You have blood on your shirt. A palm print." He frowned, peered down at his hand, then peered at her shirt. When his gaze finally met hers, she saw a flash of horror and guilt—even anguish—before it went blank.

He started to close the distance between them. She

flinched, and he planted his heels in the ground, remaining in place. "Did I hurt you?"

He didn't know? Couldn't remember?

What the heck had just happened?

If he *was* a cop, maybe…maybe the sight of the blood had taken him back to a violent memory?

"No," she said, her trembling growing worse for some reason. She wrapped her arms around her middle.

"You…should go home," he said. "Please go."

Maybe I should. Or maybe we're finally making progress. She'd just seen a side of him she'd never seen before. One that didn't just hint at vulnerability but screamed it. And though it had scared her—there was no way around that fact—it was kinda like catnip to her. She wanted to curl into his lap and purr against his throat, tell him everything was going to be okay, that they would get through this…whatever *this* was… together.

"I'm going to bandage your wound," she said.

"No."

"Yes," she insisted. "Don't argue. You'll lose. I'll meet you in your bathroom."

CHAPTER THIRTEEN

JASE REMAINED IN place long after Brook Lynn walked away, trying to put the pieces of what had happened together. He'd been removing weeds from the side of the house. That's right.

He'd thought he'd heard a noise behind him and jerked, cutting his hand on the hoe as he glanced over his shoulder. He'd thought he spied a man dressed in brown darting behind the bushes. Jase had stepped forward, intending to give chase, only to realize it had to be a deer. He caught glimpses of wildlife every day.

He'd glanced down to see a well of blood in his hand, and he'd flashed back to all the times he'd been jumped. Sometimes with fists, sometimes with shivs. In nine years he'd endured a total of twenty-three stabbings across his torso and a few more scattered over his legs. He'd lost count of the number of fights he'd participated in, only knew he'd won more than he'd lost. He'd endured several broken bones and had suffered…other things. Things he rarely ever allowed himself to remember.

Held down…too many hands to knock away…

A knee in my back…

Clothing being ripped.

His breath sawed in and out faster, hotter. Brook Lynn must have come upon him while he'd been trapped inside his head. He remembered the softest of touches on his shoulder, the softest of voices saying his name. Soft—when soft was the last thing he'd ever gotten in prison. The contrast had been enough to pull him out of the abyss. At least partway.

He'd...pushed her.

The image of his bloody palm marring her shirt would forever plague him.

He stumbled to the side until he came into contact with the house. He leaned his forehead against the brick. Little tremors slipped down his spine, dislodging beads of sweat.

He couldn't face Brook Lynn, and he certainly couldn't let her help him. He deserved castigation, and she deserved better.

West and Beck were right. Jase had judged her from the first as someone too good for him—because she was.

Something else his friends had nailed? Jase had feelings for her. Feelings he could no longer deny.

With the admission, a bright light suddenly shone inside his mind, chasing away the darkness, causing the monsters of his past to hiss and run for cover, letting him confirm what he'd suspected. His armor had indeed been cracked, and Brook Lynn was the cause. She had somehow burrowed deep, deep inside him, and he might not ever be able to pry her loose.

Panic rose, swift and sure. One day, he would lose her. That was just plain fact. If she didn't meet someone else, she'd have questions about what just happened. Even if he managed to omit the worst of the details, she would eventually find out about his prison stint,

about what he did to Pax. She could grow to fear him…
hate him.

He could have lost Brook Lynn today, even. He could
have done serious damage to her, without even realizing
it. Still could, if ever he lost control again.

Can't take that risk.

He managed to pull himself together and stomp inside the house. Now wasn't the time for brooding. It
was the time for action. He found Brook Lynn in his
bathroom, standing by the sink.

She'd anchored her mane of pale hair into an adorable ponytail, two tendrils hanging over her ears. She'd
washed her face and changed into one of his shirts.

How was she more beautiful every time he saw her?

You know what you have to do. He did, but first
things first. "I'm sorry I scared you, honey."

"Don't worry. I'm over it," she said.

At least she hadn't tried to deny her fear. "Good.
That's good."

"I hear a but."

Just do it. "I hate to say this, but…you're fired."

"No, I'm not." She motioned to the closed toilet seat.
"Sit."

"I'll still pay you," he said.

"Of course you will. Because I'm still working for
you."

"Brook Lynn—"

"Jase." She anchored her hands on her hips. "You
don't like what just happened. I don't, either, but now
we know it's a possibility. We'll be on guard against it
and handle it better if it happens again."

So that was it? No questions what had caused
it to happen in the first place?

Far, far too good for me.

The ache he'd by now grown used to intensified, sharper than ever before, as if it had sunk deeper inside him, spread and taken up more space—but he sat.

She cleaned the wound with soap, water and then peroxide. Blood continued to leak from the long slit that stretched from his index finger to his wrist, and though her touch was gentle, every bit of pressure stung. He'd endured worse countless times before, so maintaining a neutral expression wasn't difficult. He'd never allow her to feel guilty about hurting him.

The fact that she'd stayed to help baffled him. Thrilled him. Even humbled him. He felt as if she might actually...care for him.

How was that possible?

After she squeezed antibiotic cream on the injury and wrapped a bandage around his hand, she studied her handiwork and frowned. "I'm clearly not a medical professional. You probably need stitches."

"Nah. The cut isn't that deep."

She met his gaze with a gentleness that confused him. "How do you know?"

"I just do."

"Jase." She crouched between his legs. "We need to talk."

Words every man dreaded, but she was so close he could smell the sweetness of her scent, feel the sensual heat of her, and both short-circuited his brain waves. He had to grip the sink on one side of him and the tub on the other to keep his hands away from her.

Tension grew between them, sharpened, until it was utterly unbearable. He imagined his mouth on hers and had to cut back a groan. He imagined his fingers trailing over her curves and had to cut back a plea.

He was clean. He even had the paperwork to prove it. He could take her, thrust inside her and—

"Be honest with me," she said quietly.

Reason returned, and he tensed. Here came the questions.

"Were you a cop?"

Wait. What? "A cop?"

She nodded, the ends of those pale tendrils caressing his thighs.

"Why would you think that?"

"Okay, I'll take that as a no." Her mouth tugged into a frown. "Were you in the military?"

Understanding suddenly dawned, bright and devastating. She thought he had PTSD because he'd defended his country. She wanted to think the best of him, probably couldn't even conceive the horrors that had led to the incident outside.

How disappointed she would be when she learned the truth.

Another reason to get rid of her.

"Brook Lynn," he said and sighed. "It's time for you to go." He'd beg her if necessary.

She shook her head, stubborn. "No way. I'm staying until either West or Beck return. I'm not leaving you on your own."

The ache...so much worse. "It's just a cut."

"And it could open up again, and you could pass out, bleed out."

"It won't. I won't."

"Jase," she said, raising her chin with more stubborn

determination. "The only way you're getting me out of this house is if you carry me kicking and screaming."

BROOK LYNN SETTLED on the plush leather couch in the living room. Jase had not been happy with her refusal to leave and had muttered, "If you're going to stay, fine. But I'm going to work, and you're not, because you're still fired," before stomping into the kitchen to peel wallpaper. He'd admitted he eventually needed to open up the walls and replace all the wiring and pipes, but he didn't want to be without a kitchen while she was the chef.

He didn't peel long. From the sounds of it he'd noticed the sandwiches she'd prepared and dug in. A short while later, he called, "You're rehired, effective immediately."

She was worried about him. Not about the cut on his hand. He was right—it wasn't that deep and probably wouldn't open back up. But he was so closed off right now. It scared her even more than the push. And the fact that he hadn't flinched as she'd doctored him, when it must have stung like an SOB...there was something wrong with that. Though it *had* been sexy.

But mostly wrong. And sexy.

Why did he go to such lengths to keep his emotions hidden? Because he *did* have them. She knew that now. The intensity of his rage...

If he'd served in the military, he could be having flashbacks.

She remembered how Beck and West had mentioned "six months" the night of the party. Had Jase been discharged six months ago? Well, no wonder he hadn't yet acclimated.

"Need any help in there?" she called, knowing he'd finished his meal and had restarted his newest task.

He came barreling into the living room, pointing a sheet of wallpaper at her as if it was a weapon. "You're on a break. You shouldn't be offering to help."

She leaned against the arm of the couch, getting more comfortable. "Good friend that I am, I'm willing to cut the break short just for you."

"I'd rather you—" His gaze landed on her midsection, and he sucked in a breath. The muscles stretching from his shoulders to his fingers flexed as he stepped closer to her.

She glanced down. The hem of her shirt had ridden up, baring her midriff—now quivering under the heat of his masculine attention.

Her eyes flipped back up, locking on his. The whole atmosphere of the room seemed to change in an instant, the air sizzling with sudden awareness. Of him. Of her. Of what they could do together...

"Jase," she said, the neediness of her tone almost enough to make her cringe. *Let me make you forget your inner wounds. Let me feel what I haven't felt in years: pleasure.*

"Brook Lynn, I can't—I shouldn't. I—"

He turned abruptly and stalked back into the kitchen.

She pushed out a shaky breath. Despite what had happened outside—or maybe because of it—her fascination with this man hadn't lessened. She imagined his warrior hands all over her, his mouth following in their path, and nearly slid off the couch.

He was a puzzle. He was damaged by his past. He had secrets, and he would die before he admitted he needed her. He may not have realized it, but he'd leaned into her every time she'd put her hands on him, his body telling her what his expression and tone had not.

But…there was Jessie Kay. There was also the date she had with Brad, the one she'd thought to firm up later today. However, they hadn't actually set a date, so she could get out of it pretty easily.

Should she?

And what about Jase's stance on happily-ever-afters?

The guy was clearly more of a fixer-upper than she'd ever realized, and she'd sworn off fixer-uppers for all of eternity.

The end result might make all the work worth the effort.

She rested her head on the back of the couch and closed her eyes, picturing Jase and Brad side by side. What she wanted versus what she thought she needed. Passion against compatibility.

She imagined Brad trying to kiss her and shied away from the image.

She imagined Jase trying to kiss her and moaned for more. Fire ignited in her veins as her nipples drew up tight and arousal dampened her panties.

A few minutes later—surely that was all the time that had passed—she felt as if she was floating…floating… gently stretching over a cloud.

"Sleep, angel."

"Jase." A breathy sigh escaped her as she realized he had carried her to bed. "Want," she admitted, hovering somewhere between awake and asleep, where nothing but sensation existed.

"You're going to be the end of me, I know it." Strong but gentle hands smoothed over her brow, warm and calloused, comforting, but just as she leaned into the heat, it vanished.

Her eyes popped open. The bedroom was dark, all the lights out, and though there was a crack in the blackout curtains, no sunlight seeped through. Hours must have passed. But even in the gloom she could make out the strength of Jase's silhouette—he hadn't walked away.

"Come back," she begged, reaching for him.

She heard a soft curse before he shucked his shirt and pants and climbed in beside her, surrounding her with his heat once again. She snuggled close, loving the feel of his skin against the exposed parts of her. Warm, mint-scented breath tickled her scalp. The scent of soap and musk filled her nose. Tingles danced over her, driving her to move against his hard-as-stone body. She couldn't *not* move, a week's worth of pent-up desire desperate for an outlet.

A broken moan sounded in her ears. "Brook Lynn, honey. You have to stop...what you're doing... You have to..."

"Can't." Her limbs were heavy, achy, her body writhing, writhing of its own accord, searching for release.

He gripped her hips to still her with his strength.

Every bit of willpower she possessed was needed to roll to her other side, away from him—before she started up again, despite his grip. Even that innocent action was too much for her sensitized nerves to tolerate, and she moaned.

"Go to sleep," he said.

"Yes. Okay." But how could she with him so close? She needed to leave, and she would, just as soon as her body was under her control again. Deep breath in, out.

In. Out. Good. Gradually, the ache eased, but rather than hopping up and driving home, she found herself drifting off...

...and dreaming of kissing Jase, writhing against him, touching him...

...and waking up however long later facing him yet again, panting, his hand draped over her rib cage, just under her breast. She went still. The heat and ache were back—only stronger.

He was awake, his expression tight with tension. His *body* tense.

"Jase," she said. Why wouldn't this stop?

"I tried to resist," he rasped, the ragged quality of his tone making her shiver. His hand inched up, coming closer and closer to cupping her breast.

Would he do it?

A blush heated her cheeks. She remembered writhing against him...and couldn't blame it on a dream. "I don't... I mean, I..." Her voice was so breathy. "Jase."

His gaze hooded and his hand finally conformed around her breast, his thumb brushing over her nipple. His voice lowered. "Do you want me to take the edge off, honey?"

He meant...he wanted to...

Her blush deepened. "I..."

"Let me." He cupped her backside with his other hand and pulled her closer. As he wedged one of his legs between hers, his tongue thrust inside her mouth.

Every cell in her body melted, practically fusing her against him. His erection— *Oh, oh!* Long, thick and right where she needed it. She arched into him, rubbing. He grunted his approval, swiping his thumb over her nipple a second time before he tangled his fingers in her hair, fisting the strands. He angled her head to kiss her deeper, harder.

Sweet sensation poured into her and filled her up, chasing away the loneliness that had always seemed to plague her.

She wished the room were brighter. The need to see Jase's chest, to explore every ridge of muscle, every design etched in the skin that so fascinated her, proved overwhelming.

As her fingertips rode the hard ropes in his stomach, sliding lower…lower still, tunneling under his underwear…he thrust against her, mimicking the motions of sex. A hot flood of liquid pooled between her legs.

She swiped her thumb over the moist slit of his erection. As he gave another thrust, she released him to reach up and suck the taste of him into her mouth.

His nostrils flared as he watched her. "Not sure how much more I can take. Ready to spill already."

"I guess we'd just have to start all over again," she rasped.

"You are…perfect." His mouth returned to hers, actually slamming down, and it was hot. Wild. She met his tongue with her own, the two rolling together, hinting at what was to come…hard and dirty. He kneaded her breasts and plucked her nipples as he slowed to a lazy grind against her, stoking the ache inside her higher and higher.

Never been this good…and he hadn't even moved past her clothing yet!

Jase knew exactly what he was doing. Fueling a fire deep inside her, making her *want* to burn.

"You feel so good," he said.

She couldn't think of a reply. Her thoughts were frag-

mented, each broken by a single need: more. More of
Jase. More of his taste. More of his touch. More of his
hardness. She rolled her tongue against his, even bit his
bottom lip, passion driving her every action. Her fingers played with his hair, roved over his back. He was
strong, even there. Especially there. His muscles were
as hard as granite. She raked her nails over his shoulders, all the way around to his nipples, only to caress
those beaded tips gently.

His shudder rubbed him against her all over again,
and she finally found the right words to say. "I'm so
close. Need..."

"Let's get you closer." He traced a fingertip between
her breasts, down her stomach and dabbled at her navel
before playing at the waist of her shorts. He tugged
at the button, pulled at the zipper. "You wet for me,
angel?"

Angel. It wasn't the first time he'd used the endearment, but it still caused her heart to skip a beat, delight
going head-to-head with...a sudden wave of suspicion.

Had he called Jessie Kay *angel*?

Brook Lynn froze. She had yet to tell her sister about
the first kiss she and Jase had shared.

"Wait," she whispered. "We can't do this."

Jase reacted as if she'd bellowed. He stiffened from
head to toe. And then...then he withdrew from her and
scrambled from the bed, standing at the side to peer
down at her. He scrubbed a hand through his mussed
hair. "You're right. We can't."

"I just need to call Jessie Kay and—"

"No, you don't." The frost returned to his eyes, seeming to grow colder, thicker, by the second. "This was
a mistake."

Pleasure still coursed through her, and he considered what they'd done a mistake?

"I don't understand," she said, trembling inside and out.

"You want more than I have to give."

"No. I don't." Except...

I do. I really do. Once would not be enough. Not even close. Two kisses, one touch, and he'd already addicted her.

"You *deserve* more," Jase said, sounding tortured. Looking it, too.

"Why can't you give me more?" she asked softly. Maybe, if she knew his reasons, she could—

No, no. I don't try to change a man's mind. Either I'm worth fighting for, or I'm not.

He offered her a smile so sad it broke her heart. "It's like I told you. Relationships between men and women become toxic. Always. I don't want that with you. I want to enjoy the time we have together."

The time we have together... To him it was inevitable that they'd part.

"So that's it?" she asked. "You're not even going to try?"

Who am I, pushing like this?

A girl who wanted this man more than anything.

"If you knew half the things I've done..." He shook his head, adamant. "One day you'll thank me for this."

He feared her reaction to his past? "Tell me what you've done. Let me prove you wrong. Please, Jase. Give me a chance."

He opened his mouth, and for one tormented moment he looked as if he would fulfill her request. Then he said, "Go home, Brook Lynn. When you come back tomorrow, I'll be the boss, and you'll be my employee. Nothing more, nothing less. For your safety and my peace of mind, that's the way things have to stay."

TRUE TO HIS WORD, Jase treated Brook Lynn like a distant employee twice removed the next morning...and the next and the next. Each time she arrived at the house, he gave her a new list of chores that involved cooking, cleaning, keeping house and even finding a venue for a "Congrats on the GED!" party for a girl she'd never met.

Also, Brook Lynn was tasked with those stupid daily affirmations. So far she'd offered gems like *I will assume full responsibility for my actions, except the ones that are someone else's fault—which will be all of them.* And *Every part of me is beautiful and brilliant...even the ugly, stupid parts.*

At first, she simmered at midlevel anger over his treatment. Mouth-bag her and push her away? How dare he! But it wasn't long before the anger began to slip away, leaving her with curiosity. What had shaped this man? The father he'd never known? The mother who'd allowed her boyfriends to hurt him before he was put into the system? The many foster families he'd gotten to know...only to lose? The job he hadn't named?

A past as volatile as his had probably caused major attachment issues. Her eyes widened, and she gasped. Finally! Answers. Brook Lynn and Jessie Kay battled their own attachment issues, determined to hold on to everyone, while Jase must have veered to the other end of the spectrum, determined to hold on to no one, fighting with everything he had to save himself from further hurt.

Which meant...*I have the power to hurt him.*

He cared!

Her sudden flood of joy was tempered only by concern. *Not just a fixer-upper. He'll have to be torn down and put back together if we have any hope of lasting long-term.*

No question, he would resist any attempt on her part to win him over. But if she could just breach his first line of defense—those frosty walls—she'd have a shot at him.

After what had happened in his bed, she knew beyond a doubt the end result would be worth every wrong turn, every inconvenience.

I will have him. One way or another.

But first things first. Her sister.

After she had dinner with Beck and West—Jase had taken off without a word—she drove home to await Jessie Kay's return. Miracle of miracles, the girl had gotten a job plucking wild strawberries at a nearby facility, and she'd kept it all this time.

An eternity seemed to pass before the front door's hinges creaked. Brook Lynn jumped up as her sister trudged into the house.

"Strawberries suck." Jessie Kay groaned with fatigue as she threw her purse on the coffee table. When the bag slid to the floor and the contents spilled out, she flipped it off and left it there. "I'm moving to someplace called Blueberry Fields. Or Pineapple Cove."

"And they'd be lucky to have you," Brook Lynn said, her palms beginning to sweat. "I baked your favorite carrot and apple casserole today. Though I had to fork Beck's hand, I managed to come home with half of it."

"Thanks, but I snacked on my dignity on the way home."

"Too bad. Kitchen. Now."

Jessie Kay sighed. "Warden is in the house, I see. Are you fixing to start counting?"

Gotta take it down a notch. "Sorry. No." Brook Lynn warmed a plate of fried chicken, mashed potatoes and gravy and the coveted casserole.

As Jessie Kay pretended to eat, Brook Lynn drummed her fingernails against the table.

Finally, her sister asked, "You trying to tell me what's wrong in Morse code?"

Maybe. It'd be easier. "I'm just going to say it. Blurt it out and live with the consequences."

"Great. That'd be a nice change."

Brook Lynn pursed her lips. "When did you become so snotty?"

"When did you lose your lady balls?"

Good question. Okay. So. "Are you ready?"

"Been ready."

"I...well." She closed her eyes, drew in a breath. "I want Jase." And now there was no taking the words back. She peeked through her lashes. "I want him for me, not for you. And I think...I think he wants me, too."

Jessie Kay paused with her fork midway to her mouth. She peered at Brook Lynn with wide blue eyes underscored by dismay. "You...and Jase? *My* Jase."

Her stomach twisted, a single word screaming through her head. *Mine!* She bit her bottom lip, nodded. "Do you love him? Please, please tell me you don't love him. Because we kissed. He and I. While I was in the hospital, and then again while I was at his house. There might have been some grinding the second time. And I'm sorry I didn't tell you sooner. I know you want him, too, and know you had him first, but..."

"Wait. He kissed you? As in, mouth to mouth?"

Her brow furrowed with confusion as she said, "Yes…"

Bemusement and sadness warred on her sister's face. "He slept with me, but he didn't kiss me. Not on the mouth."

"No, stop," Brook Lynn said, slapping a hand over the mouth in question. "I don't want to hear this."

Jessie Kay pried her fingers loose. "I thought it was a *Pretty Woman* thing, that he didn't think he was good enough to give alms at the door of my temple." Her shoulders slumped. "Dude. He didn't think *I* was good enough for *him*."

This. This was what Brook Lynn had hoped to avoid. "He's clearly a moron."

"And yet you still want him."

"I have bad taste."

Her sister rolled her eyes.

"You *are* good enough for him. You just aren't right for him. There's a difference."

"True, but somehow I'm never the right one for the guys I sleep with. But that's my problem, not yours." Jessie Kay pegged her with a hard stare. "Are you sure Jase is the one for you?"

"Yes."

"Then I guess you need to know what to expect. Being with him was—"

"No! Don't say it."

"—weird," Jessie Kay finished, and Brook Lynn frowned.

"Weird?" Not pure ecstasy? "What do you mean? You appeared so satisfied afterward."

"Oh, I was. But anytime I touched him, he stiffened,

and not in a good way. He constantly looked over his shoulder, as if he expected someone to sneak up on us. After a while, I just had to lie back and let him do all the work. You know, every girl's dream."

He'd stiffened? Looked over his shoulder? She thought back, but couldn't remember if he'd done either of those things while they were in bed together. She'd been too overwhelmed with pleasure.

"He won't commit afterward," Jessie Kay said. "You told me so yourself."

"I know that," she said with a sigh.

"But you're going to sleep with him anyway, aren't you?" Jessie Kay leaned back and crossed her arms. "Even though you've denied every other guy you've ever dated."

"I haven't denied *every* one."

"Your short-lived romance with Conner doesn't count."

Conner, the boy who used to live next door. He'd moved away for college, met the love of his life and had never come home. "Why doesn't it count?"

"He only ever lasted a minute. Two, tops. And yes, I heard you guys. Well, I heard him. You were as quiet as a mouse." Her head tilted to the side. "I wonder if Jase will be able to make you scream."

A white-hot burn in her cheeks. She already knew the answer to that.

Conner had been kind and sweet, but Brook Lynn had never reacted to him the way she'd reacted to Jase. All in, nothing held back. Attuned to his every nuance.

"I want Jase no matter what," she said, realizing it was true. Even if he ended things after one night. With him, she would take what she could get. "Are you mad at me? Please don't be mad at me."

Jessie Kay leaned over and kissed her on the cheek. "If I was mad, my nails would be scratching out your eyes. You know this. Besides, I guess a part of me saw this coming. The way you talk about him. The way he looks at you. The things he does for you. But for once in my life I have to be a voice of reason. I don't think this is a good idea, Brook Lynn. He's going to hurt you, and then I'll have to kill him dead."

Maybe he'd hurt her. Probably.

Okay, definitely for sure—there was a chance. She couldn't bring herself to commit to the idea that she'd fail to win him. "I've been saying the same thing to you for years, and it's never stopped you."

Jessie Kay arched a brow at her. "Look at you. Doing the whole role-reversal thing. It—and you—suck seriously hairy balls right now, but okay. If you want him, he's yours. I just hope you don't end up regretting it."

CHAPTER FOURTEEN

THE NEXT MORNING, Brook Lynn called and canceled her date with Brad—the one she still hadn't put in the books. He was hurt, and she hated herself. He asked what happened, what changed her mind, and she had to go with the truth and admit she had feelings for another man. She then texted Jase to tell him she had errands and would be running late. His response came seconds later.

Feel free 2 take the entire day off.

Those freeze-out walls really needed work, didn't they?

Her response: Nah. My errands R 4 YOU, boss-man.

A minute passed, then another.

What kind of errands?

Grinning, she stuffed her phone into her pocket. He'd find out when she was good and ready and not a moment before. Until then, he could stew.

Excited, nervous, she left the serenity of redbuds and strawberry vines behind to drive into the city, where she bought a fancy frame and a bundle of heavy paper, as well as time on a computer. As she typed, she constantly glanced over her shoulder to ensure no one was reading what was on the screen.

When she finished her project, she had it printed on the paper, her cheeks burning with embarrassment—and they stayed hot the entire drive to Jase's house.

Didn't help that he was on the front porch when she arrived, shirtless and sweaty. The moisture in her mouth dried.

What if he viewed her gift as an attempt at manipulation rather than a way to ease his fears? What if he was right?

Just need a chance with him. This was the only way.

As she traversed the porch steps, he crossed his arms over his muscle-ripped chest. With the farmhouse behind him, framing him, she felt as if she'd just been transported into the pages of a Hunks of Small Town, USA calendar. A place she wanted to live forever.

"You mentioned errands for me," he said, and she would have sworn she heard excitement underneath his irritation. "You finally get me those ex-large condoms?"

"Nope." *Don't grin.* "First, it's time for today's affirmation. You ready? Here goes. I need not suffer in silence while I possess the ability to moan, whimper and complain."

He went still, not seeming to breathe. "Are you suffering?"

"In a way." She closed the distance and held out the plaque she'd made. "Here. This is for you."

He backed away from her, saying, "If this is a resignation letter..."

After all the times he'd fired her, he would complain if she quit? "Do us both a favor and read it."

He took the thing reluctantly and looked it over, his frown vanishing. His eyes flipped up to her, flames sparking to life deep, deep inside their emerald depths. She shifted from one foot to the other, waiting for him to say something, anything.

"Well?" she asked and gulped.

"'I, Brook Lynn Dillon,'" he read, the tenor of his voice husky and rough, "'hereby promise Jase I'm Not Sure What His Middle Name Is Hollister one night. Only one. Afterward there will be no tears, no clinging and no romantic gestures of any kind. I will be an employee of Hollister Slave Trade, nothing more.'"

"I even signed it," she said—with what had felt like blood.

"I see that," he replied.

When he said nothing more, she once again shifted uncomfortably. "Well?"

His stare returned to her, hotter than before, with absolutely no sign of frost. "We will discuss this after eight, when you're off the clock."

JASE HAD NEVER been so turned on, and he'd never watched a clock quite so intensely, trying to stare it into flashing the number he wanted. Brook Lynn's gift had surprised him. More than surprised him. It had set off a waterfall of the most exquisite, terrifying need inside him—one that had been close to drowning him since he'd gotten her into his bed.

He hadn't been sleeping well, his attempts to avoid her leaving him restless and irritable. Yesterday West had called him a he-beast without equal, and Beck had just flat-out announced he was an asshole. But how was a man supposed to go about normal business once he'd held Brook Lynn Dillon in his arms?

Jase had continually replayed the things they'd done together. The kissing, the touching. The way they'd writhed against each other. Afterward, as the days passed, his craving for her had begun to seem bottomless, endless, but so had his guilt. He wasn't right for her, and while he knew it, she didn't. Not yet.

He wasn't just a petty con man, like her uncle. He was a murderer. There'd never been a stronger deal breaker.

Plus, he lost complete awareness of his surroundings whenever he put his hands on her, and for someone who liked to stay on guard at all times, that left him exposed. In more ways than one.

Despite all of that, he wanted her. And now she wanted a night with him. He only wished she had demanded more for herself. More from him.

Complaining? Seriously?

Soon he would have her, all of her, and nothing else mattered. His gaze made another mad dash for the clock. Only five. Damn it!

Brook Lynn puttered around in the kitchen, preparing dinner. The smell of home surrounded him—something that was brand-new to him but quickly becoming familiar—a little sweet, a little spicy. He fell on the couch, propping his elbows onto his knees and resting his head in his upraised hands. He was going to have a heart attack before he got her naked, wasn't he?

And how the hell was he supposed to sit across from her at the table, knowing she ached for him?

He should have carried her to his bedroom the second she'd given him her gift. Like an idiot gentleman, he'd decided to wait, unwilling to let her feel cheap or as if he was paying her for sex. He couldn't offer to give her the day off, because she would just refuse payment for work she hadn't done, and the girl needed every cent she could get. Especially since she kept attempting to pay him back for the hospital bill.

He'd lost track of the number of times she'd stuffed bills in remote places, just as he'd expected. Kitchen drawers, under his bed, in his clothes. Every time he found one, he doubled it and stuffed it at the bottom of her purse or somewhere in her car.

The front door opened. West and Beck walked in, returning from a day at the office. They stopped when they spotted him.

West appeared unkempt, his hair sticking out in spikes, his shirt unbuttoned to the center of his chest and a rip in one of his sleeves. Beck was just as unkempt, but he had lipstick on his collar.

"What's wrong?" they demanded in unison.

"I'm dying of hunger," Jase replied, and it was true— just not the kind of hunger they might think. "What's up with you guys? Something happen?"

A muscle jumped in Beck's jaw. "You don't want to know."

"I went to a bar," West said, defensive. "Big deal."

"You also punched me while I was making out with your waitress," Beck said.

"Only the second and third time. You kept drinking the shots she brought me."

"None of which you needed."

"And you did?"

"Boys," Jase said. "Brook Lynn is cooking our dinner. Don't scare her away." Please. He needed her afterward.

"Dinner?" Beck brightened. "Brook Lynn Dillon," he called, striding into the kitchen, all else forgotten. "You need to speed things up before Jase faints like a delicate Georgia peach."

West remained with Jase. Shadows drifted through his already dark eyes as he eased onto the couch. The scent of alcohol was so strong it actually stung Jase's nostrils.

"What's really going on with you?" West asked quietly.

I'm in too deep with a woman I can't keep. "Don't want to talk about it." West had his own problems.

"Fair enough. But you should know bottling it inside will do you no good."

"Believe me, I do know."

West laughed, and there was a bitter tinge to it. "Yeah. You know better than me."

He couldn't help tying everything back to the time Jase had served—that he had not. "You've got to let that go, my man."

"Maybe in another six months."

He'd sentenced himself to ten years? "What about time already served? What about time off for good behavior?" Jase bumped his friend's shoulder. "I don't blame you, you know."

"You should. I could have knocked years off your sentence if I'd just come forward."

Beck's throaty laughter boomed from the kitchen and into the living room; Brook Lynn's sweet, husky chuckle soon followed. A dark wave of jealousy crashed through Jase. The two were certainly enjoying each other's company.

Were they interested in each other?

He stopped breathing. He wasn't sure why he'd never thought of that before. Beck loved a fresh conquest more than anything. And what if Brook Lynn was interested in Beck *and* Jase, as Jessie Kay had been?

Jase thought back. He'd noticed Brook Lynn's tendency to leave something new at the house every day. A pot holder hanging on a cabinet door. Curtain ties in the living room. A scented candle on the windowsill. He'd never rebuked her, had just assumed she'd hoped to make things more palatable for him, a little at a time. But what if she'd been making things more palatable for *Beck*? Perhaps gently nudging him into accepting change.

Wouldn't matter, he decided, eased only slightly. Beck knew Jase had staked a claim. Even if he'd denied it all along, the guy had eyes and half a brain. His friend would never make a move.

"Jase?"

West was here. Right. Jase uncurled his fists and said, "If I'd had a scholarship, you would have done the same for me."

"Yes, but you also wouldn't have blown the scholarship."

"What makes you think so? My stunning success in every area of my life? My Fortune 500 job? My fairytale relationship? My brilliant mental health?"

West snorted, some of the darkness at last shaking off him. "Dude, you totally suck. I'm not sure how I've remained friends with you so long."

"You can't get enough of my sparkling wit."

"Yeah." A warm smile from West. "That's got to be it."

"Dinner's ready," Brook Lynn called.

Jase practically leaped to his feet.

"Uh, a little too eager there, champ?" West asked.

"You have no idea."

In the kitchen, Brook Lynn wouldn't look at him. She smoothed a lock of hair from her brow, a rosy blush spreading over her cheeks. Beck didn't seem to notice, or care, while Jase's body practically went up in flames.

"Everyone take a place at the table," she instructed.

Throughout the meal, she shifted in her seat and blushed. *She's thinking of what's to come...* Her reaction fed his, strengthening it. He wasn't sure how much longer he could last without putting his hands on her.

Beck stuffed his face, still unconcerned, but West glanced between Jase and Brook Lynn countless times, finally arching a brow in question, all *I wonder what you two will be doing later.*

Jase flipped him off.

Brook Lynn pretended to eat.

"You guys are acting weird," West said, tone sly. "Are you not hungry, Jase, when just a short while ago you were nothing but a ravenous pig?"

Jase kicked him under the table.

West spilled his water, impact causing his glass to slip from his hand. In an act of revenge, he silkily asked, "Or are you hungry for something other than food?"

"What! No!" Brook Lynn burst out. "Shut up."

"He's subtly inquiring whether or not you plan to screw Jase's brains out," Beck said, reaching for another scoop of casserole. "I say go for it. If I were a girl, I'd already have tapped that."

Brook Lynn snatched the ladle out of his hand. "Bad Beck. Bad, bad, bad. I will not reward you for sticking your nose where it doesn't belong."

"But...but..." the guy stuttered. "I'm still hungry."

Jase tossed down his napkin, saying, "All right. Come on, honey. You and I need to talk. In private."

"While you're having your chat," Beck called, "don't forget to punish her for speaking to your friend so rudely. And wear a condom."

JASE PRESSED HIS back against the closed bedroom door as Brook Lynn sat at the edge of his bed…the very bed in which he'd rolled around with Jessie Kay before he'd acted as her very own orgasmic scratch pad. The urge to throw up battled with the urge to be held, leaving her confused and vulnerable. Was she really going to do this? Give him a chance to compare her to Jessie Kay? To find her, the less experienced one, lacking?

Maybe she should just go home.

Good plan. Did she seriously want a meaningless one-night stand? Simply for the chance to change Jase's mind about relationships and prove they could have something special? That they could have more?

She stood.

"Leaving already?" He swiped up a remote and switched on the radio. Soft rock poured from the surround sound as he met her gaze.

"Yes. No. Oh, I don't know." Even as she spoke, the tension between them expanded, thickening, until it was difficult to breathe, to focus on anything but Jase and what she yearned to do to him…what she yearned to have him do to her.

"Wrong answer." He crossed his arms, cotton pulling tight over his biceps. "I didn't want to have to remind you of this, but you signed a *legal* and *binding* contract, honey. If you don't give me the night of sexual bliss you promised me, I'll be forced to sue you for everything you've got. And that would be a shame, because I only want the best for you—and for you to take off all your clothes."

The teasing helped relax her. "Court, huh? Why don't you tell me your opening argument?" She returned to the bed and reclined, resting her weight on her elbows. "Convince me you've got a case."

He removed his shirt—as any good attorney would have done—and the absolute maleness of him staggered her. The incomparable ropes of muscles. The glimmer of his bronze skin. The delicious plethora of tattoos.

Tonight I'll study every design. Trace them with my tongue. She shivered.

"Are you ready?" he asked.

"Ready," she replied, breathless.

He cleared his throat. "Your Honor," he said and paced in front of her, the panther-like grace of him making her shiver all over again. "I want something more than I've ever wanted anything else. It's been promised to me, and it would be cruel and unusual punishment if it was taken away from me."

He paused to glance at her.

He wanted her more than *anything*? "Appealing to the judge's sense of compassion," she said with a nod. "Nice try. Unfortunately for you, I've heard this particular judge is a coldhearted witch."

The flash of a smile before his eyes hooded. "Perhaps I should show the judge what I'm bringing to the table."

"Permission to approach the bench," she said, crooking her finger at him.

He closed the distance, his hands at his sides. Her heart drummed as butterflies danced excitedly through her veins.

When he stopped between her legs, she sat up as if pulled by a rope. Trembling, she flattened her palms on his chest, over the most detailed map she'd ever seen. It covered one of his pecs, the lines of it somehow raised.

Not somehow. They weren't an illusion caused by the ink—they were scars. More scars than she could count without intense study.

She knew so little about this man, she realized. Well,

other than the fact that he had a lot of secrets, clearly more than she'd ever suspected. And they were violent secrets, steeped in bloodshed. But she also knew he was a good guy, strong and capable, and right now, that was enough.

Besides, she could guess he'd gotten the wounds while in the military—he'd never confirmed nor denied her suspicions, so she was running with it. As tough as he was, he could have been Special Forces.

And how sexy was *that*? Proving just how much of a protector he really was.

Next to the map was a tree with olives of some type, black birds perched on the branches. There was also a redbud, the root of it sinking past the waist of his pants. And on his side was a cross with crimson flowing down it, pooling to spell the word *Strength*.

She stroked the insides of the map first, her trembling getting worse. His muscles jumped at the moment of contact. The heat of him delighted her, burned away the rest of her resistance. She leaned forward to kiss and lick her way to the upper edge of the olive tree.

His fingers entwined with her hair, holding her close. She sucked on his nipple, nibbled, and he hissed in a breath. He captured one of her hands, brought it to his lips and kissed her knuckles, ever the gentleman—before tracing his fingers along her jaw, down her neck and cupping her nape, ever the possessor.

"How long has it been for you, honey?"

"Four years," she answered honestly and pulled her gaze from his chest to peer up at his face. His expression had softened yet again, only this time he looked as if he'd *melted* with tenderness.

Jase ghosted his fingertips over her cheek before crouching in front of her. "I'll take good care of you."

He gripped the hem of her shirt and lifted, her hair tumbling around her shoulders as he discarded the material.

"Just a plain white bra," she said apologetically, unable to hide the new flood of nervousness, hating that the undergarment wasn't fancy and pink. Or red. Yeah. Definitely red.

"My new favorite." He unhooked the center, and the straps fell down her arms. "Been dying for these ever since you flashed me. More so since I had them in my hands."

Cool air caused her nipples to harden almost painfully. He traced the pads of his thumbs over them, twin lances of pleasure shooting through her.

"Just so you know," he said, "I've been tested since— since my last lover. I'm clean."

His last lover. Her sister? She hadn't even thought to ask.

Stupid! "Me, too," she said. "Before you, I was only with one other…but he moved away…college… We didn't want to try the long-distance-relationship thing." *Stop babbling!* "We always used a condom."

More tenderness from him. "Only one man?"

"A boy, really." She combed her fingers through his hair, urging him to bend down and take her lips, but he kept going lower, fitting his mouth over one of her nipples. His tongue flicked it, readying it, before he sucked on her. A fever flushed her skin, liquefied her bones and short-circuited her thoughts.

"Jase." Just then, it was the only word she was capable of saying.

He flicked and sucked faster, harder, while working at the waist of her shorts. As soon as the button and zipper gave way, he leaned away from her to yank the material down her legs. When the edge caught on her sandals, he removed them, too.

Her new outfit? A pair of panties and a full-body blush. The momentary self-confidence crash faded as he urged her to her back, to the cool sheets and the soft luxury of the mattress. A second later, his hard body was pinning her down. As heavy with muscle as he was, he had to shift to the side to keep from crushing her.

She loved his nearness, even as it struck a new chord of desire in her. To have this, him, at least once a day. Like breakfast, the most important meal. "Kiss me," she said.

He fit his legs between hers and placed one of her knees against his hip, his mouth finding...her breast again, laving her nipple with even more wicked attention.

"Not...there... Oh!" The alignment of his hardness to her aching softness allowed her to grind against him, slow, faster, until she was gasping out, desperate, needy, thrashing blindly.

He cupped her hip and forced her into a slower rhythm, even slower, so exquisitely slow. "Like that," he praised.

"Yes, yes." Every point of contact took her to a newer height of awareness. Her nails sank into his back, probably drew blood, but he must have liked it because a groan left him.

"What are you doing to me, angel?" He licked and nibbled his way to her neck, sucked, and it felt too good to worry about any lingering marks people would see.

"Jase." There was his name again, escaping of its own accord. A plea or a demand, she wasn't sure which. "Kiss me."

Once again he obeyed, but once again it wasn't where

she'd meant. He drew his lips along the line of her jaw, nipped at her earlobe—*the implants!* She stiffened.

"No," she said, gripping his chin to hold him back.

His gaze flashed fire at her. "Let me."

"No," she repeated.

He cupped her between the legs, the heel of his hand pressing where she ached the most. "Let me, and I'll give you more of this."

"No," she said on a moan. Her legs parted wider, granting him better access, but he took his hand away. Oh! Dang him. If he wanted to kiss her ears, fine. He could kiss her ears. Just as long as he continued touching her.

She removed her hand from his chin, and he nuzzled all around the implant, not stopping until she relaxed into the mattress, actually…enjoying the attention. Who knew ears could be such an erogenous zone? As she arched into him, silently demanding the return of his hand, just as he'd promised, he switched tracks and licked his way to the cord of her neck, where he bit.

Raw sensation poured through her. He kneaded her breasts until every touch was like a jolt of electricity, and when she was writhing, incoherent, he slid his fingers down the center of her stomach, stopping to play at her navel, teasing her with what could be.

"Jase, please. It's good. So good, but…but you promised."

"I'll keep my promise, angel." He slid his fingers under her panties, where she was wet and needy.

"Yes!" She arched her back. "Kiss me."

He returned his attention to her neck. Again, not what she'd meant or needed, but she figured out why he kept doing it. He thought to resign her to the same forgettable fate as the ones who'd come before her.

She framed his face, met his gaze. Those emerald eyes, so bright, simmering with passion. "Kiss me."

He stared at her lips with a hunger only the most deprived ever experienced while his fingers continued to stroke between her legs—it was almost more than she could bear.

"Brook Lynn." Never had her name sounded quite so tortured.

She traced her tongue along the seam of her mouth— then his. "I want to taste you while you play with me."

He groaned, a sound of animal hunger. "I shouldn't have kissed you before. It's better if I don't…"

"To remind your women that the sex means nothing to you. I know."

His fingers stilled. "In a way, yes, but also—"

"I don't need the reminder," she rushed out. *Let me pretend…continue to hope.* She nipped his chin. "Please. Kiss me, and I'll make you so glad you did." As she spoke, she moved her hand between them, down the waist of his pants. Burrowed under his underwear and found his long, hard and extra-large length inside—he hadn't just been bragging about his size. Hot beads of moisture seeped from the tip.

His shudder rattled the entire bed.

"Don't kiss me," she whispered, "and I'll make you wish you had." She took her hand away—and he cursed. *Too bad for you, Jase. I'm learning from the best.*

"Ultimatums, angel?"

"Consider it negative and positive reinforcement." Or desperation. "Like you gave me."

His narrowed gaze watched her as she placed her fingers at her lips, opened wide and sucked deep, tasting what he'd given her. A low moan reverberated from him.

He yanked out her fingers and replaced them with his tongue. A hot, wet thrust she met with one of her own.

As fierce as the make-out session had been before… this was…was… Oh! Nothing compared. He devoured her mouth. She fed him passion. Breath intermingled. Bodies undulated. He wasted no more time, tunneling a finger deep inside her. She arched into the inward glide, needing to be filled. *Have been empty for so long.*

"So tight, angel," he praised. He worked in a second finger.

She clung to his shoulders. As he scissored the digits, she felt stretched, the sensation a little uncomfortable, and yet it only made her desperate for more. "Jase," she gasped.

He pressed in, pulled out then pressed in again, teasing her, forcing her hips to follow his motions, allowing him to go a little deeper with each plunge.

"Can you take another?"

For him? "Yes."

He worked in a third finger. Her back bowed as her body accepted him. A sheen of perspiration formed over her skin, burning her from head to toe. The most delicious burn.

"So wet," he practically purred. "So perfect."

"Jase…it's good. I'm so close."

Out went his fingers, and she moaned in protest. He sat back on his heels, placing her legs outside his thighs, forcing her wide open for him. He stared at the soaked crotch of her panties before shaking his head, as if he'd made a life-altering decision.

"Hope these aren't a favorite pair," he said and, without waiting for her response, ripped her panties away, leaving her bare, utterly vulnerable.

He freed his erection from his jeans and, using her wetness on his hand, stroked himself up and down, an easy glide.

"Touch yourself," he commanded. "Let me watch you, see what you like."

She had never before pleasured herself in front of a man, but this was Jase. Sex made flesh. Her fingers walked a path to the apex of her thighs, and his hot gaze remained riveted on their every move. She showed him what she preferred, how hard and how fast, perhaps harder and faster than he would have guessed, all while he stroked his erection.

"I'm ready for you," she panted. "Please, get in me."

"Don't stop, angel. Don't you dare stop."

"But I'm going to…don't want to…not without…"
Oh!

Pleasure had been building steadily inside her, pulling her as taut as a bow, and seeing this feast of male aggression and carnality experience the same sensations at last pushed her over the edge. She cried out his name, her back arching. And then— Yes, yes! Her eyelids popped open. He'd put his face between her legs, was licking her up as she came and came and came, the rapture never ending, her entire body convulsing with satisfaction as he lapped and lapped.

He groaned deeply with his own satisfaction and spilled all over the bed.

Panting, she said, "You didn't…we didn't…"

When his shudders ceased, he straightened his spine. His hair was disheveled. His lips were red and swollen. Underneath his scars and tattoos had to be a thousand scratch marks.

He wouldn't look at her. He'd purposely come outside her, hadn't he?

"Why did you do that?" she asked quietly.

He fell to his back. "I just…I…" He ran a hand down his face.

Jase, at a loss for words. That was new. And somehow, it doubled her hurt.

She swung her legs to the side of the bed, standing to shaky legs. Motions clipped, she swiped up her clothes and dressed. She slipped her feet into her sandals, saying, "I've got to go."

A muscle jumped in his jaw. "Don't leave. Stay."

"Why?" They hadn't had sex and clearly wouldn't. What was it, exactly, that he hoped to do with her? Confuse her to the point of insanity?

Too late.

"You're upset," he said. "I don't like to see you upset."

So…it had nothing to do with his feelings for her—him *wanting* her nearby—and everything to do with guilt. Tears welled in her eyes.

"Good night, Jase." She marched from the room, head high.

JASE FOLLOWED BROOK LYNN to her car, though he never said a word, and she never acknowledged his presence.

When she disappeared down the road, he returned to his bedroom and paced like a caged animal. He'd handled things poorly. Could he really be blamed, though? He hadn't been thinking clearly. He'd had her in his bed, naked, open and willing, tasting like melted strawberry ice cream, flushing so beautifully. The sounds she'd made…purrs of pleasure his ears would forever crave. She'd gone wild for him, and he'd been desperate to make sure she continued to enjoy it.

And she had. She'd begged him for a kiss, begged him for more, and he thought he would have killed to give her *everything*. Problem was, when it had come time to do the actual deed, he'd remembered her gift, her offer of one time only. If he'd taken her then, that would have been it for them, the end. He wouldn't get to take her tomorrow…or the next day…or the next.

Once wasn't going to be enough. He realized that now. He wanted her countless times in countless ways. Underneath him. On top of him. Beside him. On her hands and knees. Her mouth on him, his length down her throat. His mouth on her, making her go wild again and again and again.

More than that, he wanted to do everything on her fun list. The two of them, together. When she "danced for a hot guy," it would be him. No one else.

But after the way she'd stormed off, he wasn't sure she'd agree to that.

He switched off the music and heard a knock at his door. "What?"

"Everything okay in there?" West asked.

"Yeah," he croaked. "Fine." *Might never be* fine *again*.

"Glad to hear it. But next time, if you don't want us to know you're giving your employee a little strange, tell her not to scream your name."

Smart-ass. Jase threw a pillow at the door.

"I'll pretend that was a hug."

"Oh, goody. Is it hug time?" Beck asked, joining the Torture Jase game.

"Go away before I remove what's left of your balls with pliers," Jase told them.

The boys' laughter started off strong but faded as they ambled away.

Jase fell on his bed and peered up at the ceiling. He had to protect himself from future hurt.

But...he didn't want to protect himself from her.

He needed more of Brook Lynn, not less. *I can't let her go. Not just yet.*

CHAPTER FIFTEEN

BROOK LYNN HAD the next day free—though she would be on call—her first break in forever. To be honest, she wasn't sure what to do with herself. Also, it was odd, knowing she wouldn't be doing any non-wife wifing unless Jase had one of those casserole emergencies he'd mentioned. Odd...and freaking awesome. But mostly awesome. And okay, a little awful. She'd spent last night squirming in bed, remembering the way he'd touched her, desperate for everything she'd been denied.

In an effort to distract herself, she spent the morning with Jessie Kay and Kenna, trying on bridesmaid dresses and finally checking another item off her fun list: drinking whiskey straight from a bottle.

"You look different today," Kenna said as Brook Lynn moved to the dais to show off the latest gown—a floor-length lavender beauty fit for a fairy queen.

Heat pooled in Brook Lynn's cheeks. The only thing different about her was the brief taste of satisfaction she'd experienced in Jase's arms.

Jessie Kay emerged from the dressing room in a short red halter dress, smirking over at Brook Lynn and singing, "I know what youuuu diiiiidd. I know. I know. I really, really know."

"You lie!" Brook Lynn said. "You know nothing."

Kenna pointed to the whiskey. "You take another swig right this second, Miss Dillon, and then you tell me why you blush every few minutes, why you keep sighing while staring off at nothing and why you've got a bruise the size of my butt on your neck."

The hickey! Crap!

Both Jessie Kay and Kenna burst into laughter as she slapped a hand over her neck. Clearly they knew what was "different" about her, but had decided to tease her.

"I'll drink, but I'll never tell you devious slags *anything.*" Eyes narrowed, she bent down and grabbed the whiskey bottle at her feet then chugged. Oh, the burn! But with the third swallow, she actually began to like it. Her skin flushed, and a drugging numbness filled her limbs. "So get this," she heard herself say. "Jase and I made out."

It was as if she'd just let the air out of a balloon.

"Made out?" Jessie Kay gave her a thumbs-down. "I thought you'd sealed the deal."

"Hardly." She faced herself in the mirror, irritated by the sudden, defeated slump in her shoulders. "He refused."

Why had Jase denied her? Had he simply changed his mind? Men were allowed to do that, same as women— though it should be illegal for guys. Or had he not enjoyed what they were doing?

No. Definitely not that one. He'd come. Hard. Like, propel-a-rocket-grenade hard.

Men! She would never understand them.

Kenna gave her rear a smack. "Don't look so pitiful. So what if he didn't give it to you last night. There's always tomorrow, right?"

Always tomorrow.

The words played in a loop in Brook Lynn's mind. She'd only promised him a night of sex. A single night. Had he, perhaps, hoped for a second go-round? Because not actually sleeping with her left their *legal* and *binding* contract in play.

Her jaw dropped. Was *that* why he'd stopped? There was a good chance…yes, she thought, and someone might as well have tapped her vein and injected her with happiness. *I'm still in the game!*

She took another two…six swigs of whiskey before putting the bottle back on the floor and picking up her phone. Texting Jase to ask for confirmation seemed like *such* a good idea right now. The best! Absolutely nothing could go wrong.

But as her fingers flew over the keyboard, *Do you want more from me or not?* wasn't what she typed.

Guess what? U missed out, Jase Hollister. U could have had ALL this.

She waved to encompass her entire body. Wait. He couldn't see her. Should she send a video, too? Nah.

It's a treasure, & I don't go around giving it away 4 free. But U blew it, she added. Blew. It. So. Hard.
Perfect. Don't even need to proofread. Send.
Another thought hit her. She began typing again.

Guess what else? I still owe U a nite & UR gonna get it whether U want it or not. I'M LEGALLY BOUND, RE-MEMBER?? So the next time we R 2gether I'm going 2 start by running my fingers down UR chest, all the way 2 UR zipper…

Send.
His reply came within seconds.

And then?

She yelped with surprise…then nearly melted into a puddle with pleasure. He really did want more!

"What are you doing?" Kenna demanded.

Brook Lynn ignored her, typing, I will lean in soooo close…

Send.

Another lightning-fast response came in.

AND THEN? Tell me, angel. I have 2 know.

Oh, I'll tell you all right.

"Seriously," Jessie Kay said. "What are you doing? You're panting."

Brook Lynn ignored her, too. She typed

And then I will whisper "I have a headache. Maybe we can try again tomorrow."

Send.

Her phone rang a few moments later. Startled, she dropped the thing on the floor and peered down at it as if it had just begun leaking poison. Was that Jase?

With a grin, Jessie Kay swiped up the phone and handed it to her. "Answer, or I will."

Brook Lynn tentatively placed the phone to her ear. "Hello?"

"Cruel, honey. Cruel." Jase's husky voice filtered through the implants and drifted into her head, making her shiver. "I might not survive that severe of a punishment."

She tried for a tough tone. "Well, I'm hard-core. And you should have considered the consequences before you kicked me out."

"Kicked you out?" He sounded as if he'd just choked

on his own tongue. "You blazed out the door after I asked you to stay."

The girls crowded around her, whispering, "What'd he say?" and "Put him on speaker. I want to hear this."

She batted them away, got dizzy, tripped over her own feet and ended up in a puddle of silk scarves. "Jase, I need you to stop trying to place the blame on my delicate flower shoulders and come find me. This is a 911 sexergency. You have made me more frustrated than a zombie at a salad bar. Fix it!"

Behind her, Jessie Kay and Kenna burst into laughter.

"You been drinking, honey?" he asked.

"Only this much." She pinched the fingers of her free hand to indicate a little.

"Doing your fun list, then?"

"I am. And guess what? It's fun!" She pushed to her feet to twirl around the room…and then had to sit back down and stick her head between her legs before she passed out or threw up. "Or it *was*. Now it's not."

The phone was swiped out of her hand.

"Hey," she protested.

"Jase," Kenna said. "This is Kenna Starr, and I just want to assure you…" She went silent. "Yes, we are… No, no, of course not…Well, that's a little extreme." Her eyes widened and swung to Brook Lynn. "I would never let anything…Okay, all right."

Curiosity poured through Brook Lynn. "What's he saying?"

"You are…Wow," Kenna said to him, disregarding her. "I'm going to have to refuse your oh, so generous offer…What! That's blackmail!" A pause. "But I *promised* and…well, she *does* seem to like you…Fine! You win. I'm going to hang up before I change my mind."

"What was *that* about?" Jessie Kay demanded.

"Yeah," Brook Lynn said. "Tell me before things get ugly."

Kenna placed a hand over her mouth as a chuckle escaped. "I'm supposed to take you home, ensuring you do not speak to any man between the ages of sixteen and fifty. Sixty, if they look like they work out. I'm also supposed to refuse to help you with any more items on your fun list—and so are you," she said to Jessie Kay. "Jase has called dibs, and he's willing to go to extraordinary lengths to make sure he gets what he considers his. Even creating a mess at Dane's office that causes him to have to work late nights for the next six weeks!"

"Dibs," Brook Lynn echoed. *He* wanted to help her? Had insisted on it, even scaring away the competition? *And* he wanted her to avoid other men?

Was it her birthday?

"Give me that phone," Brook Lynn said. "I need to ask him where exactly we stand, where we're going with this and where he wants to end up." *Simple* questions.

"No way," Kenna said. "He'll do what he threatened and come here."

"Even better!"

"No!"

"Give me!" she demanded, lunging for her friend.

Kenna threw the flip to Jessie Kay, who dropped it and kicked it across the store. Brook Lynn crawled to her sister and grabbed *her* phone.

"Why don't you play a *little* hard to get?" Jessie Kay gasped out.

"Why should I? I gambled, and I won. Now I want my prize. I *deserve* it."

Kenna raced over and swatted Brook Lynn's wrist until she dropped the other phone. "Did you know she would turn into a needy hobag after a few drinks?" she demanded of Jessie Kay.

"No!" Jessie Kay tried to back away, saying, "It's as much a surprise to me as it is to you."

Brook Lynn grabbed hold of her sister's ankle and yanked. The girl flailed and fell, landing with a hard thud, the hem of her dress ending up bunched at her waist, revealing lacy blue panties.

Kenna tried to help Jessie Kay stand, but Brook Lynn dove on her. "I'm not needy—I'm curious. Now gimme!"

"Have we decided on a color, ladies?" The prim voice of the saleswoman echoed. "Or a design?"

The three of them froze.

"Um…still mulling things over, ma'am," Kenna said.

"I'd like to see that little light blue number over there," Jessie Kay said, pointing.

The saleswoman walked away, grumbling under her breath. Kenna helped Jessie Kay and Brook Lynn stand.

Steady on my feet—almost.

"Why don't we call it a day?" Kenna said.

While she and her sister changed into their regular clothes—after Jessie Kay ruled out the blue dress she'd made the saleswoman fetch for her—Kenna gathered the fallen phones. As her friend drove her home, Brook Lynn began to lose her buzz…but not her sense of happy.

Jase wants me!

It would be smooth sailing from here. No doubt about it.

JASE NEARLY POUNCED on Brook Lynn when she showed up for work Monday morning. Spending the weekend away from her had been torture. His mind had been locked on her, unable to think of anything or anyone else. He'd wondered what she was doing and who she was doing it with. He'd wanted to know if she missed him. If she'd thought about him at all…craved him, unable to sleep, the desire in her little body too much to bear.

Her texts had been a gift from above…or a means of torment from far, far below. He wasn't sure yet. He somehow found the strength to go out back and get to work on his own chores without hounding her with a million questions.

Have to let her do her thing during office hours.

What seemed an eternity later, she carried a glass of ice water out to him. A blush stained her cheeks. Remembering what she'd texted to him?

"Thank you." His mouth went dry and he drained the contents—if it wasn't the Oklahoma heat, it could only be the woman standing in front of him. "I'm still waiting to hear today's affirmations."

At first, she didn't respond. Finally, though, she cleared her throat and said, "I am at one with my duality."

Funny girl. A jab at his hot-and-cold treatment of her?

"So we're going to act like Friday night didn't happen and the texts Saturday stemmed only from the alcohol," he said. "Got it."

Silence.

Such tense silence.

But it was a blessing. One word of encouragement, and he would have picked her up and carried her straight to bed. Now that he had firsthand knowledge of the curves hidden by her clothes, the softness of her skin and the sweetness of her taste, being with her wasn't a want—it was a need.

I'm going to start by running my fingers down your chest, all the way to your zipper...

He handed her the glass and returned to hammering new pieces of shingle into the roof, her scent surrounding him. Vanilla and sugar today. "By the way. Your phone is a POS. I want to get hold of you when I want to get hold of you. Consider this a bonus for working for me." He pointed to the box resting beside the grill.

She picked up the device and frowned at him. "You bought me a phone?"

"Yes. And there are no take backs."

"But—"

"No buts. It's yours. Agree and save us an argument."

"I... Thank you," she said, then quietly returned to the house.

He glanced over just as she disappeared beyond the door and caught a glimpse of long blond hair swishing at the waist of her shorts, a pert little ass he'd like to sink his teeth into and the lithe legs he wanted wrapped around his head.

A moan escaped him, his body so hard he could have used it as a battering ram. Hell. He *wanted* to use it as a battering ram.

Not yet. And not just because of her work hours and pay. She'd tied him in knots, and those knots had to be undone first. Otherwise, there was no telling what he would allow to happen. Like, say, feeling more, deeper...wanting more.

His mind replayed two conversations that had taken place over the weekend, both of which had scared the hell out of him.

He'd spent some time in town...*not* looking for Brook Lynn. He'd once again felt as if he were being watched, but when he'd found no evidence of a stalker,

he'd known he had to get over these little paranoias if
he had any hope of staying sane. He'd soon come across
an elderly woman doing her best to change a flat tire.
Despite the summer heat, she wore a sweater. But his
favorite thing about her? She had quintessential old-lady
hair, white curls forming a ball of fluff around her face.

He was ashamed to admit he'd held an internal de-
bate about whether or not to help her. He hadn't wanted
any of the locals thinking about him, much less talking about him, or inevitably looking him up, but in the
end he hadn't been able to leave the woman on her own.
Especially since she hadn't been working the scissor
jack properly.

He'd parked in front of her, at the side of the road,
and walked over.

She'd stiffened, backed a few steps away and held
out her hands to stop him. "You think you're the first
stranger to approach me today? Think again. I've got
Mace, young man, and I'm not afraid to use it."

"I'm not here to hurt you, ma'am." He'd slowed his
approach and put his own hands up, all innocence. "Just
wanted to help."

"That's what the last guy said and he had serial killer
written all over him."

"I didn't know serial killers were so obvious nowadays."

She'd lifted her chin and *hmph*ed. "You just go on
now. I'll have this tire changed on my own in another
hour or two."

"I'm Jase Hollister, friends with Lincoln West and
Beck Ockley," he'd said, and her entire demeanor had
changed from suspicious to fawning in less than a heartbeat.

"I've met West and Beck. Beautiful boys. I'm Peggy,

the event planner for the Silver Foxes. You ever heard of us?"

"Uh, no, can't say that I have."

"Well, we are hot mommas still going strong. We host mixers at the assisted-living center. You should come." She'd patted his shoulder. "Look what a big strapping lad you are. And so helpful, too, stopping to take care of my needs." A calculated gleam had entered her eyes. "Are you married, Jase?"

He'd swallowed a groan, knowing where she was about to delve. "No, and I—"

"Wonderful," she'd said, speaking over him. "My granddaughter is single, too."

Yup. There.

"I know you'd love her. She's a nurse at that assisted-living center I mentioned, and let me tell you, you will never meet a girl with a better personality."

"That's, uh, great," he'd replied, while thinking: *I should have driven on*. "But I'm kind of…seeing someone."

As in…dating?

No, some part of him screamed. No!

"Who?" she'd asked, as if she'd had every right to know.

He'd ignored her, and she'd spent the next twenty minutes regaling him with reasons why city girls were inferior to Strawberry Valley girls, as well as stories about her granddaughter, while he'd taken care of the tire, a captive audience. By some miracle, he'd gotten away without having to relinquish his phone number.

For his trouble, Peggy had given him a Werther's Original. Seriously.

Afterward, Jase had helped Virgil Porter carry his groceries to his beater of a truck.

"Heard you're dating Peggy Newcomb's granddaughter," Virgil had said as he settled behind the wheel. "You sure that's wise, considering you're pinin' for our Brook Lynn?"

He'd had to swallow a mouthful of curses.

But…was he pining? What, exactly, did he want from Brook Lynn?

Irritated with himself now, Jase worked outside for hours, even skipping lunch to avoid being around the temptation of her. Of course, after a while, she brought food to him.

She's concerned for me. Caring for me.

Ruining me.

Stopping himself from grabbing hold of her and pulling her body against his might have been the most difficult thing he'd ever done.

When dusk finally descended, she peeked her head out the window and called, "Jase. I need you."

Just like that, he was hard. "Everything okay?"

"Everything's fine." When she disappeared back inside the house, he stored his tools and entered the kitchen. She bustled around between the stove and the counter, mixing ingredients.

"You need something?" he asked. *Need me?*

"Yeah. Answers. Did you tell Kenna you'd help me with my fun list?"

More like demanded. "Yes," he reluctantly admitted.

"Well, then, you need to help me. I'm ready to check off another item."

Dance for me. He cleared his throat. "How about we hustle West and Beck during a poker game tonight?"

She glanced at him, bit her lip nervously—and it was sexy as hell. "Shouldn't I learn how to play first?"

"You've never played?"

Wiping her hands on a towel, she said, "Would you be able to teach me? It isn't that hard, is it? It looks so easy and fun on TV, so I'm absolutely certain I can learn, like, superfast."

You've got to be kidding me. He retrieved a deck of cards and shuffled. As her newest casserole baked, he showed her how to pull a royal flush, straight flush, four of a kind, full house, flush, straight, three of a kind, two pair and the two least desired hands. He taught her about the flop, river and turn, and through it all, she nodded her head.

Then they played several hands. She lost. Badly.

"You'll get better," he said. *In a few years. Maybe a few decades.* "As for tonight, let's hustle West and Beck at pool. You can play *that*, right?"

The lip-biting started up again. "Sure I can…if you teach me how."

The timer on the oven went off, and right on cue the front door opened and closed. Jase had begun to suspect his friends clocked their days according to Brook Lynn's meal preparation.

West and Beck entered the kitchen, both sniffing the air and moaning with approval.

"What'd you make this time?" West rubbed his hands together. His eyes were bloodshot, his hair a mess. Once again he smelled of alcohol.

"What?" Jase said. "No greeting for me? You just go straight to the girl with the food?"

"Yeah, I'm smart like that." West slapped him on the shoulder. "Brook Lynn? I believe I asked you a very important question."

She laughed with genuine amusement. "This is called Thanksgiving Dream. It's turkey and dressing, with a mix of green beans and potatoes, and a cranberry sauce topping."

"Rename it Heaven in a Dish." Beck reached out to pinch a piece of the dressing. "And then you're going to marry me right here, right now."

Jase scowled at him.

"Bad boy." Brook Lynn slapped at Beck's hand before he could sample the dish. "Also, my answer is heck, no."

"Um, I hate to break it to you," Beck said, "but I was proposing to the casserole."

"She says she'd rather die the death of a thousand bites," Brook Lynn replied, deadpan.

"Oh, I'll bite her all right," Beck replied, equally deadpan. "And I guarantee she changes her mind. From what I hear, my mouth is pure magic."

Brook Lynn laughed again, only to grow quiet when her gaze collided with Jase's in a tangle of need.

I better unknot soon, he thought. *Or else.*

BROOK LYNN FOUGHT hard to hide the evil-overlord quality of her grin.

Hook, line, sinker.

While Beck and West took care of the dishes, Jase ushered her into the poolroom, where the mighty fine table he had never allowed her to polish or clean awaited. He helped her pick a cue. The shortest one he owned.

She pretended to pay attention when he planned the break, the first shot of the game. He told her about the scratch, when the cue ball jumped off the table, and how to continue afterward. He let her start, standing behind her to help her line up her shot, his body flush against hers.

Suddenly, fighting a grin wasn't her biggest problem. *Can't breathe...can barely stand.* Her knees wouldn't stop trembling.

"See how the balls are laid out? The solids will be easiest to sink this game, so that's what you'll pick," he said.

The connection screwed with her concentration, and missing her shot proved easy.

"Don't worry," he said. "Even the best players miss sometimes. I rarely do, but that's just me."

Oh, Jase. You have no idea what's in store for you. "But I haven't hit a single one," she said, turning to pout at him.

Had her uncle always had this much fun with his cons?

The thought sobered her. *Shake it off.* She wasn't doing this to get something out of someone, but to have a good time with someone who liked to tease her to the edge of insanity. Huge difference.

Jase sifted a lock of her hair between his fingers. "How about we play doubles eight ball? We'll be partners, and we'll alternate shots. I'll be able to set you up."

No, no, no. But she said, "That's so sweet of you."

The doorbell rang. Jase frowned, and Brook Lynn pretended not to know her sister—who she'd secretly texted during dinner—had just arrived. A few minutes later, Jessie Kay strode into the game room with Beck and West trailing behind her. West now had a beer in hand, and Beck was watching him warily while Jessie Kay just looked tired.

Brook Lynn felt a flicker of unease. Jase and Jessie Kay in the same room not long after they'd seen each other naked may not be a great idea. *Don't go there.*

Such thoughts wouldn't do any of them any good. She forced herself to concentrate on the situation at hand.

"Come here." Beck turned away from West and swung an arm back to pull her sister forward. That arm remained around her waist as he rubbed his knuckle into the crown of her head.

She giggled like a freaking schoolgirl. "Stop it!"

"Only when you pee your pants," Beck said. "You don't call, you don't write, and I'm just supposed to forgive you?"

West watched the interaction through narrowed eyes before draining his beer.

Something had obviously angered him, but Brook Lynn had no idea what it was.

"I came to speak with my little sis, but if y'all are playing pool, the conversation can wait." Jessie Kay pushed away from Beck and threw her purse in the corner. Strawberries had stained her hands red. "I'm in!"

"We were fine without you," West muttered. "You may go."

His uncustomary rudeness surprised Brook Lynn— and ticked her off. She opened her mouth to demand an apology.

"Dude," Beck said to his friend. "Don't think I can't kick you out of your own house. The lady deserves respect, and she'll get it."

"Seriously. What the hell is wrong with you?" Jase demanded.

"Yeah!" Jessie Kay bristled. "Clearly everyone else is happy to have me."

"Maybe they're just better at hiding their emotions," West said.

"Or maybe they hope my delightful personality will make up for your crappy one." Jessie Kay fluffed her hair. "Or are you just jealous you're the only one who hasn't nailed me?"

West's nostrils flared. "The day I let you in my bed is the day I want to be smothered by a pillow." He took a seat at the poker table in the corner, cut off the end of a cigar and began to smoke.

Wow. What had gotten into him?

If Brook Lynn allowed herself to dwell on it, she might unleash the viper's tongue she'd been known to use...or actually physically hurt him.

What the heck? Why not both? "Talk to my sister like that again, West, and I will rip out your intestines and use them as a jump rope."

All three men gaped at her.

Jessie Kay gave her a thumbs-up.

"Sorry, Jessie Kay," West mumbled.

"Now that that's settled." Brook Lynn cleared her throat. "Let's move on."

As soon as the boys turned away, Brook Lynn flashed her sister the signal her uncle had taught them, and it was odd, doing so without being forced. As she flashed back to childhood times she'd resented, she felt no remaining animosity, just satisfaction that she possessed the skill.

Amazing what a change of perspective could do.

"We're playing something called doubles eights," she said. "Ever heard of it?"

"Maybe from a movie?" Jessie Kay shrugged. "Either way, you'll be my partner, Brook Lynn. Of course. And I'm just certain we'll figure out the rules together."

"No," Jase said, shaking his head. "Brook Lynn is with me."

Jessie Kay bit her bottom lip the way they'd been taught. "But I came here after a long, hard day of work, and all I want to do is play with my sister. Or should I go home? Yeah, I probably should. Just like West said. I don't like to cry in public."

Jase's eyes narrowed, and he glanced between them suspiciously.

Can't laugh. Really can't laugh. "Oh, Jessie Kay. Please don't cry. I'd love to play with you. Beck? West? Which one of you will be Jase's partner?"

"I'll do it." Beck selected a cue. "Word of warning. I never let my opponent win."

"I'm glad, because we're going to wipe the floor with your face," Brook Lynn said, giving trash talk a try.

"I'll kick us off, then," Jase said tightly.

Poor guy. His plan to help her hustle his friends had failed—and he had no idea Brook Lynn had been hustling him all along.

"How about we put cash on this game?" Jessie Kay said. "I could use the cash."

"No money," Jase said. A sudden gleam in his eyes as he focused on Brook Lynn. "But we can play for favors."

"What kind of favors?" she asked, doing her best to sound nervous. He'd stopped trying to help her and now saw this as an opportunity to win something from her. Sneaky devil. At least the new prize had doused his suspicions.

"Open ended," he said. "To be named at a later date."

"I don't know," she hedged.

"Yeah. What if you ask us to count our own hair or lick our own elbows?" Jessie Kay said. When everyone gaped at her, she added, "What? Someone asked me to do that just this morning."

"Nothing impossible," Jase said. "Nothing illegal."

What about…sexual? Brook Lynn gave a faux-reluctant

nod. "Okay. We're agreed. One non-illegal favor for every game won. So go ahead. Kick us off."

What should she ask for? Because this game? *In the bag.*

Radiating fierce determination, Jase racked and broke the balls. He sank a stripe in the right pocket and then another in the left. But he missed his third shot—thanks to Brook Lynn "accidentally" dropping her new phone and bending down to pick it up.

Now she aimed her cue, choosing the most difficult shot, and met Jase's gaze. With a grin slowly blooming to megawatt, she sank the ball with expert precision.

He blinked in surprise. And when she did it a second time, he unleashed a stream of curses. Jessie Kay giggled.

"Dude," Beck said. Clearly fighting a grin, he patted Jessie Kay on the shoulder. "You girls are hard-core."

As she preened under the attention, West muttered another curse, his eyes never leaving Jessie Kay.

Jase leaned against his cue. "I just got hustled, didn't I?"

"Prepare to owe me a bunch of favors, Jase Hollister," Brook Lynn said and sank another shot.

CHAPTER SIXTEEN

BROOK LYNN UTTERLY *annihilated* Jase, showing zero mercy. *I'm heartless, and I love it!* She didn't trounce him once, but every single time. He gave up after the sixth game, which was probably a good thing, considering West and Jessie Kay could not stop fighting.

She called one of his shots "pathetic" and he said, "You'll have to forgive me if I'm not as talented as you are at handling shafts."

She'd blustered before gritting out, "Did my opinion bother you? Well, you should have heard the things I kept to myself!"

"What's the difference between what you're saying and a knife? A knife has a point."

Finally, Jase led Brook Lynn outside, where the moon glowed romantically and the stars sparkled like diamonds. The perfect setting. The scent of salt water blended with strawberries, roses and magnolias, delighting her further.

She removed her sandals and sat at the edge of the pool then dipped her feet into the warmth of the water. He claimed the spot right next to her, leaving only the slightest of gaps between them, surprising her.

"What is going on with West?" she asked. "Is he always this mean when he drinks?"

He looked uneasy before saying, "It's a bad time of year for him."

"And he's decided to take it out on my sister?"

"Appears so."

"But why?"

"Who knows? He's been different with women ever since he lost Tessa."

Tessa. The one Brook Lynn was planning the GED celebration for. "Lost? As in…she died?"

"Yeah."

How sad. "He loved her?"

"More than life."

Well, it wasn't an excuse for his behavior, but it sure did break her heart. "I think he's a great guy and all, but I will never be okay with him hating on my sister. And if he does it again, I *will* get a little Dillon girl revenge."

Jase gave a mock shudder. "Sounds scary."

"You have no idea."

"Let's forget about those two for the moment." He pulled a cigar from his pocket, cut off and lit the end then handed it to her. "For you."

Another item from her list. "Thank you, Mr. Loser."

"You're welcome, Miss Con. But I have a feeling you'll soon be cursing my name."

"Why? A little smoke can't be that bad. I didn't react to West's cigar."

She puffed on the cigar—and promptly choked.

Laughing, he stubbed out the cigar and set it aside then handed her a bottle of whiskey. "Any item on the list you check off without me will have to be repeated with me."

When the taste of ash lingered, she took a shot and wished she'd died. That horrible burn had returned!

"Consider this punishment for the hustle," Jase said.

As the inside of her chest cooled, she said, "You deserved it. I never lose," she mocked. "I could have killed you at poker, too."

He bumped her with his shoulder. She turned toward him, her gaze seeking his in the darkness. He was so close…if he just leaned in a little more…

Someone flipped on the back porch light. Gold suddenly spilled over him, adding a layer of mystery to features already suffused with raw masculinity. As smoke curled around him, creating a dreamlike haze, her need for him redoubled, shivering through her.

"I owe you six favors," he said, his voice tighter than before. "What is it, exactly, that you're going to want from me?"

How about…everything? Though, technically, he owed her *and* Jessie Kay, which made her want to dump the favors ASAP. "Help me get my tattoo, and we'll call it even."

He looked her over, his eyelids seeming to grow heavy. "Where are you going to put this tattoo?"

She took another swig of liquid courage before saying, "My shoulder. And neck," she added. "I want a vine of flowers. Wild strawberries."

He confiscated the bottle and set it out of her reach. "I'll take you to a guy who did a few of mine. He's good."

"Really good." She traced her fingertip up his arm, following the lines of several expert etchings. *Can't help myself.* Along the way, she encountered two areas of scar tissue, thick and raised, both a few inches long, though not very wide. "You were injured." Shrapnel?

He hesitated. "Yes," he finally said, his voice tight… but also husky with need. "I like when you touch me."

She shivered. Finally they were getting somewhere. "That makes two of us." He'd once accused her of adding crack to her casseroles, but she thought it might just lace his skin. When she wasn't touching him, she *wanted* to touch him. And when her hands were actually on him, she wanted them everywhere all at once.

He picked her up by the waist, and she had to straddle his lap for balance. The move did more than thrill her physically. It told her beyond any doubt that they weren't over, not by a long shot, and she eagerly pressed into him.

Playing with the ends of his hair, she said, "Thank you for my lessons today."

"Who taught you to play?" He flicked her hair over one shoulder, but she quickly brought it back into place. He frowned then tried to flick it again, but again, she moved it to cover her ears. She might have let him kiss around the devices in the heat of passion, but after their abysmal finish she wasn't going to make that mistake again.

"My uncle taught me," she said, some of her old resentment rising up. "He had a new lesson for Jessie Kay and me every time he babysat us, before my mom died. But since he always kept whatever allowance he won, we learned fast."

"He kept your allowance? That's harsh."

"Also effective."

Jase leaned in and placed a soft kiss against the hammering pulse at the base of her neck. "You got any more surprises for me?"

"Just one. This." She placed two fingers under his chin and lifted his head, then pressed her lips to his.

He opened immediately, and their tongues thrust together. Desire sizzled through her...sultry, heady. Drugging. Fogging her mind and giving her one purpose: more pleasure.

"Everyone should experience a kiss like this at least once in a lifetime," he said.

"Yes." Every inch of her body was engaged, humming and vibrating with need, burning deliciously. "They just have to be prepared to want more."

"You want more?" Jase stroked the ridges of her spine, a gentle caress before cupping her bottom and yanking her the rest of the way forward, until they were locked together. Her softest part grinding against his hardest.

She gasped at the sensation.

"I like the sounds you make," he said, the words nothing more than a growl. He arched his hips, rubbing against her dampening core.

She balanced on her knees to try to gain a little control. Then *she* arched against *him*, rubbing harder...up and down. "I *love* the way you make me feel."

He grabbed her by the hips, stilling her. "Only me." His fingers flexed on her. "No one else."

It was as if he'd penetrated her in a single thrust, so strongly did she react to those words.

He urged her into a slow grind against his erection, the friction off-the-charts erotic. Then he slid his fingers into her hair and fisted the strands to angle her head... and take her mouth in a soul-searing kiss.

His hands moved to her breasts, kneading, thrumming her nipples. And when he had her gasping incoherently, straining to get closer to him, pulling at his shirt to get it out of her way, he unsnapped her shorts and tunneled his fingers inside...under her panties.

"My angel is so hot and wet," he praised, practically purring with masculine satisfaction—and then he thrust a finger deep inside her.

"More. Please, more," she whispered, lifting to give him better access. The whoosh of the back door being opened barely registered.

"Jase. Dude."

But Beck's voice *did* register—like a hammer—intruding on the private moment.

"I'm sorry to bother you guys, but I'm desperate."

Brook Lynn stiffened, momentarily blinded by panic. *Caught with a guy's hand in my cookie jar!* But the wide expanse of Jase's chest prevented Beck from seeing anything he shouldn't, and the panic faded...the pleasure once again making itself known.

"West and Jessie Kay are about to kill each other," Beck said.

"Not now," Jase snapped. He'd stopped moving in her, and oh...oh...*dying here!*

Do not *writhe on him.*

"Yes, now," Beck said. "Nothing I've done has helped."

"I should take her home," she managed, her tone breathless, her inner walls clamping on his finger. Inside she wept.

Gritting his teeth, gaze still locked on Brook Lynn, Jase called, "Give me five minutes."

"I don't think we have five minutes. I'm predicting a murder-suicide in less than one." But the door whooshed shut.

Slowly Jase withdrew his finger, and she had to bite her tongue to stop her moan of remorse. As she watched, he put the finger in his mouth and sucked; this time she couldn't stop her moan from escaping—this one of ultimate pleasure.

"I like the taste of you," he said. "Pure, sweet honey."

Shivers danced through her.

"I don't want you to go," he said, expression one of absolute torture.

"It's for the best." Maybe. Probably. If she stayed, she wasn't sure what would come of the make-out session. Would he stop short like the other night? Or would they go all the way? And if they did, would he ever want her again?

Might as well end on a positive note, eager for more of each other.

He pursed his lips. "Why?"

"Because. Just because." After all, this was a war for his affections, not just a single battle. She refastened her shorts and stood to shaky legs. "I'll see you tomorrow, Jase."

A pause.

"Tomorrow, Brook Lynn."

There was a promise of something in his tone. But exactly what he was promising, she didn't know.

JASE HAD DEALT with his fair share of hard-ons throughout the years, but never one so determined to hang on for dear life. It wanted Brook Lynn, and absolutely no one else would do—not even his own hand. The knowledge panicked him. Made him realize just how dependent on her he'd become.

He remembered the way she'd begged him for more... *please, more*...the way he'd craved those pleas like a starving man craved food. Remembered thinking, *I will die without this...without her.*

No. Hell, no. He couldn't allow himself to depend on anyone like that.

He'd made a huge tactical error, he realized. He should have taken her while he'd had the chance, that first night inside his bedroom. He would have already moved on. Surely.

When she arrived for work the next morning, she told him the day's affirmation—*Today I will gladly share my expertise and advice with others, for there are no sweeter words than "I told you so"*—as he handed her a shopping list, cash and keys to his car.

"You're on your own today, honey." He needed distance. Perspective.

She gaped at him. "Uh, o-kay."

He strode outside to clean the gutters. She followed him out, only to stand in place for a long while, watching him, her mouth opening and closing, as if she had plenty more to say to him but didn't quite know where to begin. Finally, she left, and though he'd expected to be able to breathe again, he felt more oxygen-deprived than ever.

The weather. Had to be the weather. Though it was 8:00 a.m., it was already wretchedly hot. The temperature would probably top one hundred and five today. *But it won't even come close to how hot I am for that girl.*

Have to resist. It's for the best, just as she said.

As he worked, several town residents swung by to "check on things." Namely: to probe into his life. What did he do for a living? Was he single or dating Peggy Newcomb's granddaughter? Would he be able to fix the clock tower in town? He knew he'd invited the attention by helping out two of the town's chattiest residents, but still—small-town living was sometimes more nightmare than dream. He wasn't rude, but he definitely wasn't welcoming, either, and he absolutely did not answer any questions. Also, a handful of women brought Beck baskets of food. The disturbances put him behind schedule.

When Jase finally finished cleaning the gutters, he turned his attention to the fence surrounding the property. His mind continually drifted to Brook Lynn. He liked that she'd hustled him. That she'd enjoyed every moment of it...then kissed him as if only his lungs contained the air she needed to survive. He'd been on fire for her. Still was.

He wasn't sure how many more hours passed before she returned and called him inside for lunch.

As he walked into the house, he tried to summon all his strength.

She had her back to him, steam wafting around her as she drained a pot of noodles. "Hungry?"

"Yes." For more than food. He used a towel to wipe the sweat from his face. "I'm sorry I was so abrupt with you this morning."

"That's good."

"I'm…ready to talk about what happened last night." Maybe then he'd finally unknot.

She stiffened slightly. "Oh. You mean the fact that we made out again and you liked it?"

Loved it. "Yes."

"Well, then. Talk away."

Tell her the truth. Tell her everything—well, almost everything. "You make me feel things I've never felt before, and I don't know how to deal."

She spun, her blue eyes wide. "You feel things? What kind of things?"

"You can't tell?" He took a step toward her.

"Well, last night you were aroused. But right now? I have no idea. Like I told you before, you're very difficult to read."

The doorbell rang, stopping him from taking another step. He was disappointed. He was relieved. "I'll get it."

She sighed. "Put on a shirt at least."

No need. It was his friend Pepe, the tattoo artist.

Pepe held a big black bag of necessary equipment, and when Jase explained that he'd brought the tattoo shop to Brook Lynn, he expected her to chicken out—

he might even have wanted her to chicken out, because he couldn't bear the thought of her in any kind of pain. But he'd promised to help her, so he would help her.

She trembled as Pepe showed her the book of designs he'd created just for her, and didn't seem to notice when the guy looked her up and down with interest. Jase grew tenser by the second. He'd paid the guy to work, not to scope out a potential lay.

"Sure you want to do this, honey?" Jase asked her. Without the whiskey giving her courage, and the cigar making her feel badass, maybe she'd decide—

"Yes," she said with a nod, pointing to the design she wanted. She raised her chin, determined. Always determined. Her against the world.

He wondered how many times he'd done the same thing when backed against a wall, in prison and out, when things were at their worst. Even when things were at their best—knowing that could end at any moment. Determination and pride were all he'd had. And it shouldn't be that way for her, he thought. Not now, not ever.

Not that determination was a bad thing; it wasn't. But he hated the circumstances that had robbed her of her innocence. Circumstances he could guess. People making fun of her for her condition. Her parents dying, one after the other. Her uncle abandoning her. Becoming the mother to her sister. Worn down by too many responsibilities. Never able to do the things she wanted.

Rather than allowing her to remove her T-shirt for Pepe, Jase had her change into one of his tanks. He liked seeing her in his clothes. A lot. She pulled down one strap. As Pepe labored on her shoulder and the back of her neck, she continually flinched.

Jase took her hand in his, squeezed. She squeezed back in wordless thanks and cast him a sweet smile.

"You're doing great, honey. Better than I did."

"Oh, yeah? Did you cry?"

"Like a baby." But only the first time. Because he'd been in prison—and he hadn't wanted the tattoo at all. A group of inmates had held him down, given him a gang symbol he'd hated with every fiber of his being, nothing but a representation of humiliation and subjection.

Breath, suddenly coming too fast, too shallow.

Brook Lynn squeezed his hand again, drawing him back to the present. "I wish I had been there," she said softly. "I would have kissed your boo-boo better."

Steady. "Boys don't get boo-boos. They get wounds." He'd since covered the hated tattoo with another one.

"Too bad. I don't kiss wounds. I kiss boo-boos."

"I have a boo-boo," Pepe announced.

"Well, you're about to have a massive, gaping wound," Jase muttered.

Brook Lynn grinned at him.

A pang in his chest. "I like the design you've chosen," he said. Not just the wild strawberries, but the flowers that bloomed on the vines. White petals, yellow centers. Dewy green foliage climbing up the sun-kissed perfection of her skin. It was a bold choice. Unexpected. And undeniably hot as hell.

He wanted to lick every inch of it.

Pepe finished and tried to explain wound care, but Jase kicked him out and told her what to do. The skin was red and swollen and would be sensitive for a few days, and damn, he still couldn't get over how sexy it was—how sexy *she* was.

"Well?" she asked and held up her hair while twirling. "What do you think?"

I think you're seconds away from being tossed on my bed, angel.

On the counter, her phone buzzed, signaling a text had just come in.

He glanced at it out of habit—and did a double take. A curse built inside him, but he held it back.

"That Brad guy just asked you out," he said flatly and handed the phone to her.

"No way. I told him— Wow, he really did," she said.

The exact text read:

Thought I'd take a chance. Haven't been able 2 get U out of my mind. I'm asking YOU this time—would U like 2 go 2 dinner w/me?

Jase stepped into her personal space, realized what he'd done and made himself back off. "What are you going to tell him?"

She blinked at him. "What would you like me to tell him?"

He heard yearning in her voice…

He heard hope…

At the pool, he'd even staked a verbal claim. *Mine.* But there was no way he would allow her to put this on him. While he hated the thought of her with the other man, it wasn't his place to deny her. They weren't in a relationship, weren't even headed in that direction. Later on, she could resent him for interfering.

"Tell him whatever you want," he said, a denial screaming inside his head. What she wanted had better not be Brad.

Something flashed over her expression…something dark, almost haunted—definitely haunting.

She raised her chin. "In that case, I'll tell him yes."

DO SOMETHING STUPID because your pride was pricked—or in Brook Lynn's case, *say* something stupid—and you would have to deal with the consequences.

Why hadn't she just opened up to Jase, told him what she desired? Why had she goaded him, expecting him to prove with action those possessive words he'd once uttered?

She'd backed him into a corner, hoping he would confess his feelings—*I want you all to myself.* While he'd felt comfortable claiming she belonged to him in an intimate setting, he hadn't been ready to say the words during an argument, even if he felt the emotions.

At least, that's how she comforted herself as Brad led her to his car. A '68 Nova he'd restored himself. It looked dated on the outside, but modern on the inside.

"You are beautiful," he said, opening her door for her.

Such a gentlemanly move. *My heart should be fluttering.* "Thank you. You look very handsome yourself."

He drove just outside Strawberry Valley city limits, choosing a high-end restaurant with romantic lighting and soft music playing in the background.

"I hope you like Italian," he said.

"I do." Guilt plagued her as they were seated at their table. She'd gone from kissing Jase to *this.* Leading on the man she should want…but didn't.

A menu was placed in front of her face. She read over it—and tried not to hyperventilate. The prices! Sweet fancy. What did they put in their food? Gold?

Maybe Brad was paying. Maybe he wasn't. Either

way, she would *not* go over twenty dollars. So…it looked as though she would be one of those lame girls who ordered only a side salad and a glass of water.

"What sounds good?" he asked.

"Everything." Truth. But what sounded good and what she would be eating were vastly different things.

He smiled warmly at her.

When the waiter arrived, Brad ordered the fettuccine Alfredo with blackened chicken, and her mouth actually watered. When it was her turn, she forced herself to stick to her plan. Thankfully, Brad merely nodded, as if he was used to women eating like baby birds on a diet.

"How do you like working for the big guy?" Brad asked.

"He is…" *Sexy, thrilling, exciting. A great kisser. Good with his hands.* But she settled on, "Fun. It's a whole new experience for me."

His gaze dipped to the tattoo peeking from the collar of her shirt. "Did he encourage you to get the flowers?"

Did Brad disapprove? "No. That was all me."

"How far does the vine go?" he asked, definitely not disapproving.

She pointed, mapping out the entire span, then changed the subject, asking questions about his life, and he answered without hesitation. Quite a difference from Jase, who seemed to guard his every word.

And yet, she still longed to be with Jase.

The thought caused her guilt to intensify. Here she was with a wonderful man. A man who checked off every box on her Made for Me list. He deserved a fair shot.

She smiled and allowed him to take over the conversation. He asked her about the best gift she'd ever received, the most thoughtful gift she'd ever given and the role model who'd had the biggest influence on her life. She suspected he'd gotten the questions from a dating website, and that, too, should have caused her heart to flutter. So adorable! So sweet! A guy who cared enough to try to impress her.

Though…she tried not to feel as if she was being interviewed for a job and answered as best she could: her happy childhood, a scrapbook she'd made for Jessie Kay, and her parents.

The waiter arrived with the check, and Brad snatched it up.

"Allow me to pay for my portion," she said.

He appeared horrified by the thought. "Absolutely not."

More guilt.

As they walked through the congested parking lot, she drew in a deep breath. The air lacked the sweet scents she was used to, and she experienced a pang of homesickness. Not just for home…but for Jase.

What was he doing right now?

"I had a really nice time tonight," Brad said as they motored down the road.

"Me, too." He would ask her out again, she sensed it. But…even though she'd had fun with him, she didn't want more from him—and she never would. Her attraction to Jase had burned away all thoughts of other men. It was Jase's mouth she craved on hers. Jase's hands she desired on her body. Jase she longed to be with—in bed or out.

That wasn't going to change.

Jessie Kay's car was gone, which meant she wasn't home. Brad parked in the driveway and walked her to her door. On the porch, she paused and faced him.

Light flickered from the lamp, casting muted rays over them both.

"Well," he said.

"Well," she said.

A sudden gust of wind tousled and lifted several locks of her hair. Brad's gaze dropped to her ears automatically.

"They light up," he said, his tone conversational rather than surprised.

"Yes." She righted her hair, suddenly self-conscious. Could no one ever pretend they weren't there?

He leaned down as if he meant to kiss her, as she'd feared, but she backed away. "Good night, Brad."

A flash of disappointment showed on his face before he nodded. "Good night, Brook Lynn."

She stepped inside, closed the door and trudged to her bedroom—where she promptly screamed at the top of her lungs. But she went quiet as soon as she realized the reason for her scream—the strange man standing at the edge of her bed—was Jase.

She threw her purse at him, the heavy bag thumping against his chest. "Jerk! What are you doing here? Where's your car?"

"You once broke into my room, so I thought it only fair that I break into yours. And my car is parked down the street." His arms were crossed. "Why do you look so sad?"

"I think you mean scared." *I'm surprised my heart is still beating.*

"No, I said what I meant. Sad."

She didn't want to discuss her ears right now. "Tell me why you're here, Jase. The real reason. And it better be a good one."

A moment ticked by in silence, tension growing between them.

"Did you kiss him at the door?"

The words were a rasp, lacking any type of emotion. But she went still, not daring to hope. Was he jealous? Would he finally admit it? "That's not any of your business, Jase."

"Oh, it's my business all right, and I'll show you why." Eyes locked on her, he advanced.

CHAPTER SEVENTEEN

JASE BACKED BROOK LYNN into the door, but still he kept coming toward her until he'd pressed his body flush against hers, her breasts smashed into his chest. He'd been possessed by jealousy for hours, and his control had finally snapped.

Actually, the word *jealousy* did not accurately describe the frothing monster that had crawled and clawed through his mind.

Brook Lynn peered up at him with those wide baby blues, as if she couldn't believe what was happening. "I think I'm mad at you," she said, but she didn't sound it. She was too breathless. She flattened her palms on his pecs in an effort to push him back and create distance. "So whatever you're doing, you can just stop."

He remained firmly in place. "Whatever I'm doing? Honey, I'm going crazy for you, that's what the hell I'm doing. And if you think I haven't been trying to stop, *you're* crazy. I've been trying so damn hard, but I've only gotten worse." As the night had progressed, the thought of her with Brad had made Jase foaming-at-the-mouth wild—like a dog with rabies.

He'd imagined them talking and laughing, Brad rubbing his foot against hers under the cover of the table, holding her hand on the drive home, the guy's thumb brushing over the hammering pulse in her wrist, and he'd wanted to punch another wall. But when he'd imagined Brad taking Brook Lynn in his arms and kissing her good-night...Jase had jumped in his car and sped over.

When he'd arrived at their house, Jessie Kay had let him inside and lectured him.

You like my sister more than you liked me. I get it. She's a better person than I am. She's also endured her fair share of heartache and isn't out trolling for more, so you better not treat her like trash afterward, or I will personally separate Big Jase from Little Jase.

Then she'd gone out with a friend of hers and all he could do was watch the clock as he used to do in prison, every second a new level of hell. Finally, he'd heard the purr of a car's engine, seen lights flash through the curtains. When Brad had helped Brook Lynn out and walked her to the porch, Jase had forced himself to move into Brook Lynn's room. It had been that...or storm outside and attack Brad.

The guy might not have survived.

"Well," she said now. "Your attitude is shocking, considering you told me to go out with Brad."

"No. You're not putting this on me. I told you the choice was yours, and you made it." Was that bitterness he heard in his tone? *Get it together.*

"Because I had zero encouragement from you!"

He slapped his hands on the wall on either side of her, caging her in, then rolled his hips forward, brushing his erection between her legs. "Consider this your encouragement."

"That's great, wonderful, but let's just...stop and... and think about this," she said, panting now. "A lot's happened today. Taking time to process isn't a bad idea."

He would give her anything she wanted—except a reprieve. "It's too late for stopping and thinking."

Her eyes widened. "I just went out with another man. I can't…I shouldn't…"

"You're not his—you're mine." He leaned down, putting them nose to nose. "You promised me a night, and I *will* have it."

Those blue, blue eyes got wider. "Jase," she said on a soft sigh, and he pressed his lips to hers, silencing her, feeding her the kiss he'd longed to give her all night— Who the hell was he kidding? The kiss he'd longed to give her since the moment he'd met her. One to brand her soul-deep so that she would never forget him.

She opened for him, not only welcoming his tongue but thrusting her own against his. He tasted mint paired with a hint of fresh strawberries, each spiced with a passion he'd never before known.

"Put your arms around me," he commanded.

She obeyed without hesitation, wrapping one around his neck and the other around his waist, holding him close. Both of her hands trembled as they slid underneath his shirt, reaching bare skin. Breathing became a thing of the past. One simple touch, and yet *she* branded *him*.

He kneaded her breasts, reveled in their heavy weight. "I want your shirt off," he said, already tugging at the material. He ripped her bra in the center—*will buy her a new one*—and bared her from the waist up, flames engulfing his insides. *Gorgeous girl.*

"Your turn," she said, tugging at his shirt.

He jerked the material over his head and dropped it. He meant to kiss her again, needed to, but she stared with rapt fascination at his tattoos and scars.

He saw the question in her eyes and felt he owed her at least a kernel of truth.

"Knife fights," he told her.

"On military raids?" she asked softly, and he couldn't bring himself to nod, to lie to her so boldly. She still thought he was a hero. How would she feel when she discovered he was actually a villain?

"Fighting. Hard living." *In prison. Say it. Tell her.* But he couldn't—not yet. Not with her half-dressed before him, almost ready to be taken.

"They're ugly, I know," he said. He'd covered most of them with ink, but had left a few free. Reminders of what could happen with a single mistake.

"Ugly? When they proclaim just how strong you are? No. But I wonder…did anyone ever kiss these boo-boos and make them better?"

A tightening deep in his gut. "Never."

"Here, let me…" She traced the edge of a scar with her tongue, moving along the map to reach another.

He sizzled, as if she'd stroked him with more of those flames, experiencing a hurt so good his knees shook and threatened to buckle.

She reached his nipple, sucked.

Damn. "Harder, angel."

She did, and he fit his hands on her waist to urge her into a counterclockwise rhythm, brushing her core against his erection. As she gasped with pleasure, he tried to loosen his grip on her, knew he was squeezing too hard, but part of him feared she would float away.

"Jase," she said, need thick in her tone.

Was she already desperate for climax? "Let me take care of you," he said, tearing at the waist of her skirt, dragging it and her white cotton panties down her legs. He crouched, ripped off her sandals and yanked the clothing free. He straightened, but didn't stand, his gaze suddenly riveted on the prettiest little patch of pale curls. He remembered the honey of her taste, and his mouth watered.

"Part for me," he said.

Her hands flattened against the wall as she rolled her hips toward him, seeking, allowing him to lift one of her legs and anchor it over his shoulder. He started at her knee, kissing his way up, up, leaving a trail of moisture in his wake.

"Please, Jase," she whispered. "I want it. Need it."

She wasn't the only one. *Liiick.* Right up her center. She was hot, wet. Sweet. And he nearly came from the taste of her alone.

"Yes, yes, there!" Her scream of rapture echoed through the room, inside his head. "Again. Please."

He sucked on her and bit gently, then a little harder. As he dragged his fingers up, up her leg, she whimpered, begged some more.

He slid two into her wetness, and her back bowed, allowing him to go deeper…so wonderfully deep. Another scream ripped from her as she shot straight into a climax, her inner walls clenching around his fingers. He stilled, no longer kissing her, no longer mimicking the motions of sex with his tongue, but looking up at her—drinking in the pleasure glowing from her features—and waiting.

When she calmed and met his gaze with dazed eyes, he smiled slowly. "I hope you're ready for more. I'm just getting started, angel."

BLISS, RAPTURE…CASCADES of ecstasy. With Jase, Brook Lynn finally understood what everyone was talking about when they raved about sex. This big, strong, fierce man had her pressed against a wall, stripped her, spread her legs and pierced her with two of his fingers, moving them inside her…so amazingly deep…while his tongue took her to heights she'd never dreamed possible.

"Jase." She couldn't *not* gasp his name.

He returned his mouth to her core and continued to taste her. It was beyond erotic, watching him as unending waves of pleasure washed over her. He reached up with his free hand, cupping her breast, plucking at her nipple, and suddenly there was no part of her that couldn't feel some part of him. Everywhere he touched, sensation branched off, traveling through the rest of her.

Consumed, she thought. She'd heard Jessie Kay and Kenna talk about moments with their men when everything else ceased to matter. When a tornado could have dropped from the sky and ravaged everything they owned, but they wouldn't have cared, as long as their lover continued doing what he was doing.

I'm so there.

Jase inserted a third finger, bringing her to another swift and brutal orgasm. And as she gasped and shuddered, he kissed his way up her stomach, laved her nipples and then straightened. His hair stuck out in spikes; her fingers must have plowed through the strands. His eyes were hooded in that way she loved, his lips moist with the essence of her.

More beautiful every time I see him.

Her gaze raked over the rest of him. The scars, testaments to the violence he'd somehow managed to survive. The tattoos she was only beginning to understand. The muscles…*so strong and yet, with a simple touch I can make them tremble.* The long, hard length of him stretching past the waist of his pants, a pearly bead at the tip…

Her heartbeat reminded her of quick flashes of lightning, her blood thundering through her veins. Trembling, she reached for him, drew him closer. The heat he emitted twined around her, making every ache he'd caused a thousand times worse—or better.

"I want inside you," he rasped.

"Inside me," she agreed. "Please."

BURNING FROM THE inside out, Jase picked up Brook Lynn and gently placed her upon the bed. He kicked off his shoes, removed his jeans and underwear. The ache in his shaft had become unbearable, but the sudden freedom from the constraints of his zipper provided only the barest amount of relief.

He crawled up the bed, and she opened for him.

"I *did* buy those ex-large condoms you asked for, just never gave them to you," she said, wrapping her legs around him. "Top drawer in the nightstand."

Smart girl.

But for the first time in his life, he actually resented latex. He wanted to take her bare, feel all of her and let her feel all of him. It startled him. He'd never gone without a condom, and he wouldn't start now.

Next time, however, if she were on the pill…

Next time?

He blindly reached for the foil packet even as he bent his head and thrust his tongue into her mouth. She welcomed him eagerly, sucking and meeting his thrust with one of her own. Her nipples abraded his chest, a delicious friction that only intensified his need for her.

"You crave me, don't you, angel?" He sheathed himself and smoothed the hair from her perspiration-damp cheek. "Ache for me."

Her gaze flickered with a hint of sadness he didn't comprehend before she licked her lips, as if savoring the taste of him. She nodded, saying, "Yes, I do. Please take me."

So polite. So perfect.

Reminding himself that it had been a long time for her, he positioned himself for entry...nearly undone by her heat. He pressed in slowly. Every muscle in his body was tensed, ready for action as sweat trickled from his temples, but he never increased his speed. Her inner walls clamped around him tightly, trying to suck him in, and oh, hell, he'd never felt anything so damn incredible.

"Jase." She clawed at his back, probably drawing blood. "Deeper. Please. I need you deeper."

Hearing this woman beg for his shaft might have been the hottest thing he'd ever heard. Acting on instinct, fueled by a primal need to possess and conquer, to give his woman whatever she desired, he plunged the rest of the way in. Her hips arched, and she cried out, a sound of pleasure and pain.

He thought to stay right where he was, to enjoy the incomparable feel of her, to savor, to give her a chance to acclimate to his invasion, but already the tension building inside him was beginning to be too much, forcing him to move. He pulled out and hovered at the edge of her for a second, two, before plunging back in. She gasped, and there were no vestiges of pain, only pleasure, so he did it again. And again. Faster and faster, until the entire bed rocked with the force of his thrusts.

As he hammered in and out of her, he was pretty sure he lost his mind, but decided he never needed to find it. A pleasure fog had taken its place. He existed for this moment and no other. This woman and no other. She surrounded him—branded him all over again. Consumed him. Owned him.

As she writhed under him, her legs wound tight around his waist, her arms around his neck; her head thrashed from side to side. He stilled her with a kiss. A hard, punishing kiss with teeth, a sharp bite, his body still thrusting, thrusting inside hers.

"Jase. I'm going to…going to…" Her inner walls suddenly clenched on him, tighter and tighter, demanding their due as climax overcame her.

He managed another couple of thrusts before exploding, his own climax pulling a satisfied roar out of him. One that nearly shook the walls. He poured every throb and ache into her, experiencing a moment of perfect peace for the first time in his life.

Utterly spent, he collapsed on top of her. Her arms and legs fell away from him as she struggled to catch her breath. Not wanting to crush her, he rolled to his side.

Usually, this was the moment he jumped out of bed, dressed as if he'd just found out his house was on fire and took off. Tonight he gathered Brook Lynn close, unwilling to let her go. He was simply too tired.

She snuggled up close, resting her head on his chest… where his heart still raced like a freaking freight train.

"That was definitely fun," she said.

"Yes." He combed his fingers through her hair. "Ask me to stay the night," he said, shocking the hell out of himself.

Silence.

He swallowed a curse.

"Stay," she finally whispered.

BROOK LYNN TRIED counting sheep, and when that failed, she tried counting naked men, but one hour ticked into another without favorable results. Sleep continued to elude her.

Why? It had been years since she'd spent the night with a man, and it should have been 1) relaxing 2) comforting or 3) both. But she remained on edge...confused.

Had this truly been a one-time-only event? Or would Jase ask for a repeat?

Just then, she *hated* the plaque she'd given him.

"Why are you tossing and turning, honey?" he asked. "If anyone should have trouble sleeping, it's me."

True. The bed was only a full, and Jase's feet hung over the edge.

"Maybe we should do something to tire each other out," she suggested, tense, waiting for his reaction. *Is this where he'll begin to pull away?*

"Agreed," he said, and she released a breath she hadn't realized she'd been holding. "And I know just the thing." He fluffed the pillows, reclined like the most self-indulgent pasha—and gave her a gentle little shove off the bed. "You're going to dance for me."

She came up sputtering. "What!"

He switched on the bedside lamp. "Your list, remember? You said you wanted to dance for a man. Definitely a lover. Well." He held out his arms, all *behold my magnificence*. "I now qualify on both fronts."

She'd actually written "preferably a boyfriend," but she didn't point that out. "I'm not dancing for you, Jase Hollister."

His eyes narrowed to tiny slits. "You're sure as hell not dancing for anyone else."

The fierceness of his tone made her shiver, warmth spilling into her blood, tingles moving along her sensitized skin. If she did this, he might make love to her again. Or laugh at her.

Another gamble. But the result would answer both of her other questions, wouldn't it. If he laughed, he wasn't worth her time. If he made love to her, he still wanted her.

"Fine," she grumbled. "I'll do it."

His expression mocked her. "That's all well and good, but I already have to deduct points for your attitude."

"You're going to score me?" she gasped out.

He offered her a sad, pitying smile. "Another point lost for a delayed start—and a silly question."

Well, then. She'd have to do something to *earn* points.

"Before I begin," she said, "I should probably lay out the ground rules." Still naked, she sucked on the end of one finger and slowly traced a path down her stomach. "At no point during my *amazing* performance are you allowed to touch me."

His gaze followed the motion of her finger, only to whip up to her face and narrow as her words registered. "Did I forget to mention that every rule you make costs you one thousand points?"

Ha!

"Good thing there's only one rule, then. Ready?"

"Do it."

She began to undulate her hips, giving him a preview of what was to come, and his pupils expanded. "Hands on the headboard, Hollister. I don't trust you to keep them to yourself."

When he failed to comply, she cupped her breasts and pinched her nipples. "I'm about to change my mind," she said.

With a frustrated groan, he grabbed the headboard.

"There's a good boy."

Brook Lynn undulated her hips again…more slowly… slllooowly…

A sheen of sweat glistened on Jase's forehead, and his knuckles bleached of color. "I'm giving you a point for technique."

Turning, revealing her backside, she glanced over her shoulder and lifted her hair...let the strands tumble back into place. "Only one?"

Bad-boy Jase released the headboard long enough to cup his now-rock-hard length. "Look at what you've done to me, angel."

"And I'm just getting started." Brook Lynn bent over and slowly lifted her upper body, her gaze never leaving Jase. She heard an erotic melody in her head, though no music played, and moved to it. Bump, bump...griiind. Her hands roved over her curves, kneaded her breasts.

"Come here," he rasped. "Please, angel. I need you."

She didn't have the strength to resist. She crawled up the bed, rhythmically shimmying closer and closer to his erection before retreating. Another groan rose from him. On her knees, she continued to move her hips, sliding her hands down...down...between her legs.

"Let me touch," he rasped. "I *need* to touch."

Roll...roll...she worked her way around, so that he once again had a backside view. Roll...roll...

"Angel, please." He leaned forward, warm breath fanning down her spine. His tongue flicked out, stroking over her nape, and the contact sent shivers through her body.

"How many points have I gained now?" she asked, heart drumming a wild staccato in her chest.

"All of them."

She glanced over her shoulder. His features were taut, the fine lines around his eyes more noticeable, his lips pulled tight. A bead of sweat trickled down his temple. Knowing she affected him so strongly empowered her, and she tangled her fingers in her hair, raised her arms high in the air. She swayed her hips left, right, all the way around, always rubbing against him, as her hair fell back into place.

The beat in her head quickened, and so did her motions. Faster and faster, hardness to softness, flesh against flesh. Her breaths came faster, too. Her heartbeat. A moan from her. A groan from him.

Faster...faster... Her every nerve ending ached, tingling.

"Brook Lynn, you have to stop. I have to have you." His palms gripped her waist. He pushed her forward, to her hands and knees, and positioned himself behind her. Her hair fell over one shoulder, leaving the other bare.

The implants!

She stiffened, but he leaned forward and kissed the shell of her ear, like he'd done before, careful not to put any pressure on the implant itself, and slowly she relaxed. He didn't mind the bulky plastic and flashing lights, she realized. Didn't think she was a Frankenlynn freak.

"Please, angel. You are so beautiful," he whispered. "So damn perfect in every way."

The words titillated her more than his kiss, more than his touch. "Inside me," she said, her body aching as if it had never been filled. "Now."

"I'm going to make you feel so good, angel."

And he did.

CHAPTER EIGHTEEN

BROOK LYNN WOKE up bright and early—and alone. The
spot where Jase had lain was no longer warm, which
meant he'd been gone for a while. His clothes were no
longer scattered across her floor, either.

She pulled on a robe and checked the rest of the
house. No sign of him. She checked the driveway, only
to remember he'd parked his car down the street and she
wouldn't have seen it even if he'd been here.

It didn't matter, really. He was gone, no question.
Should have expected this.

And it was probably for the best. The thought of Jase
having breakfast with her and her sister bothered her.

Dang it. She would have to get over that. She wanted
them both in her life and—

Sweet! A wealth of happiness hit her when she spotted a note on the kitchen table.

> Dude. Thought I'd be safe coming home after
> midnight, but noooooooo. Could you have been
> ANY louder? Next time Jase comes over I'm stay-
> ing with Sunny. Love, Queen JK (Former Miss
> Strawberry or not, I'm still royalty.)

Her cheeks burned with embarrassment and mounting anger. Not with her sister, but with Jase. She'd expected the note to be from him, and now, knowing it

wasn't, she realized she *deserved* a note, at the very least.

After his bout of jealousy and his desire to spend the night with her, well...*I thought I was different to him.*

Clearly, she'd thought wrong.

She showered and dressed for work, doing nothing special with her appearance. No makeup. Not styling her hair. Clothes: a ratty T-shirt that read Zombies Hate Fast Food and jean shorts. Jase could suck it.

As she drove to his house, a car she didn't recognize pulled up behind her, riding too close to her bumper. No big deal, until the car followed her for a pretty good distance, taking the turns she took, slowing when she slowed. But...she had to be mistaken. Why follow *her*? Frowning, she took a turn she didn't need to make, and sure enough, the four-door sedan with the tinted windows stayed right on her tail. Not just right on her tail, but actually giving it a light tap.

A thousand horror stories seemed to play through her mind at once. Namely: a serial killer had targeted her as his next victim and purposely causing car wrecks was his MO. No way she'd stop to exchange insurance info with the driver. Heart speeding up, she debated between leading a potential psycho to Jase—and putting him in danger—or making the longer journey to the sheriff's office.

Another tap made her decision for her. The sheriff. Definitely the sheriff. But as she took the next turn, the car honked and sped around her, its tires squealing.

She released a relieved breath and made a mental note to be on the lookout for the sedan next time she was out and about. Being in a hurry was no excuse for such aggressive driving.

She backtracked, finally heading into the acreage.

By the time she arrived, her shaking had stopped, at least. "Jase," she called as she stepped through the door.

"He's not here," West said.

He and Beck were reclined on the couch. They'd clearly been waiting for her. As she dropped her purse on the coffee table, Beck pressed a button on the remote and turned off the football game, the TV screen going blank.

"I don't know what happened between you and Jase," West said, "and honestly, I don't want to know."

"But we're not stupid," Beck added. "We can guess."

Limbs heavy, Brook Lynn trudged to a chair and eased down. Their words could mean only one thing, and it calmed her down significantly. "He's freaking out right now, isn't he?"

West inclined his head. "He came stomping in at four this morning. Woke me up. I found him in the kitchen, pounding back Red Bull and pacing. We talked, and for hours he watched the clock, waiting for the moment you would arrive. But then something snapped inside him, and he said he had to get some supplies in town. He beat feet."

Good. A freak-out meant some part of him cared for her more than he'd realized—he just didn't want to admit it. "Has he never done a relationship before?" she asked.

"One," Beck admitted. "They were together for two years."

Hate her already. "Why'd they break up?"

West propped his feet on the coffee table, saying, "Jase will have to give you those details."

Even as curious as she was, she liked that they were unwilling to share details about their friend. Proved their loyalty. But she needed intel, dang it. "What *will* you tell me? Because I've got some decisions to make.

Like how to handle him, how to handle *us*. If we've got a chance for a future, or if I should just throw in the towel now, before either of us gets hurt." And by *either of us*, she totally meant *I*.

The guys shared a look, and Beck nodded.

West sighed and said, "He's had a hard life. Been betrayed by everyone he's ever loved. Including us."

She blinked in surprise. "How did you—"

"Again, those are details he'll have to give you," Beck interjected.

She nodded in understanding—or, pretend understanding—then motioned for West to continue.

"I've never seen him so worked up about a woman, and I don't know what to think about it." West pegged her with a hard stare. "He looks as tough as iron, but he's actually as fragile as glass. If you want him, you'll have to fight for him. But if you don't think you can handle a few internal battle wounds, it'll be better for him if you let him go now rather than later."

Oh, she could handle a few battle wounds. She'd never been as intensely attracted to a man as she was to Jase. She'd never before given herself so fully to one's possession. And she wanted more, definitely. But could a happily-ever-after be based solely on lust and sex? No.

What would a future with him entail? Those rare smiles that lit his entire face…the rusty sound of laughter only she seemed capable of summoning…a quirky wit that perfectly matched her own…unconditional acceptance for who and what she was…

Would he ever be interested in marriage? What about a family? Both were important to her.

But did she really want marriage if she wasn't sure it was with the right man? Was a family already set up for failure if the right couple wasn't at its helm?

Being with Jase would be a big-time gamble. He could decide he was done with her at any time and walk away. But so could anyone else. He was her boss, and being with him could backfire and make her feel like a whore. He could fire her if things didn't work out. Or, even worse, he could keep her on, and she would have to see him with other women.

But he could also fall head over heels in love with her...

How awesome would *that* be? She could touch him anytime the urge hit...hug him and kiss him, comfort him...take care of him while he took care of her... shiver as he offered her a smile designed for her and her alone...

She squared her shoulders. "I'll fight for him," she announced. Jase angered and frustrated her, yes, but he also fascinated and delighted her. "I need you to listen to this next part and heed it. I'll do it my way. You two aren't to interfere. No matter what I say or do. Got it?"

SEVEN DAYS.

Seven miserable days.

That's how long ago Jase had woken up in Brook Lynn's bed, her naked body curled around him. He'd experienced such bliss. Such...contentment. Like nothing else he'd ever known. But then the familiar fear that it couldn't—wouldn't—last had intruded, and panic had set in.

He'd left her, basically running for his life, thinking a little time away from her would put him back on track, strengthen his resolve to remain alone and detached... but he'd only grown to want her more.

Gritting his teeth, Jase toyed with the strawberry charm she'd given him. The one she'd made. He'd removed Jessie Kay's photo and now carried it every-where, a reminder of what he shouldn't want…but couldn't resist.

To be honest, it wasn't just sexual things he craved from Brook Lynn. It was her as a person. He was so much more…complete when they were together. She met needs he hadn't known he'd had.

If he was fire, she was water. If he was dark, she was light. She wasn't afraid to tease him, to let down her guard with him, and she actually seemed to *enjoy* him. But he hadn't come clean about his past. She deserved to know who he was—what he was—before they went any further. If she even wanted to go further. That damn contract.

He stood in the kitchen, watching as she straight-ened couch cushions in the living room. The hem of her summer dress was too short, lifting with every move she made, revealing an indecent amount of trim, tanned thigh… *One nibble wouldn't hurt either of us…*

She caught his gaze and, with a smile trying to form, said, "Oh! I forgot to tell you today's affirmation. Are you ready?"

He forced himself to nod.

"I am both dominating and submissive at the same time."

Taunting me?

He'd take the abuse and then some. He deserved it.

He just couldn't go on like this. He had to talk to her, admit to his feelings and his past so they could move on—the facts were like obstacles, so many in their way. And if they couldn't move on, he'd have to come to terms with it; at least the mental torment would finally end.

He stalked toward her, determined to confess all. Maybe.

"I promised I'd help you with your list," he found himself saying instead. "It's time to check off another item."

She stepped back, maintaining a certain amount of distance between them. "I already planned to check something off today," she said. "I'm attending a wine-and-cheese tasting later."

"I'll take you."

She beamed at him. "Thank you. I'd like that."

Relief coursed through him as he realized she wasn't going to yell at him for the juvenile stunt he'd pulled, leaving her house in the middle of the night—or his even worse treatment afterward. One obstacle dodged, at least, and as easily as a blink.

He reeled. He'd always thought his life merely moved from one crap experience to the next, but just then, he couldn't deny how blessed he actually was. He'd found a beautiful girl with a big heart, and she genuinely seemed to care about him.

He pretended to work as he watched the clock. *In just a few hours, we'll be alone in a car.*

Not soon enough.

Time seemed to tick by slower than ever before, but finally the clock did zero out, and they headed into the city. Being so close to her rekindled the fire only she was able to stoke, and he had two choices. Grip the wheel or reach for her. He gripped the wheel.

"Have you ever been to one of these?" she asked.

"No." The closest he'd come to a "tasting" was the toilet-brew one of his cellmates had offered him. Declining had been a no-brainer. "What made you want to try it?"

"My parents went to one. They came home tipsy, giggling and kissing, unable to keep their hands off each other. My mom even danced around the room, grinning so big, saying she'd never had so much fun."

Wine and cheese just became my new best friends.

They reached the three-thousand-square-foot warehouse where the event was taking place, and he quickly found a spot in the gravel, parking and racing around the car to open her door for her. He even took her hand to lead her inside the barn where the tasting was to take place, touching her at last, barely stifling the urge to kiss her knuckles. There were several other couples milling around, studying the different bottles of wine on display and countless shelves of cheese. The smell in the room was pungent but sweet.

Multiple tables formed three rows. Candles glowed in the center of each, with trays of bite-size cheese plated in front of every chair. Throughout the room, display cases were lit from within to make crystal glasses glisten like diamonds.

"Rustic meets romantic." Brook Lynn breathed deeply as she took everything in. "It's amazing."

You are amazing.

During the next hour, he was forced to endure speeches from the family of owners, each taking turns to explain every single nuance of the different cheeses and wines. Jase barely tasted the things he put inside his mouth. He wasn't sure how he stopped himself from pulling Brook Lynn into a dark corner, ripping open her shorts and her panties and taking what he craved more than breath. Actually, that wasn't true. He did know. She was having such an amazing time, he refused to end it. She grinned without ceasing, listened intently and participated every step of the way, even forgetting her inhibitions and hooking locks of hair behind her ears.

His chest puffed with pride. He liked those implants. They helped her. Why be embarrassed about that? He loved that her confidence had grown by leaps and bounds, and he couldn't help but feel he'd had something to do with it.

"—poor girl," the woman to his right said to her companion. She wasn't quiet about it, either, and she should have known better. She was in her midthirties. "I wonder what's wrong. To have to live with machines in her ears like that…well, it must be miserable."

For the first time since they'd arrived, Brook Lynn stiffened. The bright light drained from her eyes. She hurriedly unhooked her hair from behind her ears.

Jase went still and quiet—a dangerous thing. He knew it and tried to temper the storm brewing inside him.

Too late. Lightning struck his mind. Thunder boomed in his heart. The ceramic plate he held snapped in two, sharp stings erupting in his hands, warm trickles of blood dripping to the floor.

His switch had just been flipped.

He stalked toward the woman whose careless words had cut through Brook Lynn's hard-won self-confidence. He'd never hit a female before, and he wouldn't start today, but she was with a man and he'd do.

In the back of Jase's mind, a warning screamed. *Don't do this. You'll get in serious trouble with your PO.* But the scream wasn't loud enough to overshadow the rage. Someone had to pay.

The couple noticed him, paled and backed away. He kept coming.

Soft fingers suddenly wrapped around his biceps, a

touch he recognized. He jolted out of the darkness of his thoughts and stopped.

"Jase." Different degrees of upset and fear layered Brook Lynn's voice.

He whipped around. Eyes of baby blue peered up at him with concern.

"I want to leave," she said. "Let's leave. All right?"

Leave? Inside him, two needs warred. To punish those who'd hurt her...or to please her.

No contest. He gathered her in his arms and led her outside.

"I'm sorry," she said as soon as they reached the car. "I'm sorry I ruined everything."

Confused, he pinned her against the hood. "You didn't ruin anything. Why would you think you did?"

"My ears—"

"Were not the problem." Jase cupped her cheeks, his thumbs caressing back and forth. "There is nothing wrong with you, angel. You are the most perfect person I've ever met and those implants are a part of you. I think they're as sexy as you are."

Her eyes widened with every word, her breathing coming faster.

"I was about to lose my temper in there," he said. "I wanted to hurt the woman for hurting you. I wouldn't have hit her, but I would have hit the guy with her. So if anyone is to blame for ruining everything, it's me." And he needed to make up for it.

He scanned the distance. Across the street was a barn with a flashing sign over the roof, advertising gourmet desserts.

"Hungry?" he asked.

"Yes, actually."

"Come on."

A bell chimed over the door as they entered. There were more customers than he had expected for this early in the day, but he understood why they were there. The scent of coffee and chocolate laced the air, combining into an irresistible summoning finger.

Brook Lynn squealed with delight as she studied the contents of the display case. "Did we pass through the pearly gates and I just don't remember? This has to be heaven."

"What can I get you?" the young girl behind the counter asked.

As Brook Lynn continued to study the case, the light in her eyes dimmed all over again. She straightened, cleared her throat and tugged at the collar of her shirt. "Um, just water for me, thanks."

"What's wrong?" he asked her. "Don't you dare tell me you starve yourself to stay thin or I swear I'll tie you to my bed and force-feed you Twinkies and Ho Hos for a week." Maybe a few other things, as well.

"Trust me, I never purposely starve myself." Her cheeks paled as she looked up at him and whispered, "Jase, the desserts are over five dollars each."

She would deprive herself of a treat over five measly dollars? He'd taken this woman under his care—an angel who should never lack for anything—and yet she still struggled with money issues. He wanted to fall at her feet and offer everything he had, everything he would *ever* have. She shouldn't have to scrimp and save and miss out on little pleasures while he had millions he hadn't really earned sitting in the bank.

"We'll have one of everything," he announced.

Brook Lynn gasped and squeezed his wrists. Then she laughed nervously, saying to the salesgirl, "He's kidding. Of course he's kidding."

"I wasn't fuc—freaking kidding," he said. "One of everything."

The girl rushed to obey him, and within minutes, he had Brook Lynn and three large boxes at a table in the back of the shop.

"Eat," he said.

She peered at the plethora of desserts with ravaging hunger in her eyes. "I shouldn't take advantage of your generosity."

"Why? I offered. No advantage will be taken."

"Actually, yes, there will be. I have a rule. If I won't buy it for myself, I can't in good conscience allow someone else to buy it for me."

This girl and her rules. He pushed a box in her direction. "Eat, or I start buying more."

"That's blackmail."

"I'm glad you recognize that. But, Brook Lynn? I'm capable of much worse."

"Well…" Trembling, she reached out only to curl her fingers and draw back. "No. I can't control you, but I can control myself."

With calculated intent, he withdrew a warm brownie square and bit off half. She watched him, licking her lips, her pupils dilating. When he held the dessert out to her, she opened her mouth to rebuke him, and he fed her the remaining half. Her eyes closed in surrender, and she moaned in delight.

His body reacted instantly, hardening, readying—always readying for her. He had to touch her, even in the smallest way. He grabbed the edge of her chair and scooted her closer to him, until their thighs brushed together. Contract burned oh, so good.

She swallowed. "Jase." Her tone was firm.

His eyes narrowed. "Brook Lynn."

"Your actions right now are confusing me," she said, her trembling intensifying. "You had your one night. What is it you want from me?"

I want to keep you at a distance, yet hold you close. I want to give you everything and yet nothing.

I want a right to scare every other man away from you.

I want to tell you my secrets.

"I want another night with you."

BROOK LYNN DID her best to hide her elation. Her efforts to tempt and hook Jase had finally paid off.

He was trying to take care of her and had just admitted he wanted to be with her again. Both were steps in the right direction. He had feelings for her—he must. But he wanted only one more night, which sliced into her happiness. She couldn't settle for so little when she knew an entire future with him was possible.

Although...he'd certainly raised a red flag today—that temper of his wasn't just tethered to the past. He would have fought a stranger for no real reason. It concerned her, especially considering what had happened in his backyard the day he'd cut his hand. But he'd calmed himself down, so it wasn't as if he couldn't control it. And it wasn't as if she didn't have a temper of her own.

"I want you, Jase, I do, but I have to decline your offer. I'm no longer interested in a short-term fling." Her aching body shrieked in protest, the hussy. *Have some self-control!* "I'd like a commitment from you."

His features blanked in an instant, hiding his emotions. "I see."

No, no, he didn't. But he would—she would make sure of it. "If you ever decide you want something meaningful, we'll talk. Until then, I consider you a dear friend."

"A friend," he repeated.

"Yes." She sipped her water, watching him through the shield of her lashes—*want more for me and yourself. Please.*

He ran his tongue over his teeth, peering at her as he gripped the edge of the table, his knuckles leaching of color.

She let herself imagine he was thinking the things she prayed he was thinking. *Don't reach out. Don't grab her and carry her away to do naughty things to her. Do something to change her mind.*

A girl could dream.

Fight for me, Jase Hollister. Fight for us.

He released the table and settled back in his chair. "How are plans coming for Tessa's party?" he finally asked, and once again it was business as usual, his emotions well hidden.

Disappointment proved as swift and brutal as a tidal wave—*made a play, got shot down*—but somehow she found the resolve to forge ahead as if she hadn't a care. "As well as can be expected, all things considered. But I've been wondering. If Tessa is gone, why are you guys throwing a party for her?"

He pushed his chair to the other side of the table, creating physical distance between them again. A metaphor for the emotional distance he hoped to obtain? "We'd like to give her the celebration West promised her just before she died."

Ohhhh. How amazingly sweet and yet utterly heart-breaking.

Brook Lynn toyed with the edge of the dessert box. "How did you, West and Beck meet her?" The few times she'd asked about his past, Jase had given her the bare minimum or shut her down completely. But they were closer now. Had she breached at least one of his many walls?

He looked past her, saying, "We were in foster care. Me, West and Beck. We ended up in the same house, and she lived down the street."

"How long were you in foster care?" Brook Lynn had known about his time in the system, and more and more she hated the thought of him being shuffled from one home to another, losing everything he'd managed to build: friendships, family, even clothes and toys.

Tone deadened, he said, "From the age of six to the day of my sixteenth birthday, when I returned to the house I'd been staying at and found my stuff packed in a garbage bag, waiting on the porch. I was supposed to go to a new home but got myself emancipated and found a place with West and Beck."

Oh…hell. She reached out, wrapped her fingers around his.

"Don't feel sorry for me," he snapped, jerking back to sever contact.

Proceed with caution. "There's a difference between pity and sympathy," she said softly.

"You're right." The fire in his eyes gradually cooled. He drew in a deep breath, slowly released it then reached out and took her hand. "A lot of kids had it worse. At least I had food, shelter."

"But what of love?" Brook Lynn had enjoyed her parents' love, not to mention Jessie Kay's love, and both had been necessary for her survival.

"You have a soft, tender heart," Jase grumbled.

"Yes, but I also have a mean streak," she reminded him.

His beautiful mouth curved into a smile, making her

heart skip a beat. "Don't worry, angel. I'll never forget. But I should probably ask around town, find out what else you've done while worked into a temper."

"Don't you dare!" They'd tell him about the time she and Jessie Kay fell into a vat of strawberry jam—and kept fighting. The time they'd both stood at the top of the courthouse and shouted humiliating facts about each other.

Jessie Kay sometimes laughs so hard, she farts.

Brook Lynn thought a vibrator was Harry Potter's magic wand.

"Oh, honey. You shouldn't ever dare me like that. Now I *have* to know what else you've done."

She leaned toward him, saying, "Why aren't you defending my sweetness? It wasn't too long ago that you praised me for it." In bed. Did he remember?

His gaze dipped to her lips and heated. Oh, yes. He remembered. "You are sweet, that's for sure."

Shivers drifted through her, and she had to force herself to lean as far away from him as she could get without actually running out of the store. *Eye on the prize.*

"The mean streak really only shows up when I'm dealing with Jessie Kay," she said, getting them back on track, "so I guess you're safe enough."

He rubbed two fingers over his jaw. "You care about her more than you care about anyone else."

"Yes. I don't want her to end up like our uncle Kurt."

"Tell me about him."

If I want him to open up to me, it's only fair I open up to him. "He was a con man to the max, but I already told you that. He was charming and yet awful. He would teach us terrible things but make us laugh all the while. At the end of the day, nothing mattered more than money to him. He lived and breathed it, every word and action meant to get more of it. And now, looking back, I can see Jessie Kay and I were extremely blessed that he left. One day he would have run out of cash, and I don't think he would have hesitated to use us in a worse way to get it."

"Do you hate him?"

"No. You know the saying? Hating someone is like swallowing a mouthful of poison and expecting *them* to die. It's a wasted emotion. But that doesn't mean I'd want anything to do with him if he were still alive. He was a criminal… *He* was poison."

"I'm glad he's gone." Jase went quiet, stiff. His motions were clipped as he gathered the boxes of desserts. "We should go."

"But why?" she asked, baffled. Why the abrupt change in him?

He said nothing more as he left the shop. His stride was longer than hers, and she had to run to keep up.

"Jase?"

Again, nothing. He held open her car door, and she slipped inside. When the slam registered, sealing her inside, she had the sinking feeling the action was as symbolic as what he'd done with the chairs. That he hadn't just shut the car door; he'd shut the door on their relationship.

CHAPTER NINETEEN

JASE HAD REACHED a breaking point. When Brook Lynn had voiced her uncle's crimes, he'd known beyond any doubt that she would never be able to accept what *he* had done. He was by far the worse criminal.

Panic had clawed at him. He'd fought to keep people out of his heart most of his life, and yet she had been inching her way inside. How would he react to her loss?

A cold sweat beaded over the back of his neck. He scrubbed a hand down his face, barely able to breathe. She'd made it more than clear she would enter into a relationship with him, become his exclusively. If he agreed, he absolutely could not keep his past hidden. He'd already known that, but now the truth was like a nail in his chest. It was a guarantee he'd lose her sooner rather than later.

For the next week, they barely spoke to each other. He watched her, and he wanted her…ached for her. She seemed unaffected, going about her chores with barely a glance in his direction.

His mood grew darker and darker, until something finally snapped inside him. She'd turned down another night with him, but that didn't mean he couldn't work to change her mind. The benefits without the label or the necessary heart-to-heart.

By the time she arrived for work the next morning,

he'd already rearranged the living room, creating space for the next item on her fun list.

"What's going on?" she asked as she stepped inside the house.

Getting my hands on you any way I can. "You're about to learn how to defend yourself against a zombie attack."

"Really?" Excited, she jumped up and down. "Kenna is going to be so jealous."

As her breasts jiggled with her movement, his hands fisted at his sides.

"Come here." He motioned her over.

Sweet, luscious Brook Lynn waltzed over without a care, not realizing he was a powder keg set to explode. "This is so thrilling," she said.

You have no idea, angel. But you will. Soon.

"You're a beginner, but I'm still going to start you off with an expert move." *Fastest way to get you under me.* "You're going to pretend I'm a zombie," he said. When she nodded, he added, "I've just snuck up on you, intending to eat you." *One tasty bite at a time.* "What do you do?"

She thought for a moment, frowned. "How did you sneak up on me? You're in front of me."

"I'm crafty. Now put your hand on my neck."

Her features wrinkled up. "*Touch* you? But your flesh is so rotted I can see bone, and you smell like a maggot farm."

May not be as cut-and-dried as I'd hoped. The thought of rotting flesh didn't actually set a romantic mood.

"Besides, why aren't I running away?" she demanded. "Every zombie survival guide I've ever read says the first thing to do is run and hide."

Should have gone with Cinderella for a day. "I think I remember you telling me you plan to cut off heads, not run. And I snuck up on you, remember? I've grabbed hold of your shirt. You *can't* run away."

"Are there other zombies around us?" She actually twisted left and right to scan the room.

"No. It's just us." No zombies...and no humans. Last night, Jase had told West and Beck to beat it bright and early and not come back till after dinner.

"Well, what happened to the others? Zombies always run in packs. And do I have a weapon? Jase!" she said, as if the key to world peace had just struck her. "I have to have a sword. If the zombie apocalypse has just happened, I would never leave my base camp without one."

If a zombie apocalypse had happened, Jase would have already tied her to his bed. And for a moment, he kinda wished it *would* happen. He would be able to protect her, care for her, see to her every need—and she would want to be with him, no matter his past, because she would recognize that he and he alone stood between her and certain disaster.

I'm more messed up than I realized.

"Do you want to learn to fight or not?" he asked. "Put your hand on my throat."

"Fine." She wrapped her fingers gently around him. "Like this?"

The heat of her skin...the softness... "Only use one hand," he instructed with more force than he'd intended. "It's merely to hold me back." *Though I only want to be closer to you.* "Next you're going to hook one of your legs behind one of mine."

She did—and it caused her hips to arch forward, her core pressing against his erection. If she noticed the intensity of his arousal, she gave no— Scratch that. She noticed. Her breath hitched, and her eyelids grew heavy.

"Jase," she said.

"Apply pressure to my calf, pulling my lower half toward yours, while pushing my upper body back with the hand on my neck."

Her leg jerked against his.

"Ineffective," he said. "Do it harder."

She tried again, and when that failed, she tried a third time, using all of her strength. He finally teetered backward, but he had a grip on her T-shirt and dragged her down with him. They landed on the couch. Jase bounced with Brook Lynn poised over him.

Gasping, she sat up to straddle his waist. "Um, you may not have realized this, but your move comes with a fatal flaw. If you were a real zombie, I'd already be dinner."

"Well," he said, running his hands up her sides. "I *am* hungry…and I definitely think you'd make a tasty snack."

Her nails dug into his chest. "This is—"

"What we both need? I agree." He pushed his hands down the back of her shorts, past panty to skin. Goose bumps broke out underneath his palms as he urged her into a slow grind against him…

"Well, what do we have here?" Beck asked.

With a squeal, Brook Lynn leaped to her feet. Jase cursed under his breath and eased to his.

"Um, I'll get to work now," Brook Lynn said and rushed into the kitchen.

Jase glared at Beck. "You're supposed to be gone."

Beck glared right back. "I planned to leave as soon as I'd eaten the strawberry waffles Brook Lynn promised me. If you'd never had her cook for us, I would have left sooner. This is on you, my friend."

"Last night you agreed to go *before* breakfast."

Beck scratched his chest. "Did I?"

Jackass! "If you want the room the way it was, you'll have to rearrange the furniture yourself," he grumbled, then stormed to the gym he'd just finished building at the back of the house. All he had left to do was put the equipment together. But as one hour bled into two, the physical exertion failed to calm him. His body remained revved.

He heard Beck and Brook Lynn...laughing? He tensed. When the suspected laughter turned to definite arguing, he threw down the wrench and stalked down the hall. No way he would allow Beck to intimidate—

"—got to make him beg for it, the way he's making *you* beg for it," Beck was saying. "But you were seconds away from going all-in."

"Keep your voice down," Brook Lynn whispered. "And don't you remember? I do this my way."

Jase stopped. Do *what* her way?

Seconds away from going all-in...

Make him beg for it...

Sex?

His heart hammered wildly. He quickened his pace, ready to yell—

But then he paused. If Brook Lynn wanted him enough to work for him, she might want him enough to keep him—despite everything. A heavy burden seemed to lift from his shoulders. He backtracked, returning to the gym. He had to think, make a few decisions. Because once he took the next step—once *he* went all-in—there would be no going back.

BROOK LYNN PACED inside her bedroom. She'd turned her implants to silent so she could reflect in peace.

After Zombie Fighting 101, Jase had disappeared into the gym. He'd stayed there for several hours, and when he'd finally emerged, he'd acted weird. Almost... *happy*. Why?

Because Beck had stopped them from going all the way? Or because Brook Lynn had almost given in to Jase's advances without insisting on a commitment?

She turned—gasping when she saw that Jessie Kay stood in her doorway.

"You've got to tell your man to stop throwing rocks," her sister said.

"What are you talking about?" Brook Lynn asked, switching the implants on.

Jessie Kay motioned to the window with a tilt of her chin. "See for yourself. Jase has done gone eighties heartthrob on us," she said and shut the door.

Frowning—even while her heart hammered against her ribs—Brook Lynn padded to the window. *Clink.* A rock hit the glass as she parted the curtains.

Outside, Jase stepped into a pool of light...and utterly stole her breath. The man who'd turned her world upside down wore a black T-shirt that hugged every one of his muscles and a pair of jeans almost as dark. He'd recently showered, his dark hair damp and plastered around his face.

Her heart pounded a thousand times faster as she lifted the pane. A dog barked in the background. A car's headlights illuminated the man who'd obsessed her further before fading away.

"What are you doing here?" she demanded in a whisper-yell, praying she wouldn't wake the neighbors who were an acre away.

"A romantic gesture." He moved to the sill and crossed his arms over the bottom frame, leaning in.

Brook Lynn took a step back as bumblebees took flight inside her stomach. "Why are you making a romantic gesture?"

"Because I want you."

A flare of disappointment. *Not this again.* "You've said that before."

"All right, then, how about this?" His eyes glittered like freshly polished emeralds, snaring her. "You are gorgeous, Brook Lynn, and you are sweet. You are protective and loyal. I've never seen anyone care for her family the way you care for yours. It's admirable, and I want to be part of that family. I want more from you."

She rubbed her chest in an attempt to dull the ache his words had caused. "I—I've heard that last part, too."

His gaze slid over her and heated. "I'm happiest when you're nearby. You make me smile and laugh. Do you know how tough that is to do? You make me want to be worthy of more...of better. You make me want to hold on to you, hold on to what we have, and never let go."

Her knees threatened to melt. *Can't jump into his arms. Must proceed with caution.* "But...you're my boss."

"And I want to be your man. I can be both. Boss by day, boyfriend by night."

Boyfriend. He'd put a label on it.

He was deadly serious about this.

"Yes," she said, tremors running through her. "Yes, I want that. Want you."

She expected him to smile. She'd just given him the green light. But he frowned, confusing her.

"Don't agree just yet. There are things you don't know about me," he said, taking her hand, linking their fingers, gripping her almost painfully, as if he feared she would try to jerk away. "Things about my past. Things you're not going to like and that I don't want to tell you. Things that might even scare you. But I hope you'll give me a chance to explain anyway."

A tremor moved through him and into her. He'd never—never—looked at her like this, as if there really had been a zombie-virus outbreak, and he had to be the one to tell her. Her mouth went dry. What could be so bad?

Car lights flashed yet again, and in the light she caught a glimpse of his guilt, regret and sorrow, emotions he couldn't hide.

"Did you chop up an old girlfriend and put her in your freezer?" she asked easily.

"No," he rushed out. "Never."

"Are you sick or dying?"

"No."

"Do you kick puppies in your spare time?"

"No."

"Then I don't need to know. Yet." They'd just decided to try for more. The bonds between them were fragile, easily breakable.

"But—"

"Jase," she said softly, tracing her fingers over the hand holding hers. "It's okay. Really." At the moment, he only wanted to tell her because he felt he *had to*, and that's not what she wanted from him, or for him. One day he would realize sharing their pasts was a way to grow closer. But until then, he would only feel pressured, forced or coerced. They might be over before they started. "I know the man you are *now*, and I like him."

He expelled a breath, brought her hand to his mouth

and kissed her knuckles. His tongue stroked her skin, and heat only he could ignite spread through her.

"I should warn you," he said, gaze locked on her. "I might not want to chop you up and put you in my freezer, but I'm a little obsessed with you. I want you to be mine fully. Mine to touch. Mine to taste and to strip and play with. And I will do so. Often."

Was he trying to prepare her or scare her off? Well, news flash. He'd failed to scare her. She only wanted him more. To be the center of his attention, to be the object of his attraction—yes.

"No one else can have you," he said.

"Will *you* see other people?" she asked. "Because that would be a deal breaker."

"Hell, no. There is only one woman I desire, and I'm outside her window, waiting to be invited in."

Oh, this man. Tenderness welled inside her. "I would invite you in *so hard*, but Jessie Kay is here and the walls are thin."

"I can be quiet. The noise problem is all you, honey." He offered a sweet, sexy grin that weakened her knees. "Brought you a present."

"For me?"

"Yes, you." He dug into his pockets and pulled out handfuls of ripped paper. "Your contract had to go," he said, "and a new one had to be drafted." He lifted an eight-by-eight frame he must have propped against the house before he'd started throwing those rocks.

She peered down and read, "'I, Jase Hollister, give Brook Lynn Dillon all the nights, mornings and afternoons she so desperately desires. I'm in this thing long-term.'"

He was giving her more than she could ever have hoped. Happy tears stung her eyes as she set the plaque down and cupped his cheeks, her thumbs stroking over his stubble. "Get in here. Your presence isn't invited—it's commanded."

He took her hands, squeezed. "You get to command me now? That's how this works?"

"Yes," she said and heard rustling in nearby bushes. She moved aside so Jase could climb into the bedroom, in case wild animals were out scavenging. When he stood before her, she closed and covered the window and gripped the hem of his shirt, ready to tug the material over his head. "But don't worry. You'll soon be thanking me."

NAKED AND SATED, Brook Lynn snuggled into the warmth and security of Jase's hard body. They'd gone at it like animals, dozed and then gone at it again. And the sex had been amazing, just as before. But—

I'm such a slag, adding a but.

But. Since they'd committed to each other, she'd expected something…more. More intimate. More meaningful. More emotional than physical.

I'm seriously complaining about four orgasms? I think I can hear women all over the world cocking their guns to shoot me.

"Should we call ourselves Brase?" she asked to distract herself. "Or maybe J-rook? Jaselynn?"

He snorted.

"Too soon for a Hollywood nickname?"

"Considering the things we've done to each other," he said, "nothing is too soon." He smoothed the hair from her temple and stroked the shell of her ear, careful of the implant.

She tensed at first, but the more he did it, the more she liked it, and soon she was leaning in to the touch.

It was so new, a pleasure she hadn't known she could have until him. "Are you really my boyfriend?"

"I am."

"And I'm…"

"My girlfriend."

She kissed the spot just above his heart and stroked her fingers over his chest. "Then I need to know more about you. Where are you from?"

"Oklahoma City. But I've lived in Mustang, Yukon, Norman, Moore…McAlester. Even Pawnee."

"Have a favorite?"

His arms tightened around her. "Definitely Strawberry Valley."

She playfully bit his nipple. "Trying to seduce me when I'm already naked?"

"Maybe it's not only your body I'm hoping to seduce," he grumbled.

Her mind? Her…heart? She sucked in a breath. It was far too soon in their relationship for love…right?

A pang shot through her…one of longing. Was that what had been missing from their lovemaking—the love?

I want him to love me, she realized. And he could—surely. *I won* this *from him. I can win more.*

"What about you?" he asked.

"I've been here all my life," she said. "Never really wanted to live anywhere else."

"Is there somewhere you've wanted to visit?"

"Wichita Mountain." She remembered the way Harlow Glass had bragged about all the fun she and her family had there, climbing Mount Scott, seeing the patchwork of lakes, the rock formations and the bison herds.

"Camping?" He laughed. "You?"

"Hey! I told you we did it once a year when I was a kid. I excel at camping."

He rolled her to her back, a grin still in place. "I'd like to go camping right now. At Lake Bliss. And I know just where I want to stake my tent."

She moaned as he slipped a finger deep inside her.

A vibration rattled the nightstand. A ring followed.

"Ignore it," Jase said, kissing her neck. "The rest of the world no longer exists."

"But what if Jessie Kay needs me?"

He lifted his head to check. "It's not Jessie Kay. It's—" He whipped out an arm and swiped up the phone. "You've missed a call and two texts from Brad." His tone had gone flat, his eyes dark. "He'd like to go out again."

It reminded her of the anger he'd displayed at the wine-and-cheese tasting, the moment he'd gone still—a predator preparing to strike—and gave her a momentary twinge of unease. "I'll tell him no," she said, knowing she should have taken care of this already. This wasn't the first time Brad had contacted her. "Tomorrow, after work."

Jase gave a clipped shake of his head. "Now. This second."

"No way. I'll do it in person, not through a text."

"Fine," he said. "But you'll do it this morning."

I willingly hitched my wagon to an alpha. What did I expect? "First, you'll need to adjust your tone if you want results. Second, I have too much to do at your place."

"You're right about the tone. I'm sorry. As for the other thing, your very generous boss will give you an hour off."

Brad didn't love her or anything like that, but rejection was rejection, and it always hurt. "Maybe I'll let him down in stages."

"In one swoop. This is necessary to his survival," Jase said. "I don't want him thinking there's a chance he can have what's mine."

What's mine. The caveman claim of possession reverberated in her head, thrilling her.

"He's a nice guy, Jase, from a nice family. His dad is sheriff and one of the best—"

"Sheriff?" Jase asked, going still again.

"Yeah. Why? Is that a problem?"

The color drained from his cheeks. "No," he rasped. "No problem. Just…tell Brad first thing in the morning."

"Okay."

Fiery green eyes locked on her. "And bring an overnight bag to work."

"Ask nicely."

"Or what? You start counting?"

"Nope. I put your body in a time-out corner."

He arched a brow. "Going to be *that* girl, are you?"

"For sure. As long as we're together, I'm going to use sex against you."

"Well, well. I'm finally meeting that evil side I've heard so much about."

"Too bad for you she only gets worse."

"Nah. All she needs is an orgasm or two, and she'll forget all about that time-out corner." He palmed her breasts. "Let me prove it…"

CHAPTER TWENTY

I CAN DO THIS. I've got this. Except I probably can't do this, and I most likely don't have this.

Brook Lynn marched down Fragaria Street, heading toward Lintz Automotive, giving herself the best-worst pep talk of all time. She'd never had to reject someone before. *It's not about saying all the right things when there's nothing right to say. It's about believing I won't destroy his self-esteem even though I probably will.*

Jase walked at her side, his steps clipped, his posture tense.

He'd stayed the entire night. Anytime she'd inadvertently rolled away from him, he'd begun to toss and turn. When she'd snuggled up close, he'd calmed. They'd woken up wrapped in each other's arms and made love again. It had been thrilling and satisfying—but still she couldn't shake the sensation that something had been missing.

She'd expected him to head home, but he had errands in town, he'd said, and would escort her to the auto shop. When she'd refused to ride with him—no need to encourage him—he'd followed her. He wanted to ensure she made it to Brad's safely, and she understood that. But waves of anger pulsed from him, and she found herself wondering what he'd do to the guy if they ever came face-to-face.

"Go," she said, waving him away.

"Not till you're at the door."

"Don't think I'll do as ordered?"

"There's just something I need to do—ah, finally," he said and wrapped his arm around her waist.

The contact startled her, and she gasped.

Charlene Burns had just turned the corner, she realized, her steps stuttering when she spotted them. She pasted a smile on her face and skipped the rest of the way over.

"I didn't realize you'd be bringing your assistant to our meeting," she said, not sparing Brook Lynn a glance.

What! What meeting?

Jase kissed Brook Lynn on the temple and said, "I didn't. I brought my girlfriend."

Charlene gaped at him. "Oh, that's...lovely." Her tone suggested *lovely* was the new word for *craptastic*.

Warmth spilled through Brook Lynn as she realized what, exactly, was going on. Charlene must have turned her sights to Jase, and this was his way of letting her know nothing was going to happen. Meanwhile, though he had no idea he was doing it, he was proving Charlene's "use her and lose her" comment wrong.

Just like that, Brook Lynn forgave him for his brutishness last night.

"Just wanted to thank you for those muffins," Jase said. "The tin is in my car." He kissed Brook Lynn again, smack on the lips, and said, "I'll be at the house when you're done, and I'll be missing you every second, honey." He gently caressed her cheek before walking off with Charlene.

I am going to fall so hard for this man.

Charlene looked so envious, Brook Lynn actually felt

sorry for her. She patted the girl's arm, saying, "Everything will be okay. I'll see you later, Charlene."

Charlene jolted away from her and hissed.

Brook Lynn didn't let it affect her, just ambled away. About to turn the corner, her step faltered. Not because she'd reached her destination, but because she caught the reflection of a man in a store window, barreling toward her from behind. She attempted to sidestep him, but she wasn't fast enough, and he plowed into her. She tripped, landing on her knees. The pavement cut into her skin, and her purse thumped heavily against her hip.

The man stopped to help her up. "I'm so sorry…was in a hurry…didn't see you."

"Don't worry about it." She hooked her purse strap over her shoulder, letting it crisscross over her middle. "I'm fine."

As he looked her up and down, she recognized him as the tourist who'd entered her shop only to leave without saying a word. "Your poor knees. They're bleeding."

"They'll be fine." Up close like this, she could tell he was roughly her age. He had sandy-colored hair and eyes as dark as slate, but he appeared sickly. His skin had a yellow tint, and there were bags under his bloodshot eyes. His button-up and slacks were ill-fitting, with several stains.

"Well," he said, staring at her so intensely she shifted uncomfortably. "I should be going." He turned on his heel and rushed off.

O-kay, then. Weird.

Brook Lynn continued on to Brad's shop. When she stood at the door, she withdrew the sandwich she'd made for him from her purse and drew in a deep breath. *I can do this. Maybe.*

Cool air enveloped her as she entered the lobby. She

bypassed reception and slipped into the garage. Brad was a few cars down, twisting something under the hood of a car. He wore his work coveralls, and his hands were stained with grease.

What am I going to say to him?

Her mind drifted back to the breakfast she'd shared with Jessie Kay while Jase showered. As they'd munched on a fruit platter she'd bought to sample for Tessa's party, she'd explained her dilemma to her sister, asking, "How can I let Brad down easy?"

"Tell him you'll give him another chance if he'll consider a penile-enlargement surgery, and boom, *he'll* be done with *you.*"

Not going there.

Just before leaving the house, Brook Lynn had texted Kenna, but her friend's reply had been every bit as ridiculous.

Say this: Is it hot in here or is this relationship suffocating me? No? Then say this: I now pronounce you dumped and single, you may kiss my butt.

Brook Lynn thought about what her mom might have said to her, if she'd still been alive.

He's a person with feelings. Treat him the way you'd want to be treated. Be polite. Gentle.

"Brook Lynn." Brad's voice jerked her into reality.

She blinked into focus, her nervousness returning in a flash. "Hey."

He grinned as he cleaned his hands on a rag. "What a nice surprise. I'm glad you're here."

"Um, can we talk in private, maybe?"

He caught her unease and lost his grin. "Sure." He led her to an office in back.

Along the way a big burly guy she'd seen around a few times stepped into their path.

"Hey. You selling those?" he asked, motioning to the sandwich.

"No," she replied.

"Who does? Where can I get one?"

"No one. Nowhere. I made it." As usual, she'd baked the bread from scratch, and this time she'd even called to have her favorite cheese from the tasting delivered right to her door.

Interest lit the mechanic's eyes. "How much do you charge?"

"Yeah," another guy said as he walked over. "How much?"

Several others wandered over, too, listening intently.

"Smells like a slice of heaven," someone said.

That was surprising, considering it was her consolation prize for Brad, and guilt was the main ingredient.

"Thank you," she said, "but it isn't for sale."

As groans of disappointment sounded behind her, thrilling her, she continued on to the office. Inside, she leaned against the closed door and offered the sandwich to Brad. "This is for you."

"That was sweet of you." He accepted with a mix of dread and hope gleaming in his eyes. "It does smell wonderful."

Her nerves kicked up again, obliterating her excitement. Sweat moistened her hands. *Use your lady balls and speak!* "Brad, well, I'm so sorry to do this, but I can't go out with you again." Once she started, she couldn't stop, the words pouring from her. "You are such a great man, and I wanted you to ask me out for a long, long time, but you didn't, and then Jase showed up, and I wanted him, though I thought I couldn't have him, but I also thought I needed to have some fun anyway, so I asked you out, and that wasn't fair to you and, well…I'm…I'm sorry. I led you on, and that was wrong of me. I'll understand if you hate me forever, but I'm with Jase now, officially, and we're exclusive."

Brad placed the sandwich on the overcrowded desk and scrubbed a hand over his face. He mulled over her long-winded speech before sighing. "I've wanted to ask you out for a long time, too."

"So why didn't you?" If she had been with him, she would never have allowed herself to notice Jase.

Not notice him? Impossible. But she wouldn't have acted on it.

"Thought you'd say no," Brad said. "You never seemed to notice I was a man when I was inside Edna's store."

So…he'd let the mere thought of failure stop him from pursuing her, which meant the fear of rejection had meant more to him than she had. He'd been unwilling to fight for her.

The clarity of *that* caused her guilt to drain. The man she ended up with had to be willing to fight for her—her love, her life. Her happiness. The way she would fight for him and his. Otherwise, the relationship would lack a solid foundation to stand on, and they would be doomed.

Would Jase be willing to fight for her?

In a way, hadn't he already?

"Had you asked earlier," she said, "I would have said yes, yes, a thousand times yes."

Clouds of sadness drifted through his eyes, but they were soon replaced by determination. "I'll wait," he said, squaring his shoulders. "I'll wait for you to be single again."

"No. Don't," she said with a shake of her head, but on some level she wondered if he'd have to wait very long. "I'm going to do everything in my power to make this relationship last a long, long time." *Maybe even the rest of my life.*

JASE PACED HIS living room like a caged tiger, waiting for Brook Lynn to arrive. She had ten more minutes, then he was heading to Lintz Automotive, and—

What? The shop was owned by the sheriff's son.

Hell. Instinct said: *let the competition know what will happen if he touches my woman.* Self-preservation shouted: *Do I want to go back to prison?*

But…*she's mine.*

His first *"mine"* since Daphne, and the two couldn't even compare.

Must take measures to keep Brook Lynn. Can't let her leave me like I've been left in the past.

The ring of the doorbell snapped him out of his daze.

He strode to the door and found a tall, lean man with weathered skin standing outside. The brim of a white Stetson cast shadows over his eyes, and he wore an official SVPD uniform, dark polyester and a bit too tight.

The sheriff, as if Jase's thoughts had summoned him.

"Well, now. I'm Sheriff Lintz, and you must be Jase Hollister."

The sheriff must have found out Brook Lynn and Jase were dating, that she'd chosen Jase over Brad, and had come to warn him off. Worse, Sheriff Lintz had to know about Jase's past. Why else would he be here?

Cold sweat broke out on the back of Jase's neck at the same time as fire blazed in his blood. How soon before Brook Lynn learned the truth?

"I am," he said, lifting his chin.

"Good, good. I paid your boys a visit in town earlier

today, introduced myself and let them know I'm here if they need me. Wanted you to know the same."

A welcome? A trick, surely. "Thank you," he said carefully. Why hadn't the boys warned him?

The sheriff rocked back on the heels of his boots. "I hear our sweet little Brook Lynn Dillon is working for you."

"Yes." He offered no more, no less.

"Pretty as a picture, that one."

Fishing? This time, he said nothing.

"Not a very talkative fellow, are you?" Sheriff Lintz laughed, and it sounded genuine. "Well, now. Guess you've got things to do. I'll take my leave. You take care, you hear." He ambled to his black-and-white and drove off.

Jase remained in the doorway until the car disappeared from view. He swiped up his phone to call Beck—and saw his friend had left three messages. Damn it, he'd left the ringer off.

The scare with the sheriff made his need to see and hold Brook Lynn animalistic. What the hell was taking so long?

Hinges on the door squealed a few minutes later, and she sailed inside the house. His body reacted instantly, tensing, heating—readying. Just like that.

He wasn't sure how much longer he'd have her in his life, and urgency filled him. He was on her in seconds, pinning her against the wall.

"Well?" he said. "Is it done?"

She curled into him, not even a little bit upset by his manhandling. "I talked to Brad," she replied, breathless.

"And?"

"And I told him I'm seeing a Mr. Jase Hollister exclusively."

The tension he'd been carrying around, boulders on his back, suddenly dissolved. "Did he cry? I would have cried."

"Please. You are not a crier, Mr. Hollister."

"No, I suppose I'm not." He found himself adding, "I cried the time I was taken from the apartment I'd shared with my mother," surprising them both by revealing a little more of his past. "I expected her to come back... was afraid she wouldn't be able to find me if I wasn't there. And I cried the first time I was pulled out of a decent foster home. After that I had no more tears to give."

She melted against him, warm and soft—*and all mine.* "I hate that you went through those things."

"I'm learning to appreciate what I have." He nuzzled the line of her jaw. "But all that moving around as a kid gave me a boo-boo that hasn't healed, and I know how you like to kiss those."

"Yes," she said with a tremor. "Tell me. Where is this boo-boo?" She tapped a finger against his heart. "Here?"

"No." He took her hand and curled it around his erection. "Here."

She chuckled, even as she tightened her grip on him. "I'd be happy to kiss this boo-boo...after I tell you a ground rule I have."

Playing me like a piano...and I love it. "Tell me."

"As long as I'm on the clock, there will be no PDA."

It was a little after nine, and this was definitely a public display of affection. "The rule needs an addendum. No PDA, unless I fire you. Then you can tell your boyfriend all about your cruel boss, and your boyfriend will comfort you...naked...and then you can convince your boss to rehire you."

Her warm breath drifted over his skin as she leaned

in and licked his throat. "*That's* the caveat, is it?" As she spoke, she stroked his erection, the pressure building in his groin.

"I have a rule of my own," he gritted out. "You have to wear a garbage bag Monday through Friday. That is your new work uniform. Anything else is likely to be ripped off you the moment you walk through the door."

"And that would be terrible, wouldn't it?" She nipped at his collarbone.

Building…

He forged ahead. "Actually, I have a couple more rules. You aren't allowed to prance around the house if I've got a hammer in my hand. And you aren't allowed to bend over. Ever."

"Such a stern taskmaster," she said…and slid her free hand under the hem of his shirt. Her fingers traced a path of fire to his nipple.

He flattened his palm on her bare thighs and had to bite the side of his tongue to silence his groan. She was so damn soft.

"You're wearing a dress. Which means you've already broken a rule. Which means you'll have to be punished."

She pinched him lightly. "Spanking?"

"Severe tongue-lashing. But as your man, it's only right that I take the punishment for you." He unsnapped his jeans.

"You're so good to me."

He hissed in a breath as she bent her head to bite his nipple just the way he liked. Then she dropped to her knees. Watching as she freed his length from the constraints of his underwear, he braced his hands on the wall. Brook Lynn. On her knees. *For me.*

She peered up at him with baby blues smoldering all

kinds of need and licked her lips. It was the most erotic thing he'd ever seen. Until she opened her mouth and sucked him deep. He could only throw back his head and pant at the overwhelming flood of pleasure.

She worked him good and hard, sucking all the way down, licking all the way up, the pressure never ending. When her teeth scraped against the head, his hips jerked, sending him back down her throat, deep, so damn deep. He tried to gasp out an apology for being too rough, but all he managed to say was her name. When he glanced down, he saw her hand moving between her legs.

Pleasuring me...and herself.

The knowledge nearly sent him hurtling down a spiral of bliss. He cupped her nape and urged her into a faster rhythm.

"That's the way, angel. So good. You're sucking me just right."

As he hit the back of her throat again, she groaned, and the vibration sped down his length, into his sac, and oh...damn...a fire flicked to life there, smoldering, growing... Up and down she bobbed on him, never slowing, only working him faster and faster. Every muscle in his body began to clench on bone, the fire in his sac riding up his length...and finally shooting into her mouth.

She swallowed everything he fed her, still moaning against him, the vibrations little flashes of pure ecstasy.

When at last he'd emptied, she licked her way free of him and glanced up. Her eyes were bright, her features soft and tender. Her lips swollen and red.

He bent down, took her by the wrist and eased her up. She swayed as her knees wobbled, and he brought her wet fingers close to his mouth.

"Tell me how hard you came," he said.

Color flooded her cheeks as she nodded. "So hard I might have broken my soul."

"Good girl." He sucked each finger into his mouth, savoring the taste of her honey.

She shivered. "By the way," she said, dabbing daintily at her mouth when he released her. "You aren't paying me for today's work."

As he tugged up his zipper, he said, "Why?"

"Uh, because you aren't paying me on the days we have sex during work hours. I'll feel like a hooker."

Pain radiated through his jaw as his teeth ground together. He got where she was coming from, but he didn't like it. "Well, congrats. Today is a federal holiday at Chez Hollister. National Blow Job Day. No work, plenty of play, *as well as* a paycheck."

Her eyes narrowed to tiny slits. "No. Utterly unacceptable."

He wanted to say, "This is the way things are going to be, honey. Get used to it." But the need to make her happy superseded everything else. "Fine. I won't pay you, but you won't work, either." And oh, hell. West and Beck were going to kill him. They lived for her sandwiches and casseroles.

Like I don't.

She made something new every day. There was the corn dog casserole. And the tropical ham casserole. The bacon and blue cheese casserole. And his personal favorite, the turkey and white cheddar tetrazzini casserole.

The sandwiches were just as exotic. There was the one made with a doughnut rather than slices of bread. The one she made with small squares of meats and cheeses to resemble a Rubik's Cube. The one she called the Temple of Southern Doom, with two large pieces of chicken-fried steak stuffed with mashed potatoes, yeast rolls and a scoop of bacon gravy.

His mouth watered, and for a moment, he almost wished he'd waited to kick off National Blow Job Day until after dinner.

"All right," she said at last. "I'll take the day off."

He helped her right her clothing, noticed some scrapes on her knees. "You're injured," he said and frowned. "What happened and when?"

"I fell on the way to the auto shop."

Damn it. He never would have let her go down on him if he'd known she was injured.

He picked her up and placed her on the couch. After he'd found the first-aid box, he crouched in front of her to clean and bandage her knees.

"Do they hurt?" he asked.

"A little. Distract me."

"How?"

"Well...you can tell me if you've ever been in love."

"I have."

"How old were you?"

Leery of the subject—the time frame—he said, "I dated her in high school. She took off when I was eighteen."

"Do you love her still?"

"No." His feelings for Daphne had been true and solid, and because she'd been the only relationship he'd ever had, he'd thought of her often over the lonely years in prison. Also the reason he'd thought to reconnect with her after he'd gotten out. But his feelings had faded completely, nothing but an echo of a past he'd tried to forget.

What he felt for Brook Lynn burned hot and wild. He could love her. Madly, deeply.

But could she love him? The real him?

He would never know...unless he told her the truth. The realization slammed into him, undeniable. The longer he kept his secrets—even at her own request—the more she would resent his silence. The more he would feel the weight of it hanging over them.

The sense of urgency returned.

And what if she found out before he could tell her? What if she heard of his sins from someone else? This was a small town—once people found out, it would be impossible to keep it quiet. Would she ever be willing to listen to Jase's side of the story then?

He peered at her, hoping for understanding, dreading rejection. "Brook Lynn. I have to tell you something."

She tensed, as if afraid of what he had to say, then released a resigned sigh. She traced her finger along his jawline. "What you were going to tell me before?"

He nodded, knowing he had to do it, had to say it, before he lost his nerve.

Like ripping off a bandage. Here goes.

"I spent the last nine years in prison."

CHAPTER TWENTY-ONE

JASE'S WORDS REVERBERATED in Brook Lynn's mind. *I spent the last nine years in prison.*

She laughed at the joke. Because he was joking. Right? He had to be joking. Her new boyfriend couldn't be an ex-con. He couldn't have done something so terrible he'd had to spend nearly a decade behind bars.

"Don't tease me," she said.

"I'm not teasing." His tone was as hard as granite.

Ice crystallized in her veins.

"You have questions," he said.

"I mean it," she insisted. "This isn't funny."

"I'm not teasing," he repeated.

A lump grew in her throat. Jase, the man she was falling for, really had spent the past nine years in prison?

She stood, jolting away from him. He watched her, his expression losing its hard edge and going blank. The blank one she knew too well. But she didn't know *him* at all, did she?

Multiple emotions frothed inside her, and she began to pace. "How is that possible? Why didn't you tell me?"

"I tried. You stopped me."

"You should have told me anyway. Should have told me sooner!"

"Maybe. But I'm telling you now."

"Now isn't good enough."

He flinched. A reaction that kept her from bolting out the door.

"Ask anything," he said. Not only did his expression remain blank, but his voice was now deadened. "I will answer."

"Wh—what were you in prison for?"

He closed his eyes for a moment. "Voluntary manslaughter."

He'd *killed* someone. Her hand fluttered to her throat, her pulse hammering fast and hard. "Tell me everything."

He placed his hands on his knees. "I was eighteen."

A kid. His entire youth had been spent behind bars with hardened criminals. Murderers. Sociopaths. Rapists. They'd shaped the man he would become.

At least his scars made sense.

"There was a guy. Paxton Gillis. Pax. He was nineteen, in college. Tessa had gone to a frat party. He was there and he followed her to her car and raped her."

Brook Lynn flattened a hand over her stomach.

"When West, Beck and I found out, we hunted him down. I don't remember who threw the first punch. So much of what happened is a blur. I was so angry. I lashed out and just…didn't stop. I couldn't."

She remembered the picture and the news clipping she'd seen when she'd searched Jase online—the slim teenager who'd been arrested for beating a college student—and she felt sick.

"So West and Beck were in prison with you?" she asked.

"No."

"Why?"

"I took full responsibility."

"Why?" she repeated, her voice lashing like a whip.

"They had bright futures."

"And you didn't?"

He hiked his shoulders.

She stopped to stare at him, to study him. He wasn't just blank anymore—he was cold. As cold as he'd been the first day they met. He hardly seemed capable of a good mad, much less a black, uncontrollable rage. But too well did she remember the wine-and-cheese tasting. How, for a split second, he *had* looked capable of murder. Would he have hit that woman, despite his claim otherwise?

A tremor of fear washed through her. What would happen if ever he lost his temper with *her*?

That day in the yard, he'd pushed her and come at her with his hands fisted.

He might not want to, might not mean to, but...

Fear held her in its jaws, razor-sharp teeth sinking deep into her heart.

"Are you sorry?" she asked.

"Every day since," he said.

Was he really? Or was that his answer simply because it was the right one?

"You don't look sorry," she said. "You don't look like you feel anything."

"I feel. You know it." He stared back at her—giving nothing away. "Are you afraid of me now?"

"Yes," she snapped, because it was true. She understood why he'd erupted back then. His friend had been hurt in a horrible, cruel way. But he hadn't stopped himself from going too far. In his own words, he *couldn't* stop.

"I would never hurt you, Brook Lynn."

"So easy to say," she muttered.

Another flinch, as if she'd struck him. Yes, okay, he

did feel. But was it enough to stop him from unleashing on her if ever his control snapped?

"Jase," she said, hating herself—hating him. "I…I'm going to go. I need time to process this."

He didn't hesitate to give her a clipped nod, as if he'd expected the words. She waited, but he offered nothing more.

Disappointment coursed through her. Had she expected him to fight for her to stay after she'd just confessed to fearing his temper? It may have been wrong of her, but…yes. Part of her wished he would draw her into his arms, hold her tight and promise everything would be okay.

So confused!

"I…I'm sorry." Turning, she fled the room, the house…and the man she'd never really known.

Brook Lynn didn't report to work the next day, or the next. Jase's chest had stopped throbbing at least; it now hurt all the damn time. He wanted to shout "See! I knew this would happen."

He'd once heard fearing something gave it entrance into your life, and actually brought it to pass, like a self-fulfilling prophecy, because it changed the way you thought and spoke and acted. This—Brook Lynn's defection—had been his biggest fear.

And here I am. Without her.

By some miracle, during their talk he'd managed to return to the state he knew best—every emotion hidden behind armor—guarding himself against desperation, rage and even heartbreak. He'd managed to hold himself together all the minutes—seconds—since. He'd worked. He'd gone to another soccer game and cheered for the

Strikers. He'd helped plan a few details for Tessa's celebration.

Today, the armor had cracked and he'd begun to
break down bit by bit.

He should have been prepared for this. How many
people had he lost in his lifetime? He should be over
it already.

Except he wasn't.

Jase stood outside in his backyard. There was a full
moon tonight. Locusts buzzed. Crickets sang. The combination was pleasant and should have soothed him, but
he hated all of it. Brook Lynn wasn't here to share it
with him, and she never would be. One day she might
even share it with someone else. Someone without a
record.

He drained the beer in his hand then threw the empty
bottle into the trash bin he'd carried out here. A six-pack
waited on the porch table—his second of the evening.

"You want to tell me what's wrong?"

Beck's voice. Jase didn't bother turning around as
the back door slid shut and footsteps sounded. "No,"
he said.

"How about the reason Brook Lynn stopped coming
around making my dinner?"

"Nope." He popped the cap of another beer, drained
half the contents.

"Well, okay, then." Beck grabbed a beer for himself.

"You aren't going to push for answers?"

"No."

"Why? Never mind. I know why." Jase gave a harsh
laugh. "I don't know how many ways I can say it, but
you guys really need to get over your guilt issue." He
drained the rest of the bottle, swayed on his feet. Had
that been a sneer in his tone?

"I will always feel guilty for what we did," Beck said quietly. "Or rather, what we didn't do."

"You shouldn't." Had the situation been reversed, had one of them taken the blame and told him to stay quiet, he would have done it, despite his feelings on the matter. Because that's what they did for each other. Whatever the others asked.

He threw his bottle at a tree, the tinkle of broken glass filling the night. Brook Lynn had accused him of not feeling. Well, he felt. Despite his armor. He felt so much he suddenly choked on it. Bitterness, resentment. Hate. So much hate. Guilt of his own. Sorrow and remorse. Pain—oh, the pain, still there in his chest, growing worse with every second that passed. It was just better for everyone—including himself—if he didn't allow himself to feel so strongly.

"She left me." He pushed over the table. The remaining beers hit the ground, the tops blowing off. Liquid guzzled out. He was panting, fighting for every breath. "I told her about prison, and she cut and ran."

"Hey, hey, hey." Beck cupped the back of his neck, applied pressure. "You and I both know just because something is going on one day doesn't mean it will be going on the next. I've come to know that girl. I've seen the way she looks at you. Which makes something I've done especially stupid."

Confusion penetrated his haze. "What have you done?"

"Not important right now. I'm certain Brook Lynn won't stay gone."

Beck hadn't seen the panic in her eyes, hadn't heard the fear in her tone. "You're wrong."

"I wouldn't make a statement like that unless I was

one hundred percent confident," his friend said. "I know women. Well. Like, really well. Like, really *really*—"

A small spark of humor. "I think I get it."

"She just needs time. Imagine if she'd led a life you knew nothing about."

"I would want her, no matter what."

"You would also need...say it with me..."

"Time," they said in unison.

The loud crunch and grind of heavy metal forcibly changing shape suddenly echoed. He and Beck shared a look of concern before taking off in a sprint. The first thing Jase noticed as he rounded the corner to the front yard were the headlights blinking on and off—West's headlights. Smoke curled from the hood. A hood wrapped around a tree.

Jase quickened his pace. "I thought he was in his room."

"He was."

"West!" He reached the door first—the mangled door. He and Beck had to work together to wrench it open. West spilled out, blood dripping from the center of his forehead.

"Call 911," Jase said, catching West before the guy hit the ground.

"That tree had it coming," West slurred, the scent of alcohol pungent on him.

Oh...hell. "Forget 911." The law would only make things worse. "Let's get him inside." Jase slung his arm around West's left side, and Beck came up to his right side. They acted as crutches, leading him toward the door.

"You could have killed someone," Beck muttered.

"How? Didn't drive anywhere," West said. "Would never. Just reparked my car."

"And purposely hit the tree?" Jase asked.

"Told you. Tree had it coming."

"This," Beck ground out.

Jase knew exactly what he meant. This was how West self-destructed around the anniversary of Tessa's death.

Beck added, "Get ready. It only gets worse."

CHAPTER TWENTY-TWO

LIFE SUCKED.

Just when Brook Lynn had started to get things together, to step through the heaven-on-earth door, fate had closed in behind her, tied a blindfold around her eyes, forced her to turn in a thousand circles and step through the *hell*-on-earth door.

How could she have been so wrong about Jase? How could she have pegged an ex-con as a cop or a soldier?

"Okay," she heard Jessie Kay say, "you've moped enough."

Brook Lynn cracked open her eyes. Her sister was stretched out on her bed. When had that happened?

"I'm not moping. I'm brooding. Big difference."

Since the breakup— No, no, they hadn't broken up. Since the decision to take a break—better—she'd left the house only once, when Kenna had dragged her to another dress appointment, hoping the change of scenery would cheer her up…but after she'd sobbed all over the salesgirl about the unfairness of life, her friend hadn't asked her out a second time.

"Just go away." Brook Lynn rolled to her other side—and came face-to-face with Kenna.

The redhead smirked at her, all *it's not over*.

They'd surrounded her!

"Go away, both of you." She tried to pull the covers

over her face, but her sister ripped the material out of her hands…and kicked it to the floor.

"It's nine o'clock at night," Kenna said.

"So?" she demanded. "Your point?"

"So. You haven't gotten up yet."

"You and Jase broke up and—" Jessie Kay began.

"We didn't! We decided to go on a break," she corrected, depression and guilt settling over her like another blanket.

She'd just run out on him like a scared little rabbit. Because that's what she was! And it hurt, knowing she wasn't the woman he needed. Accepting. Comforting. Maybe he knew it, too. Maybe that's why he hadn't come after her. Why he hadn't done anything to convince her that her fears were unfounded.

Not that the blame fell fully on his shoulders. She could have called him, but hadn't.

If only her mind weren't at war. On one hand, she knew that while he'd committed a crime, he'd been a teenager at the time and had since paid the price. And really, he'd paid far more than a few years behind bars. Obviously, he'd paid in blood and pain.

On the other hand, she'd seen glimpses of rage in him and now didn't know if she could trust him in such a state.

Still…part of her wanted to be with him.

Part of me?

Ha! Most of her. But it wouldn't do either one of them any good if she flinched every time he raised his voice or his hand. Or if she ran and hid every time he got a little irritated with her.

Casting stones? She had a temper of her own, one the whole town feared. But she'd never really hurt anyone. Well, besides her annoying sister. Even at her worst,

Brook Lynn had never done anything seriously damaging—and Jessie Kay had ensured she got hers in return. But a temper like Jase's?

How would he react the day she pushed him past the limits of his control? And she would. That was a guarantee.

Why couldn't she be like the women in books and movies and just trust him?

Easy. Because she was real, with real reactions.

Being real sucked.

"Dane says Jase is miserable." Kenna smoothed hair from Brook Lynn's brow. "Though he won't give details. Bro-code or something like that."

"You won't go see him. You won't talk about him. What's going on?" Jessie Kay asked.

She didn't want to reveal Jase's secret, but she desperately needed advice. She'd been agonizing for days with zero results.

"I just found out... I mean, Jase told me..." The rest of the words snagged in her throat. Was she really going to do this? Betray him? Because that's how he'd see it. He'd trusted her enough to share the most painful part of himself.

Dang it! She couldn't do it. She was on her own. "I plead the ho-code and will remain silent."

Jessie Kay snorted. "Did you just refer to yourself as a ho?"

"Did he cheat on you?" Kenna demanded.

"No, nothing like that."

"Did he lie to you? Steal from you?" Jessie Kay asked.

"No and no."

"Dude. Did he hit you?"

"What? No!" she gasped out.

But…would he? It was a question she couldn't shake, a fear she'd never before entertained. The only way to find out how he would treat her while enraged was to, well, enrage him.

A frisson of distress swept through her. *I'm miserable without him, but too unsure about what the future holds to go to him.*

She couldn't afford to make a mistake. But…she couldn't let fear make her decisions for her, either. After all, she might actually be in love with Jase Hollister. All the signs were there. A need to give him everything she had…to protect him from further pain. And she treasured her time with him, delighted in teasing him, laughing with him. She thrilled in breaking through his icy demeanor to find the heat that swirled inside him.

But, dang it, the fear remained.

"I need a new job," she muttered. "Just for a little while. Just until I figure some things out." But what could she do? Who was hiring? What wouldn't destroy her soul, little by little?

Off the top of her head…nothing. Cooking was the only thing she truly enjoyed, but none of the local restaurants or bakeries were hiring. Maybe they'd make an exception for her, though. She'd never forgotten the way those guys at the auto shop had reacted to her sandwich. Name your price, they'd said, as if they'd pay anything. Even…ten dollars? Fifteen? Just for a sandwich!

She would have tried opening her own shop, but it would have required too much overhead on her part.

Although…did she really have to open a shop to sell her sandwiches?

Buds of excitement unfurled within her, giving life to a tide of eagerness. What if she operated on a delivery-only basis? People could place their orders every morning, and she could make deliveries every afternoon and evening, making casseroles for working moms and dads to easily heat and serve to their families. That wouldn't be enough to sustain her, but she could always expand into catering.

My own business, she thought, awed. She would be in control of her hours and her schedule.

She had to try.

"The job search can wait another day," Jessie Kay said. "You don't want to tell us what's going on, fine, but we're not letting you wallow a second longer. We're going dancing, and that's final. You deserve a good time. And a new man, if that's something you're interested in exploring."

"I'm not. I only want Jase," she muttered.

"I bet I can change your mind." Jessie Kay tugged her out of bed and herded her into the bathroom. "Shower. Wash the stank off."

"Fine. I'll wash the stank off, as you so elegantly put it," she said. *You're welcome, world.* "But that's it. That's all I'm doing."

Kenna grinned at her. "I'll be in the closet, looking for your sluttiest dress."

"I mean it," she insisted. "I'm staying in tonight."

"Sure, sure." Jessie Kay riffled through her underwear drawer. "Do you want to wear a thong or go with something lacy? Definitely lacy," she answered for her. "It'll drive all the guys you meet wild."

"I'm. Staying. In," she said and slammed the bathroom door.

TWO AND A HALF hours later, the girls flanked her sides, guiding Brook Lynn into the club. Of course, nothing in Strawberry Valley had been good enough for Jessie Kay, so they'd driven into the city.

"I can't believe you forced me into this," she muttered, waving a hand in front of her face. Smoke thickened the air, tickling her throat and making her cough.

Jessie Kay grinned. "I know! Isn't it great?"

Strobe lights flashed a million colors in every direction, spinning, spinning. Bright white lights pulsed in sync with the music. A thousand bodies overflowed the small space, men and women crowding the bar, standing around the occupied tables, bumping and grinding on the dance floor. She expected the seams of the building to split at any second.

I think I've walked into hell.

She switched her implants to silent, the noise simply too loud for her to function. Still she could feel the vibration of music bouncing off the floor and the walls.

Jessie Kay disappeared for a few minutes, only to return with a drink and two guys. She thrust the shot glass at Brook Lynn, saying to the guys, "This is my sister, y'all. As pretty as I promised, right?"

They looked her over as if she were a piece of meat on display at the butcher block.

One of them said something but she had no idea what. While she'd had no trouble reading her sister's lips, these boys were strangers and the lighting dim—when it wasn't exploding like fireworks.

The lack of understanding was probably a good thing.

One guy continued to leer at her, as if she were already a sure thing. The other smiled a smile he probably thought was charming but that merely creeped her out. It said: *I know how to bury a body.*

"Excuse me," she said and pushed her way into a dark corner.

Kenna wasn't far behind. Her features contorted into a grimace as she looked around. "I wasn't expecting… had no idea *this* was what your sister enjoyed."

"The sad thing is I knew, and yet here I am." She missed Jase. The way he looked at her—as if she were special. The way he touched her—as if she were a gift to be unwrapped.

She just had to find out how he'd react to being furious with her. Then they could be together.

"You gonna drink that?" Kenna motioned to the shot glass she still held.

The last time Brook Lynn had imbibed, she'd texted the most insane things to Jase. Every "what not to do" in every women's magazine.

Lightbulb! Maybe, with a little alcohol, she'd work up the courage to push his hot buttons and finally learn the answer to the question plaguing her.

I'm a sick, sick girl.

"Bottoms up," she muttered and drained the glass in a single gulp.

Oh, the burn! Just as bad as before. She sputtered, trying to catch her breath.

Jessie Kay arrived with a new crop of hopefuls— and two more shots. Brook Lynn downed the drinks without a word.

Considering she hadn't eaten much that day, just a few chips left in the bag on her nightstand, dizziness hit her fast and strong. She giggled, and Kenna wrapped an arm around her waist to hold her steady.

"You okay?" her friend asked.

"Better than." Maybe. Probably. She was going to make Jase soooo mad. He had no idea the storm about to be unleashed. "Hey, you," she said to the guy who wouldn't stop playing with the ends of her sister's hair. "Can I have your number? I lost my own."

He just blinked at her.

Jessie Kay rolled her eyes. "What she meant to say is… Here she is. Now, what are your other two wishes?"

His friend clasped Brook Lynn's hand. When she focused on him, his lips were already moving. "—scale from one to ten, you're a nine…and I'm the one you need."

He expected her to do a little mathing? Now?

Who cared! "Selfie time! Me and Numbers." This had to be the best…idea…ever. Jase would see her with another man and sink into a black pit of rage; she'd discover how he handled the emotion. In a word: foolproof.

Brook Lynn sidled up to Numbers and threw her arms around his shoulders. "I know what you're thinking. Yes, I did sit in a pile of sugar—because I've got a pretty sweet bee-hind. Now smile for the camera."

Warm breath fanned her ear, making her shudder. She snapped the photo and bolted out of reach. Surely creepy and creepier was not the caliber of male on today's market.

Or maybe they wouldn't have been so bad if she'd stopped comparing everyone she met to Jase.

"You're so hot," the other one said to Jessie Kay, wiggling his brows, "even my zipper is falling for you."

Jessie Kay slapped him on the back. "Dude. That's a good one. I know! I know! Did you buy your pants on sale…because at my house they would be one hundred percent off."

The guys laughed. Jessie Kay gave Brook Lynn a look that said *having fun already?*

No, but soon. Brook Lynn scouted the room for her next photo partner. Perfect! Young and cute. The mustache wasn't to her taste, and he was a bit on the thin side, but beggars couldn't be choosers and all that.

"We'll be back in a bit," she told her sister. "You. Come on. I might need an interpreter." She dragged Kenna out of the corner, away from the circle of bad pickup lines, and bounded over to Mustache. "Let's take a picture together."

The guy furrowed his brow with confusion, but eventually consented.

Over the next half hour, Brook Lynn took a total of sixteen pictures, each more provocative than the last.

"Jase is going to flip out," she said, opening a text to him, selecting all of the images—and pressing Send.

Kenna moved in front of her. "Are you sure that's wise? What if you lose him for good over this?"

She frowned, not liking the thought and rejecting it. "We'll be good as gold after this. I'll have my proof."

"Proof? And, Brook Lynn, I wanted to jolt you out of your funk, maybe even to get you to talk about what's going on with Jase, but I didn't want to help ruin your life!"

"You've helped make it better. You'll see." And now, the moment of truth. She opened another text to Jase.

Come over 2nite. Let's discuss the pix.

Send.

Someone bumped into her, pushing her forward. She stumbled and bumped into someone else. "Sorry, sorry." The room began to spin faster and faster, and her stomach rebelled. She tried to move toward the bathroom—

where the heck was the bathroom?—but she made it only two steps before hunching over and vomiting all over the floor.

BROOK LYNN WASN'T sure how she made it home. She woke up in bed, alone, with a splitting headache and a terrible taste in her mouth. Had rodents crawled inside it and died?

Grumbling, she stumbled into the bathroom, where she brushed her teeth and showered, dressed in a tank and a pair of panties and brushed her teeth again. As memories of last night's escapades invaded her mind, she decided to go back to bed—and stay there forever.

My picture should be next to idiot *in the dictionary.*

She turned the volume up on her implants, just in case her sister decided to make another surprise visit, and curled up under the covers. Lesson learned. Alcohol only made everything worse. She'd actually sent pictures of herself draped over other men to Jase. *Of course* he was going to rage.

A weight settled at the end of her bed. Her eyelids popped open, and she gasped. Jase! He'd flipped on the lamp, and golden light spotlighted him. Rumpled dark hair, eyes that were bloodshot but not spewing fire. He didn't seem to have shaved since she'd left him, his stubble dark and thick.

She sat up, her body already heating…burning. Readying. The man who'd pleasured her so perfectly, so many times, was here, once again within reach. His masculine scent filled her head, at last chasing away her headache.

"Wh—what are you doing here?"

He frowned, and she had to battle the urge to brush her fingertips over his lips. "You invited me. Remember?"

She did, and she had to swallow a moan. The final text.

Jase withdrew his cell phone. "Let's chat about these." He showed her the screen. "This one is of a strobe light. This one is of a crowd. This one is of a dirty table. This one is of multiple pairs of feet."

Mission fail.

Why not tell him the truth? Get everything out in the open? "I was trying to make you mad."

"You…what? Why?" He set his phone on the nightstand.

"Okay, fine. You got me. I was trying to make you more than mad. I was trying to enrage you."

"Why did you think these random pictures would enrage me?"

"They were supposed to be pictures of me with other guys."

A terrible stillness came over him. "I see."

She covered her face with her hair and peeked at him through her spread fingers. "I wanted to find out what you'd do."

Several beats of silence. Such oppressive silence. "I see," he repeated.

There'd been hints of anger in his tone, but nothing else.

"I'm sorry," she said, miserable.

"Did you do anything with these men?" he asked quietly.

"No! Gross."

He studied her features, still masking his own, before he stood. "I better go. I wouldn't want to frighten you with my temper. I'll see you around, Brook Lynn. Or not. Yeah, probably not."

That was it? All he had to say? "Now just hold on a sec."

"Why?" He pushed a hand through his hair. "You're afraid of me, even though I would rather die than hurt you. There's nothing else to discuss."

A part of her melted. A part of her panicked. "You think this is easy for me? Being apart from you? Not trusting you?"

"Certainly seems that way."

There was a hint of bitterness in his tone. She deserved it, even welcomed it. He felt! "You're so cold so much of the time, Jase. You hold everything in. Then, apparently, you have times when you boil over and can't return to a simmer."

His eyes narrowed. "This is true, but have I ever harmed you?"

"You pushed me once."

"I didn't know what I was doing."

"Exactly my point!"

He closed his eyes for a moment. "That won't happen again. I won't let it. I know to be on guard now."

"But, Jase...I don't even know what happened that day. You've never told me."

Tensing more with every second that passed, he said, "I saw blood and flashed back to prison, to the times I'd been ambushed and...stabbed. And worse things."

She flattened a hand against her churning stomach. Knowing he'd endured such horrors was one thing. Hearing about it was another. "I'm sorry."

"I'm *not* going to hurt you," he insisted. "You mean too much to me. Just give me time, and I'll prove it."

"But...if I mean so much to you," she whispered, "why didn't you come after me?"

His laugh was bitter. "You can't have it both ways. You can't run and expect me to chase you. I'm an ex-con. Do you know what a stalking charge would do to me?"

See Brook Lynn's resistance begin to crumble. "I would never accuse you of stalking."

"Will you give me time, then?" He seemed to stop breathing, as if her response mattered more than anything ever had.

Tremors skated through her as she realized this was it. Decision time. There'd be no going back after this. He'd take her at her word and proceed accordingly.

"I'm never going to be the guy who displays every emotion," he said. "I can't be. But I'm telling you, stating it plain, I want to be with you. I don't care how I get you—I just want you in my life."

How am I supposed to resist him?

"O…okay," she said. "I'll give you time."

He stepped toward her, only to stop. "Be very sure. I won't live through another separation."

"I wouldn't, either," she admitted. "I'm sure. I want to be with you, too."

His relief was palpable, his desire more so. His eyes hooded, making her tremors redouble. "I hope you're ready to cross another item off your fun list." His tone… from stoic to simmering, tentative to determined.

"Always sometimes," she said with a nod.

"Good enough." He placed a knee on the edge of the bed, then the other, and urged her to her back. "Because we're about to solve the mystery of the missing orgasm."

She half laughed, half moaned in sublime surrender. "I believe I specified a mystery dinner."

"Oh, don't worry," he said, bending down. "We'll be dining."

Her heart kicked into a wild beat, her insides immediately flashing white-hot when he crashed his lips into hers, his tongue thrusting with brutal force, and she lost track of her surroundings.

He took her mouth with the same sense of possession he'd first taken her body. It was as if a dam had burst inside him, and only passion spilled free. He began pulling at her clothing, ripping the material in his haste. By the time he had her naked, a glorious madness had overtaken her, his name the only word her fragmented thoughts could form.

"Jase…Jase…" Oh, how she'd missed him. At times like this, when they were intimate, she feared nothing.

Their tongues parried and thrust in a sensual dance of dominance, and she realized this…this was what she'd thought she'd be getting when they'd first decided to commit. Raw carnality. A passion unlike any other. Almost…savage, with absolutely nothing held back.

He kissed and nipped his way to her breast, kneading the plump flesh. He sucked her nipple so hard a cry parted her lips, her back arching—to get closer to him or put distance between them, she wasn't sure. It was a mix of pleasure/pain she'd never before experienced, and she was instantly addicted.

"More," she commanded, fingers fisting his hair to hold his head in place.

He sucked one nipple then the other, giving them the same fierce treatment, until both were swollen and throbbing with ecstasy, a mimic of the constant throb between her legs. She didn't think she'd ever been so aroused or so wet—until he anchored her feet on his shoulders and knelt at the edge of the bed, dragging her over and placing his mouth directly between her spread legs.

He…utterly…*devoured*…her.

Like a starving man who'd just discovered a banquet. Like a man who'd had too many treasures stolen and thought he would lose this, too. He was ferocious, almost like an animal. Nipping and growling his approval as she writhed against his face. She came once… twice…lost in an ocean of rapture and never wanting to be found.

When she could take no more, her body so sensitive even the slightest breeze from the air conditioner tickled her, she used her feet to push at his shoulders. He raised his head, his eyelids heavy, hooded, and his eyes devoid of color, his pupils so large the green had been completely eclipsed. Tension branched from the corners, as well as from his mouth—a mouth wet with her pleasure.

He straightened slowly. As she watched, he licked his lips, savoring every drop she'd ceded.

"Not done," he said and slowly undressed. "Not even close."

His every movement was now measured, as if he knew he'd reached a breaking point and had to make an effort to regain control. But as more and more of his beautiful body was bared, desire was stoked inside her all over again, as if she'd never reached completion.

"Are you on birth control?" he asked.

"Yes. I got a shot soon after I met you." She trembled, and she burned, and she ached. *Empty,* she thought. *I'm so empty. Have to be filled.*

"You want me to wear a condom or do you want me bare?"

"Bare."

As she watched, he stroked the long length of his erection. "There is no one more beautiful than you, angel. Have I told you that?"

Her trembles came faster. "Jase. Please."

Maybe it was the needy edge her voice held. Maybe it was the plea itself. Either way, the frenzy hit him once again—only with more force. He grabbed her knees and pried them as far apart as they could go. He positioned himself at her entrance and slammed all the way home.

She cried out, stretched and filled as she'd so desperately needed to be. Knowing there was nothing between them, that the hardness of his flesh glided along the wetness of hers, somehow shredded *her* control. The pleasure was incredible, accompanied by a rush of adrenaline every time he thrust...and thrust...harder and harder, faster and faster. She bucked against him, her hips lifting off the bed, causing him to sink deeper every time he pushed in, as deep as her body would allow.

The headboard slammed against the wall again and again, the pictures anchored over it rattling. Jase never paused, just hammered inside her with greater force. She would still feel him tomorrow, in every cell of her body, and she would love it.

When he pulled out of her completely, she shouted a denial, even reached for him. He dropped to his knees and licked the heart of her until she began to climax against his tongue. As the first spasms swept through her, he straightened and pushed back in her. His mouth met hers in a kiss that would forever blister her soul. Her spasms intensified, the pleasure too much...more than she'd ever experienced at once...

"Brook Lynn," he roared, the harsh sound of his voice bringing her back down to earth. He gave one final shove before shuddering and coming inside her, hard.

He sagged against her, and all she could do was hold him close as her mind began to return to earth...to the fears she hadn't yet shaken. Not completely. She trusted him implicitly in bed, but she was still a little nervous about everything else.

She said she'd give him time, and she would—and she'd never been gladder about something. One thing she'd learned while apart from him: she couldn't breathe without him.

A dangerous way to feel, but just then, she didn't care.

CHAPTER TWENTY-THREE

JASE WOKE IN a rush, dead asleep one moment, upright and panting the next. Sweat had created a fine sheen over his skin. He scanned his surroundings—not his bedroom, he realized. Or his prison cell.

Brook Lynn's room. He was in her bed.

His gaze jerked to the slender body lying next to him. Morning sunlight spilled from the crack in the curtains, illuminating her sleeping form. Sleeping Beauty. Blond hair cascaded around her delicate features, tangled from the clench of his fingers. Eyelashes cast shadows over rose-flushed cheeks. Her lips were still red and slightly swollen from his kisses. Everything inside him relaxed. *Back where I belong.*

But for how long?

She was scared of him, she'd said. He hated that, but he couldn't blame her for it. He knew what she'd merely begun to suspect: the absolute utter darkness of his rage. He hadn't been pushed that far in a long time, but what if she was right? What if he snapped one day and hurt her?

Suddenly sick to his stomach, he rose from the bed, careful not to wake her. She didn't have a private bathroom, so he used the one in the hall. He found a toothbrush still in its packaging and wondered if she'd bought it for him, pre-confession.

He glared at his reflection in the mirror and saw a

well-satisfied but obviously unhappy male. *I can't give her up. I just have to prove to us both I can be trusted.*

And he would. No other option was acceptable.

Noise drew him out of the bathroom. The sound of a cat being murdered, surely. But no. He found Jessie Kay in the kitchen, singing while making sandwiches. He paused as she glanced up from frying eggs and frowned at him.

"What are you doing here?" she asked. "I didn't see your car, and last I heard, you'd gotten the ax."

Had Brook Lynn told her sister about his past?

Either way, it was time for a reckoning, he supposed. He closed his eyes for a moment—*man up*—before sitting down at the table. "Beck dropped me off last night."

"I wish he'd stayed. I needed help painting my toenails."

"Well, I'm glad we're getting a little time to ourselves."

Her frown deepened. "Dude. If you're hitting on me, I'm going to take this knife and shove it up your—"

"No. I'm not hitting on you," he said, speaking over her. "I'm trying to apologize for the way I treated you. In the beginning." Brook Lynn loved this girl, and now, knowing Jessie Kay and her vulnerabilities a little better, he understood why. She had a quick wit and an easy smile, and she would burn the world to the ground if it meant saving the ones she loved. As he would.

"Can't say you didn't end up with the better choice," she muttered. "You may or may not have noticed I have a few issues."

"You and me both. But Brook Lynn is merely the better choice *for me*. Some guy is going to be lucky to have you."

She flipped her hair over her shoulder, saying, "Duh."

Then she flashed him a wry smile. "What happened between you guys, anyway? Brook Lynn wouldn't say."

She'd kept his secret, even from her sister. That *had* to mean something. "I told her how I...spent almost a decade in prison," he said.

"What!" Jessie Kay spun around and gaped at him. "You're freaking kidding me."

No more hiding, he decided. It caused too many problems later on. For others and for himself.

Jase clenched the edge of the table. He had to pry his fingers loose before he snapped the thing in two as he told her the entire story. She listened intently, never interrupting. Her expressive face registered more shock, disbelief, horror and finally understanding.

"Dude." She arched a golden brow at him, an expression he'd often seen on Brook Lynn. "I always thought I'd be the Dillon sister to end up with an ex-con."

"You still could," he replied drily. "Your soul mate is still out there."

"This is true. Well, fingers crossed."

"So?" he asked. "Is this the part where you warn me away from your sister?"

She peered at him for a long while, studying him, thinking. Then she sighed. "No. But if you ever hurt her..."

"I won't." He'd run like hell out of her life first.

"Good. Because I don't want to have to spend time behind bars for the murder *I'll* commit."

Please. There'd never been a woman with more bark and less bite. "You're a good person, Jessie Kay. My... friend." She was, wasn't she? She could have tried to stop Brook Lynn from dating him, but she hadn't. She'd encouraged the girl. "Don't ever settle for less than the best. It's what you deserve."

"Truer words have never been spoken," she said, and he wished she'd sounded as if she believed him. "But right now I don't have time to listen to you wax poetic about my awesomeness. Brook Lynn woke me up while you were sleeping and told me about her new business idea—making and delivering sandwiches. We're partners, and we're calling it You've Got It Coming. She baked the bread, cooked and spiced the meats, and even mixed the condiments before crawling back into bed with you. I'm putting everything together to hand out as samples to the people in town."

And he'd slept through it all, which shocked him. Considering how much time he'd spent wondering when he would next be attacked had made him a light sleeper. Guess he was more comfortable here than he'd realized.

"You guys are destined for success." Though he hated to lose Brook Lynn as his non-wife wife.

"I will *not* fail her," Jessie Kay added staunchly.

He needed to get home and check on West, but he found himself saying, "Anything I can do to help?"

She tossed him an evil grin. "You are so gonna regret asking that."

Together they made thirteen sandwiches, everything from a ham, egg and cheese bagel to a huevos rancheros wrap for the breakfast lovers, and roast pork with pickled cucumber to smoked salmon salad sandwiches for the lunch crowd. He felt it was his duty to test most of the ingredients for poison, the same way Brook Lynn once tested baked goods. He was diligent like that.

"You're eating our profits, you douche," Jessie Kay finally cried, throwing a handful of cheese shreds at him. "And I will get them back, whatever it takes!"

He laughed and threw a pickle at her. She was reaching for a slice of bacon when Brook Lynn walked in, wearing a tank, a pair of short pink shorts and fuzzy house boots. He hardened instantly.

She pasted a too-bright, clearly fake smile on her face. "Morning."

"Uh-oh. Warden's here," Jessie Kay said, the food fight over before it had really begun.

"So the fun has to stop, right?" Even Brook Lynn's fake smile vanished.

"I didn't mean… Oh, never mind. You're clearly in a mood. One too many orgasms?" Jessie Kay started bagging sandwiches. "I've got some deliveries to make before my boss, the Dragon Lady, decides to fire me." She snickered. "See what I did there?"

Brook Lynn rolled her eyes.

"I'm off." Jessie Kay kissed Brook Lynn's cheek before she left.

"You okay?" he asked her. Jase studied her, this woman who'd stolen his heart.

He froze. The words echoed in his mind. *Stolen his heart.* She had, hadn't she? He'd known he could fall, but hadn't realized he'd long since fallen. He loved her. Loved her with every cell in his body. Loved her with every bit of light in his soul. She'd somehow snuck past his defenses to become one of the most important parts of his life. More important than his lungs.

"Do you want me to go?" he asked, fighting the urge to go to her, draw her in his arms and *show* her how he felt.

"I…don't know."

"Why?"

"I don't know."

"This isn't going to work if you refuse to tell me what's going on inside that head of yours."

Baby blues he'd so often drowned in implored him

to understand. "I'm a horrible person. I ran away from you, stayed away from you, tried to make you angry—and now I want to complain because you were alone with my sister."

She was…jealous?

Don't smile. "Your reaction is understandable. I slept with her."

The color vanished from her cheeks. "I know. The image is burned into my brain."

He wished she hadn't walked into his room that night. Even the thought of her with another man… Deep breath in, out. "Like so many other things, I can't change it," he said. "What's done is done."

"I know that, too," she said, shoulders sagging with dejection.

He sensed a "but" and leaned against the counter, crossed his arms.

"Do you compare us?" she asked.

"No!" he burst out. How could she think that, even for a second? "There is no one who compares to you."

She flinched. "I just…I don't…"

Forcibly controlling his tone, he added, "Tell me what you want me to do, and it's done. Burn my bed and get a new one? Done. Buy a new house? Done. The only thing I won't do is stay away from Jessie Kay. The two of you are a package deal, honey, and that's never going to change. You know it, and I know it. Besides, if I ignored her, it would hurt her, which would hurt you."

"I don't want you to ignore her," she said. "I don't want any of those things. I just…I don't know." She stomped across the room, but she didn't draw him closer when she was within reach. She pushed him, as if daring him to react. "I'm so frustrated with us both right now. There's no quick fix for any of this."

"Trust me, I know."

She looked down at her hands, as if she couldn't believe what they'd done, before turning away from him.

He gently latched on to her waist, stopping her. "You do whatever you need to do to me, as long as you stay with me."

My resistance is melting all over again, Brook Lynn thought.

Seeing Jase with her sister had caused the darkest, most primal surge of jealousy to shoot through her. It had been irrational. It *was* irrational, not to mention illogical. She trusted him not to cheat. And she trusted Jessie Kay. But...

The emotions were still there, frothing, propelling her toward madness. Even knowing she was out of line didn't help. And now she couldn't shake the questions rapid-firing through her mind. Questions she voiced. "What sets me apart from my sister in your mind? What makes you want one of us but not the other—when you once wanted the other, too?"

Warm breath fanned the curve of her neck, making her shiver. His chest pressed against her back, the strength of him buffering her from the rest of the world. He picked her up and turned, placing her on the kitchen counter. Parting her legs, he stepped into the cradle she provided.

He framed her face in his big, callused hands. "You've known hardship, and yet you've never allowed it to define you. You are serious...about having fun. You carry responsibilities too heavy for your shoulders, and yet you don't seem to notice. And I have never wanted a woman the way I want you. Never needed one the way I need you. You were made for me—she wasn't."

"Jase," she said softly. Had more beautiful words ever been spoken to her?

"I'm not done." His hands moved to the back of her neck, fisting her hair. Ravaged, he said, "You are pleasure to my pain, hope to my fear. You are everything I've ever needed but didn't think I'd be lucky enough to have. I adore the way you think and the things you say." Voice going husky, he added, "And don't even get me started on the way you move."

A tremor danced along her spine as she played with the ends of his hair. "That's the sweetest thing anyone has ever said to me."

"Brook Lynn," he said.

"Yes, Jase."

"I love you."

Oh…wow. She'd been wrong—more beautiful words had been spoken to her. "But…you can't. You shouldn't. I abandoned you when you needed me most."

"Not your fault. I started our relationship in the wrong place. But we're on the right track now. You know everything. I can prove myself. I will."

Well, it was suddenly clear to her that she had things to prove, as well. "Jase, I—"

"Still not done, honey. I love you with every fiber of my being." His thumbs caressed her cheeks with reverence. "I'm happiest when I'm with you and resent any time apart. I think of you and smile. I think of you and crave. There's nothing I wouldn't do for you."

She melted against him, and in that moment, that instant, that snap of time, the fear left her. Just, *boom*, it packed up and moved out. This man—this amazing, precious man—might have a temper, but he loved her. He loved *her*, defective Brook Lynn Dillon. And she knew without a doubt that he would never turn his rage on her.

She might not have forgotten his rages, but she *had* forgotten his reaction to her, at least for a little while. He'd snapped out of his darker emotions at her command, at her touch, and his first thought had been of her, of her safety.

How could she ever have doubted him?

"So…" she said, kissing the center of his chin. "What I'm hearing is, you are totally whipped."

He laughed, the sound of it rusty but magnificent. "I think 'tenderized' is a more apt description."

"Like chicken?"

"For sure."

Feeling more lighthearted than she had in days, she couldn't help but tease, "You think I'm a mallet?"

"A very beautiful mallet." He kissed the center of her chin, as well, then the edge of her mouth. "I was serious about proving myself. And the only way I know to do that is to make sure you know everything about me. Nothing held back." Thin lines of tension formed at the corners of his eyes. "And there *is* something else I haven't told you. Something I haven't told anyone, not even Beck and West."

When he said no more, she petted at his chest. "Whatever it is," she said softly, "I'm not going anywhere. Not this time. And I want you to know I kept your other secret. Whatever you tell me stays with me. Always."

He thought for a moment, nodded. But the lines of tension only deepened. "I…when I was first locked away…I was…I was scrawny, and the things you've probably heard about prison life…they're true." He cleared his throat. Beads of sweat dotted his brow. "The 'worse' things I told you happened to me…I was held down and...forced...and it happened more than once, until I got stronger and learned to fight back."

Hearing the confession was like taking a baseball bat to the head: jarring, shocking and horrific all at once. Reeling, she wrapped her arms around him, held him close. "I'm so sorry, Jase." A thousand emotions seemed to bubble up at once, nearly choking her.

He squeezed her tightly, holding on as if she were a life raft. He'd suffered, and was still suffering, with the aftereffects.

His body began to shake. Something wet splashed on her neck. Tears?

"Oh, Jase," she whispered. No words would be good enough, but she had to try. "You are a wonderful, amazing man, and I am so blessed to know you. I hate that you were hurt. I hate it so much. I would take away your pain if I could. I would bear it for you."

He held on to her long after his shaking stopped. When he lifted his head, she wiped the moisture from his cheeks, her heart pounding against her ribs. She'd been right before. This man felt *too much*. Too deeply.

A buzz sounded from his pocket, followed by a ring.

"Answer if you'd like," she said and gave him a quick peck. "Then I want you to take me to bed." *Where I will confess my love for* you. After everything, it would be better if she showed him before she told him.

"No. Bed now. Actually, counter now. You'll help me forget the past and remember I have a future."

Before he could lift the hem of her shirt, *her* phone started ringing.

He sighed and straightened, then checked his phone. "Missed call. Beck."

She checked hers. "Missed call. Beck."

She gave him a little push, and just like before her

mountain of a man remained in place. He dialed his friend. As the two men talked, she unbuttoned Jase's pants. But the one-sided conversation soon captured her full attention, and she stilled.

"What do you mean?...No, impossible...She isn't... she can't..." Jase turned away from Brook Lynn, and dread slithered through her. "Okay. I'll be right there."

He hung up, but didn't face Brook Lynn right away.

"What's wrong?" she asked.

The longest moment she could ever imagine passed before he turned. He'd grown pale, waxen. "Beck's secret. He tracked down my ex-girlfriend. Daphne. Had emailed her once he found her, so now she's here. In town. At my house."

"What!" Chilled to the bone, Brook Lynn hopped to her feet.

"That's not all." Jase tunneled a hand through his hair. "She has a kid—and she says the girl is mine."

CHAPTER TWENTY-FOUR

THOUGH BROOK LYNN was in a knock-down-drag-out fight with her nerves, she was able to hide it behind the warden persona. A stern expression and clipped, efficient movements. The talent came in handy as she and Jase climbed into her car.

"We will get this figured out," she said. Would they, though? Would they, really? He might have a kid—and a former girlfriend he might want to support.

He mumbled an agreement, too dazed to respond any further than that.

She took extra care on the road, going slower than usual as her mind lobbed questions and statements at her as if they were baseballs and she held a bat.

Jase…a father?

Jase…a family man?

A family that did not include Brook Lynn, but *did* include Daphne, the girl he'd once loved.

He loves me now. He said so.

But does he love me more than he once loved her? Brook Lynn had a major mark against her. She'd walked away from him the moment she'd learned the truth about his past. Did this Daphne person have *any* marks?

By the time she reached his house, her fingers had clenched the steering wheel so tightly the two were practically fused together. Her legs trembled as she trailed Jase to the porch and inside the house.

Beck waited by the door, and as they passed him, he marched outside, casting Brook Lynn a pitying glance and saying, "I'll give you guys some privacy."

He wanted Jase to have a choice, he'd once told her. Now she understood. The choice between Brook Lynn and Daphne, present and past.

The moisture in her mouth dried when she noticed the floral-printed luggage stacked in the foyer. How long did the woman hope to stay?

Jase stopped in the living room, and Brook Lynn moved beside him. A pretty brunette in her late twenties sat on the couch. She wore a crisp gray blouse and black slacks, and despite the heat outside, she looked as fresh as a newly bloomed rose. Her makeup was perfectly applied and demure. The slenderness of her bones gave her a regal air Brook Lynn would never be able to achieve.

Studying the competition, she began to feel like an idiot for ever being jealous of her sister, who would never make a play for Jase now that Brook Lynn was dating him…and Jase would never do anything with Jessie Kay to jeopardize their relationship. But this Daphne person was a whole different story. She had what Jase never had but had probably always wanted. A family.

A little girl sat at Daphne's side. She wore a white sundress and shifted uncomfortably, tugging at one of the dress's straps. She had a shoulder-length crop of dark hair that was straight as a pin and eyes as flawless as the most expensive emeralds. A thought Brook Lynn had often had about *Jase's* eyes. The little girl had his mouth, too, with an upper lip plumper than the bottom.

Calm. Steady.

Brook Lynn's gaze returned to Daphne…who was

staring at her with curiosity, probably speculating about her relationship with Jase.

"Daphne," Jase said, his voice rough. "It's good to see you again."

"You, too. Although you look so different. So *big*." Her attention returned to Brook Lynn. "And who do we have here?"

"This is Brook Lynn," he said.

She waited for him to add, *She's my girlfriend.* But the words never came.

Feeling like an interloper, she moved in front of him, giving Daphne her back, and whispered, "Do you want me to go?"

Deep down, she prayed he would grab hold of her and command her to stay with him, then tell her he needed her support now and always. But he could barely peel his gaze from the woman who consumed his past.

"Yes," he finally said, and it was like being stabbed in the heart. "Thank you for understanding. Text me when you get home and let me know you're safe."

Officially dismissed. The hurting only magnified as she turned away from him. "Sure thing."

Without another word, she walked to the door. Her legs shook the whole way.

"What are you doing here?" she heard him ask Daphne.

Brook Lynn hesitated, hovering between inside and outside, her hand resting on the door's knob. All she had to do was give a little tug and the partition would close, stopping her from becoming a dirty eavesdropper. But the need to hear Daphne's reply locked her in place.

"Beck emailed me. I thought you wanted to see me... that maybe you'd heard... Well." Daphne cleared her throat. "Jase, I'd like to introduce you to your daughter, Hope. Hope, this is Jase. Your father."

Hope. A beautiful name for a beautiful girl.

Jase's girl.

Brook Lynn stood there, struggling to breathe for one minute...two...as she waited for Jase's response. But he didn't give one, and she couldn't risk staying there any longer. The door snickered closed, and she stumbled to the car.

Maybe Daphne was lying. Maybe she was telling the truth. But Brook Lynn suspected the latter—and knew her relationship with Jase was about to change drastically.

Even...end?

She wasn't sure how she made it home without crashing. By the time she pulled into the driveway, the tattered remains of the warden facade had completely burned away.

Less than an hour ago, she'd realized just how deeply she had fallen in love with Jase. Now she could lose him.

Once inside her bedroom, she texted Jase as requested. Minutes ticked into an hour, but a response never arrived.

A daughter, she thought, dazed. Jase had a daughter. He was a dad, with a ready-made family. What place did Brook Lynn have in his life now?

I can make a place.

He just has to give me a chance.

The thought mocked her. He'd asked her to give him a chance, too, and yet she'd hesitated.

She tossed and turned all night. Jessie Kay never came home, and for once she didn't go out looking.

In the morning, Brook Lynn dressed with special

care, choosing a pink T-shirt with cutouts of lace and her best shorts, the ones with the fewest frays at the hem. Jase still hadn't texted her.

She drove to his house and found Daphne's minivan still parked in the driveway.

Dread made Brook Lynn's limbs feel as if they were a hundred pounds each as she made her way inside, using the key Jase had given her. The luggage bags were no longer stacked beside the front door, which wasn't actually a good sign. It meant they'd been moved into one of the rooms. And since there were no spare bedrooms...

There were no blankets or pillows on the couch to suggest someone had slept there.

Jase isn't a cheater, she reminded herself. But that didn't mean he wouldn't make a clean break from her and go back to Daphne.

The scent of bacon saturated the air. Since Brook Lynn had started working here, she had been the one to fix breakfast every morning. Maybe Beck had an overnight guest, and he'd decided to make his famous morning-after meal. His consolation prize for the woman he'd never see again. But Brook Lynn doubted that was the case. For the most part, she'd taken over that duty, too.

She tripped her way to the kitchen. Daphne stood at the stove, and wave after wave of jealousy rolled through Brook Lynn. *I may not work for Jase anymore, but cooking his meals is still my job.* No way in hell this girl was going to take over.

"Where's Jase?" Brook Lynn asked.

Daphne glanced over her shoulder and offered a tight smile. "You're Brook Lynn, right? The maid?"

I'm far more than that. But it looked as if the claws had come out. "Where's Jase?" she asked again.

"Out back. But would you mind staying inside for a bit? He's getting to know his daughter, and I'd really like to give them more time."

Her hands tightened into fists. "More time? Where were you nine years ago?" *I'm acting like a green-eyed she-beast. Don't like this side of myself.*

Daphne turned off the stove and faced her full-on, features hardening by the second. Today she wore a blue tank and shorts that came to just over her knees. Casual chic. Her hair had been pulled back in a ponytail, showcasing the many piercings in her ears. Her feet were bare, her toenails painted a delicate pink.

"I've already discussed that with Jase," Daphne said, her voice stiff. "I owed him an explanation. I don't owe you anything."

Do not react.

Should she go?

The back door slid open. In strode the little girl. She'd looked uncomfortable and nervous last night, but that wasn't the case today. Happiness radiated through her pores.

Jase came in behind her, wearing a soft, tender expression. Seeing him with his daughter only made her fall deeper in love with him—but when he spotted Brook Lynn, he frowned.

Perspiration dotted her palms. She was suddenly transported back to her childhood, before she'd gotten the implants. Jessie Kay would drag her out of the house to play with other kids, only to have those other kids run away, not wanting anything to do with Earmuff Girl.

"Brook Lynn," he said in greeting, his voice tempered, revealing zero hint of his emotions.

Back to square one.

"This is Hope. Hope, this is Brook Lynn."

Again, he left off the *girlfriend* identifier. "Hello."

"Hi. I guess." The girl certainly had her mother's unwelcoming attitude. But she'd inherited more than Jase's eyes and mouth, Brook Lynn realized. She had inherited the shape of his face. They were like carbon copies of each other, and a pang tore through her chest.

"Don't be rude," Daphne admonished, surprising her.

Hope glared up at Brook Lynn as if she was the enemy. "She started it! We're having a family day, and she's not family."

Translation: go home. "Don't worry. I'm not staying," Brook Lynn croaked.

Jase tousled Hope's dark hair, earning a grin from her, before he claimed Brook Lynn's hand. "Excuse us for a moment." He ushered her out of the kitchen, into his bedroom, where he released her to scrub a hand down his face.

"I'm sorry," he said. He plopped on the end of the bed.

Both sides were mussed, both pillows flat and well used.

"They stayed the night," Brook Lynn said hollowly.

"Of course." He sounded mildly offended, as if she'd just accused him of throwing the pair into the street.

"Daphne slept in here," she said. A statement, not a question.

Understanding dawned, and he snapped, "With Hope. Not me. I crashed in West's room. Both he and Beck stayed out all night."

She exhaled a breath she felt like she'd been holding all her life. Okay. All right. "I'm sorry. I don't know who I am anymore. This situation is just so…"

"Screwed up. I get it." A tense pause before he added,

"But it's about to get even more so. Daphne and Hope are going to stay for a few weeks."

The jealousy she felt now made a mockery of the jealousy she'd felt only seconds before, though she tried not to show it. "I'm glad you'll have a chance to get to know your daughter." That was the truth.

"She is…perfect," he said, and Brook Lynn would have sworn there were stars in his eyes.

It warmed her heart to see the deep love he'd already developed for the girl. "Why is Daphne just now telling you about her?"

"Because I was in prison."

"That's an excuse."

A sardonic flash of teeth. "Really? Because I seem to recall you wanting nothing to do with me for that very reason."

Ouch. "Do you still want to be with me?" she asked quietly.

"I do," he said without hesitation. "I wasn't kidding when I told you I loved you."

Relief was like the first rain after a long drought. "But…why didn't you tell Daphne I'm your girlfriend?"

"Honey, the last I heard from you, you were giving me time. I didn't know you were accepting me back as your boyfriend."

"I—"

A light tap sounded at the door.

"—want you," she finished. "I want *everything* from you."

He reached for her, only to fist his hands just before contact as another knock sounded. His arms fell to his sides. "The door," he said.

"Right." Trembling, she turned the knob.

Hope stepped inside, wide-eyed, a plate of food in hand. "Um, hi." She glanced between them.

"Hey, sweetheart," Jase said, his tone gentling.

Hope unveiled a devastating smile, preening under his attention. "Momma wanted you to have your breakfast while it was still hot."

Well, wasn't that nice. Too nice?

Had Daphne come here hoping to win Jase back?

Brook Lynn's knees nearly gave out. If she were to war against Daphne, she would lose. Daphne had the ace.

Be that as it may, Brook Lynn wasn't giving up without a fight. Not this time. She'd walked away once already, and it had brought her nothing but heartache. Jase deserved better. He deserved her best, and that's what she would give him. *I'm coming at you guns blazing, Mr. Hollister.*

"Eat your breakfast." She strutted over, kissed him on the forehead and whispered, "Your days belong to your daughter, and I'm glad about that, I really am, but your nights are mine."

JASE GLANCED AT the clock. 10:07 flashed in bold red numbers. Hope had been asleep for an hour. And for the entirety of that hour he'd wanted to go to Brook Lynn.

But Daphne sat on the couch, telling West and Beck what she'd told him last night—her story since they'd last seen each other. Neither interrupted her. Neither accused her of lying about Hope's paternity.

Jase didn't need a DNA test. In his heart, he knew the truth. *Break out the pink cigars. I'm a dad.*

He was scared as hell he'd do a bad job with Hope, maybe scar her emotionally because he had no idea how to love a kid, and she'd have to spend a few decades in therapy, but he did love her. Just a few minutes alone with her had sealed the deal.

You're really my dad?

I am.

I'm glad. I've been dreaming of you my whole life.

He'd toppled head over heels then and there. And yeah, for a guy who'd professed to never want kids, he'd sure fallen for this one fast and hard. But then, he hadn't known what he'd been missing.

"I found out I was pregnant the day before Jase's sentence," Daphne said. "I was scared, but I thought I could find another guy and everything would be okay. Jase had no money, no prospects and no future. I wanted someone who had those things. But the one I picked stuck around only until I began showing. I got a job as a receptionist at a law firm and went to night school to become a court stenographer, knowing I'd need a way to support the baby on my own. And I did it. I finished, was making something of my life, but Jase was still in prison. I just...I didn't want Hope to see him behind bars."

Good call. But if he'd known about her, at the very least, he could have been there for her, providing money, a home, food, clothes. Anything she'd needed, everything she'd wanted.

"Where does she think he's been?" Beck asked.

Daphne plucked a piece of lint from her shirtsleeve. "In another country, helping starving children."

A saint rather than a sinner. Of course. "I'll be telling her the truth," Jase said. "Soon." The thought of his own daughter fearing him caused him to break out in a cold sweat, but he wasn't going to lie to her or risk someone else telling her. He also wasn't going to allow her to think he'd put other kids before her.

"He's been out for over six months," West said, anger tightening his voice. "You've had plenty of time to create another lie about her dad's return." The wound on his forehead had begun to heal, but the wounds in his soul had begun to leak their poison.

He once again smelled of the most potent alcohol.

"Well," she said, casting Jase a look filled with remorse. "I thought about it, I did, but I wasn't sure how Jase would feel, if he would care. But I was just fooling myself. I see that now. I was scared. I've been in a stable, loving relationship for almost three years now, and I didn't want to screw that up. But Tyler is in the military. The army. He's currently overseas, left last week, and he'll be gone for six months. That's why I decided to answer Beck's email."

"Is he good to Hope?" Beck asked.

It was a question Jase had asked, as well.

"Very. He loves her like she's his own."

But she's not *his. She's mine.* And he adored that little girl with every fiber of his being.

"You'll have to tell him about me, Daph." Jase pinned her with a hard stare. "I'm going to be a part of Hope's life." Now and forever.

"I know," she said, surprising him. "If he's able, he's going to video chat with me later tonight. I plan to tell him then."

"And that's going to make everything better?" West exploded. "You left without a word, hid a secret for nine years and think you can come back as if you've done nothing wrong?"

Daphne stiffened.

"West," Jase said. "I love you, man, but I won't let you talk to her like that."

"Someone has to look out for you." West's gaze practically spewed fire as it landed on Jase. "I didn't before, but I will now."

He closed his eyes for a moment, drew in a breath. This was what guilt did, he realized. Tore down. Left you in a rut. Unable to move forward. And Jase didn't want to live like that any longer. He didn't want his friends to live like that.

He stood, walked to the couch where West and Beck sat and eased onto the coffee table in front of them, his attention remaining on West. "Let it go," he said softly. "It's time. The past is a noose around your neck, and it's choking the life out of you." He looked to Beck. "You, too. You just hide it better."

Both men focused on something other than Jase and remained silent.

"I want better for you. I want better for *me*." He patted each of their knees. "I want my friends back. The ones who see me as an equal, not someone they owe."

Again, silence.

"I'm asking you to move forward. Therefore, you have to move forward," he continued. "You've paid enough. I've paid enough. We're going to enjoy life. Finally." He gave them another pat before standing and meeting Daphne's watery gaze. "I'm really glad you found your happily-ever-after."

"Me, too. I hope you find yours."

"I'm working on it."

CHAPTER TWENTY-FIVE

BROOK LYNN SANG and danced through the kitchen as she put together orders for You've Got It Coming. Twenty-three sandwiches and six casseroles. But the growing business wasn't what had put her in such a great mood. Jase had come over last night, and he'd rocked her world. Stripped her, touched her. Loved her.

I think we broke the mattress. And the world record for the number of orgasms achieved in one night.

Before he'd left early this morning to be with Hope, he'd kissed her so tenderly she would have sworn her soul melded with his. Afterward, when he'd lifted his head and peered deep into her eyes, his thumbs caressing the line of her jaw, she'd experienced the most sublime sense of contentment.

I belong in his arms.

As she made her deliveries, the air smelled sweeter and felt less stifling. The trees seemed greener, the flowers lusher and everyone in town nicer. More than one person remarked on her smile.

Even Edna—who had ordered a sandwich, expecting a discounted rate—had noticed. *You're positively glowing, Brook Lynn. New vitamin?*

Yes. Vitamin J.

Finally, there were only three orders left. West, Beck and some guy staying at the Strawberry Inn. His name was Stan, no last name, and she decided to check him off the list first so she could spend a little extra time with the boys.

Inside the lobby, Brook Lynn waved to Holly Mathis, the owner's teenage daughter, who manned the counter. "Delivery to room twelve," she said to the girl.

"Whatever," Holly replied, chewing her gum and returning her attention to her magazine.

Brook Lynn had barely tapped the room's door when it whisked open to reveal the guy who'd plowed into her on the street...forever ago, it seemed. She blinked in surprise, saying, "You."

A flare of something appeared in his bloodshot eyes... something that took her aback. "Yes. Me."

His skin was sallower, his hair unkempt. He wore a long-sleeved shirt despite the heat outside, with shorts. She thought she could make out the tail of a snake or dragon tattoo curling around his calf.

"How are your knees?" he asked.

"Completely healed, thanks." She cleared her throat and held out his sandwich. "Uh, that'll be fifteen dollars, please." Ten for the sandwich, five for the delivery. It may be considered pricey in these parts, but she'd been told her sandwiches were well worth it.

He handed her wadded-up bills that were slightly damp.

"Thank you, and I hope you enjoy it."

"I know I will."

She turned to leave.

"Hey. I heard you're friends with Jase Hollister," he said. "Is that true?"

Frowning, she faced him. "Do you know him?"

"Better than you. Be careful." He shut the door in her face before she could respond.

Her stomach twisted. How did he know Jase? Because honestly, if she judged solely by appearance, she would have to guess prison.

She headed to Fragaria Street. The building West and Beck had purchased was made of crumbling red brick, copper and wrought-iron trim. The guys were in the process of fixing it up, though the inside already resembled something out of a magazine, with plush rugs, gleaming wood floors and wainscoting on the walls.

At the front was a massive, intricately carved desk and the woman who manned it, Cora Higal. She used to teach at the local elementary school, and no one had ever gotten over their fear of her index finger. When it pointed in your direction, you were likely to melt into a puddle of guilt and shame.

A sign hung on the wall behind her. WOH Industries. For West, Ockley and Hollister.

"Brook Lynn Dillon," Cora said with a firm nod, the phone ringing beside her. "Mr. West and Mr. Ockley are expecting you. You may head back."

"Thank you."

There were three offices, each surrounded by glass walls, but both men were inside the one on the far right. Beck spotted her and waved her in.

"Hey, guys." She handed off the requested sandwiches and tried to deny payment, but Beck stuffed the bills into her pockets. Fine. No reason to fight. She'd simply drop them at Cora's desk on her way out. "How's it going?"

"Better, now that you're here." Beck gave her an appreciative once-over. "You're looking more gorgeous than ever. I'm thinking I need to seduce the hell out of you right here, right now."

"As if you could," she quipped.

His eyes twinkled with merriment, his smile carefree. "Oh, I could. You're just lucky I've never released the full measure of my sexual prowess on you."

"*So* lucky," she said and rolled her eyes.

"But once again, I wasn't talking to you, Brook Lynn." He kissed the wrapper of his sandwich. "You're the only one for me, baby."

As she snickered, West stood from behind the desk, his chair skidding backward. He scowled at Beck then at her then at Beck again. Like Stan, he had bloodshot eyes and wrinkled clothes. Though his were clearly more expensive. "I can't work under these conditions."

"Then we'll leave," Beck said easily.

"Don't bother." West stormed from the office and out of the building.

Brook Lynn didn't have to ask what was wrong with him. Tessa's party loomed ever closer.

Speaking of, she had some more planning to do. She might not be working for Jase, but she wasn't going to leave him in the lurch. "I have bouquet samples to show you guys, but I didn't bring them."

"Worry about it tomorrow."

Good. She had to run a few errands she planned to run today—it was time to check another item off her fun list.

"Well," she said. "I better go."

"I'll see you later." Beck offered her a sad smile. "I'm sorry about that."

"Don't be. I get it. The loss of a loved one leaves a big hole in your heart, and if you aren't careful, sorrow and regret fill it."

"He'll be sunshine and smiles a few days after the party. It's his cycle—after the actual anniversary date, things always look up."

"I'm glad." Not just for West's sake, but for Jase and

Beck. They hurt when their friend hurt. "Let me know if there's anything I can do to help."

"Will do."

As she tromped to the door, Jase entered the building. Warm delight instantly spilled through her and she had to fight not to throw herself into his arms. Daphne and Hope were with him, and Brook Lynn wasn't sure how he'd react to displays of affection.

Both females looked lovely in summer dresses, dark hair pulled back in matching ponytails. Though Daphne's eyes were rimmed with pink and a bit swollen, as if she'd spent the night crying.

Jase narrowed his focus on Brook Lynn and closed the distance, a ravenous predator determined to enjoy his prey. She shivered in pleasure as he wrapped her in the strength of his arms.

"I missed you," he whispered against her ear, answering her question about the PDA.

"I missed you, too." Even though they'd been parted only a few hours. A minute was too long. She rubbed her nose against his neck and breathed in the masculine scent of him. *Can't ever get enough.*

"Sandwich deliveries?" he asked as they pulled apart.

"Yeah, but I'm all done now." She peeked at Daphne, expecting the woman to be seething with dark jealousy. Or hatred. Something. Anything.

But Daphne merely smiled at her. "It's nice to see you again, Brook Lynn."

"Uh...you, too?" A question when it should have been a statement. Jase hadn't told her anything about Daphne's situation—when they'd seen each other last night, they'd been too eager to get to bed—and she made a mental note to ask. "What are you guys up to?"

"Getting to know the town," Daphne said, adding hesitantly, "Jase has asked us to move here."

"I was going to talk to you about it," he rushed to tell her.

Did he expect Brook Lynn to protest? "Have you taken them to Strawberry Jam?"

At first, he remained silent, peering down at her with surprise…which soon turned into a potent mix of affection and desire. "You are an amazing woman," he said and kissed her softly, gently. "You know that, right?"

Tonight I'm going to climb him like a tree. "Strawberry Jam is where Jessie Kay, my sister, used to work," she told Daphne. "They pluck wild strawberries from several hundred acres and create the best jellies you'll ever taste. If you sign up for a tour, you'll get to sample all the different flavors."

Hope jumped up and down. "I want to go! Can we go? Please, please, Momma."

While Daphne promised her daughter a tour, Brook Lynn ran her hands over Jase's shoulders, smoothing the lines of his shirt. "I almost forgot. Do you know a guy named Stan?"

He thought for a moment, shook his head. "No. Why?"

"I delivered a sandwich to him at the Strawberry Inn, and he asked about you."

"Me?" He frowned. "Reporter?"

"I don't think so. He didn't have a professional look. And he told me to be careful around you."

His frown deepened, a spark of anger in his eyes. "I'll look into him."

She nodded and decided to change the subject, asking quietly, "What's wrong with Daphne?"

He responded just as quietly, saying, "She told her

boyfriend about me, about her trip here, and he broke up with her."

She'd had a boyfriend? Wow. Brook Lynn had all but accused the woman of coming here to steal Jase. *Looks like I owe her an apology.*

"Hey. What are those weird things in your ears?" Hope asked, pointing to Brook Lynn's implants. "Are you part robot?"

Jase stiffened against her but for once Brook Lynn felt no embarrassment. Something the man beside her was responsible for. "I *am* part robot," she teased. "Is it hot in here or did my internal fan system just crash?"

Hope didn't understand, but Jase did, and he chuckled, whispering, "Is ten inches your maximum RAM capacity or can I try for eleven?"

"Requested log-in denied," she quipped.

He only laughed harder, and it thrilled her to her soul. *You'll never be one of those guys who displays emotions, my love? Think again.*

"I'm so sorry about that," Daphne said, looking mortified.

"No worries." Brook Lynn crouched down to Hope's level and said, "Why don't you and I hit the town together?" She looked at Jase, Daphne. "If that's okay with you guys?" The little girl was a permanent part of Jase's life. A part of him. "We can get to know each other."

"No way," the girl said, shaking her head. "I want to stay here. With my *parents*."

A twinge in her heart. "We'll have fun, kid. Promise."

As Hope opened her mouth to issue another protest, Brook Lynn added, "I'm headed to an animal shelter. I plan to reduce a dog. If you don't want to go, I can just show you pictures later and—"

"A dog?" The girl brightened. "My mom says dogs poop in your house and ruin your carpet, but I like them anyway." She hugged her mom...hugged her dad. "See you guys later."

Jase's expression had just softened, his eyes going wide with wonder. "You are *amazing*."

She kissed him smack-dab on the lips. "Right back at ya."

JASE PACED IN the living room and watched the clock. It was 10:01 p.m., roughly nine and a half hours since he'd last seen Brook Lynn, and there'd been no word from her.

He was worried about her and Hope. When he'd stepped out of the WOH offices about an hour after the pair took off, he'd discovered trash dumped all over his car. He would have blamed punk-assed teens—if someone hadn't spray-painted the word *DIE* on the shed in his backyard sometime during the night. Two cases of random vandalism? Not likely. He'd been targeted.

Even remembering caused his blood pressure to boil. *Calm. Steady.* This wasn't the first death threat he'd received in his life, and he was sure it wouldn't be his last. At least he'd had a lead. Since a stranger named Stan had just asked about him, Jase had left Daphne with Beck and gone to the Strawberry Inn. Even though the owner's daughter refused to tell him the name of the guests, she'd purposely stepped away from the counter with the sign-in list visible. There'd been a handful of names, but he'd known which one belonged to Stan. The only illegible one, the last name indecipherable.

Jase had gone to the room, but it had already been cleared out.

Had an inmate he'd wronged behind bars come to town?

It was a possibility, and yet it didn't freak him out as it once would have. He wasn't on his own anymore. He had West and Beck as backup. And he had a woman and daughter who needed him to keep his shit together, so he would. It was as simple as that.

"Jase," Daphne said from her perch on the couch. She sighed. "What if I decide not to move here? What then?"

He kicked into a fast pace and plowed a hand through his hair. "I might move into the city." He wanted to be near Hope. But would Brook Lynn be willing to move with him? Just pack up everything and say goodbye to her sister? Could he even ask her to?

She'd never left Strawberry Valley and had never really wanted to. This was her home, the only one she'd ever known. She had roots here. And shockingly enough, he now did, too.

"How long have you and Brook Lynn dated?" Daphne asked, tracking him with her gaze as he moved back and forth, back and forth.

"Not long." *Not long enough to ask her to uproot her entire life.*

He remembered the way she'd looked at him today, with reverence and awe. Every cell in his body had reacted, burning with those same emotions themselves. How was he supposed to live without her?

"Is she the one?" Daphne asked.

He didn't pretend to misunderstand. "Yes. I love her. I'd have her physically attached to me, if I could. But I won't miss any more of Hope's life."

Daphne's shoulders sagged.

"I told Hope about prison," he said. "This morning before you woke up."

"Oh." She blinked in surprise. "She didn't mention it to me."

"I don't think it mattered to her. She took it better than I expected." She'd asked him why he was sent there, and he'd told her that he'd hurt someone for hurting someone else. How wrong he'd been.

Did they make you eat dog food in prison? she'd asked. *I watched a show where the guard made the inmates eat cans of dog food.*

He'd almost laughed at the innocence of the question. She couldn't have imagined the horrors he'd actually endured in there, but no, dog food wasn't among them. He was so grateful that she hadn't been—wasn't—scared of him over the revelation.

All his worries for nothing. After hearing his answer she'd raced off to catch a butterfly, constantly glancing back to make sure he watched. All she'd wanted was his attention.

"I'm glad," Daphne said. "And I'm sorry. I really am. I handled things poorly over the years."

"You did what you thought was right. I can't blame you for that."

"You should." She pushed out a breath. "Tyler called me a liar. Said he couldn't trust me."

"Give him time. He'll either forgive you or move on. And if he moves on, you're better off without him." Easy to say. Jase would *never* be better off without Brook Lynn.

Car lights shone through the window. He rushed to the front door. Outside, a dog barked. Feminine laughter echoed. His heart pounded against his ribs. With desire. With relief. His girls had returned safely.

He battled the urge to rush out and sweep them both into his arms, an eternity seeming to pass before Brook Lynn and Hope made it to the porch, a dog in each of their arms. Both animals were of indeterminate parentage. Brook Lynn's had salt-and-pepper scruff and a lower jaw that protruded over the upper. Hope's was solid black with half an ear missing.

"I called," he said, his gaze drinking her in. She had never looked more beautiful to him, illuminated by the golden light of the moon, as if cut straight from a dream. "No answer."

"Oh," Brook Lynn replied. "My bad. I turned the cell to silent."

"The barking made her ears hurt," Hope said matter-of-factly.

He released what remained of his fear and panic on a long, heavy breath and decided not to waste another second feeling that way. There were other things he could be doing. "Do your ears need to be kissed all better?" he asked softly.

Hope heard and cringed. "Gross!"

Jase fought a smile. "By the way, I bought you something." He pulled a can of pepper spray from his pocket and stuffed it in Brook Lynn's purse. "Never leave your house without it." The dog squirmed in her arms. "Now. Who do we have here?"

"This is Steve," Hope said, proudly grinning at Half-ear.

"And Sparkles," Brook Lynn said.

Sparkles?

"The names were chosen long before we arrived, and I'm thinking Sparkles belonged to a toddler princess." Her gaze moved to his daughter and softened. "Thank you for going with me. I had fun with you."

"Me, too." Hope cuddled her dog close and peered up at Jase. "Brook Lynn said I could ask you if I could keep him, and if you say no she'll take him home with her. But can I keep him? Please. He wanted a home so bad. He cried when I tried to leave him. Please, Daddy."

Daddy.

He basically liquefied into a puddle at her feet. "Of course you can keep him."

"Uh, I'm not so sure about that," Daphne said, approaching his side. "Dogs hate me. All dogs. There are no exceptions. You know this, Hope."

As though wanting to prove the validity of her claim, both Steve and Sparkles growled at her.

"See!" she squealed, paling and backing up.

"I think they smell your fear," Brook Lynn said.

"Just don't be scared, Momma. Please."

Daphne shook her head, her gaze never leaving the dogs. "I'm sorry, baby, but that's impossible."

Jase hated watching Hope's features fall. Unable to bear it, he chucked her under the chin. "Don't worry. Steve can live with me. You'll get to visit him whenever you want."

Hope unveiled the toothiest, cutest grin he'd ever seen.

Brook Lynn reached out and ruffled the girl's hair. "Whenever you want to set our doggy date, call me."

"I will!"

The sight of Brook Lynn interacting with his daughter… Yeah. If he hadn't already been in love, he would have fallen in that moment.

"There are dog supplies in the trunk of my car," she said.

Both dogs began to wiggle, wanting to be put down. Daphne raced to the couch and jumped up. Steve managed to work his way free of Hope's arms. When he landed on the ground, he took off like a bullet and ran circles around the coffee table in front of Daphne. Hope tried to wrangle him, but he leaped onto the couch and nipped at Daphne's ankles. As she screamed, he lifted his leg and peed on her foot.

"This is my nightmare!" she shouted, diving over the side of the couch.

Beck rounded the corner. He was shirtless, his hair mussed, and there were scratches all over his chest. Well, well. He'd clearly smuggled a female through his window. "What's the racket?" he said, just as Steve tried to rush past him. "A dog? Seriously?" He grabbed the animal by the collar, stopping him. "No. Absolutely not."

Steve licked his hand and settled at his feet.

"Suck it up, Beck, and help me get the supplies," Brook Lynn said.

"But—"

She clapped her hands, all *chop chop*. "Now! Don't make me start counting. If I get to three I will never bake for you again."

"Yes, ma'am." Beck followed her outside.

Jase swallowed a laugh. "Hope, why don't you take Steve to my room?"

Hope gathered up her dog without any more problems and disappeared down the hall.

"Stay in Strawberry Valley," he said to Daphne. "Let me buy her all the animals she wants."

"I—"

"Please. I will pay your bills. You won't have to worry about anything."

Daphne seemed to roll the possibility through her mind. "We'll see."

Beck entered the house with a big box in his arms and several sacks hanging from his wrists, but there was no sign of Brook Lynn. "She told me to give this to you," he said and handed over a folded piece of paper.

Jase read the note. *Don't forget your nights belong to me. I'll be waiting...*

BROOK LYNN MOTORED down the winding country roads, dirt blowing behind her tires. What a day! Hope had warmed up to her and told her stories about the kind of dog she'd always and forever dreamed of having. A white puppy with blue eyes she would name Snowflake.

They'd spent hours at the shelter, going through the different rooms, petting the different dogs. Even walking some. Brook Lynn had to stave off tears more than once—and the desire to try to abscond with every single animal. It had just been so sad, all of those dogs desperate for a home, looking at her with a mix of fear, hope and loneliness. It had affected Hope, too, and she'd decided a puppy wasn't what she wanted, after all. Instead, she'd asked the employees to introduce her to the dog most in need.

Brook Lynn had never been so proud of another human being.

After they'd filled out the paperwork, they'd taken Steve and Sparkles to PetSmart for necessary supplies, then the local vet to be examined. The experience had bonded them. At least, Brook Lynn hoped so.

Were those car lights flashing behind her? Thinking someone had an emergency, Brook Lynn eased to the side of the road. But the driver didn't pass her. He stopped behind her and got out.

Jase.

She would recognize his towering silhouette anywhere.

Sparkles slept in the passenger seat. Trembling with
a sudden deluge of concern, she entered the night. The
pulse in her throat thundered.

"Is something wrong?" she asked.

"Yes. You're not in my arms."

She felt instant relief...followed by a flood of need.
She stopped, allowing him to come to her... He pinned
her against her car, his nearness playing havoc with
every inch of her body. She trembled. She flushed with
languid heat. She had to fight to breathe.

"You couldn't wait until I got home?" she asked,
winding her arms around his neck. "I'm glad."

Moonlight couched his features, painting him with
fantasy and shadows. "I would wait forever for you, but
I'm also glad I don't have to." He flattened his hands just
over her shoulders, letting his strength completely surround her. "Besides, I have to talk to you about something, and waiting was killing me."

Her heart skipped a beat. "What?"

He licked his lips. "If Daphne won't move to Strawberry Valley, I might have to move to the city. I have
to be near Hope, Brook Lynn, but I don't want to be
without you."

His tone begged her to understand, but he needn't
have worried. She'd begun to wonder what would happen when Daphne's visit ended. And the more time
she'd spent with Hope today, the more she'd come to
realize Jase would be filled with a need to protect the
girl, to give her what he'd never had. An unbreakable
family. Brook Lynn would never deny him that chance.

"I don't want to be without you, either, and I won't.
I'll come visit you as often as—"

"That's not good enough. I want you to come with me," he said softly.

She had wondered if he'd ask—and had already made up her mind. "Yes. Yes, I will go with you."

He closed his eyes, expelled a breath.

Oh, this man. "I love you, Jase Hollister," she said.

His lids snapped open.

"That's right," she continued. "I love you so much I don't want to imagine my life without you. I would follow you to the ends of the earth."

Like a panther, he moved quickly. He was flush against her and framing her face with his big, hot hands in less than a second. "You love me?"

Chin trembling, she nodded.

"I have to have you. Here. Now." He didn't give her time to respond, but slammed his mouth against hers, his tongue thrusting deep and sure.

Her inhibitions burned to ash. She grabbed hold of him, certain she had reached a point where she couldn't let him go ever again. His taste invaded her senses, reminding her of all she'd been missing. His chest, so close to hers, felt like a wall of steel, a drum beating beneath it.

He tore at the snap of her shorts, jerked the material down, along with her panties, then tore at the waist of his pants. The moment they were open, he pulled his underwear down just enough, lifted her by the waist and, as she wrapped her legs around him, surged inside her, filling her up. She'd grown wet the second he'd kissed her—the second he'd backed her up against the car, really—and now her body welcomed him with a rush of hot relief.

He fisted the hair at her nape, forcing her head back. The next kiss he fed her was hard, punishing…luscious.

Fire ignited in her blood, burning her up, burning so perfectly.

"You feel so good," he praised. In. Out. He thrust and thrust and thrust, and she felt the car rocking against her backside. Their moans blended with the hoot of an owl, the call of a coyote. She inhaled the sweet scent of strawberries and wildflowers.

"Not letting you go," he said.

"Never."

"You're mine." He reached between their bodies and pressed against her sharpest desire. Climax came hard and fast, and she erupted, crying out as satisfaction claimed her. He followed her over the edge, spilling inside her as she clenched around his length.

They stayed like that, locked together, shuddering against each other, until the muscles in her legs gave out. Slowly she slid to the ground; but still Jase didn't pull away from her. He sagged against her, the bulk of their combined weight held up only by the car.

His warm breath fanned over her neck, tickling. She toyed with the ends of his hair.

"Move in with me," she blurted out. "While Daphne and Hope are here."

The darkness hid his expression. "You'll have to forgive me. My brain isn't functioning at optimal levels right now. I think you drained the smart right out of me. But...did you just ask me to move in with you?"

"Yes." She chewed on her bottom lip. "If you don't want to—"

Lights flashed in the distance. With a screech, she pushed him away and scrambled to right her clothing.

He laughed before tucking himself back into his pants. "You are too cute when you're about to be caught in a compromising position." In a snap, he sobered. "Get inside your car, honey. Now. Lock the doors."

Thinking about Stan, maybe? She opened her mouth to protest—no way she'd leave him out here on his own—and he gave her a little nudge. She took a step then another, thinking she'd grab her new pepper spray, only to stop when Edna eased her car beside them.

Jase relaxed and waved Brook Lynn back over.

"You two having car troubles?" Edna asked.

Her daughter sat in the passenger seat, took one look at them and covered her mouth with both hands. "Drive on, Momma. They ain't having no car troubles."

"But—" Edna said.

"Drive," the daughter commanded with another laugh.

Edna gave an uncertain wave and motored on.

Brook Lynn flushed with heat and hid her face in the hollow of Jase's neck.

He kissed her temple. "Yes," he said. "I will move in with you."

CHAPTER TWENTY-SIX

JASE MARVELED. HE'D just spent his first night with his new live-in girlfriend. And now, as the sun rose and pushed bright rays through the curtains, with her snuggled in his arms, he finally experienced the peace he'd craved his entire life.

She stretched her arms over her head, her back arching as she blinked open her eyes. The sheet had fallen to her waist, revealing pretty pink nipples and breasts with faint marks from his beard stubble.

"Good morning," she mumbled.

"Morning." He traced his fingers over her tattoo. "And yes. To answer the question you're probably asking yourself, I *am* ready for my breakfast." First and foremost, he wanted the strawberries etched into her flesh.

"Too bad for you." She kissed the globe on his pec... grazed his nipple with her teeth. "You'll have to earn your food."

"The hard way?"

"Ha!"

"I'm assuming you accept orgasm."

Her husky laugh filled the room, delighting his senses. "Today only, I accept—"

The bedroom door swung open, and Jessie Kay surged inside...only to grind to a halt when she spotted Jase.

Brook Lynn squealed and jerked the sheet up to cover them both.

"Dude," Jessie Kay said, covering her eyes. "A little warning next time." She peeked through her fingers, her dark blue gaze settling on Jase. "You must be losing your touch. I don't recall hearing any screams for more last night."

As Jase laughed, Brook Lynn threw a pillow at her.

"Does this mean there'll be no breakfast?" Jessie Kay asked.

"Not for you. Out!" Brook Lynn shouted, also trying not to laugh.

"Okay, okay. By the way, Sparkles chewed up another pair of my shoes, so be sure to add the cost to my paycheck. And just out of curiosity, are you sure you didn't rescue him from hell?"

Another pillow hit her in the face. Jessie Kay flipped her off before backing out of the room and shutting the door.

"And *that* is what you signed on for," Brook Lynn muttered.

He heard no jealousy in her voice and realized just how far they'd come. "Honey, I definitely got the better end of the deal. Are you ready to face what *you* signed up for?"

"You mean West's drinking, Beck's flirting and Daphne's looming decision? Sure. Why not?"

"Family" was all he said.

"Yes, they are certainly your family."

As Jase rose from bed to shower and dress, those words played through his mind. Did Brook Lynn think *they* were his family but *she* was not?

"Hey," Brook Lynn said, slipping her feet into a pair of sandals. "I've been wondering. Should we cancel

Tessa's celebration? Is it too much for West? He seems to be getting worse."

"We probably *should* cancel, but we won't. I think he needs some sort of closure."

"Very well, then. Onward and upward. I'll continue planning. Oh, and don't forget I have Kenna's bachelorette party after my dinner deliveries tonight. I'll be in late."

"Where are you going?"

"Some fancy restaurant in the city." She tapped her ears. "Thank God Kenna decided to forgo clubbing."

Yes, thank God. He had a feeling he would have followed her inside a club and warned away every guy who dared come sniffing. But honestly, the thought of her being *anywhere* out of his sight right now made him nervous. He could handle death threats against himself, but if anyone tried to hurt her...

"If you see that Stan guy while you're out, call me. Do not approach him. In fact, I'll come with you and remain in the shadows. Just in case."

She rolled her eyes. "Stay. Be with your daughter. I want to invite Daphne to the bachelorette party," she said. "Think she'd be interested?"

He just peered over at her, reeling. This was one of the many reasons he'd fallen for her. "I know she would."

"Good."

A sense of urgency settled inside him, driving him onward. "Come on," he said. "I want to show you something." It was time.

On the way out the door, he scooped up Sparkles—who wasn't exactly comfortable with him, but hadn't yet tried to bite him. He scratched the mutt behind the ear, and the stiffness gradually left the little guy's body.

"How's my baby?" Brook Lynn asked, kissing Sparkles's small, wet nose.

"I'm well, thank you," Jase answered.

She gave Sparkles another kiss. "Don't listen to Jase. He knew I was talking to you."

Too damn adorable. She'd make an amazing mother one day.

He blinked as realization settled deep in his chest. *I want to give her children.* He would love nothing more than watching her body grow to support his kid, would love being there for both her and the child, protecting and loving them. Because of Hope, he'd realized just how special being a dad really was and knew it was the most fulfilling role he would ever play.

He'd once assumed he would ruin a child's life. Now he thought he could actually make it better.

Jase drove Brook Lynn and Sparkles to his house. The moment they were inside, the little guy started barking, on the lookout for Steve.

"Come on," he said to Brook Lynn. He picked her up and carried her out the back door, to the entrance of the shed, which was closed.

She laughed. "What are you doing?"

"Close your eyes," he commanded.

"Why? What's going on?"

"Close."

With another laugh, she finally complied.

He shouldered his way inside and set her on her feet. He'd been working on this in his spare time, waiting for the right moment to show her.

Her gaze widened as she spun. "It's…" She gaped at him. "Oh, my gosh, Jase. It's a bunker to see us through the zombie apocalypse."

"Yes," he said, knocking on one of the walls. "I reinforced the perimeter with steel. I built shelves and stocked them with food and weapons. I researched everything you might possibly want or need and made sure you had two of each."

Tears brimmed in her eyes. "Jase." She pressed a hand over her heart. "This is the sweetest thing anyone has ever done for me."

"I want to be the guy you rely on, always. I don't just want to live with you—I want to be a part of you. I want to prove every minute of every day just how special you are to me."

"Jase," she said again. Then she launched herself into his arms. "I love you," she said, kissing his face. "I love you, and I can't believe you did this for me."

"For you, I will do anything."

She grinned up at him, and for that split second of time, he could almost believe they'd finally achieved their happily-ever-after, that nothing bad could ever happen to them again. Almost.

That old sense of foreboding swept through him, both taking him by surprise and yet feeling all too familiar. In the past, anytime he'd experienced even the slightest glimmer of happiness, something terrible had happened to push him back into the pit of despair.

Brook Lynn's smile faded, and she brushed her fingertips over his frowning mouth. "Is something wrong?"

A cold sweat broke out on the back of his neck, but he forced himself to shake his head. "Things have never been better."

BROOK LYNN DECIDED to cross another item off her fun list. Be another person for a day. No Worries Girl. That's right. She wasn't going to worry about the dark look that had come over Jase's face earlier today or his refusal to share the reason behind it.

He was such an amazing man, but he carried too much on his shoulders and had for the whole of his life. He had a heart capable of giving what it had never known but had always craved: love. He possessed an innate sophistication, yet it was coupled with a sharpness he'd honed through rejection and pain. He was urbane, polished, yet still so rough around the edges. A warrior determined to protect. A seducer determined to possess. Powerful. Compelling.

And he's mine.

Fingers snapped in front of her face. "Again?" her sister said on a sigh.

She blinked into focus. The dinner! Here she was, No Worries Girl, at a fancy restaurant with Kenna, Jessie Kay and Daphne, and she kept spacing out.

"Sorry," she muttered.

Laughter broadcasted at her right, and she glanced over to ground herself in the here and now. A spacious room with dim lighting, the only illumination coming from what seemed to be a thousand candles flickering here, there, chasing away shadows. The vaulted ceiling cascaded downward, giving way to lower tiers, and elaborate murals decorated the walls. Re-creations of famous artwork. The Mona Lisa. A Monet: *Nimphee.* *Starry Night* by Van Gogh.

Kenna—well, Dane—had procured a private room for the bachelorette dinner, but its double doors were open to the rest of the restaurant, where couples and families enjoyed food that Jessie Kay said was "almost as good as Brook Lynn's."

"Let's try this again," her sister said, motioning to Kenna.

Kenna lifted her glass of champagne. Everyone else followed suit. "To love, laughter and sexy men."

"Hear, hear," Jessie Kay said.

The champagne tasted like liquid candy, a decadent invitation-only party in her mouth, but there would be no more for her. She'd learned a hard lesson: she and alcohol were not a good mix.

Daphne drained her glass. "Right now, I'm zero for three."

Brook Lynn patted her hand. "I'm sorry about Tyler."

"Boo." Kenna flashed a thumbs-down. "Exes suck!"

"Did he end things because you turned every celebration into a cry fest?" Jessie Kay signaled the waiter for another round. "Why are you upset, anyway? You are living with two superhot bachelors."

Daphne actually cringed. "They're like my brothers."

"So?" Jessie Kay said. "I can personally vouch for Beck. Yes, you should totally choose Beck. He's perfect for you."

"Half the world can vouch for Beck." Kenna ran her finger over the rim of her glass. "He'll never commit. Go for West."

"No, West would be a mistake," Jessie Kay said quickly, shifting in her seat. "He's obviously going through something. He's so not in the right place to start a relationship."

Oh, oh, oh. What was this? Brook Lynn detected a *warning* in her sister's tone. To stay away from the guy?

"How long have you been infatuated with West?" Daphne asked.

Well, well. Brook Lynn hadn't been the only one to notice.

"I'm *not* infatuated with West," Jessie Kay insisted.

The waiter arrived with a new bottle, and instead of

doing a taste test, Jessie Kay drained what he poured and tapped the rim of her glass for more.

The second he left, she said, "West was clearly an experiment in Artificial Stupidity. Truth be told, all of my problems end with West—lo*west* paid, slo*west* on the road to success, fe*west* good times."

"I think the lady protests too much." Proper manners be damned. Brook Lynn propped her elbows on the table. "I don't know how I missed the fact that you want to marry him and have a million babies."

Jessie Kay threw a buttered roll at her. Kenna snatched the bread bowl before Brook Lynn could retaliate and cuddled it to her chest, muttering, "My precious."

Daphne snickered. "I wish you could have met him before Tessa died. I wish you'd met all of them. Cocky as hell, but unbelievably kind. Hotheaded, but protective. Each of them would have sold their organs on the black market if I'd asked."

Brook Lynn leaned back in her chair. "Actually, not much has changed."

Daphne focused on her. "I've been wondering. Are you still working for Jase? I keep hearing about your amazing food but you haven't come over to cook."

"No, I'm not working for him," she said. "We have a rule. There's only one place I will take orders from him, and it's not his kitchen."

"First, if you want our food," Jessie Kay said to Daphne, "you'll have to pay for it like everyone else. Second…" She faced Brook Lynn. "I didn't know you'd gotten the kinky gene. Good going, little sis."

Her cheeks heated. Movement from the corner of her eye drew her attention, and she welcomed the distraction. She expected it to be the waiter. Instead, she met the narrowed gaze of…Stan?

He stared at her for several prolonged seconds then said, "Tell Jase it's almost time for a reckoning. I'm going to make sure he pays for what he did."

She jumped to her feet, her chair skidding backward. Stan pivoted and soared out of the private room, through the restaurant toward the exit.

"Dude. Who was that guy?" Jessie Kay asked.

"I think I'm being followed." No way this was mere coincidence. She was thirty miles outside town. And had he just *threatened* Jase?

As the girls rapid-fired questions at her, she dialed his number. He answered after the second ring, and she wasted no time. "I saw him," she said. "That guy. Stan. He's here and he's looking for you, said there would be a reckoning. That you would pay for what you did."

"Are your eyes on him now?" he demanded.

"No. He took off."

He cursed. "Stay there. Do not go after him. I'm on my way." He hung up.

The manager came inside the room a few minutes later, taking a stand at the doors—standing guard. Jase must have called Dane, who must have called him.

"What's going on?" Kenna asked, the color drained from her cheeks.

Brook Lynn wrapped her arms around her middle. "I don't know."

CHAPTER TWENTY-SEVEN

JASE CALLED DANE from the road. They arrived at the restaurant within seconds of each other and rushed inside. The manager had known they were coming—Dane must have phoned—and had instructed a member of the staff to wait for them.

Of course, it helped that Dane was one of the richest men in the world.

"This way," the hostess said, motoring forward. But she didn't move fast enough.

Jase shot in front of her, scanning the faces in the restaurant—finding no one familiar. "Brook Lynn," he called.

"Back here."

He followed the sound of her voice. Relief washed through him as he stepped into the private room and drew her into his arms. Her little body trembled against him. He hated that he'd brought this to her door.

"Kenna. Sweetheart. Are you okay?" Dane cupped the redhead's face, looked her over.

"I'm fine. Really. Nothing happened. The guy creeped us out, that's all."

Another tremor from Brook Lynn.

"Yeah, I'm okay, too," Jessie Kay muttered.

"What she said." Daphne hiked her thumb in the girl's direction.

Jase kissed Brook Lynn's temple. "I will find this guy. I won't let him near you again."

She trembled against him. "I don't want you to go after him. I don't want you in trouble."

He'd once thought he would rather die than go back to prison, but the truth was, he'd rather go back to prison than see Brook Lynn hurt. But he kept the thought to himself, not wanting to worry her further.

"Come on," he said. "Let's get out of here."

Dane took Kenna with him. Jase took the others.

"Don't let Hope see me like this," Daphne slurred from the backseat of his car. "Please."

"Don't worry. You can spend the night at my place," Brook Lynn said.

He made sure to scout the land surrounding the house before allowing the girls to exit. As Brook Lynn tucked the pair into bed, Jase checked the locks on the windows and doors, making sure everything was secure. He even put Sparkles in the foyer as a guard dog. Tomorrow he would be installing a security system.

He drove Brook Lynn to his house and scouted that land, as well. No sign of foul play. But he could feel old habits fighting their way to the surface, the urge to glance behind him every few minutes intense, as was the urge to jump at every noise.

Once inside, Brook Lynn rested her head in the crook of his shoulder, and it felt like his lifeline to sanity.

In the kitchen, Beck and Hope sat at the table, playing a game of Monopoly. Hope punched the air in front of Beck's face, saying, "Suck it, Uncle Beck. You owe me two bazillion dollars in rent."

"Hey," Jase said.

"Daddy! You're back!" Smiling, the little girl raced over to hug him. "Where's Momma?"

"She's having a sleepover with her friend Jessie Kay."

"No fair." Hope pouted up at him. "I want to have a sleepover, too."

He was going to be putty in her hands for the rest of his life, wasn't he? "How about you have a campout on the couch? Uncle Beck can sleep on the floor."

"Sweet!" She waved at Brook Lynn, and Brook Lynn waved back.

"Where's West?" he asked Beck.

"Holed up in his room."

Good. "I'll be holed up in my room with Brook Lynn. We've got a few things to discuss." Tension had been crackling inside him since he'd reached the restaurant. He strode over, kissed Hope on the cheek then whispered to Beck, "There's been trouble. Guard her with your life. Brook Lynn and I will take your place in a few hours."

Beck nodded without hesitation.

Jase took Brook Lynn's hand and stalked to his bedroom. He shut the door behind her, sealing them inside, and faced her. He'd been so scared for her safety. He needed to reassure himself that she was here, that she was with him, that nothing was wrong.

He gathered her into his arms, taking comfort from the warmth of her body against his. "I need you," he said and jerked off his T-shirt.

"Yes." Brook Lynn pulled off her top, and arousal blistered through him, the flames too hot to bear. As many times as he'd been with this woman, as much as he craved her, he'd never wanted her like this.

Her bra came off next, and then she dropped her arms to her sides, staring over at him with wild anticipation. She had to feel it, too. The need to be cemented in the here and now...to drown in pleasure. He closed the distance in three long strides.

"I don't want to lose you," he said. "Ever. To anything."

"You told me that you wanted to be a part of me," she said, "and you are, no matter how far apart we might be. You got your hooks deep, deep in my heart, and they aren't ever coming out. I'm not ever going to leave you, Jase. I'm yours. Now...forever."

In a lightning-fast move, Jase picked her up by the waist and carried her to the wall, where he pressed her flat, her feet dangling in the air. She gasped as the cool plaster met her back. He held her there, suspended, her breasts at eye level. Her nipples puckered for him. Just then, they were the only two people in the universe. He couldn't think past the bliss of having her in his arms.

"Do you," he said sharply, giving her a tiny shake with each word, "have any idea how gorgeous you are?"

UNDER THE INTENSITY of this man's emerald gaze, she *felt* gorgeous. He radiated a rawness she'd never seen from him before, laced with something that went far deeper than hunger...animal starvation.

Slowly he lowered her, a sultry glide that left her panting. They were so close, her bare chest moving against his every time she breathed.

Then he stepped back, as if the contact was too much. His lips peeled back from his teeth in an almost-scowl.

"Undress," he said. "Remove it all."

Bossier than usual tonight, but she understood the reason, knew he hadn't quite let go of concern for her. She licked her lips, nervous and excited, aroused to the point of pain. They'd done so many things with each other and to each other. Stripping should have been more of the same, but there was something different this time, something even more than the rawness and starvation.

Trembling, she removed her skirt and underwear. Completely naked, she stood in place, pinned by the fervency of his emerald gaze.

"You know I love you," he said. "But I'm not sure even *love* is a strong enough word for what I feel for you. You've wrecked me, angel, broken me and put me back together again. I will never be the same—I don't want to be the same."

The beauty of his words stunned her, electrified her to the depths of her soul. Trembling legs carried her around him, across the room. She draped herself over the edge of the mattress facedown, shivering with an arousal so sweet she'd never known its like.

Glancing over her shoulder, she whispered throatily, "Come here and take me," surrendering all to him.

Waves of heat reached her before his hands ever slid down her spine, yet she jolted at the first moment of exquisite contact. Goose bumps broke out over her skin, sensitizing her to his touch. And touch he did. Again and again, dragging his fingers over the ridges of her spine, over the globes of her bottom, down her legs. It was like being licked by flames. As if, as the flames burned, they wafted dark, drugging smoke through the air, every inhalation filling her head with a fog of desperation.

He circled his hands around both of her ankles and forced her legs to part. She craned her neck to catch a glimpse of him. He caressed his way up her calves, dabbled at the backs of her knees and finally reached the curve of her rear. He traced a heart-shaped pattern around one side, all the way to her lower back, and then down the other side of her.

When he knelt, his face directly in line with the soaking heart of her, she rested her cheek on a pillow and closed her eyes, savoring every illicit sensation. It felt as though she were being worshipped.

Soft lips pressed into the underside of one globe, then the other. Tremors consumed her. He angled his head and— Oh…oh! His tongue. It stroked her where she ached, her body rejoicing even as it demanded more. She arched her back to allow him better access, and he took full advantage, thrusting his tongue inside her. He pinched her directly between her legs and slid his fingers through her wetness, allowing them to take the place of his tongue, moving in and out of her. He scissored them to open her wider, his thumb sliding up to her center and circling, pressing.

She fisted the sheets as moan after moan was ripped from her. Both the position and the pleasure left her vulnerable to him. Like this, there was nothing he couldn't do to her—and she wanted him to do everything. There was nothing she would deny him.

Thoughts disintegrated then, the way he worked her a testament to the endless depths of the starvation she'd seen in him. Her tremors intensified. The heat inside her built, becoming an inferno. Pressure…so much pressure, building just like the heat, *with* the heat, and any second she expected to—

Shatter.

His hand swiped at her ankle, sending her legs farther apart, allowing his fingers to sink all the way in, and the pressure exploded inside her, the most sublime satisfaction clamoring through her, shaking her. But even as she shook, Jase took her by the hips and flipped her over, so that she lay on her back.

He towered between her legs. His lips glistened with her arousal, his chest rising and falling with a swiftness that matched her own. As she watched, he unfastened the button of his pants and lowered the zipper, freeing himself.

He lifted one of her legs and set her foot on the mattress, then did the same with the other, leaving her spread wide. His gaze locked on the heart of her, heating...burning...and he traced a fingertip down the center, drawing another cry from her...and a consuming need for more.

"I thought Strawberry Valley had become my home," he said. "But it's you. You are my home, angel. You're where I've put down roots."

The words cauterized a wound she hadn't known she had—one she'd carried most of her life, festering every time she'd wondered how good people could die too young. Why her uncle couldn't love her and her sister more than money. Why Jessie Kay had often chosen a party over helping Brook Lynn.

Yet here was this man—her love—telling her she was home to him.

She arched her hips in silent benediction. He fisted his erection at the base and placed himself at her entrance, letting the tip slide in...before stilling, hovering there, teasing and tormenting her with what could be.

"You're mine," he said. His gaze captured hers, emerald completely ensnaring blue, and he slid the rest of the way in, filling her, stretching her, fusing with her. "Never forget."

"Never."

He flattened his palms on her knees, keeping her

spread as he slowly pumped in and out. Her nipples were so hard they could have cut through diamonds, her belly so hot with need she wasn't sure she would ever be satisfied again, but he just kept pumping. The hardness and the need grew stronger, until the pleasure poised at the brink of agony.

She reached back, curled her fingers around a pillow, arching her hips to propel him into a faster rhythm. He resisted, even...slowed down...until she could only writhe and beg incoherently.

"Please, Jase. Oh, please. Jase, Jase. Please."

He slammed forward with all of his considerable strength. Yes! Yes! But he only slowed down again, his gaze once again capturing hers. Sweat trickled from his temples, and tension tightened his skin, but the adoration he projected at her...the tenderness...the hope and the gratitude...

"Please."

Another hard slam.

It was too much, finally pushing her over the edge. She shouted with her pleasure—a burn that might have started slowly but one that exploded just as savagely as the other, no, more so, breaking her down into a quivering pulse of sensation.

Jase launched into the hard-and-fast ride she'd begged for, thrusting, thrusting inside her, rattling the entire bed, somehow prolonging her orgasm, keeping her suspended on clouds of unending carnality.

Like an out-of-body experience, she thought, dazed. Slowly she floated back, finding Jase collapsed over her, little shudders still rocking him.

He lifted his head and smoothed damp locks of hair from her face. "If I've got my hooks in you, it's only right you bear my name. Wouldn't you agree?"

Her jaw dropped. "Are you…asking me to *marry* you?"

He laughed. "Asking? Oh, no, angel. It's too late for that. I'm telling."

Had those words come from any other man, she would have balked. From Jase…

With a squeal, she used what little strength she had left to wrap herself around him. "I'm going to make you the happiest man in the world, Jase Hollister."

"Angel," he said, kissing her. "You already do."

CHAPTER TWENTY-EIGHT

I'M ENGAGED.

Me. Miss Brook Lynn Elizabeth Dillon. To Mr. Jason... what was his middle name?...Hollister.

When she told Jessie Kay the next day, the two of them danced around their house. When she told Kenna while they lunched at Two Farms, they squealed so loudly, Mr. Calbert stomped from his office to shush them.

Through it all, Jase never left her side. And he'd smiled more than once.

Even Daphne seemed genuinely happy for her.

"Hope and I are going to have to move here, aren't we?" she said and sighed. "I just can't pull Jase away from all of this. He needs it. And I think...maybe we do, too."

Life was better than ever. The only damper on her happiness came when Jase failed to learn anything new about Stan. He still didn't know who the guy really was, or what his connection was to Jase, or why he wanted revenge on him so badly. But he did suspect the guy was responsible for the vandalism of his shed and his car, and had talked to Sheriff Lintz about a possible restraining order.

But Brook Lynn wasn't going to think about Stan right now. If she did, she'd just sink into a pit of nervousness, wondering what would happen if—when—

Jase confronted the guy. Nothing good, that much she could guess. He could be hurt. He could do some hurting of his own.

Worst-case scenario: he could be sent back to prison.

It was a fear he shared. Yesterday he'd said, "If this guy approaches you again, I don't know what I'll do, how I'll react, but even the thought of it is enough to work me into a black, black rage. Does that scare you?"

She'd replied, "I love that you're so protective of me. I just want to make sure nothing bad happens to you."

She'd then done her best to talk Jase into canceling Tessa's party, thinking it was too much of a risk, but again and again he'd assured her that he'd put a lot of money into security. There would be guards posted at every door. They knew who to look for, because she and the girls had given a description—though it hadn't jogged Jase's memory. Even still, Stan would never be able to get inside, and if he tried, he would finally be detained and hopefully arrested.

Put like that, she almost wished he'd try. She wanted this to be over so bad, she could taste it. Then she could start planning her wedding.

"Well, the day has finally come," Daphne said. "Tessa would have loved this."

Together, she and Brook Lynn double-checked every detail to ensure nothing was out of place. Jase had beautifully refurbished the old barn situated at the edge of his land, and the new wood planks on the walls and floor gleamed as sunlight streamed in through the stained-glass windows. Roses of every color hung from the ceiling and down the walls, small golden lights sprinkled throughout. A sweet perfume saturated the air, creating a heady paradise.

The buffet tables lined the back walls and were piled

high with all different kinds of bite-size sandwiches and pinwheels. All thanks to You've Got It Coming.

"I also think there's no way in hell you could have done this good a job without me," Daphne said, bumping her shoulder good-naturedly. "I want you to know I mean that from the bottom of my heart."

"Oh, how sweet." Brook Lynn bumped her shoulder right back. "Your compliment has brought a tear to my eye."

"I do what I can." Her head tilted to the side, and she frowned. "Guests must not know the meaning of fashionably late. Someone's here already."

Brook Lynn skipped toward Jase. He and Beck waited at the door, ready to greet the early arrivers as they made it past the guards. West was...well, no one knew where. He'd taken off yesterday and hadn't come back, and it was a shame, considering this whole party was his idea—his way of seeking the closure he so desperately needed.

Jase smiled when he spotted her. An intimate smile filled with promise, causing her heart to skip a beat. She wondered if her reaction to him would always be this strong.

"I missed you," he said.

"Because I'm the light of your life. Duh."

"You certainly are." He kissed the tip of her nose. He was in a good mood today, some of the tension he'd been carrying now gone. "Later, I'm going to make you beg for every kiss, every touch."

She shivered. "I'm looking forward to your attempt. But this time I think *I'm* going to make *you* beg."

He sucked in a breath, his muscles going rigid. "I'm looking forward to it." He looked as though he wanted to say more, but a steady stream of guests began to pour inside the barn. Residents of Strawberry Valley, as well as people who'd driven in from the city. Kids—adults now—from Jase's past.

He shook hands with some, bumped fists with others and always introduced her as his fiancée.

When finally there was a lag, she gave Jase a soft peck. "I'm going to check on the food. I won't be gone long."

"It'll still feel like forever."

She smiled dreamily as she moved through the crowd; guards dressed as guests followed behind her. There was Jessie Kay, Sunny and Charlene, surrounded by a group of men. All of them were smiling and talking, probably flirting. There was Kenna and Dane, cuddled close while Dane answered the questions of those surrounding him. Norrie played with Hope and some of the other children in attendance, and something lurched inside Brook Lynn's chest. Hope would soon be her family. And then, one day, she and Jase would have children of their own, giving Hope little brothers and sisters.

Last night he'd said, "How many kids do you want, angel? Because I'm thinking we give that eighteen-and-counting family a run for their money."

She'd twisted his nipple until he'd cried out. "I'd like two, but I could be talked into three or four. Any more than that, and you'll need to find another new wife."

"I'll only agree to that if you're cloned."

Remembering, she could have thrown out her arms and twirled. *Must concentrate on the party before I run back to Jase and demand we get started on those babies* now.

One of the barn's stalls had been turned into a makeshift pantry, and she was happy to learn all was well behind the scenes. Though the crowd was going through the sandwiches as if tonight was their last meal, the staff she'd hired was keeping the buffet well stocked.

She returned to Jase's side, and they mingled for the next hour. She was able to relax, even though women stared at him as if he was the last piece of chocolate in the world. Actually, he kind of was.

Daphne approached her side and tugged on her arm. "I'm going to steal her away, Jason. Don't protest, or I'll start counting. And yes, I'm stealing your girlfriend's material."

He held up his hands, all innocence.

"What about *my* protests?" Brook Lynn asked.

"They will be ignored." Daphne dragged her across the room, only to stop and point. "Who is that?"

"Who?"

"Tall, with dark hair and a god among men."

Brook Lynn's gaze cut through the crowd... *You've got to be kidding me.* "That's Brad Lintz." Brad was out of his greasy overalls and in a white polo and slacks.

"I want to meet him," Daphne said.

Of course she did. Because this was a game of musical love interests. Life was funny sometimes. "He's an excellent choice. Kind, reliable and capable."

Arching a brow at her, Daphne said, "But?"

"But...I went on a date with him, and he said he'd wait for me and Jase to break up. I just thought you should know."

Daphne waved a hand through the air. "Sorry, blondie, but by the end of the evening, he will have forgotten your name." She pushed up the cups of her bra, enhancing her cleavage.

Had to admire that kind of confidence. "Come on. I'll introduce you." Brook Lynn led her over and did as promised, heartened by the interest in Brad's eyes.

As the two got to know each other, Brook Lynn searched the crowd for Jase. Her mouth went dry when she caught sight of someone else, sidling through the crowd.

Stan.

How had he gotten past the guards?

He glanced over at her, as if he'd known where she was all along, and their gazes clashed. He kept moving, soon disappearing among the sea of bodies.

No. No, no, no. She excused herself from the flirting, blushing couple and crossed the room. Not to chase Stan but to find...not Jase. She didn't want him getting into a fight. Beck. Yes, Beck would know what to do. When she caught sight of him, she picked up speed.

He had a woman pressed against a shadowed corner, one of his hands sliding under her skirt as he whispered in her ear.

In public? Really?

Shameless! I would never—

Uh. Never mind.

Brook Lynn tapped him on the shoulder. He turned, frowning, probably thinking he would curse whoever it was, but when her identity clicked, he released the woman and focused on her.

"Something wrong?" he asked.

"Yes." She pushed out a shaky breath. "That Stan guy somehow got inside."

An instant darkening of his expression. "You're sure?"

"Positive."

He cursed. The woman grabbed hold of his arm, clinging to him, but he extracted her to kiss her knuckles. He told her he'd be dreaming about her later and probably sobbing like a baby that she wasn't in his arms then took Brook Lynn's hand to lead her away.

"Sorry," Brook Lynn mouthed to her.

The girl glared at her as if all the world's problems began with her—and maybe she should be buried six feet under.

"Show me," Beck said.

"He knows I saw him, so maybe he left," she said, ushering him to the area Stan had been headed. Of course, he wasn't there. She spun, determined to ferret him out. "I don't see him."

"Doesn't matter. Jase is going to lose it."

She chewed on her bottom lip. "Maybe we shouldn't tell him."

"He has a right to know."

"Yes, but—"

Beck peered down at her. "There's no way I can keep this from him."

"Just find Stan and force him to leave. *Then* tell Jase." She gave him a pleading look and knew he was thinking the same thing she was—they had to do whatever proved necessary to protect Jase from his own temper and the consequences thereof.

Beck pursed his lips as if he'd just sucked on a lemon. "Come on." He covered her shoulder with a muscular arm and moved forward, stopping only to have a whispered conversation with the guards, who rushed off when he turned away. "We'll keep looking for him together. I don't want you out of my sight."

As they pushed through the crowd, she withdrew her pepper spray from her pocket. Once...twice...she thought she spotted their target, but when they reached the spot he'd stood in, he'd already vanished.

They checked the stalls that had been blocked off from the guests—and finally found West. A half-undressed woman sat on a bench before him, her back to the door,

West's body between her legs. His hands were fisted in her long, dark hair.

Beck cursed, and the woman jerked around. Her identity registered, and Brook Lynn scowled. Though Jessie Kay would probably pretend not to care, she was not going to like this. At all.

Charlene Burns tugged up the straps of her dress and leaped to her feet. Without her as an anchor, West stumbled backward. His hair was mussed, his eyes bloodshot. Dark stubble dusted his jaw. There were smears of lipstick along the column of his throat, and his shirt was unbuttoned to the navel, revealing a set of washboard abs that might have been sculpted from granite. His pants gaped open at the fly, and Brook Lynn immediately averted her gaze.

"Y'all here to chaperone?" Charlene asked with a sneer. "How sweet."

Beck stomped over to West. "At Tessa's GED party? Really? At the party *you* wanted to throw for her, this is how you commemorate her? By picking your next two-month-stand?"

"She's not my next. Was just fooling around. And you're one to talk," West replied. "You sleep with anything that moves."

Beck was unfazed by the insult. "This isn't you, man. You need to pull your head out of your ass and think."

"Just back off." West shoved Beck.

Beck could have shoved back—or worse—but he merely held up his hands, palms out, a *do what you feel you must* pose. Still, his eyes were on fire with anger.

Brook Lynn calmly faced Charlene and pointed to the exit. "Go. Now."

"Hell, no." Charlene slapped her hands on her hips, though she barely spared Brook Lynn a glance, too enraptured by the guys. "West invited me back to the house, and I accepted. I'd be rude to leave him now."

Must control myself. Shouldn't attack.

"You will leave the party," Brook Lynn said, "and you won't contact West again. He's in a bad place, and you're taking advantage of him."

"Advantage?" Charlene snorted. "*He* came on to *me*. I was talking to your sister and he interrupted, asking if I wanted two orgasms or three. I wasn't willing to settle for anything less than four, so we decided to get started right away."

So…he'd come on to her in front of Jessie Kay, who crushed on him despite his abysmal treatment. That must have stung something fierce. Was Jessie Kay spiraling even now?

"Get out," Brook Lynn insisted, fingers tight on the can of pepper spray. *I will not use it. I will not freaking use it.* "I mean it."

Charlene looked over at West and Beck. West barely seemed to register her presence, he was in such a drunken daze.

"Go," Beck said. "Now."

"One," Brook Lynn said. "Two." She stepped forward.

"Okay, okay." Charlene stomped from the stall.

"Come on," Beck said to West. "Let's get you to the house and sobered up before you cause any more trouble."

Brook Lynn tried to branch away from them, thinking to find Jessie Kay, but Beck grabbed hold of her wrist, stilling her.

"You're going with us," he said.

She shook her head. "I'm going to find my sister and stick by her. I'll be okay."

He hesitated to let her go. "I don't want you maneuvering through the crowd on your own."

"I don't care."

"Fine. West and I will help you find her."

West jerked from Beck's hold. "No way. I'm not going near Jessie Kay. Not sure whether I'll insult her or screw her."

Screw her?

Beck had to fight him to restrain him, gritting out, "I'll find her, then. And Jase, for that matter. It's time. Just do me a solid and stay here with Brook Lynn. Guard her. Don't let anyone approach her. I'll be back in a few minutes."

"Fine," West grumbled.

"Brook Lynn?" Beck asked, his brow raised.

"I'm good with that plan."

Beck took off without another word, and West leaned against the wall, only to slump to the ground.

"You okay?" she asked.

"Not even close," he said. "But I will be. Tomorrow." His head fell forward, his chin banging into his sternum.

Falling asleep?

Yep. The next thing she heard was a snore.

Brook Lynn paced the small confines of the stall, kicking pieces of straw out of her way, as well as— Gross! A pair of panties. Not wanting anyone else to discover them, she picked them up and, grimacing, flicked them into the trash can.

A pair of brown boots came into view. Expecting to see Beck, she glanced up—and spotted Stan.

Gasping, she scrambled backward. He'd changed the color of his eyes with contacts, and he'd shaved his head. His lips were chapped and pressed into a thin line.

He wore a staff uniform, white button-up and black slacks.

"Alone at last," he said, sparing the unmoving West a glance. "I've been waiting for this moment all night. Hell, long before. I heard about the party and decided there was no better time or place. Only fair."

Only fair? "Dressing as a waiter. Is that how you got in the building?" she demanded, stalling as she scrambled to plan her next move.

"After our little chat at the Inn, I knew Jase would be coming for me, so I moved in here, where you planned to have Tessa's party. You may have hired guards to keep me out, but I was already inside. Now sit," he commanded, pointing to a chair that had been pushed against the wall. "We'll wait for Jase together."

Her heart seemed to tumble into her stomach as she locked her finger on the lid of the pepper spray. "I'm not sitting. I'm leaving." Actually, no, she wasn't. She couldn't leave the vulnerable West with this guy. And she didn't want to wake West up, either. In his current state, he might say the wrong thing, provoking Stan, and might get himself stabbed.

Stan lifted the switchblade he held, the sharp silver glinting in the light. "You'll sit or you'll bleed. Your choice."

Her legs trembled as she weighed her options. She could close the distance and spray him, risking being stabbed...or she could do what he wanted and risk being stabbed anyway. "I don't care what you threaten. I like where I am and I'm not sitting."

West smacked his lips and mumbled something unintelligible, and Brook Lynn inched her way in front of him, blocking him from Stan's view.

"Look, I don't want to hurt you, okay," Stan said. "I've

never wanted to hurt you. I want to show you what he is, prove he's a monster. I want this town to know. I've heard everyone talk about him, and you'd think he wears a halo. So if you want to stand, stand, but one way or another you will be calling out for him, screaming his name. I've been waiting for this moment, and I know what will happen the moment he arrives. Everyone will find out what kind of man he really is."

Her eyes widened. "You *want* him to beat you up?"

"Why not? I'm happy to suffer the same fate as my brother, as long as Jase suffers in the end."

Her stomach churned. Playing dumb, buying time, she said, "I don't understand. Your brother?"

"My name is Stanton Gillis. The man you're planning to marry beat my older brother Pax to death. And for what? Taking what some skank bitch offered before changing her stupid mind?"

Oh…no. No, no, no. "I'm sorry. I'm sorry for your loss, but getting Jase to hurt you isn't going to bring your brother back."

"It might make me feel better."

"It won't."

"I think that it will." Stanton ripped at the buttons of his shirt. His chest and arms were covered in tattoos, and most of them were of Jase—being murdered. In one, he was being stoned. In another, he was being dismembered. In another, he had a gun to his temple. But mixed in with the many deaths of Jase were multiple deaths of *him*, Stan. He wanted to die?

Tremors nearly shook her off her feet. The crazy pouring out of him was off the charts. There would be no talking him around. No reasoning with him.

"Pax had a brilliant future, but it was stolen from him." He took a step toward her, hate, rage and bitterness simmering inside his eyes. "Jason only had to serve nine years for his crime, but my brother is gone forever. Where is the justice in that?"

Underneath the tattoos, she could see the tiny scars running up his arms. Like tiny pinpricks. Track marks? Was he high on top of everything else?

"But Jase has been out for months," she said, doing her best to sound calm. "Why strike at him now?"

"At first I didn't mind that he was free." Stan scratched at his arms. "I liked watching him, knowing he was miserable, suffering. But then you came along, and he smiled. He laughed. He shouldn't have laughed." Another step closer, more scratching. "You ruined everything."

Have to act! Now!

Brook Lynn jumped forward and reached out to spray him in the face. He hissed, dropping the knife to rub at his eyes. She tried to grab it, but she moved so quickly her foot sent it flying.

A hand clamped around her calf, a shackle, tripping her. She fell, losing both the can and her breath upon landing. The guy maintained a hard grip on her and jerked her backward, even as she kicked. She slid across the floor, clawing for purchase, but he proved far stronger.

Stan lumbered to his feet and yanked her up by the hair. As he dragged her to the chair, picking up the knife along the way, she remembered what Jase had taught her about fighting zombies. As soon as Stan faced her, she planted one foot while hooking the other behind his leg. At the same time, she grabbed him by the neck with one hand and latched on to his wrist with the other. Then she shoved and kicked in unison. He fell back, trying to take her with him, but she released him and popped him in the mouth.

When he hit the ground, she raced to the doorway screaming, "Help us! Someone!"

Stan scrambled to get to her, but West must have awoken at the sound of her scream and sobered, because he leaped into action, snatching Stan by the ankle, tripping him.

"Brook Lynn, run," West gritted out, subduing his prize.

"Brook Lynn!" Jase bellowed.

No, no. "Stay back." She couldn't let him give Stan what he wanted. But he didn't stay back and she barreled into his chest, would have floundered backward if he hadn't wrapped his arms around her. He'd been running into the stall. He looked her over and then looked at Stan, who was still wrestling with West.

"You hurt her." Just like that, Jase's entire countenance morphed. From concerned to maddened beyond all control.

"No," she said. "He didn't hurt me. Let's call for the guards and wait for the cops. Don't go near him. Okay? Please. It's what he wants."

He didn't seem to hear her. He stormed forward, as if he'd just been struck by a cattle prod. He wrenched Stan from West's grip and slammed him into the floor, following him down so that the two were a tangle of limbs. Jase displayed masterful skill as he disarmed the other man in seconds. He should have backed off then, but he just…started…whaling. Blood sprayed from Stanton's nose, filled his mouth.

She knew, because he smiled, blood all over his teeth.

Then Jase's fists rained again. Stanton's body jerked with each whack. People flooded into the stall, witnesses now.

Brook Lynn tried to stop Jase but someone grabbed

her by the waist and held her back. "Please," she shouted. "Please. You have to stop."

He didn't stop.

"Jase!"

He only hit the guy harder.

Around her, people gasped with horror.

"Jase," West said. "Man, please. This isn't the way."

"Jase!" Beck's voice now. He'd returned just in time for the finale. "Enough."

Jessie Kay sidled up to Brook Lynn's side, taking her from whoever gripped her. "Calm down, sis. Just calm down."

"Jase. I mean it. Stop right now." Brook Lynn broke free of her sister and raced forward, latching on to his wrist and tugging.

He flew back, moving away from Stan as if he'd been kicked, even though Stan hadn't moved. He looked at Brook Lynn then at the crowd. There were crimson droplets splattered over his face and dripping from his knuckles.

He was panting, struggling to rein in his temper. Meanwhile, the crowd whispered among themselves.

He ignored them to grab fistfuls of Brook Lynn's hair. "Are you okay?"

She'd wondered how she'd react if she saw him in that kind of a rage—if she'd be terrified of him. Well, she hadn't been. She'd only been scared *for* him.

The lump in her throat prevented her from speaking. She managed a nod. She was okay, but he might not be. His parole…

I can't lose him…just can't.

Jase gathered her close. As she buried her face in the hollow of his neck, a sob escaped her. She clung to him,

pouring out her fear of what could have gone wrong—
and what was to come.

"He's Pax's brother," she said. "He wanted you to
hurt him and suffer for it. And if that didn't satisfy him,
he planned to kill you."

His arms tightened around her. She would have liked
to remain in his embrace forever, but all too soon he
handed her off to…Jessie Kay. She tried to hang on to
him, but he kissed her cheek and stepped away from her.

She soon discovered why. Sheriff Lintz had just
stepped out of the crowd, his sights on Jase.

JASE WAS ESCORTED to Sheriff Lintz's office while Stanton
Gillis was taken to the hospital. Knowing the drill, Jase
refused to speak with anyone without his lawyer present.

Sheriff Lintz promised to call the guy and left…
and then just never came back. Hour after hour passed,
Jase's tension mounting. His lawyer never showed up,
either.

Was this a Strawberry Valley interrogation technique? A form of torture?

Whatever. *Already been tortured tonight,* he thought.
This was nothing.

Hearing Brook Lynn scream his name, pain and ter-
ror in her voice…and then seeing her with a bloody cut
on her lip and a hard knot on her jaw… Yeah, he'd lost
it. He'd been overcome by a rage far worse than the
ones he'd once unleashed on Pax and inmates who'd
attacked him.

Jase's switch hadn't just flipped. It had fried, the cir-
cuits blown. By some miracle, Brook Lynn's pleas for
him to stop beating Stanton had reached his ears, and
he'd managed to pull back before he'd actually killed
the guy. But honestly? He doubted the end result would

matter. Assault and battery was assault and battery no matter how you sliced it, and it was a major violation of his parole. He'd be charged tonight, face a judge within the next few days, and then he would most likely be sent back to prison.

He waited for panic to come…but…no. There was only a cold sense of calm. He'd protected his woman, and he would *never* regret that. As long as Brook Lynn was safe, he was at peace.

Was Brook Lynn scared of him again? She'd wondered what would happen if his temper ever overtook him, and finally she'd gotten an answer. The worst possible scenario.

Hinges on the door creaked, and Sheriff Lintz finally ambled his way back inside the room.

"Lawyer" was all Jase said.

The sheriff pushed back his Stetson, revealing a receding salt-and-pepper hairline. "You're free to go, son."

Jase blinked at him. "Excuse me?" Was this a trick? The guy must know about his past by now. And he was just going to let him loose in the wild?

"No charges will be filed against you at this time. Or at all," the sheriff added, striding deeper into the room, his boots thumping against the tile floor. He sat across from Jase, who hadn't risen. "Me and my boys talked to all the party guests. We were told time and time again how Brook Lynn and West were attacked and you came to their rescue. How you defended them. Now Stanton Gillis, on the other hand, is being charged with assault and, considering the things we found in the trunk of his car, attempted murder. He'll be locked away for a long time."

Jase's relief was palpable, and any resentment he

held against Stanton Gillis evaporated like mist. A day hadn't gone by that he hadn't felt sorry for the pain he'd caused Pax's family—and tonight he'd finally seen the extent of it. The guy had held on to his bitterness all this time, letting it drive his every thought and action, and nothing good had come of it.

"You know I'm an ex-con," he said, still refusing to believe that he was being freed.

"That's right, I surely do. I've known who and what you are since the moment you moved to town."

Jase blinked in surprise. The sheriff had known, and yet he had never harassed Jase. Never tried to convince him to move away. Never warned him away from Brook Lynn.

"And the people of this town know, too," the sheriff added. "I made sure of it."

Jase's heart almost stopped. How long had they known? Nobody had said anything or treated him any differently. "I get why you did it, but not why—"

"No, you don't get it. People would have found out sooner or later, and then we would have had ourselves a lynch mob, one person's outrage feeding everyone else's. I decided to be proactive and save us all the trouble."

"Save me, you mean. But why? You don't know me."

"Son," the sheriff said, resting his boot on the edge of Jase's chair. "I like to think I'm a pretty good judge of character. I've seen the best, and I've seen the worst. I don't know you, you're right about that, but I've watched you. You got you some faults, that's for sure, but who among us doesn't? You've also got you some character, and that's more than a lot of others can say."

It was almost too much to take in. This was the first time in his life he'd lived somewhere that truly felt like home, where he was accepted, faults and all. "You have to know there are conditions to my parole…"

"Your parole hasn't been violated. Even ex-cons have a right to defend themselves and their loved ones."

"I…don't know what to say."

"Well, then. Don't say anything. Like I told you, you're free to go."

Damn if tears didn't burn the backs of Jase's eyes as he pushed to his feet. Second time this week, when he'd gone years without shedding a single one. He'd become a puss, and he didn't care. "Thank you."

"You've got a very concerned fiancée out there waiting for you."

The sheriff opened the door. Jase shook his hand before striding into the corridor.

Brook Lynn paced in the lobby, and when she spotted him, a whimper left her. She raced over and threw herself into his arms. He caught her and held on for dear life.

He closed his eyes, breathed her in. Contentment like he'd never known poured through him. Just like that, in a single snap of time, all of his worries—the familiar fear that things were destined to fall apart—fled. This was it, he realized. The fresh start he'd wanted. It started now, this moment. With this woman.

"I was so worried about you," she said.

"I'm okay. I'm not going back to prison."

Her hold on him tightened. "Thank God."

"I'm sorry I didn't back off. I'm sorry I let things go so far."

"Hey. Hey, now." She pulled back to frame his face in her hands. "You did back off, and I'm proud of you."

Proud of you. He'd never heard those words before. Not directed at him.

"You're not afraid of me?" he asked.

"Never."

The contentment gave way to happiness, and he swung her around, overwhelmed. This wasn't just a fresh start, he realized, but everything he'd ever wanted.

"You," he said. It was all he could manage at the moment.

"Us," she replied.

Stronger together than apart. Better together. Meant to be.

"I've waited my whole life for you," he said. "And you were worth every second."

THE LOVE OF his life beamed at him the entire drive home. Daphne and Hope were there, waiting for him. So were Beck and a sobered-up West. Even Jessie Kay, Dane, Kenna and Norrie. Jase was hugged by every single one of them. He explained the situation, told them what the sheriff had said, and there was a collective sigh of relief.

Afterward, West pulled him aside. Dark shadows formed half circles under his eyes, and his lips were pulled tight, but he gave Jase another hug, holding on as if the world was about to end.

"I'm sorry," West said. "For everything."

Jase pulled back to pat his shoulder. "This wasn't your fault, either."

"But I certainly didn't help."

"No." No reason to lie. "But you're still one of my favorite people, if that helps."

The semblance of a grin cracked his remorseful expression. "Yeah. It kind of does."

Beck joined them, and for several seconds, they stood

in a circle each of them knew well. Once it had been the three of them against the world.

"Never thought we'd end up here," he said. "Not just Strawberry Valley, but with *them*." He motioned to the others.

Jessie Kay, grinning as she rubbed her knuckles into the crown of Hope's head. Hope, laughing too hard to get away as Steve and Sparkles ran circles around her feet. Daphne, watching the pair with misty eyes. Dane, at Kenna's side, rubbing her arm. Kenna, holding Brook Lynn's hand as the two talked weddings.

My family.

"I know," Beck said. "They are proof miracles still happen, I guess."

West's gaze locked on...Jessie Kay. "Yes," the guy said, his voice gruff. "Too bad I treated one of them like dirt."

"Give her time," Jase said. "Isn't that what you once told me?"

"But I'm an idiot," West deadpanned.

"That's never been in question."

Brook Lynn caught his eye. She smiled and ambled toward him. He met her halfway and wrapped his arm around her.

"When do you think we can politely kick everyone out so we can be alone?" she asked softly.

"Now." He looked up. "Everyone out."

She chuckled as she combed her fingers through his hair.

"Y'all need to get a room," Jessie Kay muttered.

"That's what we're trying to do," Jase told her.

Beck *tsk*ed. "Jase. My man. You lack my skill. If it were me, the good stuff would have been over and done by now, without anyone ever knowing."

"You call that *skill*?" Daphne said.

"Skill for what?" Hope asked.

"Yeah," Norrie said. "What?"

"Uh..." Kenna shifted uncomfortably.

"Well." Dane pulled at his collar.

Brook Lynn rested her head on Jase's shoulder and traced a heart over his chest. Loudly she said, "I'll give you guys one minute to disappear before I unleash that famous Dillon temper."

They were out the door in thirty seconds.

Jase was the one to chuckle this time. He stared down at his happily-ever-after. "A lifetime isn't going to be enough. I want forever with you," he said.

"Good. Because that's what you're going to get."

* * * * *

GENA SHOWALTER

77991	THE DARKEST PASSION	__ $7.99 U.S.	__ $8.99 CAN.
77891	THE DARKEST TOUCH	__ $7.99 U.S.	__ $8.99 CAN.
77844	BURNING DAWN	__ $7.99 U.S.	__ $8.99 CAN.
77775	THE DARKEST CRAVING	__ $7.99 U.S.	__ $8.99 CAN.
77743	BEAUTY AWAKENED	__ $7.99 U.S.	__ $9.99 CAN.
77698	WICKED NIGHTS	__ $7.99 U.S.	__ $9.99 CAN.
77657	THE DARKEST SEDUCTION	__ $7.99 U.S.	__ $9.99 CAN.
77622	THE PLEASURE SLAVE	__ $7.99 U.S.	__ $9.99 CAN.
77621	THE STONE PRINCE	__ $7.99 U.S.	__ $9.99 CAN.
77581	THE DARKEST SURRENDER	__ $7.99 U.S.	__ $9.99 CAN.
77568	CATCH A MATE	__ $7.99 U.S.	__ $9.99 CAN.
77567	ANIMAL INSTINCTS	__ $8.99 U.S.	__ $9.99 CAN.
77549	THE DARKEST SECRET	__ $7.99 U.S.	__ $9.99 CAN.
77535	THE NYMPH KING	__ $7.99 U.S.	__ $9.99 CAN.
77525	HEART OF THE DRAGON	__ $7.99 U.S.	__ $9.99 CAN.
77522	THE DARKEST NIGHT	__ $7.99 U.S.	__ $9.99 CAN.
77461	THE DARKEST LIE	__ $7.99 U.S.	__ $9.99 CAN.
77451	INTO THE DARK	__ $7.99 U.S.	__ $9.99 CAN.
77437	TWICE AS HOT	__ $7.99 U.S.	__ $9.99 CAN.
77392	THE DARKEST WHISPER	__ $7.99 U.S.	__ $8.99 CAN.

(limited quantities available)

TOTAL AMOUNT	$ _____
POSTAGE & HANDLING	$ _____
($1.00 FOR 1 BOOK, 50¢ for each additional)	
APPLICABLE TAXES*	$ _____
TOTAL PAYABLE	$ _____

(check or money order—please do not send cash)

To order, complete this form and send it, along with a check or money order for the total above, payable to HQN Books, to: **In the U.S.:** 3010 Walden Avenue, P.O. Box 9077, Buffalo, NY 14269-9077; **In Canada:** P.O. Box 636, Fort Erie, Ontario, L2A 5X3.

Name: _____
Address: _____ City: _____
State/Prov.: _____ Zip/Postal Code: _____
Account Number (if applicable): _____
075 CSAS

*New York residents remit applicable sales taxes.
*Canadian residents remit applicable GST and provincial taxes.

HQN™

www.HQNBooks.com

PHGS0415BL

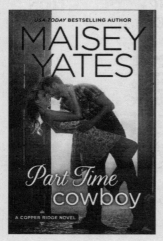

REQUEST YOUR FREE BOOKS!

2 FREE NOVELS
FROM THE ROMANCE COLLECTION
PLUS 2 FREE GIFTS!

YES! Please send me 2 FREE novels from the Romance Collection and my 2 FREE gifts (gifts are worth about $10). After receiving them, if I don't wish to receive any more books, I can return the shipping statement marked "cancel." If I don't cancel, I will receive 4 brand-new novels every month and be billed just $6.24 per book in the U.S. or $6.74 per book in Canada. That's a savings of at least 22% off the cover price. It's quite a bargain! Shipping and handling is just 50¢ per book in the U.S. and 75¢ per book in Canada.* I understand that accepting the 2 free books and gifts places me under no obligation to buy anything. I can always return a shipment and cancel at any time. Even if I never buy another book, the two free books and gifts are mine to keep forever.

194/394 MDN F4XY

Name _____ (PLEASE PRINT) _____

Address _____ Apt. # _____

City _____ State/Prov. _____ Zip/Postal Code _____

Signature (if under 18, a parent or guardian must sign)

Mail to the Harlequin® Reader Service:
IN U.S.A.: P.O. Box 1867, Buffalo, NY 14240-1867
IN CANADA: P.O. Box 609, Fort Erie, Ontario L2A 5X3

Want to try two free books from another line?
Call 1-800-873-8635 or visit www.ReaderService.com.

ROM13R

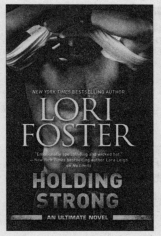

Limited time offer!

$1.⁰⁰ OFF

THE *Hotter* YOU BURN

From *New York Times* bestselling author

GENA SHOWALTER

comes the second sizzling book in *The Original Heartbreakers* series, where an irresistible charmer is about to meet his match!

Available July 28, 2015, wherever books are sold.

HQN™

"A-are you done yet?" she finally asked, sounding breathless. "Because this totally isn't working."

"Done yet?" He chuckled huskily. "Honey, I don't think I'll be done with you for several hours, at least."

"Mental anguish," she echoed.

"Probably the worst case the world has ever seen. A part of me died with the loss of that pie."

"Died." Another echo. She shifted from one foot to the other, licked her lips.

He should have remained unaffected, but Tammy—Tawny?—had gotten him worked up; that was the only reason his blood heated and his body hardened. *Play it cool.* "Are you trying to trick me into doing a little of that mouth-devouring you mentioned, sweetheart?"

Her eyes narrowed. "There you go, flirting again."

Hardly. "If you want a taste of my flirting, I'll give you a taste." In a practiced move, Beck let his head dip forward, his gaze remaining locked on his prey. Slowly he made his way around the counter, closing the distance between them. A shiver danced through her, goose bumps breaking out over her arms, and she took a step back. But he just kept coming, focused, determined... until the stove stopped her and she had nowhere else to go.

He placed one hand at her left and the other at her right, caging her in. For a long while, he said nothing, just continued to study her, letting her get used to his nearness and the heat radiating from his body.

She blinked up at him with those long, long lashes; they were as black as her hair, almost blue in the light. Her mouth floundered open and closed as she searched for the right words to say. The scent of her wafted up to him, a heady mix of strawberries and pecans, and he liked it far more than he should have, considering she was right—he did have a woman waiting in his bedroom.

The Hotter You Burn

"What do you mean, what am I?" Harlow asked.

"Are you a doctor? Lawyer?" Beck's gaze swept over her, lingering on the parts he liked best. Namely: all of them. "Femme fatale?"

Again, her chin went up. "I'm not a heartbreaker, that's for sure. Not like some people I know."

"Meaning me?" A tendril of guilt and regret swept through him, and he ran his tongue over his teeth. He was always clear about what he wanted from women, what he could give. A single night, nothing held back, nothing taboo—but nothing more.

"Yes, you," she said. "You've got Tawny in your bedroom, and yet you're out here flirting with me."

He waved a dismissive hand through the air. "This isn't flirting. This is an interrogation."

"Ha! An interrogation implies I'm being threatened, but the only part of me currently in any danger is my mouth. You just looked at it as if you were about to devour it!"

"Please. I look at everyone's mouth that way. But this isn't about me. It's about you and the fact that you owe me. Not just for the pie you stole, but for the mental anguish I've suffered. I asked what you are because I need to know how I can extract a sufficient payment from you."

Melt butter over low heat, then stir in flour, salt and pepper to taste, and stir until smooth. Stir in broth and cream. Keep stirring until the mixture thickens.

Add sherry, then stir in pasta, meat and both cheeses (and mushrooms if using). Mix thoroughly. Pour into greased baking dish and bake until bubbly and lightly browned, about 30 minutes. Enjoy!

Brook Lynn's Famous Cheesy Chicken Spaghetti

Ingredients:
16 oz spaghetti noodles
2 chicken bouillon cubes
A dash of olive oil
1 lb ground chicken breast
Pepper and salt to taste
½ cup butter
½ cup flour
1 cup chicken broth
1 cup heavy cream
2 tbsp sherry
1 can of mushrooms (optional)
8 oz Gouda cheese, shredded
8 oz creamy Havarti cheese, shredded

Directions:
Preheat oven to 350°F. Lightly grease casserole baking dish of choice.

Bring a large pot of water with bouillon cubes and a dash of olive oil to a boil. Cook spaghetti for 10 minutes. Drain and set pasta aside.

While pasta boils, brown ground chicken breast in a separate large saucepan, seasoning with salt and pepper to taste. Set aside.